The Cook's Curse

A Witherspoon Mansion Mystery

Book 2

Jax Daniels

ISBN-10: 1-946236-00-4
ISBN-13: 978-1-946236-00-5

Published by Golden Grail Books, an imprint of InQuest Productions, LLC

Cover art by Tim Neil

For *Laura*.

ACKNOWLEDGEMENTS

- To Jennifer, Denise, and Jason, who always know what to say, and what I should say.
- To Jeanette and Glenn, best parents ever.
- To Russ, diligent editor and loving husband.
- To Toastmasters, for helping me find my voice.
- To Angel, Bill, Elizabeth, and Lola, for sacrificing their time to read something imperfect.

Without you this book would never exist. Thank you.

Chapter One

THE SILVER NEEDLE twinkled fiendishly in his hand.

I tried not to watch, turning my head as the delicate sword penetrated my flesh, but my eyes always betrayed me. Each and every time. My heart raced, my breath quickened—

"*Mon Dieu!*" Hercule exclaimed in his heavy French accent. "This has happened, how many times now? Why still do you fret so much?"

"Yeah, Mrs. W," Mr. Smith agreed. "You had your head cut off by a ten foot lobster, for Pete's sake. What's a little poke with a needle?"

They just didn't understand. "I never liked needles," I sighed as Mr. Wesson removed the implement of torture from my arm and gingerly applied an alcohol-soaked cotton ball. Safety first.

Mr. Smith and Mr. Wesson, whom I dubbed my mad scientists, came with the house I inherited. Not that most mansions in New Orleans have mad scientists, but who knows? Mr. Smith (sorry, I don't know either of their first names) was a tall man, barrel chested, with long black hair pulled harshly back into a pony tail. He painted his fingernails black as well. His lab partner was a short skinny man with crazy curly hair, somewhere between Harpo Marx and Albert Einstein.

These days they had a new daily routine for me. They used to make me run obstacle courses, or spar, or practice my *time guardian* talent, which was what people in the know called my ability to slow down time. But, after the events eight months ago—when I supposedly conjured a gun—they've focused solely on recreating that result. *Conjuring*. Unsuccessfully, I might add. Almost daily they take a little of my blood, analyze it, and try to come up with explanations for why I just can't do it again.

I rubbed my sore arm. "What's wrong with yesterday's sample?" I huffed.

"Nothing's wrong with it," Mr. Smith explained. "We need a daily sample. We've explained this to you already." Actually, only Mr. Smith explained things. Mr. Wesson never says a word. "We're having a hard time nailing down your energy signature since it changes almost every day. So, we're analyzing it, yes, *every day*, trying to understand how you're changing. We're making … progress," he smiled, pointing at a monitor from over Mr. Wesson's shoulder, but he didn't sound so sure.

I'd heard those words many times now. I scowled my discontent.

About eight months ago, I was tricked into believing Nathan Marble, my lawyer, had killed my husband. In a rage of hatred and vengeance I conjured a gun, right out of thin air. Not *my* gun; I don't own one. Not a gun any of my staffers ever saw before. But there it was, in my hand, locked and loaded, ready to make Mr. Marble another New Orleans urban statistic.

It didn't happen, I'm happy to report. I didn't pull the trigger. He confessed at that moment that he was my husband's brother. That was just enough to quell the rage. Just barely.

"*S'il vous plaît,*" Hercule Poirot said, "I will try to explain." It has taken me a long while to get comfortable with his small stature, his shiny brown body … and his six legs. And talking, no less. The Great Hercule was a cockroach. He preferred the term *cafard*. "You are not yet complete in your manifesting. You are still growing. Still changing. When you are fully grown you will have five talents."

Talent is what we called *magic* in this world. We don't like to use the word magic. Apparently, it reminds everyone of the Salem witch trials.

"Yeah," I sighed, "This I know."

"You've barely achieved two talents so far. The intention of the science monkeys, I believe, is to monitor you daily and see how you change. Thus, the buffoons with lab coats can predict how your talents manifest and help you tap into those energies you have yet to possess."

Mr. Smith muttered a "hey" at the buffoon reference. He seemed content, however, being called a science monkey.

"What if that's all I get? Two talents, I mean. I wasn't born talented. Maybe, because of how I got my talents, they're limited. Or uncontrollable." In addition to the house, I inherited my ability from my husband. It was his last act on this earth. Sort of … it's complicated.

"Possible, yes," the roach continued. "However, I know you are not complete because you still have no shining."

I cocked an eyebrow as I donned my powder blue leather jacket, flipping my stark white hair free of it. "Shining?"

"Yes. The shining. The illumination of the eyes."

"The bug's right," Mr. Smith said, overhearing the conversation. "You never shine."

"Recall, *chére*, when Nathan, or the one you call Jeeves, or any of the others … when they use their talents, the eyes have a different appearance, do they not?"

They did. Their faces would grow gaunt, almost skull-like, their eyes shining bright green—"Ah. *Shining*."

"*Oui*. It is a sign of maturity," Hercule said. He perched himself on the lab table, seated upright on the edge, with his back legs dangling and his topmost folded. His middle legs braced upon the metal. Count 'em: six. "And you have no shine. Or wit, for that matter."

"Fine. I still have talents coming," I told the *cafard*, immune to his sharp tongue. "What I don't get is why my blood is needed. Isn't energy, well, energy?" I waved my hands in the air in a type of demonstration. "What does my blood have to do with it?"

"Your energy is in your blood," Mr. Smith said, "as well as your skin, your hair, and so on. This way, we can study it without you being here." With that, he made a "shoo" motion with his fingers.

Thank goodness. Officially dismissed, I spun on my heels and headed out.

Such was my life.

~ ~ * ~ ~

Taking a walk up St. Charles Avenue always lightened my mood, and the February sunshine felt glorious. The crisp winter air motivated quick steps over the broken and uneven sidewalks. The boughs of the grand oak trees lining the street reached for the sky overhead with equal enthusiasm as they did for each other, creating a lush, green canopy over the neutral ground. A little less so this time of year. A street car rumbled by stuffed with tourists and commuters, sporting an advert on its side—a King Cake dressed gaily in purple, yellow, and green sugar. Mardi Gras was fast approaching. Every Crescent City citizen's favorite time of year.

I turned left heading for Magazine Street and a certain Jamaican eatery called The Rum House that specialized in their own version of street tacos, Nola style. I ordered a variety, settled up the bill, and took my to-go bag to a little unassuming office building a few blocks away. On the lower floor was a woman's clothing store called "The Girl's Got Money"—okay, that's what *I* call it having browsed their goods a while ago—and above it, in a small room with just enough space for two desks and a water cooler, lodged the private investigation firm owned by my lawyer, Nathan Marble, and his partner, Jack Frost. The small sign on the door read, "Lost Souls Investigations: Specializing in Missing Persons." Good at it, too. But the name didn't come from their specialty. It came from them.

Both of them had to give up their old lives—family, friends, relatives—to come work for me at the manor. *They* are the lost souls. I suspect they picked this particular focus, missing persons, out of that pain, hoping to spare others from being permanently lost.

I entered through the downstairs door, rattling the cheery bell that announced my presence. I trotted nimbly up the steep and narrow steps to their office. The staircase always struck me as in need of repair: the smell of mildew, heavy and wet, in combination with the creaking floorboards beneath my feet. Thankfully, not so the office itself. Bright and shiny windows spanning floor to ceiling let copious shafts of sunlight into the room, most of the day. Brick walls, new carpet, and exposed hefty cypress joists decorated the space. A tiny and round pot-bellied stove squatted in one corner, trying to hide. Being here was a bit like stepping back in time.

The two men sat behind their desks, eyes up to see their unexpected guest. Nathan smiled when he saw me crest the stairs. Jack stood.

"Winki," Nathan called out. "Please don't take this the wrong way, but what are you doing here?" Nathan stood around six feet tall. He had dark, almost black, naturally wavy hair, which he kept short and high off his forehead. He had full lips and a square chin, which added to his warm smile, if you were lucky enough to see it.

"Bearing gifts," Jack said, watching my tote. Jack Frost was the detective of the small company, having come from England as a former Detective Sergeant. He also was my, well, healer. With just a touch of his hand he can take away a cut, cure a cold, or reattach your head. Sadly, the latter I know from experience. Born in London,

Jack speaks with an highly-educated English accent. "Your timing could not have been better, ma'am." When Jack called me "ma'am" I swear it sounds like "mom."

"At ease," I chided him. I sincerely wished we could have a less formal relationship.

"Aren't you supposed to be with Smith and Wesson?" Nathan asked.

Nathan handled the legal part of their investigation team, making sure the two men's actions didn't conflict with any laws or law enforcers. And if you needed to *become* a lost soul, as in "disappear completely", he could create all the credentials to give you a new life while making your past utterly vanish. He liked to say he doesn't just find lost souls but makes them, if necessary.

"I was," I answered. "And now I'm here." I started to unpack their lunches. "Bringing food," I scolded, "yet again … because—"

Nathan sighed. "I'm working on it."

This was a conversation we'd had repeatedly over the last eight months. The manor needed a cook. Our last cook, while overwhelmingly wonderful in her culinary skills, tried to kill Nathan and turn me dark … as in evil, not healthily tanned.

"You've been saying that for months," I added, which I'll admit wasn't the first time. I knew he was tired of hearing it, as much as I was tired of saying it.

"I'm working on it!" Nathan gave me a hand unloading the assortment of tacos. "It will happen," he said.

"We'll get a new cook?" But I knew he'd changed the subject.

"When you're ready, Winki. Your new talent. It will happen." He gave an encouraging smile.

"I'm more concerned that when it did happen I was filled with such hate and anger …" Even months later I felt so ashamed.

"You don't think you'll feel that way again?" He took out the creole duck tacos for himself. They were his favorite.

"What if that's the only way I can make it happen? If murder is the path to darkness, and that kind of hatred is my path to magic … well, maybe it's best left alone." I took out the wrapped jerked veggie tacos and tossed them to Jack.

Jack gave a small bow upon catching his food. He wore his blond hair spiked upright which made his already long face look even longer and his lanky frame even taller. He sported one of his overly large suits (one of four he owned, the fourth I bought for him a month ago, bored with his couture), complete with tie and gloves. Jack always wore gloves. Another ridiculous rule for healers; he's not allowed to remove them unless he's healing someone. Or I tell him to.

As he took the food he avoided eye contact with me. Come to think of it, I don't think we've looked each other in the eyes for nearly eight months. We hadn't really worked through our issue. He won't bring it up and I just can't … I can't even bear the thought. He lost his soul to me. He was … my …

"Thank you," Jack said as he took his first bite.

I took the remaining two tacos, the voodoo lamb tacos, the specialty of the joint. I wanted to ask the waiter what voodoo they do to the tacos, but I thought better of it. In my world, sometimes it's best not to know.

Nathan looked over at the spiky-haired thin man who surfed the net while he ate his veggies. "I'm curious, why are you a vegetarian?"

Without looking away from the screen Jack answered, "I've had to stick my digits into many a creature, and touch every different organ and tendon and muscle to heal them. Frankly, I simply can't bear the thought of chewing on the very meat I heal." He looked at Nathan. "But don't let that stop you. Please, enjoy the flesh."

With a sigh I set my food aside, his words turning my hunger to complete disgust. It had no affect on Nathan, as far as I could tell.

The door bell sang its clang. As the two men wiped their hands and set their meals aside. They shot glances at each other, appearing to ask, "Are you expecting anyone?" and shrugging "no" at the same time. I suspected they had done something similar when I arrived.

Creaking stairs announced the visitor approaching. The three of us watched the pony wall that separated the room from the staircase. Nathan, with a smooth dance-like maneuver, got around his desk. As a *thought catcher* he must have realized who had come to visit.

I recognized her. Jack's old partner, Detective Duplantier. A kindly Southern woman from the New Orleans Police Department.

"Detective!" Nathan welcomed. "How nice to see you again."

Confidently, she entered the tiny room and shook hands with him, then with Jack, who stood to greet her. Her tiny frame contrasted with Jack's tall lanky one. He stood nearly a foot taller than the detective.

"I remember you," she said to me. "Winki Witherspoon. My, how long has it been since I last saw you?"

I hesitated to answer. Several months ago she showed up to take me in for questioning about a late night motorcycle chase. Thankfully, we had a shooting in our house that day, um, well not thankfully, but it distracted her enough to leave me alone. I'm still concerned one day she's going to remember. "It's been a while," I smiled.

"Do y'all have a moment to spare?" she asked.

"Sure." Nathan gestured to an open chair for her to take. "Please." He and Jack sat tall with interest.

She reached into an abundant purse and retrieved a thick, phone-book-sized manila envelope. From it she retrieved an 8 x 10 photo of a Caucasian woman. "Have y'all heard about Saffron Jolly, the chef?"

Hard not to. Even without the picture I knew whom she meant. TV, radio, paper, and internet news spouted off about her almost constantly. Saffron Jolly was New Orlean's favorite daughter. Born right here in New Orleans (we love our own), married the Saints quarterback, Harrison Jolly (we love our WHO DAT!), devoted Catholic (we love our religion), an acclaimed chef (we love our food), and opened five successful restaurants in the city (we *really* love our food). But her name has been on everyone's lips for much darker reasons. In less than a month she had lost her husband, three sons, and the family dog in three separate accidents. The youngest boy only last week.

"Yes," Nathan answered, solemnly. "We have. It's truly a tragedy."

"I was assigned to all of her cases," she said. "All of them. And I tried, I swear to the great creator himself that I tried to find some connection, some reason for what happened. Because what other possible explanation could there be? My technician, Bobby's his name, he told me that the odds of one person losing everyone she loved in three separate incidents in the same month was smaller than her chances of being hit by a meteor from space." It was a shame she was talking about such bad news. Her accent was just darling to listen to.

"How can we help?" Nathan asked.

She handed him the bundle. "This is the Jolly file. It's everything we could collect from that poor woman's life, everything about each of the accidents, everything about anyone she'd ever known who might bear her any grudge. We couldn't find a thing. No reason, no connections, no history, no bad blood. Nothin'. This morning my Captain told me to close it, sayin' it was just one of those things." She shook her head, and her auburn-gold locks shook with her. "But I just can't bring myself to give up. If there were any truly lost souls in New Orleans, Mrs. Jolly's would be the most broken. Fact is, I'm worried she isn't long for this world."

"Has she been threatened?" Jack asked.

"No. I think she's thinking of taking her own life. I can't imagine what that kind of grief will do to a woman. But I suspect all y'all do."

Probably true. Each of us knew grief well.

Last summer, Jack quit his job with NOPD. From Duplantier's point of view, it was unexplained, ill-thought, and abrupt. But Jack had no choice. The fault belongs to me. I exposed him for what he was, a *healer*. Healers are, in the talented community, trophies to be possessed. Once I outed him, I either had to claim him for my own or let him be captured and enslaved by a darker force. I did what I thought best. But he couldn't work both as a cop—a job that could expose our world as well as endanger innocent lives—and for me. So he quit. I don't think he'll ever forgive me.

Nathan's wife and two boys vanished overnight, never to be seen again. Detective Duplantier believed his family simply ran out on him. But we know he made it happen. He put them in a safe place. As far as I know they think he's dead, so they won't come looking for him. He did it to protect them. My fault again—when I exposed him as my husband's brother, his family risked becoming a target. He walked tall and proud, but I could see the lingering loss in his eyes.

As for me, I shared Saffron Jolly's grief intimately. My husband died in a motorcycle accident over a year ago, the despair nearly killing me. He left a hole in my heart you could sail the Titanic through. I would have traded my life for his without hesitation.

"So, I'm asking you two," she said to the men. "Would you look into it?"

"Uh," Nathan said holding the bundle. "Is this legal? I mean, isn't this," he gestured to the fat envelope, "police property?"

"You know, I just don't know what happened to that danged file. It got lost this morning," she smiled. "I'm sure it will turn up soon."

"Ah," Jack said. "We won't be paid, I take it."

Nathan ignored him. "We'll make copies of everything and get it back to you."

"What?" she said loudly, "I can't hear you over that construction noise."

No sounds filled the room, but Nathan took the hint. "Ah. Well, madam detective, thank you for stopping by. We'll give you a call."

"Thank you, thank you very much," she sang as she waved and creaked down the staircase.

By the time Nathan turned around Jack had the envelope open, pulling out the separate folders within. "Which one would you like to look through first?" he asked Nathan, reading off the headings from each. "The accident on the causeway? The hit and run? Or the fall off the roof?"

"None," Nathan said. "I want to talk to her."

Jack frowned. "We should have some understanding of what has already been asked."

"What do we need to understand? She lost everything. We understand that perfectly well."

Maybe I shouldn't be here. "Well, whatever you two decide. I'll see you at home."

"Yes, ma'am," Jack said.

As Nathan grabbed a folder something fell out. A photo. I picked it up, making the mistake of looking at it. It came from the first accident, the one where the eldest boy and husband-quarterback inexplicably drove off the The Causeway and drowned in Lake Pontchartrain. The picture perfectly framed the two sitting in the front seats, seat belts still fastened. They looked peacefully asleep. My own memory flashed to Will, seeing his body in the casket. The dead might look peaceful, but grief and uncertainty undermine any hope you have that it's true.

I recalled the story from the late night news. Mr. Jolly drove his eldest to football camp whenever he could, given his own football schedule. But the trip never included the drive over the long bridge called The Causeway. Why they were there was the first mystery. The second, why he swerved at an incredibly high speed and ran the SUV off the road and into a watery grave. Witnesses claimed he just sped up for no reason.

Staring at the photograph I whispered, "Nathan's right. Go talk to her."

Nathan tried to take the picture from my hand. "I don't think you should look at these."

Before he could reclaim the photo I held out the picture for them both to see. "It never made sense. Why he was there, why he sped up, why he swerved." I gave Nathan a hard look. "Just like it never made sense why my husband drove his motorcycle right into an oncoming semi."

Jack's eyes narrowed at the picture. "You think Saffron Jolly might be talented, and the deaths were done by some dark intervention?"

"I think you'll both have a better idea once you've seen her," I said as I started down the staircase and left through the side door.

Chapter Two

"WHAT ARE THE names of the five planes?" my butler, who doubled as my tutor, asked me. He stood proudly in his pseudo-tuxedo, one hand behind his back, the other holding an open book.

When I'd returned from the Lost Souls Investigations, I kicked off my shoes and peeled off my socks, diligently resuming my duties as the Champion of the Gateway Manor, which meant schooling. Now that I had the *fighting* part of the role down, we've moved on to the finer points of the talented community, like species identification, talent definitions, and which fork to use during the *limace* course of a fancy troll-hosted dinner (turns out that's a trick question, as I'd never partake in one since *limace* are garden variety slugs).

"Air, Water, Fire, Earth, and Ether," I answered him.

"Their proper names, madam," he corrected.

I sighed. "Zephyr, Aqua, Radiant, Midland, and Phantom."

"In order," he sighed.

I rolled my eyes. "Phantom, Zephyr, Midland"—because it's in the middle, get it?—"Radiant, and Aqua." I made the mistake of asking Jeeves why Phantom was considered the first plane. That led to a long and tedious historical iteration of battles, kings, more battles, a treaty, some princess, and a final battle. I think. I regretted the question after the third battle.

Jeeves, the butler, glanced at the book in his hand with the aid of a monocle. His suit accentuated his tall and thin frame. He spoke with a painfully posh accent, being British born like Jack. In fact they were father and son.

"Correct," he said unenthusiastically. "What persistent characteristic is the Radiant Plane known for?"

"Their curious preparation of foie gras."

"Madam, please," he sighed with disapproval.

"Fire," I answered. "Jeeves, we've been at this for hours now. I'm hungry. Isn't it time for dinner?"

"You're not hungry. You're bored."

"You know me so well," I said.

Jeeves's lectures covered the history of the talented community, most of which still baffled me, three afternoons a week. My maid, Mrs. Black, took the alternate the other three afternoons, teaching me etiquette, protocols, and the manner in which planes interact. You'd think that would be interesting … and yet.

Thankfully, I got Sundays off.

Mrs. Black is also my seamstress and makes the most fabulous clothes for me, including my armor which looked like nifty motorcycle leathers.

"Please, madam. Focus."

"The Radiant Plane is known for its mastery over fire." I rubbed my face. "I'm not bored, Jeeves, but you're not telling me things I want to know. Just what you want to teach me."

"You need to know all of this."

"No, I don't." I folded my arms in protest.

He closed his book. "What is it you wish to know?" Before I spoke, he looked in the direction of the front door. "The gentlemen have returned," he said as he set down the tome and gracefully stepped out of the room. One of his talents, a *doorman*, gave him insight as to who was coming and going, and even if the people walking through the front door lived here (like Jack and Nathan, *the gentlemen* of which he spoke) the act of greeting them belonged to him. He always took his job seriously.

"What is it you want to know, *ma chère?*" said the small French voice from the other end of the sofa.

"I want to know about the healers."

"You know all about the healers, *madame*. There is no more." Hercule Poirot came into view.

"I know that they caused the last great war," I answered, "and that good and evil fought against them, side by side. I know they themselves are neither good nor evil, and therefore incorruptible, and therefore hated by both sides."

"Not just hated. *Feared.*"

"But why? How did it go from hatred or fear to complete subjugation?"

He gave a little chuckle. "To prevent it happening again, *oui?*"

"Not good enough," I scowled as I ran my fingers through my stark white hair.

"I suspect, *chère*, that the history is not what you wish to know. You wish to know how to change what is. You wish to free him without consequence." I visibly shuddered at the word "free." "But that cannot be done. You can release him from your service, but another will come for him. That is certain."

Nathan knocked on the living room-slash-classroom's door jamb. "Got a minute?" He asked. He tried to remove his tie but grimaced at the effort.

"You okay?" I asked.

"Yeah. I mean, I will be. Got a headache. I need something to eat. And some aspirin. Maybe some sleep."

Handy, then, that the dining room held tea and snacks. Before the lunch caterers leave they fill an overly large buffet top with cucumber sandwiches, pates, cheese, crackers and an assortment of fruit. Frankly, I love this time of day. British teatime. So civilized!

Together we made our way to grab a bite, Nathan rubbing his temples the entire distance. We found Mrs. Black wiping the long table in preparation for our snacks. There isn't a more witch-like looking person in the world. Her wiry long silver hair gets arranged every day in a dizzying-array of styles, sometimes a beehive bun on the top, sometimes a long pony tail with a bright red bow on her head. Piercing grey eyes behind her coke-bottle lensed *pince nez* glasses (I often suspected one of her magical talents was keeping them on) emphasized her thin, frail frame.

When she saw Nathan, she stood erect. "My boy, are you all right? Can I get you something?" She always called Nathan "my boy" once she learned he was Edward Witherspoon, a man she raised from childhood.

Nathan consoled her. "I'm fine, Mrs. Black. Thank you."

She nodded, unconvinced, took another wipe, and left the room.

Mrs. Black used to have a little fire in her belly, prone to snarky quips. But she'd lost her best friend last year, our cook, Mrs. White. She did her best to hide it, but the betrayal truly devastated her.

Mr. Marble poured cups of tea as I put together plates of munchies. We took our usual seats, Nathan at the head of the table, running the length of the room, I on his right. That way I got a view of the lovely portrait over the fireplace. My late husband gently smiled down at me from his perch.

"How did it go with Mrs. Jolly?" I asked.

He slid my cup to me. "Detective Duplantier had cause for alarm. The lady's a mess. Looks like she's been beat up; dark rings under her eyes. But she didn't want to talk about it. About anything. Hell, I tried to just talk about the weather."

"You have that *voice thing*. Can't you make her want to talk about it?"

What I call the *voice thing* he calls *the power of suggestion*. Nathan uses it to manipulate people. He boasts he can make anyone do anything at least once. It's how he got me into this house.

"I also have the ability to catch thoughts," he winced again. "Trust me, she's a quiet wreck on the outside, but she a torrent of rage on the inside. Screaming at the world around her." Nathan continued to rub his temples ... *ah!* I understood. Nathan physically suffered from that poor woman's emotion.

He took a bite then continued. "Suggesting anything in her mental condition would have bad side effects." He took a sip of tea. "She gave me a splitting headache."

"Is the detective right? If she's that bad off maybe she will kill herself."

"I don't think so. Yes, she wants to die because she wants to join her family, but she's Catholic. And Catholics believe taking your own life might not get them to ..." He pointed skyward. "Hence, the rage in her head. And mine."

"Not talented, then?"

"I have no idea. I couldn't sense anything through the pain."

Behind us Jack came in. He put a few items on a plate, poured some tea, and left the room. He never acknowledged either of us.

Nathan noticed the unhappy twist in my mouth. "What do you want from him?"

"Conversation, for butter's sake. A 'hello' would have been nice." I shook my head. "I actually like the guy."

"Winki, I'm sorry if this bugs you, but he doesn't have to like you. You can see his point, right? A gilded cage is still a cage."

I scooted myself from the table. "Of course I see his point. I don't want him to be in a cage anymore than he does," I seethed at him. He winced as he rubbed his already sore skull. I took a calming breath. "Sorry."

Grabbing my tea and plate I followed Jack into the media room where he sat with the TV on. When he saw me enter he started to move.

"Stay!" I ordered as I sat down in one of the overstuffed leather chairs. I moved a TV tray into use and snapped off the flat panel screen. "Time's up. We need to talk." The "time's up" comment was for my benefit; I didn't want to do this anymore than he did.

Jack slumped back. Despite the suit he still wore, the slouch made him look like a sullen child.

"Look at me," I said. "For once, will you please look at me?"

With a swallow Jack turned his head to me. For the first time in over eight months I saw his blue-green eyes. Shame suddenly filled me. *I did this to him.* I dropped my own.

"You can't look at me anymore than I can look at you," he spat.

I pushed my own emotions aside and brought my eyes back up to meet his. "What do you want?" I asked, defensively. "How many times do I need to apologize? I'm sorry. I'm am so very sorry about this. I don't want this anymore than you do."

"Yes, I'm certain being the master in this relationship is a hard path to walk."

My belly grew hot. "I suppose I should have let Nathan die that day and spared you this wretched life."

I gave him a moment to think about my words. His face flushed.

I went on. "I didn't know the consequences of asking you to help him. I didn't know that, by saving his life, I damned yours. All I knew at that moment was I had a brother-in-law. My husband left me a family, not just this stupid house and this stupid life with its stupid rules!" He didn't move a muscle. "And the only reason, the *only* reason, I bound us into this miserable partnership was to keep you from being bound by some other Hades-know-what demon into an *even more* miserable partnership."

There. I'd said what I needed to say. The tight lipped Brit sat there. I leaned my head back into the chair and stared at the ceiling, ticking off the moments of silence.

"You don't know everything," he whispered.

I blew an exasperated breath. "I know *nothing*. That's why we need to talk."

"I mean about ... healing Nathan." He moved, finally, reaching for his tea and taking a drink. "I made a promise. I owe Mother a favor."

"Mother?" I squinted. *Okay, I need to buy a vowel.*

"Mother Earth. *My* mother."

"Mother Earth?" I turned my head. "The *planet* is your mother, and you owe it, um, her a favor?" Yep, that sounded just as quacky coming out of my mouth as it had in my head.

"Yes. That is where my ability to heal comes from. It is she who gives me the gift. It comes from the ground, the earth itself. Technically, the dead belong to her. I can't just heal them, not without her permission. Or, now, yours. She allowed me to save him in exchange for a favor."

I recalled the incident; Jack had us take Nathan's body outside. He took off his shoes and socks and knelt next to Nathan with his eyes closed. That must have been when he asked permission to save Nathan's life.

"Not only did I expose myself to be enslaved," he ranted, "but I actually had to pay for the privilege." He raised his head proudly, as if some heavy load had been lifted off his back.

I could see why he was so peeved these last months. "Okay. So you owe Mother Earth a favor. What, like world peace?"

"As of yet she has not called for payment. But," he sighed, "her favors are never cheap. Nor small. And once she does let me know what's expected, I will have only until the end of that day to fulfill the debt. Otherwise ..."

"Otherwise, what?" I pressed.

He shrugged. "I genuinely don't know, ma'am. She might take my life. She might take back Nathan's, since his was saved. She might make San Francisco fall into the ocean. I have no idea."

Someone cleared their throat behind us. Startled we both turned to see Nathan somberly darkening the doorway, arms folded and leaning against the molding. "Since it was my life that got saved I think I should be part of this conversation."

"But she asked nothing of you," Jack said. "It's my burden. That's how it works."

"Not if my life is the penalty. Look, Jack, whenever she wants her favor, whatever the favor is, please, let me help. Just let me—"

"No," I said. Both men looked at me. "When she asks, you will tell me, Jack. I'm the one who pushed you into this, I'm the one who'll pay the price."

"It might not work that way, ma'am."

I gave him a stern look. "When she asks, you will tell me."

"Yes, ma'am." He sat a little taller, and took a proper sip of tea. For the first time in months I recognized Detective Sergeant Jack Frost.

"Are we good?" I asked. "Because I'm tired of tiptoeing around you. This is my home, and it's your home. Avoiding one another, as big as the place is, has become a bother for everyone. No more. Is that clear?"

"Yes, ma'am."

"And if there's something you want or need just tell me. Even if you know it's going to start an argument."

"Yes, ma'am."

I dropped my head back into the chair. "And for pity's sake would you please stop calling me 'mom'?"

He gave a small sigh. "I should point out a law prohibits me from addressing my … *employer*, let's say, in the familiar. However, I quite frankly can't bring myself to utter the word 'Winki'. I am British, after all."

The sound of my name coming from the English gentleman made me smile. "I see your point." I noticed Nathan, too, thought it amusing. "You feeling better?"

"Yeah, thanks. Time and distance is helping."

Jack tilted his head. "You're a *thought catcher?*" Nathan nodded. Jack's face frowned, which, considering its length, looked very sad indeed. "I'm sorry."

Nathan shrugged. "Eh. It's not a big thing."

"Why?" I asked. "What am I missing?" Again. *I'm never in the know.*

Nathan explained. "Healers don't throw thoughts. They can't be read. In fact, it's almost like they're not there. They seem empty to me." He turned to Jack, "No offense."

"None taken."

"One of the reasons I never trusted them," he said. "I can't tell what they are thinking."

Jack asked, "How did you not suspect me, then, when I came to investigate Mrs. Witherspoon last year? Didn't you know I was a healer? Not hearing me should have been a dead giveaway."

"Not everyone throws thoughts. Some people have mastery over their minds and can keep them calm and simple. I just assumed that about you. If I had to spend much time with you, I would have noticed the lack of thoughts, sooner or later."

"Working with me must be hard for you," Jack said.

"I've come to think of it as *peaceful.*" He rubbed his eyes. "Especially after an encounter like today. In fact, I'm gonna take a nap. And some—" Jeeves strolled up at the moment with a small silver platter bearing a tiny dish with pills and a glass of water. "—ibuprofen," Nathan nodded. "Thank you." He took them, gulped, and gave a small wave as he left the room.

Once alone I asked Jack, "You think Mrs. Jolly is going to be all right?"

"Hard to say. You don't need to be a *thought catcher* to understand she is in a world of pain. The kind I can't heal, either." He stood, taking his food and drink. "If you'll excuse me, ma'am, I'm going to change my attire for the evening."

I nodded, and moved myself to the sofa and stretched out.

"*Ma chére?*" a little French voice called.

"Yes, Hercule."

"I have found you a book I think you will find most interesting."

I scrunched my face in hesitation. Over the sofa I saw the book jigging its way toward me just inches off the floor. It stopped within reach. I took a deep breath and gingerly picked it up. I knew what would happen next, so I closed my eyes. Well, one anyway. Once unburdened twenty or thirty cockroaches scuttled in every direction. I quietly shivered at the sight. I walk around in bare feet, mind you. Not a pleasant thought to know a roach might be hiding about.

"Thank you," I said, hoping my voice didn't show my utter disgust.

"*De rien.*"

I read the title. *The Asclepium Order; a Memoir.*

Chapter Three

ANY OTHER DAY, once Nathan came home we'd spend a couple of hours in the training room sparring. After, around nine in the evening I'd crash on the sofa to watch an old black and white or, even better, a silent film. Those were particularly entertaining since my cockroach familiar perched himself next to me and, between nibbles of a single piece of popped corn, enough to sustain him for a whole movie, muttered insults and remarks at the screen, as if I had my very own *Mystery Science Theater 3000*.

In Nathan's state, however, sparring wouldn't be on the table this evening. He used to be a master at the halberd; for some reason, I'd gravitated to learning the old weapon. It amused me. Part axe, part staff, part spear, making it versatile for both blocking and attacking. Its only limitation was its size, too long for small spaces. I had a hammer for that.

Unwilling to go into the training room by myself, which would lead me to deal with Smith and Wesson in their unrelenting pursuit of my conjuring talent, I stayed in my own room. I intended to read the book Hercule gave me, but my mind wandered. *What if it wasn't me who did the conjuring?* I couldn't keep that thought from my mind.

I tossed the unopened tome on my little table spread beneath the window. It landed on the multitude of pages filled with my thoughts on Will's latest riddle.

The sentence, the burden, and the falter make three
The fourth is where the next clue will be

It baffled me as much today as it did the first time I heard it. Will had confidence that I would figure it out. Me, not so much.

I picked up one of the pages at random, snapped it out from under the book like a magic trick, and headed to the outdoors for some fresh air. I opened the French doors that lead to the wrap-around gallery. Dusk fell upon the house, and the long shadows cast from thin cypress trees streaked across our garden like ominous claws. The winter's air pricked my skin as I stepped barefoot onto the decking.

I kept my feet bare year round, more challenging these few winter months. My house communicates with me, but only if I have physical contact with it. Being barefoot allowed it to *talk* any time it chooses. Suddenly, I'd find myself in a different room, at a different time, witnessing whatever the house saw, whatever memory it wanted to show me. The experience overwhelms me at times, seeing my late husband as a child, or my staffers as darklings. But I've learned to wait. And watch. There was always a reason.

To my surprise, leaning against one of the black scrolled wrought iron supports stood Jack, gazing out over the backyard. He'd traded his suit and tie for casual couture: pair of skinny leg jeans, a blue, long sleeved t-shirt with the words "Defend New Orleans" splashed across the front, and red high-top tenny runners with black checkered laces. His normally spiked hair laid flat and swept off his forehead. His wardrobe change took him from thirty-five to seventeen.

He looked up as I stepped outside. "Ma'am," he acknowledged.

"Do you want to be alone?" I asked before stepping onto the deck.

"I wanted to be outdoors," he quickly waved a gesture to the grounds. Our perch overlooked the vast sculpted garden, filled with herbs and flowers, now brown and brittle from the winter, with a small glass house smack in the center. Jack nodded to the land. "All of this is yours. I can be wherever you want me to be."

"Jack—" I seethed.

"I'm not trying to be contentious," he explained. "Nor am I trying to anger you. You have to understand my position. We are not equals. We will never be equals. You can give me a long leash, but I'm not confused that it is a leash. And neither should you be." He approached me. "You need to own up to owning me. I have. Until you have accepted this you leave us both at risk."

"I disagree," I snapped back. "Just because these rules have been around forever doesn't mean they're right. Or just. Or demand blind acceptance. Just look around you. This very house has seen the ownership of people and the bloody war that fought to free them. Now it's deemed not just immoral but outrageous to consider another human as property."

"My binding is not man's law. It is a 'talented community' law." He used air quotes to make his point. "And the last war—*our* last war —created it. It will take much more than a war to change those laws. They will only be undone by total annihilation of my kind."

I shook my head. "Only shows your lack of vision."

He stood tall, folding his hands behind his back. "I genuinely hope you are correct, ma'am. Until that time, though, I urge you to embrace what is. I am yours. You are my protector and my authority." He came to me and stood before me. "I am content with that relationship, ma'am. You need to know that."

"You're angry all the time." I pointed out.

"I suspect that has more to do with my disposition rather than my circumstance." He flashed a small smile, the only kind I've ever seen him give, even when he was a free man. With a deep, contented sigh he looked over the gardens. "I miss fog," he changed the subject. "We could use a good, dense fog."

Someone knocked on the hallway door with growing volume. I

stepped back inside, calling, "Come in." Mr. Smith poked his head into my room. I sighed. "Look, guys, I'm not in the mood—"

"No, no," he held up his hand and stopped me. "We have an idea and we just wanted your okay."

If he had to ask, odds were this was not a *good* idea. "Yes?"

"Well," he started as he opened the door wider, allowing Mr. Wesson to step into the room, "we have a hypothesis. *You're* having a hard time manipulating your energy field and *we're* having a hard time guiding you because we're only just learning how your magnetic matrix affects—"

I raised my hand to stop him. "English. Please."

"Wesson here," the small man waved, "has a theory. Maybe it's not your blood or energy at all. Maybe it's due to your gender."

"You think my talents differ from Will's because I'm a woman?"

"Close." *I never get this stuff.* "We think how you *tap into it* might be different because you're a woman."

The conversation had drawn Jack's attention. "What are you proposing?" he asked.

"We want to examine another female in the Witherspoon lineage. Someone who had talent. We'd like to compare your chemistries." I stood there, my head tilted. "See, we've only studied Will's use of his talents, you know, how they interact with his body and cell structure, but he'd already mastered them by the time we even met the guy. All we had to do was create items with energies that meshed with his own energy signature and quantum fields. Anyway, if we could analyze a *female* we could compare your energy signature, maybe get some insight into what motivates and inspires you, what tools would help you tap into that energy." Wesson nodded quickly in earnest agreement.

Instead of confessing my confusion I just asked, "What do you want? There aren't any Witherspoon women, that I know of."

Mr. Smith cleared his throat. "No. Not … *alive.*"

Jack frowned. "You want to go grave digging?"

"Not for valuables or anything. We just want to take a couple of samples of—"

"But but but," I held up a hand to stop him from saying what I thought was coming next, "there weren't any. Women, I mean. The talents were all on the male side, right?"

"Will's mother was," Jack said. "She was the champion of the manor before Edward and William."

My mouth dropped. I had no idea. I'd gotten the impression Will's father had talent and passed it onto his sons. "How do you know that?"

"I know my house's history, ma'am."

Of course he did. I'd gotten used to never knowing anything, even though I'd received an extensive education the last few months. You'd think someone would have mentioned that small detail.

"You geeks need the entire body?"

"No, no," Mr. Smith waved dismissive hands. "Just a piece."

I shuddered. "Fine. I have no opinion. But Nathan might since she's his mother. He's resting now but talk to him at dinner. If he has no problem with the request, I don't either."

Mr. Smith nodded and waved as he left the room.

I asked Jack, "How is it you know so much about this house?"

"It's my father's house, of course. I researched him once I left school, kept tabs on his whereabouts. When the opportunity to work in New Orleans came across my desk I decided to take it, largely to arrange a happenstance meeting with him."

With a smile I said, "You wanted to reach out to your dad? That's sweet."

"I hoped to bump into him around town, ask him for the time, talk about the weather." He sighed. "I never intended on living with him under the same roof."

I winced. "Bad?" I asked, concerned.

He turned his gaze to the yard and stuffed his gloved hands into his jean pockets. "Better than expected."

~ ~ * ~ ~

We stumbled our way through a cemetery, the one closest to our house. I wore my baby blue leathers, my strongest protection, but hardly felt safe. Nothing feels right about tiptoeing through a graveyard in the dead of night, even if you're not alone. On this little adventure were Mr. Smith, Mr. Wesson, Nathan—also wearing his armor, black leather with red piping—and me.

When Smith and Wesson had asked about grave robbing, I didn't think the outing would include me. And yet.

New Orleanians understand the need to watch their feet constantly, since uneven roads and sidewalks buckled by the force of oak tree roots make walking in daylight a challenge. But at midnight, in the winter's cold, aided only by a couple of dim flashlights, made worse by a thick fog that rolled in within the hour, steady feet eluded us all. I hoped Jack was happy, since he had wished for fog.

Our talents made Nathan and me formidable, yet as we led the two lab coated geeks through the maze of mausoleums I felt unnerved. Tall crypts adorned with angels, crosses, crowns, and flowers loomed above us in the mist and moonlight. Nothing as humbling as being surrounded by dead people.

"This way," Nathan whispered, leading the little group with a flashlight in one hand and a halberd in the other. The halberd was his favorite; that's a term we use for weapons that blend well with our own energies. My favorite, a small but weighty silver hammer, hung from a loop on my hip. I couldn't help but rest my hand on it as we walked.

I got the impression the fog confused him, making him periodically stop, look around, read the street sign (don't your cemeteries have street signs?), before moving on.

I didn't really expect the dead to rise up and attack us. Having discovered this talented community, however, I knew there were dangerous things that hid in the dark, like goblins who answered to my nemesis, Malador. While we hadn't notified anyone about our trek through the eternal home of hundreds, that didn't mean we were undetected. We'd been betrayed before. I swallowed at the thought, removing my hammer from its hook.

After what seemed like hours Nathan led us to a big marble edifice, one of the largest on the grounds. "Here it is, guys," he whispered. "The family crypt." Many of the mausoleums and structures around us showed signs of decay and neglect. Some listed a bit, or were covered in graffiti, or revealed their brick construction due to chunks of missing plaster. Not this one. Its polished exterior reflected our flashlight beams around us. Perched on top was a stone dove with a tiny stone bell dangling from its mouth. Framing the doorway was an arch supported by two columns, symbols of victory in death and a noble life. Knowing the family's history they seemed fitting.

From his pocket he produced a jangly set of keys, using one on the heavy padlock that secured the iron gate. It opened with a loud spine-chilling creak. I instinctively looked around hoping we didn't alert anyone, living or dead, to our presence.

Despite their skeptical scientific nature, the two lab coats behind us nervously looked as well.

"Tell me again why we're doing this in the middle of the night?" I asked Nathan.

"Well, we can visit the mausoleum anytime we want, but this way," he pressed firmly on the granite wall just behind the gate, which stubbornly scraped the floor as it swung inward, "we don't run the risk of bumping into any curious curators or tours." He looked over his shoulder. "This isn't exactly a mission on the up and up."

Single file the four of us tiptoed up the two steps, over the stingy-headed threshold, and onto a floor covered with a fine dust layer. Once inside we spread out. The surprisingly spacious interior gave each of us enough room to stand and walk around. I'd seen this trick before; the manor, too, is "bigger on the inside." I don't know why it surprised me. After living in a talented house I should have assumed the family crypt, too, would be talented.

The two flanking walls from the entry all contained visible caskets running lengthwise, all stacked on top of each other like high-density bunks amidst granite shelving. A mosaic of the same symbol that sat on the roof adorned the far wall; a flying white dove holding a small bell twixt its beak. It gleamed in the glow of our flashlights. Under each casket a thin brass plate named and dated each tenant. Wilted and dried bouquets decorated the shelves, tucked in tarnished brass holders.

Nathan pointed to one of the brass name plates. "Charlotte Emilia Witherspoon Lavalle," he said, "my mother." He swallowed a small frown. "You guys are gonna have to do this on your own. I … can't." He turned, and occupied himself with reading some of the other names.

As Smith and Wesson inched their way by us, I put a hand on Nathan's shoulder. "You okay? We don't have to do this."

"Nah. I'm good. I just can't see her is all."

To distract him I pointed to the mosaic. "The bird and bell, symbols of eternal life and mourning."

Nathan chuckled. "Will made you go on cemetery tours I take it."

"He loved 'em. Been on a number. Three in this cemetery alone." I shrugged. "He never told me this one belonged to his family, though."

I waved my flashlight slowly about to take a good look around. I'm no mausoleum expert but from tours I've taken—we have many cemetery tours in New Orleans—this interior was, well, quite different. Due to the nature of New Orleans soil, which is just inches above the water table, we bury our dead above ground, creating the cemetery cities we're so well known for. That puts the housing in the sun and heat. As I understood it, the interiors could reach temperatures upward of five hundred degrees, meaning the residents are essentially "baked". To cinders. It's not uncommon for entire families to own just one slot in a wall; next time someone needed to use it, the previous occupant would be either brushed up and placed in a urn, or simply brushed aside.

But these caskets, save for the cobwebs and thick dust, lay in near pristine condition. Apparently another aspect of a talented crypt.

Nathan broke the silence and I gave him my full attention. "Our mom died when I was, I don't know, eight? The flu, or so we kids were told. Will was, god, barely a toddler. He didn't remember her much. But I do. She was always so kind to us boys. Made wonderful cupcakes and cookies, almost daily. Played with us." He shook his head. "She taught us about our family and its secret, but never lived long enough to see either of us develop our talents."

Smith and Wesson pulled the casket from the wall. "Guys, we could, ungh!" Mr. Smith moaned, "use a little help."

Nathan and I helped the two men heft the casket from the wall and set it on the floor.

"Lavalle?" I asked. The sound of a small electric drill used by Wesson filled the room; the motor's whine insulted the solemn quiet.

"My dad's name. When he died, Will and I changed our last names back to hers. Witherspoon." He smiled wanly. "Will and I never understood how they got together. Mom never told me. Too young I suppose. I suspect the marriage might have been arranged, or done out of convenience. I don't think she would have picked him out of a crowd of eligible bachelors."

I had but one memory—one shown to me by the house—of

Will's dad. I remembered a dark and abusive shadow of a man. With a shudder I distracted myself by reading some of the plaques around me. "Do you think Will should be here?" I asked him.

"Will was very specific about what he wanted after he died. Where he ended up wasn't on the list. He and I left that to you."

"Parts got donated," I nodded, "and the rest cremated. I could have him moved." The carbon bits of his remains were in storage; they were in our home when I was moved into Gateway Manor. Until that very moment I hadn't thought about the jar. I mean ... I had the portrait.

"Your call," he smiled. "We both know he's not in the dust, Winki. He's in the painting. Besides, moving him here would mean you want to be here as well. You don't know any of these people," he swept his arm wide. "Hell, I don't know any of these people."

Dust filled the air as Mr. Smith wiped away the years of soot while Mr. Wesson worked on the lid with a crowbar. "Huh," Mr. Smith said.

"Huh what?" I asked him as Nathan paced off. Mr. Wesson pushed hard on the crowbar, using his foot for leverage.

"The crest on the lid. It's different." His flashlight wandered between the mosaic on the wall and the engraved design on the coffin top.

"How so?" I asked.

"Looks like a snake coiled around a horseshoe, I think."

"A horseshoe," I thought out loud. "Doesn't that mean—"

"*No! Wait!*" Nathan yelled. He trotted toward the coffin just as Mr. Wesson gave a final push against the lid. It opened with a loud crack.

A blast of arctic air whipped through my hair, blowing out the candles. Um, we had no candles, but the flashlights flickered, then failed. *So much for modern technology.*

A loud boom shook the floor as the massive mausoleum door

shut us inside. In the pitch dark, I heard someone thump their flashlight attempting to turn it on.

"No one move," Nathan whispered.

Dazzling blue light flooded the room, seeping out from under the coffin's lid. We all shielded our faces against the brightness. I stole glimpses between my fingers of the blazing blue gel-like substance that bubbled within the casket, turbulently lifting the lid with eerie thuds as it spilled onto the floor.

Nathan sternly said, "Everyone back away, slowly."

No arguments here. We all slowly stepped backwards. I dropped my hand and squinted to take a good look.

"Uh, Boss?" Mr. Smith asked. "What is that?"

The goo moved like a lava lamp, dripping onto the floor in globs and goops. Growing, they began moving on their own, seeping towards each other, making a large pile of cerulean light. I watched in awe as the shimmer defied gravity, growing upwards in front of us.

"It's a sentry," Nathan answered. "Some of the coffins have them to prevent people from doing exactly what we're doing."

"I take it that's not good," I said, frowning.

"The horseshoe and snake?" Smith asked.

"A warning." He commanded, "Smith, Wesson, get that door open. Winki," he raised his halberd, defensively, "get behind me."

Mr. Smith snapped, "And you didn't mention it before because —?" He kept moving fingers around the door jamb, feeling for a way out.

"I forgot, all right?" Nathan hollered in retort. To me he said, "No matter what happens, use no talent."

"But I could slow it down—"

"No. Nothing. Not in front of it. It will use it against us. Trust me." He exhaled in frustration. "That's what they're designed to do."

I blinked, trying to process what I was seeing. The light began to fade and a figure emerged, as if the goopish mass had hardened into a human. Female, I thought, wearing a dress.

"Oh, god," Nathan whispered. "It looks just like her."

"Wait … this is your mother?" I asked. He didn't answer.

She stood tall before us, head held high. She wore a dated dress of bright yellow with large white polka dots, short sleeved and tight fitting. Her dark hair was pulled up and piled into a towering beehive. Her white Naugahyde go-go boots came up to her knees and matched the Naugahyde gloves that came to her elbows. Clothes-wise, she looked like a cross between Jane Jetson and an extra from Austin Powers. In fact, only two things kept me from laughing. First were her eyes, which looked like large, black, wet marbles in her head.

The second was the mace in her hand.

She stared at Nathan. His Adam's apple bobbed.

With the butt of his halberd he rapped on the floor three times. "I am Edward Ethan Witherspoon," he said with as much confidence he could muster, "son of Charlotte Emilia Witherspoon Lavalle. It is my right to see her. We have broken no law."

The figure raised a hand, arm outstretched and palm spread wide, and slowly waved it over Nathan's head. He reacted, his body rocked forward, nearly knocking him off his feet. His halberd clattered to the floor as he gasped.

"Nathan!" I grabbed his arm.

"No," he squeaked, "let go. She's … scanning me. It's okay …"

The goo-lady's hand moved over his body, never touching him, as she worked her way to the floor. When she finished doing whatever she was doing, Nathan fell to his knees, one hand on his chest while the other clumsily searched for his weapon. My eyes fixed on her.

She tilted her head. "No. You are not the son. Nor are you champion." I couldn't help but wince at her voice, which grated like fingernails on a chalkboard. "For that you must die."

"Wait!" he cried out, "Let me explain—"

Lightning shot out of her fingertips, one from each digit, and attached themselves at different points all over his body. He twisted and writhed, falling to the ground.

I lunged to help him only to get majorly shocked myself. He screamed ... rage filled me.

"Enough!" I hollered, throwing my hand into the air.

Everything stopped, frozen in the moment. My jaw dropped. I can slow things down but not freeze them. *Maybe the light quarters amplified the affect?* The lightning froze in crooked trails mid-air, Nathan's body lunged off balance yet remained rigid while his face contorted with pain, and Smith and Wesson were pulling on some lever near the door. Even the small particles of dust stopped in their drift.

I grabbed Nathan, pulling him from his torture. As soon as I touched him he snapped into my time. He scrambled to his feet, panting, and looked at the frozen ... whatever it was.

"Dammit, Winki," he hissed.

"She was killing you!"

He gave the frozen go-go dancer a hard look, pulling me toward the lab coats. As I touched them they, too, snapped back into time. The four of us wrenched the lever down. That effort wiped out my brother-in-law. Nathan collapsed again.

"Help him," I told the geeks, "let's get out now!"

The scientists, each hoisting one of Nathan's arms, helped him find his feet and they headed out into the waiting fog. I turned to look back at the sentry when—

Boom!

I didn't have to look. I'd already heard that sound tonight.

The frozen lightning disappeared. She slowly turned to me.

What had he said? "I am Winki Witherspoon," I said out loud, "wife of William Witherspoon and your champion."

She scanned me as well. I felt the most curious sensation, as if she moved a piece of cellophane through my body; it was light and yielding, yet intrusive and sticky. I quaked in response.

"No," she rasped, "this energy is not familiar. You are not the champion."

I knew what would come next and decided not to wait. Hammer in hand, I swung hard. With her mace she blocked my blow. I let my momentum turn me three sixty, and cross kicked her hard in the mid section. I felt the impact but it wasn't familiar. Her body yielded, dividing. I'd cut her in half with my foot. The clothes disappeared with the form leaving two shining piles of blue goo. They immediately started to meld together.

I heard a grating sound as the door swung open. "Winki!" Nathan called. "Come on!"

With long strides I headed to the door. As I neared it moved to close. I shoved my hammer longwise, bracing it open.

I started to wiggle my way through the small gap, but only got a leg through when Nathan called out, "Behind you!"

I ducked as I spun around, narrowly avoiding the whipping mace that seated itself in the stone wall near where my head would have been. I leapt out at her, forcing her to the floor. With a somersault I gathered into a crouch, waiting for what was next. Her mace gone, I assumed she'd come at me with her lightning. I looked around for something, anything, to fight her with, since she blocked the exit, standing between me and the door.

She raised her hands.

"Hey, lady!" Nathan said, rushing up behind her. With the staff end of his halberd he swiped at her feet, taking her to the floor in a single blow. "Come on!" he called to me, tossing me my hammer.

I didn't hesitate. I leapt over her, taking one last swipe across her jaw, which threw a spray of blue light against the wall. I joined Nathan as she scrambled to her feet. We didn't hesitate. We dashed outside and joined the scientists whose eyes were as big as a full moon.

"You okay?" Nathan asked.

I nodded. "Fine. You?" He nodded. I looked back at the crypt. "Now what?"

He shrugged. "I don't know. I don't think it can exist outside the mausoleum so we're safe out here."

"And what if someone else goes in there?" Mr. Smith asked.

"We can't leave it like that," I agreed.

Nathan scratched his head. "Lemme see, the horseshoe and snake … the horseshoe is a protection against evil and the snake is everlasting life, so what we need—"

"Everlasting life?" I asked. "As in, that thing will never die on its own?"

I heard a clapping. We looked up to see Mr. Wesson frantically trying to get everyone's attention. He pointed at the crypt.

Standing in the doorway, just visible through the fog, was—I gulped—the late Mrs. Witherspoon Lavalle. Not the youthful, gaily dressed, mace wielding, goo monster representation we'd just dealt with. This was the real deal, a corpse reanimated. Her frayed and filthy funeral gown gently swayed in the night air just visible through the wisps of fog. She stood there staring at us with eye-less sockets. Her hands, rotted and missing in patches, braced on the door frame. Her grey skin was leathery with large blotches of flakes.

"What the …?" I whispered.

"It's inside the body," Mr. Smith surmised. "That goo thing is … is …"

"She can't step out of the crypt," Nathan assured us.

Then she did.

I smacked Nathan in the shoulder with the back of my hand. "What was that, just wishful thinking?"

With a wave of her ossified hand she drew the dense fog around us, obstructing our view. I heard the scraping of bare and bony feet making their way down the two steps onto the soft ground of the cemetery.

Through the fog I saw Nathan raise his hand. "Behind me, quickly, get behind me," he said. With a flick of his wrist he summoned up a shield, a barely visible shimmer of white light that opened like an umbrella in front of him. Given what we just went through I wasn't sure how effective it would be. I must have said that out loud.

"This will stop it," Nathan said. "Well, slow it anyway."

He wasn't batting his usual thousand tonight, but I had other reasons to doubt him. We couldn't see it. If it were as clever as I am, it wouldn't have to go against the shield; it could simply move behind us. I turned around, keeping my back to the lab coats, and my eyes on our six, trying to see any movement through the churning blanket. The quiet Mr. Wesson spun to join me.

"Stay still," I whispered. "And listen." Everyone obeyed, listening for the sound of movement in the thick night. But the only sound I could hear was my heartbeat. The fog had gotten so dense I couldn't see three feet in front of me. I closed my eyes and concentrated.

A grunt came from my right, and something grabbed my arm, yanking me off balance. I allowed her to move me earthward only to tuck into a roll and end facing her. She came at me fast. I could scarcely dodge her. I felt my blood curl when she screamed. She scratched my leather, but not me, as she hastened by. *Spry old gal.* I held up my hand to stop her when I realized that would stop everyone.

I quickly looked around. I stood alone. The fog prevented me from seeing any of them, which meant they couldn't see me, either. But, they would if she used her electricity on me; that would light up her location in spades.

I had faith in my leathers and my own strength. *Time to take one for the team, Winki.*

I lowered my hammer and braced for the pain. She raised her fingers...

Thwack!

The head neatly fell from the shoulders, and the entire form collapsed, deflated. From the neck oozed blue gel, like someone had left the top off a bottle of spilled shampoo. It hissed as it touched the ground, disappearing in small wisps of blue smoke. Nathan remained in his stance, halberd in hand, making sure his blow had well and truly ended the sentry.

"Awesome!" Mr. Smith celebrated as he gloved a hand. He picked up the head by its hair. "This will be perfect."

Nathan's face went white.

"Hey," I scolded Mr. Smith. "Show a little respect." I gestured to the man who just decapitated his mother's corpse.

"Oh. Sorry," he said, as he and Wesson put the head into a plastic bag.

"You okay?" I asked him.

He nodded. "It's not her. It was the sentry. It used her body to protect itself outside the crypt, that's all."

I put my hand on his shoulder. "That's not what I asked. I asked if you're okay."

Our eyes met, and he swallowed, slowly nodding. "I will be." He chuckled, "There are times this line of work is a little gruesome."

"You're timing was great," I said, hoping to lift his spirits a bit ... no pun intended.

"I could hear you," he tapped his temple, and frowned. "And never take one for the team, dammit. That's our job."

"But I thought—"

"And if you get killed, what happens to the rest of us? Never. Got it?"

I nodded like a scolded child.

Once the scientists were happy with their catch, I made them return the headless body to its rightful home, then we, reward in hand, returned to ours.

Chapter Four

I YAWNED AT the dining room table, trying to enjoy the coffee, exhausted after last night's ordeal. But every time I drifted off, I had visions of a dead old lady coming at me in a graveyard. I slept, but it wasn't restful.

No sparring, no testing today. Smith and Wesson spent the time working on their theories regarding our gruesomely acquired head and my talents. My skin crawled thinking about what the two men were doing. Best to avoid the basement for a while.

Jack and Nathan came down the stairs, both dressed in suits, ready to tackle another day of reading news on the internet. Besides the Jolly case, which was looking rather like a dead end right now, they had little more to do. Maybe they'd get lucky.

Jack made himself a bowl of cereal from the selection of cute, little boxes that lined the buffet before taking a seat across from me. Nathan picked out a couple of soft boiled eggs, toast, and bacon from various chafing dishes. There was a time when we got served a proper breakfast, however, we no longer had a cook. Pointing that out led to bad feelings, so I kept my discontent to myself. A catering company fed us twenty-four-seven, and while I appreciate the food, the selection bored me. Thus, just coffee for me. I planned on walking to Surrey's after the boys had left for work. A ginormous peanut butter and banana pancake sounded wonderful to me.

Hercule took his position smack in the middle of the table, seated on a saucer splashed with coffee and a lone cube of sugar. I could hear the roach chewing away.

Nathan poured coffee for Jack and filled my cup. "Sleep well?" he asked.

Nightmares of corpses and floating heads filled my dreams. "Fine. And you?" I asked him.

"Ah," he said thoughtfully as he poured his cream. "It was a rough day and a rough night. Needless to say, a rough sleep."

"A rough night?" Jack asked.

"Yeah, Winki and I took Smith and Wesson into the cemetery to get some samples from—"

"Wait?" he rose his head. "Without me?" He looked at me, "You left the house to venture into a cemetery without *me?*" I furrowed my brow as I looked at Nathan, who shrugged. "Did you wear your armor?"

"Uh, oh," Hercule giggled.

"Well, yeah—" I started.

"But you didn't bring *your healer?*" he said, raising his voice. "Look, when you're in this house you can get chopped and stabbed and sliced and diced and I don't give a bloody damn because I know this house will heal you."

"Okay, I just—" I tried to defend.

He continued, his voice raised. "But when you walk out of these doors you're liable to get yourself killed. That's when you *need* me. That's why you *have* me."

"Hey, Jack, take it easy," Nathan tried to sooth. "I swear to you, if anything happens to Winki I'll make sure you're taken care of."

An awkward silence filled the room as Jack's mouth slowly dropped in disbelief. "Is that what you think of me?" he finally said. "Is that what you think this is about? That I'm only concerned about *my* well being because I certainly couldn't be at all concerned about *hers*. Is that it?"

"I just meant—" Nathan surrendered.

He slammed his utensil down. "No, I know *exactly* what you meant. That the healer is only worried about himself." He stood and pointed his finger. "It's just like you to act like a friend but treat me like a damned leech, certain my only concern is my own well being."

Nathan stood, too, hands raised in submission. "Okay, okay," he said. "That's not what a I meant. I'm sorry."

"That's exactly what you meant."

They stared at each other for a moment, speaking only with glares. Jack folded his arms. "Tell me that as you look at me now you don't see a healer."

Nathan sighed. "Sometimes I do," he confessed. "But not usually. Sometimes I see the detective sergeant that asks brilliant questions to help our cases. Other times I see my partner, a guy who I share an office with, and talk to, and joke with."

"But mostly, what do you see?"

With a frown Nathan shook his head. "I'm ... They just beat it into your head, over and over. And even then I didn't really buy it until ..."

"Until what?" Jack pressed.

"Until ... until Will went missing. Until a healer betrayed him."

I gasped, clasping my mouth. *Son of a blessed mango, I screwed up big time.* The two men and chewing bug turned to me.

"Winki? You all right?" Nathan asked.

"*Bloody hell*, how did I forget this?" I looked at Jack with my hands to my mouth, knowing what I was about to say next would cause his already red ears to burst into flames. "It wasn't the healer. Will wasn't betrayed by his healer. It was someone in the cloak, but not his healer."

"How do you know this?" Jack asked.

I swallowed, hearing Will's word so clearly in my head.

Listen to me … It wasn't the healer. They killed him on my behalf, before I had my faculties back to defend him. I'm asking you, please. Don't let that poor man, whoever he was, go unspoken for. Clear his name. Make sure they know. They killed an innocent man in the Citadel.

"Will told me." I let a moment pass. "It was on the last DVD."

I hated sitting there, seeing those blue-green eyes bore into me. "*The* DVD? The one I gave you, what, eight months ago? Don't tell me you only now watched it."

I swallowed. "Jack, I'm sorry—"

He turned on his heels and stormed out of the room. I followed, calling his name, with Nathan behind me. He finally turned to me. "Tell me, what could possibly have been more important than the murder of an innocent man?"

"Knock it off!" Nathan hollered at him. The grave look on his face caught my attention. "Don't you see what this means?" he asked Jack.

"Yes. Perfectly. It means that she's no different than you or anyone else. Without the training and the constant reminder of our station—"

"She's the one person in the world that couldn't give a rat's ass about what you are," Nathan shouted. "You know that. She didn't forget it because she was trying to hurt you, or because you mean nothing to her. Hell, she goes out of her way every god-damned day to make you comfortable in this house."

Jack's reddened eyes bounced from me to Nathan. He took a cleansing breath.

When Jack seemed more in control, Nathan turned to me. "What did he say, exactly?"

I rubbed my face. I recited the words from memory as my face flushed. "He even said it was the most important thing on the DVD, and that I needed to tell you," I fought back the welling tears. "I just got so damn fixated on the stupid riddle and the stupid conjuring that

I just … I'm sorry." I licked my lips, and through my blurred vision tried to find Jack. "I'm so, so sorry."

Nathan whispered to Jack. "I ask again, do you know what that means?"

"*Oui, mon ami*," the bug said, who'd crawled onto the sofa back nearest us. "I know." Even the roach sounded grim.

The tall man nodded, solemnly.

"Well, feel free to fill me in," I sniffed, wiping my cheeks with the back of my hand.

"It means," Hercule answered, "the Citadel Plane will crumble."

"It's already started," Nathan added. "You remember what happened outside the Citadel walls? Your talents didn't work, not properly anyway. " He pointed at me. "You told me you couldn't make things slow down. And when Malador touched you, but there wasn't a lasting effect." He said to Jack, "You couldn't heal yourself until you got back into the Citadel." His eyes darted between us all. "Don't you see? I thought something might be wrong with the tree but it's the energy that built the place." Nathan pressed on. "Jack, explain it to her. Why was the Citadel built?"

Hercule answered first. "It was made so good and evil could battle without damage to themselves or their planes."

"Or," Jack added, "even with the awareness of normals living on those planes."

Normals were what we called *muggles*.

"Exactly," Nathan nodded. "It was created out of justice and integrity, it was created with the blessings and support of both the Dark and Light Lords. And it would always be a beacon of peace and prosperity so long as it remained *just*. But if an innocent man was killed there …"

"It's no longer a just place," Jack finished.

"*Oui*. Nor is it a safe place."

"Winki," Nathan took me by the shoulders. "Will was right. That was the most important thing."

I exhaled, hanging my head.

"This doesn't just impact us or the talented community, this impacts all of mankind." His angry eyes burned down on me. "If the Citadel falls, humanity could be plunged back into the dark ages. You have no idea what could happen, or what has happened in the past. Before Light and Dark forces played in the sandbox we call the Citadel, they played in the world. Once the Citadel stood, that's when mankind truly flourished."

My knees barely held up my own weight. "What do we do?" I asked. "We should tell someone, right? The Chancellor?"

"I would wager," Hercule said, "they already know. But we need to meet with them, *d'urgence!*"

Nathan bit the inside of his lip, his mental wheels turning. "I'll have Jeeves send Hercule and me there this afternoon. I made an ultimatum when we left last year—Ah! Jeeves," he looked up to see the butler floating into the room (he doesn't really float, it just looks that way). "Please set up a meeting with the Chancellor of the Citadel this afternoon. Remind him that he has to convince me that the Citadel is safe for our Champion, and if he doesn't, this house will not attend the tournament. If that isn't motivation enough, tell him I'll make sure none of the white houses do."

"Indeed, sir, consider it done. However," he spoke with a English accent, "you and Jack can expect a client this morning, one of some import. I recommend you all, including you, madam," he said to me, "hasten to the office. That is, of course, if you are quite finished arguing with one another."

"Yeah," Nathan said softly. "I think we've all said our piece."

I hugged myself wallowing in self pity, standing in front of Jack. *How could I have been so stupid? How did I forget this? Will even told me it was important.*

I licked my lips. "Jack …"

"Please," he said, twisting his long face a little, curling his mouth into a half smile. "I accept your apology. Please accept my own apology for raising my voice to you. It's unbecoming of a healer to lose his temper."

"Not to mention rude," Hercule added.

"It's understandable," I whispered. I wiped my eyes with the back of my hand again, "I spent so much time with Smith and Wesson or on that stupid riddle, fixated on what I wanted. Stupid girl doesn't realize the world is going to end."

"It isn't quite as bad as he made it out to be."

"No, no," the bug scolded, "it is that bad." The cockroach scampered out of the room muttering as he went. "And never again are you allowed to watch the DVDs on your own! If the Great Hercule had watched with the silly woman he would have known. He would have warned the right people …"

I rolled my eyes and sighed.

"Maybe you should put on your armor. We'll meet you at the office."

I nodded, and sulked my way up the stairs.

Chapter Five

Taking Jeeve's sense of urgency to heart, I coaxed my Duck, my Ducati motorcycle, along Magazine Street and parked her on the sidewalk. Nathan had her painted a pretty powder blue, to match my leathers.

I crept up the musty staircase and into the office. I had managed to convince Hercule to join me, a small challenge after this morning's demonstration of my complete and utter lack of judgment. His sharp tongue pointed out that I only received the motorcycle back recently after an accident we had on its first time out, demonstrating, yet again, lack of judgment. Nathan sat on the repair for a while, I think to punish me for the mishap. The bug wouldn't let me forget it.

Nathan was on his cell phone when I arrived. I opened my pocket and let loose the *cafard*, who scurried down my leg and disappeared into the paneling of the room.

"Good, good," Nathan said. "I'll be home shortly. Thank you, Jeeves." He pushed the end button. "The Chancellor," he filled us in, "is coming to our house around two this afternoon."

Jack sat upright. "To *New Orleans?*" he pointed downward, at the earth below us.

"Are you sure, *mon ami*, you heard the butler correctly?" Hercule said from somewhere.

"Yeah," Nathan mused. "Isn't *that* interesting?"

"Is that some code for *we're going to get attacked,* or something?" I asked.

"No. It's code for *we don't want you at the Citadel,* that's for sure. You always take guests on your home turf when you can. Coming here is very ..."

"Abnormal?" Hercule finished. "Unusual?"

Jack shook his head. "I believe the words you are looking for are 'unheard of.'"

The door below us opened, its tiny bell tinkling. Instinctively, we all stood, waiting to see who Jeeves deemed so important. Before the visitor came into view, Nathan leaned on the desk with one arm bearing his weight, while the other grasped his forehead. *"Son of a ...,"* he hissed.

Once the woman crested the staircase I took a second, disbelieving look. Saffron Jolly. Or a shell of her former self. I'd seen her cooking shows on TV, not to mention the assortment of adverts on the interior of streetcars, sides of buses, and billboards. I could barely recognize her now—her face splotchy, probably from crying her eyes out, her short strawberry-blond hair limp and greasy, and her hazel eyes sunken and sallow, hovering over purplish-blue half moons. She hunched a bit, as if carrying a heavy burden. Probably was.

I leaned to Nathan and quietly asked, "Did I look that bad?" When he didn't answer, I glanced at him. He clenched his eyes, then pinched the bridge of his nose with his fingers, trying to massage away the screaming voice filling his head. I got out some ibuprofen for the poor man. As I poured him some water, Jack greeted the guest.

"Mrs. Jolly," Jack said with his hands behind his back. "I must say, after our last encounter, your presence is quite unexpected. But most welcomed. Please, have a seat."

Sitting, she nodded. We all waited for her to speak.

Beats passed as she seemed to search for words. Finally she asked, "Are any of you Catholic?" We all exchanged glances. "Religious at all?"

I didn't know how to answer that. Thankfully, Jack did. "I sincerely hope our faith, or lack of it, doesn't preclude you from asking for our help," Jack said. He was very good with words.

"In my religion, it's a sin to take your own life. So I won't consider it. My family, I know, wait for me in heaven, and I won't do anything to jeopardize my chance of spending eternity with them." She licked her lips. "But recently I find myself wondering, if I know someone *wants* to kill me and I do nothing to prevent it, is that a sin? Is that considered suicide? Am I putting my soul at risk?"

Jack looked like his mind raced for the right words. I spoke up. "Mrs. Jolly, I'm not sure we're the best guides for your soul, or your faith. But I can't help but believe that laws insist you endure because, well, living is always a better choice than dying."

"Have you ever lost anyone you loved? Truly loved?" I didn't need to be a *thought catcher* to hear the pain in her voice. The suffering in her eyes tore my heart. My own memories, the ones I worked hard at pushing away, came flooding back.

I answered honestly. "My husband died unexpectedly just over a year ago. In November." I let those words hang in the air a moment. "Yes. He was my world."

With a deep nod Mrs. Jolly reached into her hand bag and handed Jack a crumpled piece of paper. "This came for me in the mail a couple of days ago. After your visit yesterday, I decided maybe you should see it."

Jack gingerly unfolded it. Immediately his eyebrows shot up at the letterhead. I watched his eyes scan each line. With a thoughtful sigh he passed the letter to Nathan.

As he read the letter, his eyebrows, too, shot up. "Rather polite of them, don't you think?" He continued to rub his temples.

"Do you recognize the letterhead?" Jack asked.

He nodded. "I thought they were a myth."

"It would seem that's not true. Apparently, they have an office right here in New Orleans."

Nathan passed the letter to me, asking Mrs. Jolly, "Can we make a copy of this?"

"You can keep it."

It read:

> Dear Mrs. Saffron Jolly,
>
> It has come to our attention that you are, in fact, working on a remedy for our condition, one that will, for lack of a better word, destroy us entirely. We loathe to use the word "genocide," but your pursuits will eliminate us from this world.
>
> To that end, should you continue your efforts, we will respond in kind. Consider yourself warned, good lady. We will not hesitate to use force.
>
> Our sincere regards,
> The Asclepium Order

That name sounded *so familiar* to me. "Asclepium Order?" I mused out loud. "Talented?" I asked.

"Very. We'll talk about it later. Mrs. Jolly, you said you got this a few days ago?" The woeful woman nodded. "Do you know what they're talking about? Are you making anything?"

"No. I haven't even been in a kitchen in over three weeks. I can't bring myself to … to create anything at the moment. Hell, even oatmeal is a stretch right now."

"How about before the accidents?"

"I was always cooking something. It's what I do. But nothing harmful, nothing that was going to hurt anyone."

Jack asked, "Any new ingredients? Something you'd never used before? A new vegetable or spice?"

Mrs. Jolly just shook her head.

Jack shoved his hands his pockets. "Have there been any attempts on your life?"

She shrugged. "Don't know. Not that I'd care. Unless they've been trying to kill me all along."

Nathan tried to stifle the grunt, hung his head, and rubbed the space between his eyes. "I, um," he moaned, "I'm gonna let you two run with this. I have a meeting I need to prep for." He inhaled deeply trying to clear his head and focus. "Mrs. Jolly, please forgive me, but I think I speak for us all when I say we'd love to handle your case. Jack here is a fine detective and our partner, Winki, will do everything she can to keep you safe. May I call you this evening, if I have further questions?"

"Yeah. Sure."

Nathan handed the letter back to Jack, gathered his things quickly, stuffed everything into his briefcase, and nearly ran down the stairs.

To distract Mrs. Jolly from his hasty escape, I offered my hand. "We haven't been introduced," I said. "I'm Winki Witherspoon."

"Saffron Jolly," she said without emotion. "Call me Saff."

Jack walked around his desk and leaned against the top. "I'm not sure what changed your mind, Mrs. Jolly, why you chose to show us the letter. But I feel I need to warn you, this group is not to be dismissed. They are very dangerous."

Mrs. Jolly folded her arms. "'Kay."

"If you're serious about letting us help you—"

"You told me yesterday you think someone killed them," Mrs. Jolly stated. "Do you really think that? Did these people," she pointed to the letter, "take my family from me? Was that a mistake … did they mean to kill me?"

"Did you receive any such letters or threats from them prior?"

"Or from *anyone* before?" I added.

"No," she said.

"Then, no, I don't think so."

"You just said they're dangerous," she pressed.

He frowned, glancing at the paper. "I hardly think they'd kill your family only to send you a rather polite letter saying you're next."

"But you think someone did. You think someone killed them."

Jack shot me a quick glance, looking for help. "I live in a world of statistics, ma'am. I was recently told the odds of your family dying in three random accidents within one month are smaller than the odds of you being hit by a meteor. So, yes, I do believe you are being targeted, and not by incredibly bad luck."

"What do they want … this *Order?*"

Jack answered, "I intend on asking them as soon as you've left here. In the meantime, ma'am, I'd like to send Mrs. Witherspoon here home with you." I opened my mouth to protest, but he continued. "Let her look around your home, just to see if anything is obviously wrong."

"I think I'd notice something obvious," Mrs. Jolly retorted.

"At this point in time," Jack said, "I don't think you'd notice a cockroach climbing up your leg."

My eyes widened at the sight of Hercule doing just that. The poor woman screamed. "Hercule!" I called out as I scooped my roach-familiar off Mrs. Jolly. I tucked him away, hoping she didn't notice my odd behavior. Not many people put roaches in their jacket pockets.

"My apologies," Jack said as she hastily stood, brushing her pant leg. "The office is scheduled to be fumigated tomorrow." Mrs. Jolly cursed herself, the roach, and the city, and as she did Jack said to me, "Please, go with her."

"*You're* the investigator," I argued in hushed tones, "*I'm* the guns, remember?"

"Right now she needs protection more than anything. But you'll know if something's," he whispered, "talented."

"Are you really going to visit this Order?" Not that I had any idea of who they were. I was used to being the last to know anything.

"Yes, ma'am. With your permission, of course."

I frowned. "Not wild about you going alone."

"They're healers, ma'am."

I took a shocked step backwards. "Healers? That threaten?"

"I won't do anything foolish, I promise."

A small consolation. However, without a good-bye, the bug-frightened woman stormed down the staircase.

Jack nodded after her. "You'd better hurry."

Great. Now, I'm a baby-sitter. "Should I be looking for anything in particular?"

He shook his head. "We can assume her home was combed over by the police. So look for what seems out of place." With a heavy sigh I trotted down the stairs after the miserable lady who made it clear she wanted nothing to do with me. "And, ma'am?" Jack peered over the railing. "Please. Be careful."

I fired up the Duck and followed Mrs. Jolly to her home.

Chapter Six

FROM MY SADDLE, I watched Saffron Jolly slog to her porch. I recalled lazy Sunday mornings when Will and I would make brunch with crepes, poached eggs, toast, thick-cut bacon, topped off with mimosas or the poinsettias. Then we'd snuggled together on the fluffy sofa, watching "Spice the Kitchen with Saffron" while she cooked some outrageous southern foodstuff. Now, she walked hunched under a tone of invisible bricks. What a difference a year makes. Or a month.

I'd followed Mrs. Jolly to an elegant Craftsman house in an equally elegant neighborhood just outside the city limits. The enormous structure occupied a good-sized chunk of the large, well groomed, lush green yard. An empty swing set out front stood testament to her recent loss.

A man sat on the porch. He stood when Mrs. Jolly finally reached her destination, quite a walk from the driveway. I kept a watchful eye and ear as I stowed my helmet.

"Saffron, damn, where ya been?" the man asked.

Mrs. Jolly walked by without a word as she fumbled in her bag for her keys. I silently crept up the steps as she and the man made their way into the Jolly home. When the man saw me coming he held out his hand to stop me. "Hey, lady, Saffron isn't seeing anyone just now—"

"It's all right, Simon," she said to him. "She's with me."

I didn't even know she was aware I was around. I nodded at the new person as I stepped over the threshold.

"Simon, this is, uh … what's your name again?" Mrs. Jolly asked me.

"Winki. Winki Witherspoon." I held my hand out to the gentleman, but he didn't take it.

Mrs. Jolly thumbed the man staring at me. "This is Simon, my brother."

"And what are you again?" Simon asked me. Mrs. Jolly disappeared into the house.

I took a hard look at her brother. Handsome-ish with styled, brown hair swept across his brow. His shadow of a beard gave him a rugged look. Hazel eyes, like Saffron.

"I work for Lost Souls Investigations. I'm here to watch Mrs. Jolly for a while. Make sure she's not in any danger."

Simon looked me up and down, sussing out the white-haired chick in leathers that claimed she would keep his sister out of danger. Oh, yeah, I understood his concern. He squinted his eyes. "What are you, fifty?" he asked.

Yes, I was insulted. Without answering I walked by the rude man and into the home, running a hand through my white (not *grey*, dammit!) hair. I came to do a job, best start doing it, and not worry that my hair makes me look … older.

Beyond the front door was a lovely staircase entry and an expansive living room. The floors and woodwork shined in polish, the peach colored walls newly painted. I removed my gloves and touched a wall. I half-expected the house to talk to me, sending me a flash of its past or present like my home frequently does, but I only felt the hard, cold surface. Talking to houses … now *that*, I thought, would be a cool talent.

But you had to look hard to see its beauty since most every

surface, floor, and piece of furniture was covered in tossed clothing and fast food boxes. Popeye's, McDonald's, Cafe Du Monde, Reginelli's, Domino's; cups and mugs and partially eaten leftovers littered everything.

Mrs. Jolly planted herself on the cognac-colored Stickley sofa, which I could barely see beneath the layers of blankets and bedding. I closed my eyes, lost in my own memory. I understood completely, not wanting to sleep in an empty bed. But unlike Mrs. Jolly, when Will passed, I couldn't eat. Nothing looked good, nothing tasted good. I'd lost my appetite. I'm guessing she found comfort in food.

"Saffron, really?" Simon brushed past me, nearly knocking me aside. "You hired detectives? Man, it was just all a terrible—"

"Why are you here, Simon?" she cut him off. "If you want more money just write yourself a check and leave."

Simon put his hands on his hips. "They want to see you, Saf. They want to know you're okay." He sounded sincere.

"I'm not. I don't want to see anyone right now. Just … please, just leave." Mrs. Jolly slouched deeper into the sofa and turned on the large flat panel screen across the room. Another painful memory washed over me.

"We had a good month," Simon offered, trying to get his sister's attention. Of course they did, I thought. Many patronized the Jolly restaurants to show support, including Nathan and me last Tuesday. I'd wager most the city did.

"I don't care. I really don't."

Simon persisted. "Saf, Jenny wants to cook you dinner tonight, and the kids want to see you. How about it? You need to get out of this damned house."

"Give her my thanks and love, but no. I was just out," she pointed at me without looking. "I want to stay home."

Defeated, Simon turned away. I grabbed him by the arm as he opened the door. "She needs time," I tried to console.

"Lady," he scolded, pulling from my hand, "you don't know Jack." And left.

My bad. Shouldn't have interfered. Tragedies, like families, are way too personal.

Back to the task at hand. "Mrs. Jolly?" I asked, "would you mind —?"

"Saffron. Call me Saffron," she rasped, without looking at me.

"Saffron, would you mind if I looked around upstairs?"

"Go ahead," she said in monotone.

As quietly as I could I crept up the staircase. The creaks felt warm and loving, like at the manor.

I widened my jacket pocket and whispered, "You can come out now." Hercule crawled up and onto my shoulder. "You love to make trouble," recalling his stunt in the office.

"What I love," the French-accented *cafard* said, "is to see how people react to me. It is very enlightening, *n'est-ce pas?*"

The top of the stairs gave way to a hallway full of doors. Sticking with the right-hand rule I turned to my right.

Grand double doors greeted me, encased in a thick, ornate molding. I entered the dramatic master bedroom. High ceilings, two large bay windows, a small fireplace, an attached bathroom, a little living room all its own, and in the center a canopied king-sized bed. Everything looked organized with no signs of recent use. Running my finger over a dresser left a trail in the dust.

I picked up a framed photograph. Saffron and her husband on their wedding day. Smiling, happy faces of long ago. Looked like a pair of kids.

"The bathroom, *ma chére*," Hercule urged.

Bath*room* hardly sufficed. Bath*house* was more like it. Completely covered in limestone tile, the room had two sinks, an enormous bath-slash-hot tub, separate open shower, and (count 'em) two roomed commodes. Both Hercule and I whistled, which echoed off the walls.

"Go through everything," Hercule urged. "Open all the drawers."

"You think she's hiding something?"

"No. I just like going through people's personal items."

I chortled in disgust but did as he directed. Among the normal, everyday sundries we found a number of prescriptions. I picked up a bottle. "Sleep aids," the roach said.

I looked him over. "How do you know?"

"I know. Trust me."

The dates were old, over a year. "Nothing new, though. Wait—" I found a two small bottles tucked behind the toothpaste, hiding. "What's this?" Each was made out for Harrison Jolly, and each was current ... and each was unpronounceable by yours truly.

"You can look these up, *oui?*"

I got out my phone. One was a barbiturate, and the other a newly approved drug for memory loss. I recalled a news report about Mr. Jolly suffering a possible head injury during a game last year. They said he was fine. Maybe it was worse than anyone let on. I took pictures, replacing the items as I'd found them.

Leaving the room I continued down the hallway, dragging my hand along the wall, a habit from my own home. Next was a child's bedroom, smaller and, judging by the blue walls and fire truck motif, made for a boy.

"It would be my guess," Hercule said, "the youngest was here. Closest to the master bedroom."

Also the most recent death. The small child somehow got on the roof of the home and fell. I ran my hand against the wood grain of the door frame. "She must just hate this house," I whispered. I thought I would.

"Did you hate your home, *ma chére?*"

"No. But Will didn't die in it."

The next room, a bathroom, felt more lived in. I guessed it was the boy's. I started through the cabinets, but found nothing out of the ordinary.

We briefly explored the boys rooms. Each had its own style and color scheme (one of the boys aspired to follow in his father's footsteps, judging by the posters, the black and gold colors, and the Saints bed covers).

I descended the stairs. To my right lay Saffron in the expanse of a living room, to my left a double door. Behind lay a large office. On one side, a number of cases displayed football trophies, awards, and an obscenely ornate diamond encrusted ring. In the center of the room was a massive desk. I sat, opened drawers, pawed through papers and files, mostly about the restaurants, some personal tax documents, credit card bills, and bank statements. You know, *life.*

Nothing of import. To me, anyway.

With a huff I pressed my chin on my interlocked fingers, elbows on the desk top.

"Bah!" Hercule said. "Let's go in the kitchen."

I noticed a discrepancy. From what should have been the center of the desk to the leftmost side seemed a slightly longer distance than to the right. I wouldn't have seen it if it weren't for the intricate inlayed design on the top, which was smack in the center ... except for a little extra space on the left side.

"Come on, *chére!* I am bored. And hungry."

"Just a sec," I said as I got down on hands and knees, looking at the woodwork on the left. I ran feeling fingers underneath, where base met the top. Something gave with a small click.

"That sounded promising," he said, crawling across the top.

The entire left panel of the desk base swung open. Exposed was a petite set of shelves the height and width of the base, about one inch deep. Hidden there was another ring (identical to the one in the case, likely the real one I guessed), other pieces of jewelry, credit cards, and ... a small memory card.

"Oo," I said, gingerly picking up the tiny micro SD. "Eureka!"

"*Trés bon, ma chére.*" I started to pocket the item. "Wait, why not see what is there?"

"How?" I asked him.

"Your cell phone, of course. *Mon Dieu!* I'm a cockroach and I know more of the things technical!"

I took out my phone and—*what do you know!*—inserted the chip into a small slot on the side.

"Quickly," he said, "copy the items on it and put it back."

After a painful amount of poking at apps and flipping screens, my familiar helped me do just that. "Are you sure this is legal?" I managed to ask as I fumbled with my phone.

"Hmmm ... let me see. We find a hidden compartment and open it without asking, then we find a hidden disk and copy it without asking. I'm going to go out on a limb here and say, '*no.*'"

I gave him a glance, removed the disk and put it back on its tiny shelf, closing the desk's side with a solid click.

My cell rang, startling me enough to drop the phone. The caller ID said "Jeeves." Rattled, I sent him to voice mail.

Intending to asking Mrs. Jolly if I could take the disk, I returned to the living room. I'm not a thief by trade.

Saffron hadn't moved. Like a stone she reclined there, eyes on the television across the room. She didn't even look up when I came in.

"Saffron?" I asked. No response. "Can I get you anything?"

"No. Thanks." No emotion. I didn't think she heard the question.

I pressed, moving between her and the TV to make sure I was seen. "I'd like to ask you a couple of—"

Before I finished, her dull eyes looked at me, then widened. She jumped off the couch, throwing her blanket to the floor, and leaped thirty feet from me in one bound. "There's ... there's ..." She pointed to her own shoulder.

Great Guacamole, I'd completely forgotten. "Yeah," I tried to dismiss it, "He's a ... pet." I pointed at Hercule, who I knew would take exception to the "pet" comment. To the roach I whispered, "If you poop on me just to spite me, I swear I'll flick you across the room."

Hercule quietly grunted his discontent.

"In the pocket, please."

With surprisingly little drama he made his way down the front of my jacket and took his position. He perched himself within so he could watch, with his front legs clinging to the top and his little antennae twitching to and fro.

Saffron quaked, rubbing her arms as if she were cold. "I don't like 'em in my house."

"He won't come out of my pocket, I promise."

With a frown she timidly returned to her sofa. A prescription bottle fell to the floor. I picked it up as she asked, "You were saying?"

It was the same prescription as the expired sleep aids I found upstairs.

"Having a hard time getting any shut eye," she mumbled.

I set the bottle down. I decided to finish looking around before asking about the disk, in case I found something. Or before she got angry and kicked me out of the house. "Where's the kitchen?" I asked.

She jerked a thumb in the air. "Just go 'round." She sat up a bit. "I don't want that bug in there."

"He won't touch anything. I swear."

I heard her audibly shudder.

Once out of earshot Hercule gave a little laugh. "You see? Having me around is a good thing," he said.

"How do you figure?"

"You didn't notice, *ma chére?* When she saw me, for just the moment brief, she forgot her troubles."

That was true; she seemed greatly distracted.

"Focus, bug," I told him as we discovered the kitchen.

Again the cell rang, again from "Jeeves." He never calls so I knew it was important, but I wanted to get through my prying as quickly as I could. Even with Saffron's permission, snooping through her life felt wrong. Again, I sent him to voice mail.

The word *grand* didn't do justice to the room; her kitchen was *humongous*. Eight burner gas cooktop, three ovens, two refrigerators (one eight feet long), two separate double sinks (one in the island), several magnetic strips on the wall stuffed with various knives, and enough cabinets to run the country. All the gleaming surfaces were either brushed stainless steel or polished granite slab. I spun in a circle admiring the place. "Googly moogly!"

"*C'est vrai!*" Hercule said.

We started the search for, well, I don't know what. I just opened each cabinet and inspected their contents. Everything you would expect in a kitchen: spices, powders, ingredients in one section, home-made canned goods in another, cleaners under the sink, rags and towels over here, plates and silverware over there. All very neatly organized. Just a *lot* of it.

"You lookin' for somethin' in particular?"

I startled at the voice in the entry. Saffron leaned against the doorway, arms folded, and hair dangling in her eyes.

"No," I said. "I'm sorry for the intrusion," I scratched my head.

She looked me up and down. "Where's the roach?"

"Still in my pocket. He hasn't touched a thing. And won't."

"Good call. I don't like roaches in my kitchen. And the hammer? What's with that?"

Saffron gazed at the silver mallet that dangled from my hip. "Ah, well, um, you never know when you're gonna need a hammer. You know, late night, lots of nails taunting you. Looks cool, though, don't it?"

She didn't answer me, not sure she even heard me. She chewed on her lip. "You must think I'm pitiful." Her eyes started to glisten.

I took a deep breath. She was so much like me ... I could feel her pain; it had once been my own.

"A year ago, I was you," I nodded to the living room, "the one watching TV from the sofa. Not, you know, *that* sofa." She smiled a little, making her recognizable for a brief moment. I tried to channel Jack, who would use this opportunity to ask casual questions as a guise for gathering information. "Is Simon older or younger?"

"Older. By a couple of years."

"How many were in your family?"

"Just us four. Ma, Pa, Simon, and me."

"Did everyone cook?"

"Yeah. Pa and me enjoyed it the most. The two of us did almost all the cookin'." She had one of those sneaky southern accents, the kind that only flares up with the right word, like "cooking." Most New Orleanians talk that way, no real accent, just a flourish now and again.

"I have to ask this question, so please don't take it the wrong way," I started, "but how was your family? Your relationships? Any arguments?" *With say, your brother?*

She shifted her body weight uncomfortably. Made me a little nervous. "You mean was there any reason for anyone to kill my entire family?"

"Just ... asking how things were."

"Things were fine. No lying, no cheating, no arguing. We were happy. We were *all* ..." She wiped her cheeks and sniffed. "You planning on staying?"

My cell phone buzzed. It was Jeeves. Again. Something's wrong. "I'm so sorry but I have to take this. Please, excuse me. Hello?"

"Madam, where are you? I've tried to contact you several times."

I know, sorry. "I'm at Saffron Jolly's house. Why?"

"You'll be receiving a *visitor* soon."

I squinted in confusion. "Where ... ?" My eyes grew wide. *Great bats of Baldwin.* Jeeves was a doorman; he knows when we we'll be receiving ... "Oh, you mean *here?* Suggestions?"

"Leaving would be the best course of action."

A dull roar came from the living room. Saffron wheeled around. "What the hell is that?"

"Too late, Jeeves," I said as I poked the off button, angry that I hadn't spoken to him sooner. I raced to stop Saffron by grabbing her arm as she headed for the noise. "Stay behind me," I commanded and pulled her back.

I trotted into the living room to see the fully formed sphere of distorted light. We called them portals. *Something wicked this way comes.*

"What in the world is that?" she cried out.

I had no idea who would be so bold as to punch a hole into the house of a normal, but I for one was impressed.

I called to the wide eyed woman behind me, trying to be heard over the roar, "No matter what happens you stay behind me, got it?"

She swallowed with a quick nod, eyes fixed on the distortion.

Short and stocky green men with skin pocked in boils and pus marched out of the portal, taking positions around the living room. Two by two, side by side, the muscled men, armed with medieval weaponry and metal armor filed out of the sphere.

"Jesus," Saffron screamed. "*What the hell are those?*" She grabbed my waist and hid behind me.

"Just stay calm. Let me handle this. Stay right here, behind me, got it?"

After a dozen of the little green warriors came through, out stepped a familiar and loathed face. Albeit gorgeous. *Malador.* Tall, dark and oh-the-stars handsome. Decked out in black leather from head to toe, his deep brown eyes spied me and opened in surprise.

The hands on my waist vanished. Upon seeing the long-locked, chiseled-jawed, chocolate-eyed man, Mrs. Jolly took a step toward him. I held her back. "Behind me," I reminded.

With a windy pop the portal vanished.

"What are *you* doing here?" Malador asked me.

"Said the incubus who stepped through the portal," I retorted.

Malador's eye bounced from me to the woman behind me, um, next to me. I pushed her back again. Malador has that way about him …

"Playing protector, I see," he hissed.

"So, you wanna just turn around now or do you need me to kick your butt back home for you?"

He gave a darling smile. *Damn*, I wished he wasn't so overwhelmingly … suave. I knew my own reaction wasn't actually attraction; Incubi, by their very nature, exude massive quantities of animal magnetism and lust. Knowing that didn't make him any easier to ignore.

Malador took a stalking step towards me. "I'm here to rescue the damsel who's so distressed," he held out a hand to Saffron, and gave a soothing smile.

She started to move towards him, and I pushed her roughly behind me, hoping my aggression would break the trance. I succeeded. She gave me a hateful glance. "Think about Harrison," I said. "Think about your husband and kids."

"That's why I've come," Malador purred. "I can take that pain away, my dear." He took a step closer, hand still outreached. "Just … take my hand, and all your pain will vanish. I swear it."

He was convincing. Hell, even I wanted to go.

I grabbed the woman by her shoulders, turning her to me. "Stop. Don't listen to him. Don't look at him." Her eyes were glazed, her face turned to the man in the center of the living room.

I shoved her back, and yelled to him. "Why? Who is she to you?" I narrowed my vision. "She's just a normal."

"Normals can do the most *extraordinary* things." Some small smile dashed across his lips. I sensed something sinister, something he hid.

"Did you do this to her? Did you take her family?"

"Wait … *what?*" Mrs. Jolly said, finally—and thankfully—looking at me.

Malador laughed heartily. "My dearest love, you're ignorance is always so refreshing. So innocent. I simply dream of the day you come to me. I intend on sharing everything with you. My past. My future," he licked his lips, "my bed."

I rolled my eyes. One of his goblins laughed.

"Silence!" Malador scolded. Then smiled at me. "I can ask the same question, wife-to-be, who is this woman to you?" I couldn't help but swallow at the title he gave me. "Look. Give me the woman. I will make good on my promise. I will take away all her pain." He looked at her. Once their eyes met she was hooked again. *Dammit.*

I spun my hammer around my middle finger. Showy, but it got his attention. "Malador, go home."

"Fine. Let's do this the hard way," he sneered. Malador drew his sword and rushed at me. The goblins moved aside, some of them heading behind me. Toward Saffron.

I stomped my foot, raised my hand and yelled, "*Not in this house.*"

Everyone and everything slowed down, to an absolute crawl; Malador, Saffron, the lot of them. I looked around quickly. Yes, I could bash them all in and create a ruckus for this home, possibly destroy it, and attract a whole bunch of attention from the neighborhood. But …

Jeeves had told me to run. Jeeves was a *very wise man.*

I grabbed Saffron by the wrist, which snapped her out of slow-motion. "Time to go!" I urged.

"But … I … what?"

I hustled her out the door and raced to my motorcycle. I handed her my helmet. "Put this on." I jolted my bike awake. Once her arms wrapped around my waist, we tore out of the driveway and into the quiet safety of New Orleans.

Chapter Seven

"YOU BROUGHT HER here?" Nathan asked for the fourth time.

"What part of 'Malador attacked her home' don't you understand? I can't protect her there, but I can here. My strength is here." I didn't want to confess Malador's allure felt way more powerful in the Jolly house.

We argued out of earshot of our guest. Saffron sat curled up into the palm of a leather chair; her feet on the seat, and her knees drawn up under her chin. She looked small, almost childlike. I suspected that was how she felt, too. She'd just been exposed to the world of magic. I knew exactly how overwhelming that felt. When it first happened to me, I ran.

"There are a thousand reasons why this is a bad idea, Winki, not the least of which is I can't be within a mile of that lady without getting a migraine."

"You're doing okay now," I pointed out.

"She's a jello-head right now. It's just a matter of time before it all comes flooding back."

"What about Smith and Wesson? Could make you a gonzo or something?" *Gonzo* is a silly name for a magical charm or talisman, one of the many silly names I've had to contend with over the last year. "Something you could wear that deadens the effect. I mean, they've known you and your talents for years now. That should be pretty easy, no?"

He stood upright. "You know, that's not a bad idea." He looked at Mrs. Jolly, whose eyes focused on a distant point. Nathan quietly approached her and leaned over to take a closer look, mouthing the words, "She's freaked out."

"I remember how I felt my first day."

Nathan whispered, "But she was never supposed to know. You were." He twisted his lips a bit. "Malador, huh?"

"Yeah. And I got the impression he knows way more than he's letting on." I pulled Nathan away, back out of Saffron's hearing. "Could he have done this? Could Malador have killed her family?"

"Could he have, sure. But it's not his style. Malador likes his victims to beg for … you know. He's an incubus."

"He wanted Saffron. He asked for her. It was all I could do to keep her from him, too."

Jack joined us, having returned from his own outing. "Did I miss something?" He saw Saffron Jolly tucked in the chair. "I'll take that as a resounding 'yes'."

I led the two men into the hallway beyond the living room doors. I filled them in on the attack, the drugs I'd found, and the information I had on my phone.

Nathan tilted his head when I mentioned the prescriptions. "Sounds like he had possible head trauma. You should ask Mrs. Jolly about it."

"Me?" I asked. "Why me?"

"You found them. Do you have your cell?"

I handed Jack my phone, and while poking at it he mused, "A cleverly hidden panel? That explains why the police didn't find it." He gave a small smile. "Two sound files. Shall we listen?"

I looked at Nathan, the lawyer, for a lead.

Nathan opened his mouth to argue, then reconsidered. "We've already crossed the Rubicon. Go ahead."

It started to play:

"I said 'no.'"

"Look, man, I just need a co-signer." I recognized the voice of brother Simon. *"Nothin's gonna happen—"*

"'No' means 'no', man, get it? Saff and I are tired of all your little schemes. All your great investments, all your fancy toys and big ideas. I don't want you asking her for any more handouts."

Nathan softly spoke, "I think that's Harrison Jolly."

"I'm not asking for a handout!" Simon yelled. *"I'm asking for a signature."*

"For a quarter of a million dollars!"

"It's just a signature."

"You're always asking for something. Every time I see you. A job, money, a signature. For God's sake, leave her alone. Leave us alone."

The sound of movement, possible shoving, could be heard.

"Back off! You're not my sister's boss."

"Let me put it to you this way. You ask for one more goddammed thing and I will slap you with a restraining order so fast your face will be found in Houston, got it?"

"Screw you, man!" Actually, "screw" was not the word he used.

"Fine. You know what? I'm not going to wait. I'm heading to the police first thing in the morning."

"Screw you!" Simon yelled again, more distant. A door slammed shut, a little shuffling sound, and the recording ended.

Nathan looked at Jack. "Things weren't so peachy in the Jolly family after all."

"Sounds that way," Jack nodded. "But we know no such restraining order was filed or it would have shown up in Detective Duplantier's investigations."

"Play the next one," Nathan encouraged.

"Hey, Saff, it's me." Harrison Jolly. *"Look, I just want you to know that I'm not taking this lightly at all. Your brother's a jerk sometimes. I think we need a break from him for a while. I taped my last conversation with him, where I*

confront him on his latest scheme. I don't want you to sign anything for that guy, okay? You've worked hard. Yeah, you had some lucky breaks as well, but that's not a reason to give him everything he wants. I think he's a jerk for even asking. It's time you stand up to him, got it? I'm heading out to take Sammy to practice. I love you, babe."

We all went pale, looking at each other. "If he was planning on going to the police the next morning—" I said.

"And there was no restraining order …," Jack continued.

"And he was heading out to take the kid to practice right after he made this …" Nathan nodded.

We all gulped at the same time. It didn't need to be said. Harrison Jolly made this just minutes before driving off the bridge.

After moments of quiet reflection Nathan asked, "Why did he make the second recording?"

"It sounds like a voice mail message," Jack said.

I described the drugs Hercule and I found. "Maybe he was having trouble with his memory?"

Jack nodded. "We'll have to talk to her and see if she received this," he said to Nathan, who was already rubbing his forehead.

"Before I do anything around that woman I need to go see Smith and Wesson."

"Hold on. Don't you want to hear about my visit to the Asclepium Order? The address on the letterhead led to a small law firm in the CBD." (The Central Business District of New Orleans.) "At the firm, however, no one seemed to know what the Asclepium Order was. However, I sensed a sort of shimmer. Much like when a portal starts to open."

"Some kind of *perception shield?*" Nathan asked.

"Possibly. I'd wager it hided the real doorway to the Order."

"*Who the hell are you people?*" I nearly jumped out of my skin at the cry. Saffron stood by the living room door, pointing an accusing finger. "All of you! You're demons from hell!"

I raised my hands. "You've seen some bizarre things today, I get that."

"Stay away from me!"

"But it was all just illusions. Just like a magic show. Nothing was real. Think about it."

Chest heaving, she narrowed her eyes as a beat or three passed. "Those ... things. Those green things. They're *demons*."

"Just, um, midgets in green paint," my mind raced to explain. "They were meant to scare you, like a Halloween costume." Plausible, if I do say so myself. I hoped she bought it.

"The windy ball. What was that?"

"Another magic trick. Like you've seen a thousand times on stage. Nothing to it. Just smoke and mirrors." I kept smiling and calm, pretty pleased with my performance. I flipped my white hair, making a casual gesture to distract her.

"*You!* You made everything slow down."

I opened my mouth but this time my brain failed me. "Wow, I got nothing for that."

"That was your own illusion," Jack said in a calming voice. "When your adrenaline kicks in things move slowly. You were very frightened. We're so sorry for that. Nevertheless, the threat was real. The man who came to your home was dangerous."

Nathan's turn. "So, we'd like you to stay here, we would, we would." I winced hearing that voice he used when he manipulated people; overly chipper, grating, and with a thick Boston accent. He called the talent *the voice of reason*. I called it no end of annoying.

It was working. Her shoulders released a bit, her face softened. He continued.

"Please, be our guest. Just for a couple of days. Just until we can sort this all out."

Out of nowhere Jeeves wafted up to Saffron. He handed her a cup. "Madam, I've taken the liberty of preparing you some tea. I think you'll find it quite soothing."

She thanked him. We returned to the room and seated ourselves. Mrs. Jolly took a sip, no small challenge considering the quake in her hand. Her tense body ease as her back slumped comfortably in the chair. "A magician, huh?" she convinced herself. Her eyes drew distant.

I nodded. "That's what we do here. We make magic tricks." Not a complete lie, since Smith and Wesson, in their free time, do exactly that, and for some big-named illusionists.

Nathan spoke to Jack. "I'm going to visit Smith and Wesson to get some kind of buffer from Mrs. Jolly before she cracks open my skull. Maybe you should join me and see what they can about the Order's *perception shield.*"

Jack nodded.

"We'll be …"

I followed Nathan's gaze back to Saffron, who slumped unconscious in the chair. I turned to Jeeves. "Soothing? She's passed out! You drugged her?"

He cleared his throat. "My apologies, madam. It was not my intention. I used the tea Mrs. White left. Apparently, I don't know how to dose it correctly."

"Apparently." I had to admit, she looked peaceful. "Could you and Mrs. Black prepare her a room?" I politely asked.

"Already done, madam. Shall we take her there now?"

"Allow me," Jack offered. In a smooth sweep, he lifted the sleeping woman off her chair and into his arms. Jeeves and I followed him up the stairs. In yet another new room I'd never seen before, he carefully reclined the woman on the bed. Jeeves drew the shades and Mrs. Black tenderly arranged a throw over her. With a small click the door closed behind us.

~ ~ * ~ ~

I returned to my own room only to realize, yet again, what an idiot I was. I picked up the book on my table, the one Hercule gave me. *The Asclepium Order; a Memoir.*

I flopped into my chair and scanned the room for my familiar. "Hercule?" I called out.

"*Oui?*" I didn't see him.

"Why didn't you tell me? You knew Jack got a letter from the Order. Why didn't you help me make the connection?"

"My job is to guide you, not give you the answers."

"You have way much too much faith in me," I grumbled. I looked up at the spider perched in its web in the corner of my room. My own personal body guard. "Can you please tell Annabelle I'd like a word?"

He … she … whatever, danced in the web, plucking out its communication to the other spiders in the house, like an arachnid text message. There was always at least one spider in every room of the mansion. Some can talk. This one only watched.

While I waited for Annabelle, I told Hercule, "I'd like a few spiders sent to the Jolly home, just a small battalion, keep an eye on things there."

"That is a profoundly bad idea. She won't like it. Firstly, getting them there is dangerous. The outdoors is exposed and birds love to eat spiders."

"Have Jeeves create a portal."

"Stupid girl! What if a neighbor happens by? What if the portal knocks down a candle and starts a fire?"

"There were no candles when we left." I'm used to his tongue. "How about a teeny-tiny portal?" I demonstrated with my fingers.

He scoffed at me. "*Of all the stupid* … wait … that … is brilliant, *chère!*" He twitched to and fro, which I've come to know as "the thinking *cafard.*" Then he looked up. "Still not wise. People dislike them. They could have guests that swat, or exterminators." He gave a small shudder.

"You wished to see me, my lady?"

Annabelle drifted her way down from the ceiling and into my view. She had many roles in my life; head of security, martial arts trainer, and sparring partner. And the polar opposite of Hercule when it came to manners and humility.

"Annabelle, good to see you."

"And you," she said, happily.

I told her my idea. "Since Malador was there, I want to know if he returns and what he's up to."

"Very wise. And I concur. I will dispatch a team immediately." As she drifted upward she called back, "I do love the wee-portal idea. Not sure why we hadn't thought of it before!"

Once she was off, Hercule spoke. "To be clear, I never have too much faith in you."

I ignored him and started to read.

The Asclepium Order, the book said, was as old as time itself. In the beginning they were an organization of healers, and they bartered for healing services. Light or Dark, they didn't care which side, apparently, only getting paid. It didn't specify the form of payment: Gold? Favors? Chickens? But their willingness to work with either side bothered both. Eventually light and dark joined together to put an end to the Order. That part I knew. More or less.

Turns out healers have one and only one talent, which of course is to heal. While the rest of the community have five talents—five is always the magic number—healers only heal, another reason talented people saw them as inferior. Despite the hatred, the talent was coveted, and healers were always in demand.

The book confessed a darker truth; that a healer's touch could alter your emotions. With a touch he could make a healthy being do or think or believe anything. The Order was accused—the book didn't say if it was true or not—of creating armies with a simple touch of the hand, armies that unwillingly fought in the last great war. I bought this. Not only did I think of the gloves Jack always wore, but I instinctively put my hand on my cheek where Malador once touched me. Touch is a big thing among the talented. Some creatures can completely possess you with a simple stroke of their hand.

All healers were male. Women never gained the healing gift. The book provided no explanation. It didn't specify human males, but in recalling past tournaments, I'd only noticed human-shaped beings beneath the robes—I would have distinguished a goblin or lich, for example, by their stature and frame.

No one could predict a healer would result from any parentage or house, good or evil. It just happened at random. Few are talented, fewer still are healers. They are a tiny minority.

The last interesting point from the book described how to, as they put it, *undo* healers. If a healer engages in the act of, well, the birds and the bees, he becomes *undone*. In other words, completely and utterly normal. This news excited me. *Could the answer be so simple? Could I free Jack if I took him to a brothel, for goblin's sake?* A footnote added by some Duke Such-and-such deduced that the undoing could only happen if the act was one of *true love*. Dang. Not sure how said Duke knew, but that sounded just silly enough to fall under my growing list of "stupid rules associated with this world." In any event, the thought of a healer taking matters into his own hands, the book said, meant that ... *great lengths* were taken to prevent them from losing their powers. *Lovely*. I groaned aloud at the thought.

After the great war, many laws were put in place to prevent healers from gaining that kind of power again. Any child discovered with healing talents was taken from their home and raised in a special school. I knew this still happened; Jack was taken from Jeeves when he was only eight. And of course, healers could never touch anyone except to heal. Violators were executed immediately.

A knock on my door forced me to close the dreadful tome. "Yes?" Nathan peaked his head in. I asked, "Hey, how'd it go with Smith and Wesson?"

"Good. They think they can come up with something pretty quick. You got a minute? I want to fill you and Jack in about my meeting with the Chancellor."

"Right," I snapped my fingers. "End of the world. It's all coming back to me." I set the book aside, muttering, "There's way too much going on in this house."

Jack, already seated at the dining room table with a plateful of biscuits and a piping cup of tea, nodded as we entered. *Geez, Louise, tea time already?* My stomach's growls reminded me I hadn't eaten anything since breakfast, and only coffee then.

"How is our fine Chancellor?" Jack asked as Nathan and I busied ourselves at the buffet, piling on some crumpets and jam.

Nathan sighed. "Well. Stubborn. The usual. I told him our theory, but he disagrees. He knows there's a flaw in the energy of the Citadel Plane, but he offered an alternative explanation." Nathan paused for dramatic effect, seemingly. "He thinks the tree's been abused. What with people sticking DVDs in it." He looked at me.

The last DVD Will left me I found in the cherry tree on the Citadel Plane, the only living thing in the place. Legend said as long as it thrived, so would the plane. "Oh, so he's blaming *Will and me,* and not the killing of an innocent healer."

"Precisely. We are going to need proof, Winki, something that proves the healer wasn't involved, and his death was unjust. He's not going to acknowledge something like that without definitive proof."

Jack took this surprisingly well. I, on the other hand, saw red. "How are we going to do that? Is that even possible?"

"First, we need to know who he was, the poor man who was executed. Jack, how does this work? You guys show up and …?" He waved his hand to gesture for Jack to finish the sentence.

"We report to the Chancellor, already covered in our robes. Only in his office, in private, do we state our names and show our faces. He keeps a handwritten ledger, recording our check-in times and names. We're assigned a number for the rest of the tournament. He's the only one who knows who we are. Even we don't know who the other healers."

"Do you know where he keeps the ledger?"

Jack shook his head. "I've never seen it other than when I check-in, and it's always on his desk. I have no idea where he stores it."

"Sounds like we'll need to get into his office."

"Ah," Nathan said. "We'll have an opportunity. To convince us that the Citadel Plane remains safe, he's invited us to join him and the other mages for a friendly meal. He welcomed Winki and me to test the plane's stability ourselves. He hopes we'll keep this little matter between us."

"You want to break into his office during that visit?" Jack asked.

"One of us might be able to get away for a few minutes," Nathan said.

"That is a supremely dreadful idea," I said. I raised a finger. "However, sending in a scout to look for the ledger might work well, while he's distracted with entertaining his guests."

Nathan smile. "I like the idea. Once we know its location, we stand a better chance of getting a hold of it, say, during the tournament."

"We can send Hercule and some spiders to search the office." I explained my tiny portal idea. "When's this dinner?"

"Next week." Nathan shifted uncomfortably. "I hate to ask this because I know Will left them for your eyes only, but can I see the DVD? Just the part where Will talks about the healer."

"I doubt you'll get more from it than me, but sure. I'll go get it."

I dashed upstairs to fetch the disk, then, with the same

enthusiasm, hastened downstairs to join Nathan in our media room. Jack still sat in the dining room.

"Jack," I called. "Aren't you coming?"

"I, well," he stammered, searching for the words. "I assumed this was a family matter."

"Yeah. It is," and I motioned with my head. "Come on."

After prepping the player I stood in the back behind Jack and Nathan seated on the poofy leather sofa. I pressed *play*. Will's face popped up on the screen. "So, wife. Clever girl I knew you would be."

I folded my arms and watched again. This was the second time I'd seen the disk, hearing the words of guidance from my late husband. There were other DVDs out there, somewhere. Funny, I wanted them all, and now, even though this one was hard to watch. I swallowed the lump in my throat.

Right at the start, Will talked about the event at the last tournament, how a healer lured him to his kidnapping and subsequent torture at the hands of Esmeralda, the evil, maniacal sister of Malador. (I could only guess what their family gatherings must be like.) Nathan hung his head when Will talked about the experience. He'd been the one who found and rescued his brother.

Then my husband spoke a bit about his conversion, a process where dark individuals undergo a cleansing, a rebirth into the light and good. Will had been forced into it, but afterwards said he wouldn't have changed anything. I'd only known him as a good and noble man. No one's told me specifics, but I knew that wasn't always the case. He had killed someone. Maybe several someones. Sometimes I think I want to know. But I'm always certain that if I did, I'd wish I hadn't.

Occasionally Will would talk to me. I would answer back, just as I had the first time. Jack's jaw dropped at the "conversation" we had. I gave him a wink.

"Listen to me, this is what's important on this DVD," Will said. I rubbed my forehead, still amazed at my idiocy in ignoring that. *"They killed an innocent man in the Citadel."* And I did nothing, even though I promised I would.

I paused the disk. Jack looked at me. Nathan subtly wiped his cheeks, hiding the action as best he could. I knew seeing his dead younger brother had to be as gut wrenching as I found seeing my dead husband.

"Are you all right, ma'am?" Jack asked.

"The next part is a riddle," I said. "I … I'm sorry. It was the part I focused on all this time. Now I'm embarrassed to show it to you."

"We might be able to help you solve it."

Unsure, I hit *play.*

"All that's left is the riddle for the next disk," Will said.

"Just spare me and tell me where it is." My line.

"Where's your sense of sport, woman?" Will smiled.

"Would you at least put it on this plane?" I asked.

"I make no promises, dead man's prerogative. Now pay attention. *The sentence, the burden, and the falter make three. The fourth is where your next clue will be."*

Initially I protested, but this time round I stayed quiet.

"Take your time, Winks. Don't rush these. In fact, the more you learn before collecting the disks, the more you'll gain from them." Will leaned forward to turn off his recorder. "I love you." The screen went black.

Nathan hadn't moved. From behind I put comforting hands on his shoulders. "Nathan?"

"It's my fault," he whispered. "I'm to blame."

"For what?" I asked.

"I did the investigation," he poured, "I'm the one who found witnesses that said they saw Will and his healer together, I'm the one who pointed my finger at that man." He buried his face in his hands.

"I killed him."

"The Chancellor had you perform the execution?" Jack asked shocked.

"No, no," he moaned. "But I might as well have. I brought him to them and blamed him. I demanded retribution." He moved my hands, refusing my consolation. "I witnessed it." Nathan swallowed, looking into the past through distant eyes. "He just knelt there. He didn't argue. He didn't run. He didn't beg. He just ... waited for the blade."

"You sound surprised," Jack said in disgust. "It's what we're trained to do. We're trained to accept our life as worthless and to welcome its end." With a deep, steadying inhale he closed his eyes. "Please forgive me. I'm often plagued by my own existential malaise." He stood. "Thank you, ma'am, for sharing your disk with me. Alas, I have no insight into the riddle. When you solve it I will be interested in what it means."

"At this point, I'm not sure I will," I said.

"Your husband seemed confident. I suspect that's a clue in and of itself." With a small nod he left the room.

I sat next to Nathan, taking Jack's vacated seat. Something about all this nagged at me. "I'm sure I'm not going to like the answer to this question, but why wasn't Esmeralda punished? Why didn't they kill her? She was the one who tortured Will, not the healer."

His red eyes met mine. "Such ... *indiscretions*, for lack of a better word, are typically dealt with by the insulted house. *Our* house. But every time I talked to Will about revenge, he didn't want to hear it. Said it didn't matter and that he needed to get his affairs in order." Nathan shook his head, lost in the memory. "He acted like he was going to die soon. And he did—*Ah!*" He grabbed his head as if keeping it from splitting open. "*She's up, dammit.*" He nearly fell off the sofa, knocking some decorative flowers on the coffee table to the floor.

"What's going on? This looks way worse than before."

"I think it's the house," he rasped, eyes clenched. "I've gotta get out of this place."

"Go," I said. "Check into a hotel. I'll call when Smith and Wesson have a solution."

He got up and ran off. I heard the front door slam shut.

Chapter Eight

FEET CROSSED ON the small table in front of me, I slouched on the sofa next to a roaring fire. I kept pondering the question: Could brother Simon have orchestrated the gruesome demise of his sister's family? Mr. Jolly died first with the eldest boy in the car accident. The second child was killed crossing the street in a hit and run. When arrested, the driver swore the kid jumped out into the street, leaving him no time to react. Shaken, he'd panicked and fled rather than report the accident. The youngest, a toddler, fell from the roof of their home. Assuming someone—say Simon—wanted the family dead, there had to be an easier way than taking them out, one by one.

But the odds of the entire family dying in a single month's time was too great to put it in the life-just-sucks bucket.

One by one ... what could you gain this way over a single accident ending them all?

I heard Saffron's footsteps on the stairs. I saw the look in her eyes. Fathoms of deep, dark pain ... By the deities, *that's* what you could gain. Prolonged, agonizing, excruciating suffering drawn out piece by piece. As an added bonus, you'd get to witness it, blow by blow.

Someone really hated her.

I stood. "Sleep well?" I asked.

"Best in a while, I gotta admit." She'd taken a shower; her strawberry-blond bangs, no longer weighed down with oil, lightly bounced over her brow.

"You look better." I meant clean, but ...

"Thanks. I feel a little better. I guess I hadn't realized how much I needed to get out of that house. But, uh, I need some clothes." She tugged on her sweatshirt.

"We'll take care of that. Dinner's about ready. Do you know where the dining room is?" She shook her head. "Follow me."

As we walked, I gave her a quick tour. I pointed out the portrait of the Gateway Manor's founder, T. T. Witherspoon and covered some of its history, how many rooms it had, you know, the usual ... skipping the part where the rooms change almost on a daily basis.

The caterer finished up as we entered the dining room. Tonight's dinner was barbecue ribs, collard greens, corn on the cob, mashed potatoes, and biscuits. The caterer's eyes opened wide when she recognized Saffron, and narrowed as realized who would be judging her work. She giggled nervously, shook Saffron's hand, admitted to being a fan, and left the room.

Saffron looked over the spread. "Hm," she said, unimpressed.

"We use a variety of caterers so we don't get bored. We had a cook once who made all the meals, but she ... got fired. We haven't been able to replace her."

Fired was a major understatement. In fact, Mrs. White, whom we had lovingly called Mama, betrayed the house last year by framing Nathan for the death of my husband. And nearly succeeded. Nathan had tried to find someone else talented in both cooking and the community, but such individuals are few. Thus the caterers.

"I could give you recommendations," Saffron offered, filling her plate with small portions. "I know lots of great chefs."

"Sure," I said. Not going to happen, though. We just couldn't hire normals to work in this house, but I couldn't tell her that.

"On the other hand," she said poking the mashed potatoes, "if I'm going to stay here a while, I could cook for you." She gave a small smile. "I could do much better than this. I'd like to earn my keep."

"That's not necessary."

"It would give me something to do. I need to keep my mind busy. After dinner maybe you could show me the kitchen."

Jeeves appeared, anticipating my needs as always. "Madam?"

"Jeeves, Mrs. Jolly would like to see the kitchen after dinner. She's thinking of cooking for us while she's here."

"Indeed." Jeeves sounded dubious.

I shrugged. "Her idea. And she needs clothes."

"I will have some of her wardrobe brought tomorrow morning, if that will suffice?"

"Yeah, that's great," Saffron said.

"Jeeves?" I jerked my head to the dining room door. "A word?"

"If I may, madam," Jeeves said once out of earshot, "Mrs. Jolly cooking here is a terrible idea."

"She's staying here anyway. Keeping her busy should distract her from her own life as well as ours." But that's not what I wanted to discuss. "I want to know if you can call a particular being for me."

"*Being*, madam?"

"A goblin," I whispered. "Do you recall Theodore?"

"Theodore, the Goblin?"

I took that as a "no." "Last I knew he worked in the Realm of Gentilly for King What's-his-name."

His eyebrows went up.

"Oh, that guy, half seahorse, not Triton …" I snapped my fingers. "Hector!" I said triumphantly.

"Yes, madam. Very good. I'm glad to see your education is paying off, albeit slowly."

"Can you do it?"

"Of course. May I inquire as to why? I ask because they aren't known to simply come when called."

"Theodore used to work for Malador. Assuming there's some goblin camaraderie, I'm hoping I can convince Theo to talk to his buds, you know? Do a little information gathering. Malador wants Saffron for some reason. One of his henchmen might know why."

"Interesting strategy, madam. I will see what I can do." He gave a bow and left.

Two lab coated men ran past us and into the dining room. "Oo!" Mr. Smith said. "I love ribs!"

Saffron, seated at the table with some roast beef and mashed potatoes, watched the two men race around the buffet like whirling dervishes, dodging each other, lifting lids, and filling plates.

I took a seat and leaned over. "It's not the ribs," I said. "They do this at every meal. It's like we never feed them, or something."

"Who are they?"

"Not obvious? These are my mad scientists. Mr. Smith is the tall one and Mr. Wesson the short one." Her brow furrowed. "Bond has Q. I have Smith and Wesson. They generate income for the manor. Magicians from all over the world buy illusions and magic tricks they design. Just last month, David Copperfield was here."

"Really? Is that why you knew that guy was a magician today?"

No. "Yes. His name is Malador. And I've … *we've* dealt with him before."

"What's he want from me——"

"Mrs. W," Mr. Smith said joining us, "we've finished with Nathan's … uh," he looked at Saffron, "*jewelry*. Do want to call him or shall I?" Mr. Wesson stood next to him, shoveling food into his mouth. They don't often sit and eat; they usually come running in, grab heaps of food, and dash away again.

"I'll call. Can I see it?" From an ample lab coat pocket Mr. Smith pulled out a copper amulet dangling from a chain, like a long necklace. The bauble looked like a coin, roughly two inches in diameter, but had no markings of its own. "Kinda plain," I noted.

"It's what he asked for. It's a bit ..." he looked at Saffron, searching for words, "*comprehensive*, which means he's not going to like it. But hopefully he won't need it for long."

"And what of Jack's request?"

"What of Jack's request?" echoed Jack, who had quietly joined us and begun filling his plate with veggies.

"We're, uh," Mr. Smith stammered, "still working on it. Tricky problem. So far we can expose the ..." he looked at Saffron, "*doorway* but everyone will see it. We're trying to limit, um, who—"

I helped him out. "You're trying to make the doorway is only visible to the magician and not the audience."

Mr. Smith loudly snapped his finger. "Yes!"

Jack sat opposite of Saffron. "Welcome to the crazy house."

"You live here, too?"

"It is an unfortunate necessity," he mused.

"How many people live here?" Saffron said between small bites.

"Jeeves, Jack, his son. Smith and Wesson. Mrs. Black, the housekeeper, my brother-in-law, Nathan, and me. Seven. Plus my cockroach, but he doesn't eat much. And now you, so eight."

"The spiders feed themselves," Mr. Smith volunteered. He realized his mistake when Jack slammed down his fork and gave him a glare. "So ... don't worry about them." Juggling plates he and his partner dashed from the room.

"Spiders?" Saffron nervously echoed.

I took a deep breath. "Remember my trained roach? We've trained some spiders, too." I pointed into the corner of the room where one of the eight-legged sentries sat tucked in its tangle. "In other words, don't kill them."

Jack added, "We're a bit unorthodox here."

Saffron looked unconvinced. And unnerved.

We finished our meals without further incident. I gave Nathan a call. He was eating at The Irish House on St. Charles. Excusing myself, the Mighty Duck and I headed out to deliver his new amulet.

~ ~ * ~ ~

A few hours later, Nathan and I stood opposite each other in the five-sided boxing ring, armed with halberds and sporting our leathers. Despite the late hour we needed a workout given the stressful couple of days. He seemed dramatically better with the gonzo hidden beneath his armor.

He spun his weapon as he talked. "Footing. That's what I want you to pay attention to today."

"My footing?"

He smiled. "No. *Mine*. I want you to watch where my feet are. I want you to know what step I'm going to take next. Where's my center of balance? Where can and can't I reach with my weapon? Knowing that gives you a big hint on where you need to be, understand?" I nodded. "Wood ends only, to start."

That meant we could lunge and strike each other with the blunt ends of the weapons, which was fine by me. Even though Smith and Wesson constantly fiddled with my armor, improving its ability to repel knives, arrows, and whatnot, I still keenly felt—and didn't relish —the impact that jarred me whenever Nathan struck. I had yet to repay the favor and take him down.

Perched on a ring post was my personal trainer, Annabelle. Squatting comfortably, she identified my mistakes and offered encouragement. "Watch your left side, my lady. Don't drop your shoulder. Keep your eyes up!"

I found the exercise incredibly difficult. Handling the staff felt so awkward to me that my concentration remained largely on my hands. I couldn't keep my eyes on his feet as well. A hard and sudden blast of wood hit my ribs with a sickening thwack. Despite my formidable protection, I buckled to my knees.

Nathan gave me a moment then helped me stand up. "You okay?"

I nodded. "Didn't see it coming." I rubbed my sore side under a cloud of disgruntlement.

"That's because your eyes are fixed downward," Annabelle explained. "Your mind is in your hands. Keep your mind on his feet."

"Winki, you know you're doing well, right? You've only been at this a couple of months, and we're practicing at an advanced level. Don't get discouraged."

"Easy for you to say. You've yet to get smacked."

"Oh, he's been smacked plenty," she giggled, "trust me."

We started again. This time I purposely ignored my hands, and within moments, he disarmed me, sending my halberd sailing out of the ring. He spared me the subsequent bludgeoning.

I left the ring as he called to me. "You can't keep track of any one thing, Winki. Don't think about what I'm doing or what you're doing, it doesn't work that way."

I picked up my halberd. "You told me to watch your feet."

"My lady," said the spider, "that's the point of this exercise. Watching his feet isn't literally watching them, not with your eyes. More like your peripheral vision. Soften your vision, soften your mind. Take it all in. Like a sponge."

I hoisted myself up and over the ropes and took my stance. I closed my eyes for a moment. *Soften your vision.* When I opened my eyes I purposely avoided watching his eyes or his feet. I looked at nothing in particular, letting my eyes rest wherever they felt most comfortable.

We began again. This time I could feel my hands and hear his footsteps, while keeping my vision and my mind soft and uninvolved. I felt him shift to one side, and my hands reacted. I heard his feet shuffle to the right, and my body lunged aside, avoiding the blow. My hands spun my staff, and a loud crack broke my concentration. The sound came from his halberd and it bounced off the floor outside the ring.

I stood tall and smiled.

"Well done!" she called.

"Now *that*," scratching his head, "is what I'm talkin' about!" He athletically leapt over the ropes to retrieve his weapon. Back in position he wheeled his halberd upright, the ax blade and spear reaching skyward. "You ready?"

I nodded. With a blink I put myself back in a trance, softening my eyes, all senses alert. We battled furiously, blades whirring in the air, staffs clashing. After several minutes, he called a time-out.

He took a sip of water, as did I. The activity turned his usually kept hair into wild waves. "Much better," he said as he cooled his forehead with the glass. "Much, much better. Now, I'm going to try some tricks on you. Remember, you need to keep this impersonal."

"In other words, don't get angry," the spider said.

They both knew from past experience I anger easily, largely with myself. Rage has been the gateway to my talents. That concerned us all.

Annabelle instructed me again. "I'm liking what I see, my lady, but you still drop your guard on the left side. He will take advantage of that."

We took our positions. *Tricks, eh? Left side ... Maybe I could try some of my own.*

With a nod we came at each other, blades flying. He spun, I jumped out of the swing, then swung myself. He manipulated my momentum, pulling me toward him. I thrust my staff end up, just missing his jaw but catching his blade. I pulled him off balance.

He jumped, rolling in a somersault, only to face me. He smiled. "Clever." Then he waved, wanting me to attack.

I did. I swung the blade in a circle across my body, and flicked the blunt end toward him, purposely exposing my left side, coaxing him to attack. Then, with a great grunt, I swiped the blade downward. It hit its mark.

With a gasp Nathan sank to his knees ... my halberd's stuck in his side, buried to the staff.

"*No!*" I cried out as I opened my palm out of instinct focused my talent on him, slowing him down to a crawl. As he collapsed in slow motion, I dashed for the stairs. "*Jack. Jack!*"

Nearly breaking his own neck Jack ran to my rescue, only to see Nathan hitting the mat slowly. He ripped his gloves from his hands as he rushed to the dying man's side. With a grunt, he yanked the halberd from the ribs, then stuck his fingers into the gaping wound.

That's how they heal. Healers make as much contact with the wound as they can to close and seal the injury. I had experienced it many times during the last tournament, and witnessed it again a few months ago when Jack saved Nathan from a bullet wound. A wave of guilt washed over me. *By the stars, I did this to him.*

Jack lurched to the side with a grimace, favoring his own ribs, the same side as Nathan's wound, blood pouring down his shirt. He swallowed large lungfuls of air in the same rhythm as Nathan. Within seconds, however, everything calmed. Jack slowly pulled his hand from Nathan's side, his eyes distant and pained. He sat on his heels, palms on his thighs, taking slow and deliberate breaths, while Nathan moaned and pushed up on his elbows.

Nathan looked at his stomach, then the healer. "Thank you," he whispered.

Jack nodded, stood up and turned to leave. I stopped him by his elbow, noticing his unstained shirt. "You don't just heal people, you have to feel it, too?"

"Through my own healing, I heal you. That's how it works."

"But you must suffer horribly."

"That's how it works." He turned to leave again.

I'd never realized that each and every time he healed he literally experienced the injury himself, pain and all. My pain, terrible as it was, was lessened by shock. He knew what was coming but accepted it willingly. That seemed so unfair. "Jack?" He looked over his shoulder. "Thank you. So very much."

He put his hand on his heart and, with small smile, gave a little bow.

I noticed that my personal trainer still sat, unmoving. "Annabelle?"

"I think she's stuck in slow mo," Nathan jutted his chin.

With a finger, I delicately brushed the arachnid, who immediately screamed, "No! … Oh. I see you are well, Nathan."

"Yes, ma'am."

Our commotion attracted the attention of everyone else in the house, including Saffron. Thankfully, the healing was complete before she came in. I convinced everyone that they didn't need to see and sent them back upstairs. Everyone except my mad scientists.

I helped Nathan to stand. "I'm sorry, I'm so, so sorry."

"It's not your fault," he said, dusting off his leathers. "You took me by surprise. See, uh," he nervously chuckled, "I have a confession. I've always had the upper hand." He pulled out the copper amulet from under his armor.

My eyes widened. "You cheat!" *He knew my thoughts.* Every time we sparred he knew what I was going to do before I did it.

"I do what all your opponents do; use my talents. But this," he twisted the coin in front of him, "definitely changes everything." He looked at Smith and Wesson. "You were right. I don't like it."

"Told ya," Mr. Smith smirked as he rocked back and forth on his heels.

"Why didn't your armor protect you?" I asked. I addressed my geeks. "Surely, his should have stopped my blade."

"Uh ... um ..." Mr. Smith swallowed. His eyes bounced between his partner, who'd been writing on a computer pad, and me. "We were afraid of this. His suit syncs with his energy. We think the gonzo's interfering with *all* of that."

"Don't you know?"

"Playing with energy signatures is like playing with DNA. There can be unforeseen consequences. It's not like we have huge panels of test subjects to draw experience from. We have just you folks. It might take an iteration or three." Mr. Wesson nodded.

"So, what you're saying is I'm basically *normal* with it?"

"Yeah." Mr. Smith cleared his throat, acknowledging that the information would have been more useful, say, an hour ago. "We'll need another sample of your blood. Now that it's been at work, we can identify which signature modulations—"

"Yeah, yeah," Nathan held up his hand, then said to me, "Call it a day?"

I agreed. As I put my weapon away I watched over my shoulder into the happenings of the lab—the one that had replaced the ring, the one that wasn't there just moments ago. Mr. Wesson wrapped Nathan's arm with a rubber hose, wiped down his vein with alcohol, then stuck a needle in his arm. Nathan winced, just briefly. That had to be nothing compared to what he just went through.

Another wave of guilt washed over me. I had nearly killed him. Again.

"You know it isn't your fault, my lady. These things happen."

I wasn't consoled. *No. I don't ever want to hurt him again.*

Chapter Nine

NO WOMAN LIKES to be roused from slumber by the sensation of something crawling on her. I was no different. I screamed as I sat upright.

"Forgive me, my lady!"

Annabelle. "You could have gotten yourself killed," I scolded.

"I called out but I could not wake you."

I rubbed the tickler's traces. "What's up?"

"I thought you should know. Someone entered Mrs. Jolly's home this evening. He removed some items from the house."

I turned on a small light and checked the clock: three thirty in the morning. "Tall man? Looks a little like Saffron, but dark hair? Scruffy mustache and beard?"

"That would be the man, my lady. Do you know him?"

"Simon. Saffron's older brother." I didn't know if Saffron had told him she wouldn't be home. "What did he take?"

"Jewelry and money. He opened a safe and removed some documents as well. We don't know what they were."

Disheartening. After all the poor woman had been through I'd have to tell her her brother's stealing from her. "Thank you, Annabelle. And I'm sorry if I hurt you."

She gave a small spider laugh. "You are good, my lady, but I am better." Up her little web she went.

I rolled over and tried to return to dreamland but the news aggravated me. I didn't like the guy when we first met. I liked him less, now. I threw off the covers. I needed a cup of tea if I had any hope of going back to sleep.

To my surprise I found Mrs. Jolly going through the kitchen cabinets. And by "going through" I mean she'd taken almost everything out, covering every counter top.

"Whachadoin?" I lazily asked, spinning slowly to take in the mounds of mess.

"Hey there. Sorry. I couldn't sleep, and when I can't sleep, I organize. Always helps. Like counting sheep." I recalled how organized her own kitchen was.

"You call this organizing? Looks more like a recurring nightmare I have."

"My kitchen, my way."

"Technically, it isn't your kitchen," I yawned. "But you're the only one to express any interest, so have at it. I came for tea, myself. I, too, can't sleep."

"I'll make you a pot. Give me a minute."

Our kitchen, though not as spectacular as the one in Saffron's home, covers a bit of real estate, but it wasn't designed for guests to sit and talk with the cook. I sat at the tiny table for two wedged in a small corner.

She put water on to boil then searched for tea. "I slept a good part of the day yesterday, which I suspect is why I'm up now. Remind me to ask Mr. Jeeves where he keeps that tea. Packs quite a punch. Aha." She opened a tin and sniffed. "Not very fresh, I'm afraid." She looked over the assortment. "Preference?"

"Chamomile helps me sleep."

She wrote "tea" on a list of items written on the blackboard-faced refrigerator. It included vegetables, beans, pasta, and rice.

"We have no rice?"

"Not that I could find."

"We have a big pantry somewhere. Be sure to ask Jeeves. I bet we have half that stuff."

She served me a cup of tea.

I hated bringing this up now but … "Look, Saffron … I have some questions that aren't going to be easy or comfortable."

She scowled a little. "Okay."

"How are things with Simon?"

"What do you mean?"

"Let's start with money."

She gave a relieved sigh. She must have worried I'd accuse him of killing her family. "Simon isn't great with money," she said, continuing to empty cabinets. "Made a lot of bad investments. A few years ago he asked for work. He's been managing two of my restaurants since. It's been fine."

"You know that for sure?"

"Yeah." She furrowed her brow. "Why?"

I swallowed my hesitation. "Did you talk to him last night and tell him you wouldn't be home?"

"Yeah. Of course. I asked him to drive by if he had a chance, just to make sure everything was all right. When we left that *guy* was in my house. I told him to be careful."

"Did you tell him where you were?"

"No. I don't really know, anyway. I wasn't paying attention. Why?"

"He did more than just drive by. He took some stuff. Money, jewelry, and some documents from a safe."

Her shoulders sagged. She returned to pots on the counter. "He can have anything he wants."

"Did he ask before—"

"*He can have anything he wants!*" She swept her arm across the countertop, sending pots and pans and skillets and lids crashing to the floor. I hopped up. *Way to go, Winki.*

Saffron collapsed, her legs buckling. Palms pressed against her eyes, she wept without control. Her heart visibly broke into more shattered and sharp pieces. "God … I miss them so much …"

My chest ached as she uttered those familiar words. I'd said them myself, how many times? *How can I help this poor woman?*

Nathan stumbled into the doorway wearing only pajama bottoms, the amulet dangling from his neck. He braced himself outside the room, extending stiff arms against the jamb. His lean abdomen heaved as he gulped for air, his face twisted in a grimace. "Winki, you've got to do something," he rasped. "Even with this," he grabbed the coin, "*I can hear her.*"

My eyes darted between them, out of each other's sight. Both in worlds of torment and grief I recognized. The sharp and bright and unrelenting knife thrusted in your heart with no way to remove it. I knew it well.

Out of instinct I pressed my hands and forehead against the wall of the manor. "Please," I whispered, "*please*, help her. You're so big and she's so small … please, can you help?"

Saffron gasped suddenly, her lungs filling with air, as if breathing for the first time ever. With each inhale, she quieted as she took one deep breath after another, each slower and calmer than the last. Eventually, she sat up straight, back against the cabinets, her calming face wet with tears. *Did that actually work?*

Nathan stood a little taller, his relief apparent. He rubbed his forehead. With a wan smile, he mouthed the words, "Thank you." Apparently another trip to Smith and Wesson would be in order.

I could see the shadows of others in the hallway, no doubt coming to see what the commotion was about. I barely heard him say, "Tell Jack I'll be at work." Jeeves and Mrs. Black came in.

"It's okay," I told them before they could say anything. "It's fine. Please go back to bed."

They looked over the mess and the woman on the floor, exchanging glances themselves. "Please," Mrs. Black offered, "don't hesitate to call me. I can help clean up."

"We'll be fine. Thank you."

As they left, I approached the recovering woman and sat next to her on the floor. "I'm sorry," I said. "I didn't ... I wasn't ..."

"It's not your fault. I just miss them so damned much." She wiped her face on a dish rag. "I'm so tired of crying. God, my ribs hurt." She took a long and shaky breath. "Does it get any better?"

My own eyes glassed a bit. I knew I'd never be over my husband's death, but after a long journey I'd reached a place of ... acceptance. "I can honestly say you won't stop missing them. One day, though, instead of mourning for the lost time you should have had together, you'll feel happy for what time you did have."

She thought about my words for a moment. "That's encouraging. Thank you."

We sat there, side by side, saying nothing. The windows lightened as dawn's twilight filled the sky. I kept my hands on the floor, quietly thanking the house for its help.

Saffron hoisted herself erect and began picking up the scattered cookware. I gave her a hand. Out of the blue she said, "If you think Simon had anything to do with this you're wrong."

Uh.

"I don't think he could hurt me like that, or would want to hurt me like that. I mean, even if he were furious with me for ... *whatever.* He and Harry weren't the best of friends, but why kill him? And I know he loved his nephews. Our kids had great play dates. I can't fathom him hurting any of them." She shook her head. "If it makes him feel better to steal from me, so be it. He can have whatever he wants. I don't want any of it any more," her tone so matter-of-fact.

I headed for the dining room to discover my familiar waiting in the hallway for me, mounted on the wall at head height. As we walked I asked, "Did what just happen, happen?"

"Did the house heal the woman because you asked, *ma chére?*"

"Yes."

He scurried quietly for a moment. "Even I, the Great Hercule, do not know."

~ ~ * ~ ~

The morning unfolded: the caterers came, set up the dining room, politely bade me a good morning, and left; staff and household members wandered in, filled bowls or plates and coffee cups, ate, and talked, and left as well.

I didn't want to move. Saffron's misery overwhelmed me. I sat stirring the same tea she'd poured me hours ago, worrying about her well being. I understood. I knew that nothing could be done or said that would ease her suffering. Unlike a gaping wound, or a broken bone, matters of the heart were singularly your own. Even Jack couldn't heal you.

Nonetheless, I felt helpless.

My *cafard* danced to and fro, looking between me and my cup. "*Chére*, are you going to eat that?" he asked, pointing to the sugar cube on the saucer. I set it on the table in front of him. "*Merci.*"

Jack was the last person to come for breakfast. As he grabbed some toast and jam I finally broke my silence and informed him Nathan already left for the office.

"Did he mention how I would get there?" Jack doesn't own a car anymore. Once he moved here, he sold it.

"You could just walk," I offered. "It's a lovely day."

Rudely, and very un-Britishly, he swung a foot up onto the table. My mouth dropped, shocked. Something in his eyes smiled. For the first time in, well, *ever* Jack looked happy.

"In these shoes?" he gestured. "These are a thirteen hundred dollar pair of Berluti shoes, ma'am. One does not *walk* in these."

I didn't even look at them, just him. "First, why would anyone buy shoes they can't walk in?" He rolled his eyes. "Second, if you spent less on your shoes you'd have more than thirty dollars to spend on your suit." His jaw dropped, feigning insult. "Lastly, how much do I pay you?" I smiled at him as he removed his foot. "I can take you to work."

"On your motorcycle?" he huffed behind the smallest of grins. "The last time you gave me a lift I ended up horizontal on the garage floor." My turn to feign insult. "I will change my shoes."

Jeeves cleared his throat. Honestly, I hadn't even noticed him enter. He put an urgent hand on my shoulder. "Madam, quickly! Put on your armor. We will …" His eyes glowed bright green, his face turned grotesquely gaunt as he looked at the entryway. "It is too late. They are here."

I cursed myself for not having my hammer. Note to self: *Put some kind of hammer in every room for unexpected guests.*

Jack loosened his tie and stood behind me. Mrs. Black, sensing the change, came racing into the room, armed with a small sword. Everyone here is always on alert for attacks; you never know when Malador might stop by.

The air in the entryway shimmered, like heat off pavement, only pulled into a sphere. Smaller, about half the size I've come to expect. Maybe that's why Jeeves didn't sense it until it was too late.

Wind whipped through my hair, knocking small pictures from the wall. We all took a few steps back, bracing ourselves for whatever would step through.

For an eternity, nothing happened. Then he appeared. A small creature, only four feet in height, green skin with warts and bumps, blood red eyes. A goblin. The portal shut behind him, disappearing completely.

"Hey hey! Stand down!" he called, waving a piece of parchment.

"I got a summons!"

I recognized his voice. "Theodore!" I stepped up and gave the goblin a fist bump. "Dude! Thank you for coming."

"Anytime, Winki. What can I do for—?"

"*That's not green paint.*"

All of us wheeled around to see Saffron pointing a rolling pin accusingly. Silence shrouded us as we searched for some explanation.

"I should hope not!" Theodore answered, standing on tippy toes to see the woman over us. His red eyes went wide. "Hey, aren't you Saffron Jolly, that chef?"

A shocked Saffron stammered, "Yes."

"Oh, man," Theodore said and he pushed through us, "It's an honor to meet you, ma'am. I think you're cooking is just ... *inspired.*"

Theodore shook Saffron's hand, aggressively. "Why ... thank you." She cast me a worried look.

"Handle the goblin," I whispered to Jack. I took Saffron by the arm and led her down the hallway while her neck craned to see the green visitor. "Saffron, Theodore was born with a skin condition. We try not to appear to notice."

Saffron looked in my eyes, incredulous. I held her gaze. Finally, she nodded. "Oh. Sorry. I can apologize if I insulted him," Mrs. Jolly said, "but he looks like the ones from yesterday. Are there others with the same condition?"

"Yes," I nodded. "Yes, there are."

"Why haven't I seen or heard about it before? And how'd he get here? What was that bubble thing?"

"Okay, well, they stay hidden mostly, largely because people scream when they see them. And the bubble? Well," I smiled coyly, "a good magician never reveals his secret."

She returned to the kitchen, shaking her head, clearly unconvinced. And I returned to my goblin guest.

Jack had him waiting in the sitting room. "Oh, Winki,"

Theodore started, "I'm so sorry. I didn't know you had a," he whispered, *"normal,"* then continued, "in the house or I would have come in the back door. They can be dangerous, you know. Even the successful ones."

"As can goblins, so I'm told."

"So true, so true," he laughed. "What can I do for you?"

"You mentioned you worked for Malador in the past."

"Indeed. Lousy boss. Terrible pay."

"Do you still have any, oh … I don't know, connections there? Friends?"

He cocked his head suspiciously.

"Malador wants Saffron Jolly for some reason. He came to her home yesterday demanding I hand her over. I want to know why. I want to know what Malador wants with her."

The goblin's head bounced in acknowledgment. "And I get …?"

I shrugged. "What do you want?"

"Frogs."

I nodded. Goblins eat frogs. Exclusively, from what I understood. "What's the going rate on something like this, a covert operation kind of thing?"

"Doesn't really happen. Usually, we're just hired away."

"I'm willing to pay you for your time in addition to your current employment. I just can't guarantee you a permanent position."

He twisted his face a bit as he stroked his chin thoughtfully.. "I am owed some vacation … Okay, let's say five hundred frogs."

I had no idea where one gets one frog, forget five hundred, but before I could agree, Jack broke in, "Two hundred."

"Four."

"Three hundred," he said, pointing a finger, "and not a single frog more. That's more than a fair price. You don't want Mrs. Witherspoon to feel like she's being taken advantage of, now do you?" The goblin started to argue. "Keep in mind the possible future employment opportunities with this house."

The goblin grumbled. "Half up front," he insisted. "For the kids."

"Fine," I said.

"And not the tiny ones, either. I want big, fat—"

I stopped him there before the gruesome details. "You choose the vendor. Put them in contact with me, and I'll get you the frogs."

He spit in his hand, then offered it to me. Jack gave me a committed nod, so I screwed up my courage—thank the fates I had skipped breakfast—and did the same. We shook.

Satisfied, he stepped into the center of the room and waved his arm in as big a circle as he could muster. A portal started to form. "Would you like me to use a door next time? So as not to scare the normal?"

"Coming by portal is fine, just give us a head up … like knock three times or something, so I know it's you."

"See you soon." He disappeared into the bubble.

Jack casually put his hands behind his back. "Do you have any idea how much frogs cost, ma'am?"

"Not a clue!" I laughed. "That's Nathan's problem."

"No, you don't understand. He'll choose a *goblin* vendor. They won't want money. They'll want gold, or emeralds, in exchange for the beasts."

"Still Nathan's problem."

"When are you going to let him know?"

"Oh, I'm not. You are. As soon as you see him." Handy having paid staff at times, I must admit.

With a sigh, he hung his head. "Of course, ma'am." He went upstairs and changed his shoes.

Chapter Ten

MR. SMITH'S AND Mr. Wesson's preoccupation with … *the head* (just the thought made me quiver) left me free to visit good brother Simon. Rather than upsetting Mrs. Jolly by asking his likely whereabouts, I guessed he'd be working at one of her restaurants. After I googled their names and locations I headed out.

Simon sat in a back office of Plates, a steak house in the French Quarter.

He looked up when I poked my head in, "Ah," I smiled, "There you are. You're a hard man to find."

It took him a bit of time to recognize me. "You're that chick Saffron hired. What do you want?"

I decided to take 'chick' as an improvement over his earlier jab that I looked fifty. "I'd like to talk to you about Saffron. Got a minute?"

"Sure," he gestured to a wooden chair across from his desk.

"You know, she's in quite a state of mind."

He nodded, his eyes distant. "I can't imagine what she's going through. Her husband was fantastic; she had great kids. It's like God is trying to tell her something."

"What would that be?" I asked.

He gave me a hard look.

"I mean, can you think of anything she's done to deserve this?

Anyone who hates her so much as to take her family from her?"

"I thought … I mean the police say they were accidents. All of the deaths."

"One's an accident. Two's just bad luck, but three? That's a statistical impossibility. I'm coming at it from a different direction. If I find out who wanted her to suffer," I let that word linger a bit, "we can see if they had means to do so." His expression became guarded, as if he was hiding something. "Any ideas? Who'd want to hurt her so badly they'd kill her family? Someone from her past, perhaps? An old high school enemy?" I paused. "A disgruntled family member?"

"No," he shook his head. "I can't think of anyone. Everyone loves Saffron. Lawyers, employees, community leaders, even city council members. She worked with lots people, and I don't recall any conflicts. Or even arguments."

I nodded, all serious, like I'd seen them do in movies. "How well did you two get on?"

"Great." His voice lacked enthusiasm.

"I heard you needed some money."

"Where'd you hear—" The light bulb went on. "Wait. You think *I* had something to do with all this?" He stood abruptly. "You think I killed them? Why would I do that? *How* would I do that?"

Slowly, with confidence, I stood, too. "Simon, I'm just trying to piece Saffron's life together, her last few days with her family, to see if I can find a pattern, or a person, or a reason. I assume you want to help your sister."

"Of course, I do," he raged.

"Then why did you steal from her last night?"

"What? You've got surveillance on me?" I braced for an attack. I'd seen that kind of anger before.

"Yes, sir. I do. We know you took money, jewelry, and documents from—"

"So what if I did! It's no skin off her nose."

Maybe he really did hate her. "Certainly not now. Not after losing what she loved the most. Money means nothing to her now. Was that the point? Tear her to such tiny pieces that you could just take anything? Everything?"

"Get out!" he exploded, nearly throwing his desk over. "Get out now, you witch!" Okay, at least it rhymed with witch.

Sure, let's poke the bear. "I'm curious, though, why you didn't just manage it in one big accident? Why three? That had to be harder to pull off." He seethed. "On the other hand, if you *could* pull it off, Saffron would be all the more devastated. She would be, well, shredded."

"Getoutgetoutgetout!" He pounded on his desk, spitting as he hollered.

I'd said what I came to say and saw what I needed. I left.

As I closed the door behind me, something smashed into it from the other side. Good arm. I looked into my pocket. "What do you think?" I whispered.

"I think a concerned brother would have asked how Saffron was doing. I think a concerned brother would have wanted to talk to her, or at least ask where she was."

"Would you stick around? See what he does next now that I've rattled his cage?"

"*Oui.* That would be most interesting, I think."

"Be careful. Remember, you are in a restaurant. They're not bug tolerant." Hercule wiggled his way down my leg and under the office door. My cell rang. Nathan and Jack. "Yeah?" I asked, heading out.

"Ma'am, could you stop by? We have something to show you."

Never a dull moment.

It's a quick ride from Plates to the office of Lost Souls Investigations.

They looked so serious, sitting behind their desks, exchanging glances as I crested the stairs.

"Is this about the frogs?" I asked.

"Frogs?" Nathan cocked his head.

I glared at Jack. "I haven't had the opportunity, ma'am, I swear. I only just arrived."

How long does it take a guy to change his shoes?

"What frogs?" Nathan repeated. I quickly recounted the visit with Theodore. He took it surprisingly well. "We have some useful assets we could trade. But, Winki, in the future don't do that without me."

"Do what? Spend money?"

He shot me a glare. "Make deals with goblins. They can be tricky."

"So what's up?"

Jack held out a piece of paper. "Letter number one."

```
Dear Mr. Frost.

It has come to our attention you
attempted to visit our office within the
last twenty-four hours. We take great
effort to avoid unsolicited callers; but
in your case, sir, we're happy to make
an exception.

You might be aware that we are an
organization of and representing beings
such as yourself. We believe we have
shared interests, including the
cessation of Saffron Jolly and her
experiments. However, we have learned
Mrs. Jolly is your client. This puts us
in an unfortunate position; but one we
are willing to discuss.
```

```
Please stop by our office at precisely
six thirty this evening. Bring no
weapon. Bring no partner. Bring no
police. If you follow these rules we
will receive you. If not, your life and
the lives of those you care for will be
at risk.

Warmest regards,
      The Asclepium Order
```

"This came in the mail?" I asked.

"No. Someone slid it under the door." Jack said.

"It was here when I got in this morning," Nathan added. And he'd come early.

"So polite, and yet so … ominous."

"Clearly they believe Saffron Jolly is up to something," Jack said. "We need to know what. Maybe this is just a misunderstanding."

"And maybe they're the ones who killed her entire family," Nathan huffed. "I agree, we should know. But I don't think you should go alone."

I had to agree. "We're sending you to a doorway we can't find, which means we can do nothing if you don't make it back out. I don't like it." After what I've read about the Asclepium Order, their wanting an audience with my healer didn't appear to me to be a random occurrence.

Jack spoke thoughtfully. "I confess the idea doesn't thrill me. The order, the *real* order, fell centuries ago. As in 'The Fall of Rome' centuries. Maybe these gentlemen just liked the name, or maybe there's some real connection. It's in our interest, and our client's, to find out."

I had to agree with that, too. When in doubt, go to the geeks.

"Nathan, between now and six thirty tonight, can Smith and Wesson come up with some kind of tracking device? Something that works through portals or across planes?"

He nodded. "In fact, I seem to recall Will asking for something similar a while back. Jack, let her look at the next letter, and I'll give 'em a call."

Jack held out another piece of paper. "Letter number two."

Dear son,

Unclear who that was, I jumped to the bottom. It was signed Mother Earth. *Mother Earth?* I looked at him. "Son?"

He smirked.

I started again:

Dear son,

Perhaps my dearest. I granted you the request because I have such great plans for you. Only one with your determination and skill can accomplish what lies ahead. So know that my confidence in you is the reason I allowed the saving of one I deem unworthy.

I stopped. "Are you sure you want me to read this? Seems ... personal."

"You wanted to know when she reached out to me. Besides, you showed me your husband's DVD, ma'am. This seems only fair. I can't help but feel this will affect us all in the end."

My seer has informed me that an upcoming

```
conflict may conclude unacceptably. I
will ask you to undo it. Be ready. It
will cost you dearly. I regret that. I
wish I could give you happiness at all
points of your life. But I promise you,
abundant happiness will be yours.

I will have an emissary come to you with
specifics if, indeed, events warrant. Do
not fear her. She will take you where
you need to be.

I love you, my dear Jack Frost. Know
that first and foremost,
Mother Earth
```

"Mother Earth writes letters?"

"Dictates, I'd wager. She has a comprehensive organization, complete with an executive staff, a personnel department, and public relations."

"Mother Earth needs a PR department?"

Jack gave a crooked smile.

"They need to be fired," I scoffed. "Or hasn't Mother Earth been paying attention to the state of the world."

"Oh, she has, ma'am. You misunderstand what, exactly, she cares about."

"And you're her *son?*"

"Spiritually. Not literally."

Because *that* would be weird.

I re-read the letter. "What's a *seer*? Is that like *sight*, your dad's talent?"

"No. Father is able to see the near future, which does not vary or only varies slightly. Seers are vastly more powerful. Their vision ranges much further, enabling them to see all futures at the same time. The talent is highly uncommon and much coveted. Most cannot endure it. They tend to go mad."

Before I could ask more Nathan interrupted, "Good news. I was right. Smith and Wesson have a tracking device, but it's untested since Will never had a chance to use it. They're checking it out now."

I rubbed my face in frustration, not liking the idea of Jack walking through some unknown portal to an unknown location without Nathan or me.

Nathan waved the first letter. "I know it's not ideal, but they asked for him. Best to play along." He shrugged.

"Am I the only one who smells a trap here? The Asclepium Order, an order of 'healers,' asks for *my* healer? I mean, *our* healer," I corrected myself. Neither man responded. "Jack, do you want to go?"

"Yes, ma'am."

"Nathan, do you want him to go?"

Like a lawyer he hedged, "*Want* is a strong word. *Need* is better."

I nodded, unconvinced. "Jack, I will never get in the way of you doing what you want." *Even though, deep in my core, I know it's the wrong thing to do.* "Don't get yourself killed."

"I'll do my best, ma'am."

Chapter Eleven

"THIS MIGHT HURT a little," Mr. Smith warned Jack as he pressed some medical looking gun-thingy against his arm. It made a loud click.

"*Ow!*" Jack protested, rubbing his shoulder. "A little?"

The as-always quiet Mr. Wesson busied himself with the console of six monitors, multiple keyboards, and panels of buttons and flashing lights filling most of the van we sat in, parked a few blocks from the Order's offices. He clapped his hands gleefully, pointing to a monitor labeled Midland. On it a small, green light blinked.

"Great," I said unenthused. "He's somewhere in Louisiana."

"Give it a minute," Mr. Smith said. "Actually, give it ten seconds. That's how long it takes us to pinpoint a location." He addressed Jack. "By the way, once you stepped through the portal if you could stop for ten seconds before moving, we'd appreciate it."

Jack rolled down his shirt sleeve, pulled on his blazer, and straightened his tie. "How do I look?"

"Like a dignified fly about to go knowingly into the web."

"Just what he was shooting for," Mr. Smith giggled.

Jack opened the back doors, cutting me off before I told him yet again to be careful. "I fully intend on being your healer at the tournament this year. I promise, I will be careful."

Nathan sat in the driver's seat. "Mrs. Witherspoon? Can I have a word?"

He only called me that when he was angry at me. I delicately made my way through the cramped space of the van to the passenger seat. "Yes, *Mr. Marble?*"

He watched Jack disappear into a busy intersection downtown. "I really don't know how to start this conversation …" Great. More bad news. "You need to keep Jack at arms length."

"Come again?"

"He's a great healer, and the hallowed stars know I owe him my life, twice over now. I like him, and I know you do, too. But …"

"But?"

"But I don't … I don't trust him. Not entirely."

"Why not?" More to worry about. I thought the two of them got along so well.

"I'm certain he's broken laws that govern healers at least once. I'm telling you this so you see things more clearly. So you understand the risks you face."

"What laws? To be clear, I'll be shocked if it's something I agree with or care about."

Nathan looked over his shoulder, ensuring Smith and Wesson couldn't overhear. "At the tournament last year, he touched you. You weren't injured, he touched you anyway. He didn't think I saw but I did." I furrowed my brow trying to recall the incident in question. "Just before your bout with Esmeralda. He put his hands on your face. That's a big no-no. Healers are forbidden to touch anyone except to heal the injured."

Now I remembered. I had crippling stage fright when I saw the crush of patrons attending the bout. Jack put his hands on my face and showed me this calm and peaceful expanse of … I don't know what. But once he was done, I felt calm and centered. I knew nothing of Healers at that point, nor that Jack was one. "If he hadn't," I told Nathan, "I would have lost that battle. He got me to focus."

"Don't you see? Of course you think you needed his help. He could have put that very thought in your head. You can't be certain, one way or the other."

"You're talking about *Jack!*"

Nathan raised a hand to stop me. "I already said I owe him my life. So I'm trying to give him the benefit of the doubt."

"That's not what it sounds like."

"Winki," he gripped the steering wheel tightly. "Everytime he's around your mind ... I don't know. Something changes." He pulled out the talisman from under his shirt. "Before this stupid *thing* I picked up these odd vibrations from you. I could never put my finger on it exactly, but it only happened with him around."

No. Not possible. "I'm worried about him, of course. This stupid relationship foisted on us makes me crazy. I just want us both to be as happy as possible under the circumstance." I thought about what Nathan could possibly have been reading from me. "I know I feel tense around him ... at times."

"And you're sure that's all?"

"What?" I huffed. "Are you asking if I'm in love with him?"

He threw me a quick glance.

I folded my arms and steamed. *If only!* I wished I had feelings for someone, anyone other than my late husband. I adored Will. Too much. Having feelings for someone might help ease the pain I felt each and every time I gazed at that portrait, which I can't stop myself from doing. "I don't think I'll ever love again," I whispered, mostly to myself.

My eyes wandered to the passenger side rear view mirror. I sat up taller. "What the ... Is that Saffron?"

Nathan looked over his shoulder. "Son of a bitch," he seethed, opening his door.

"No, I'll go." I jerked a thumb behind me. "Watch Tweedledee and Tweedledum."

"Hey!" Mr. Smith objected.

I smiled at Nathan. "I was sure they were listening." I got out and made for Saffron. *Dammit, I was supposed to be guarding her.*

By the time I reached the corner she'd disappeared. I spun around slowly. "Where did you go?" I finally caught a glimpse of her, halfway down the block on the other side of the street. Frogger-ing my way through traffic, I watched her go into a church, St Patrick's Cathedral. What would bring her here at six thirty on a Thursday evening?

I jogged my way to the hefty double doors, but stopped before entering. I put my hand on the bulbous brass handle. I really didn't want to go inside. I have never liked churches. They claimed anyone could enter, but if you did, you knew you didn't belong. *Dammit, Winki, you fight goblins, wraiths, and Hecate knows what else, just walk into the stupid church.*

I heard yelling inside. I put my internal dread aside and hastened through the doors.

Tiers of small tea lights in red glass bounded the entryway. As the door softly closed the flames reacted, dancing and sputtering in every direction. Before me stretched an expanse of white marble floor checkered with black dots. Thick wooden pews lined the grand aisle to the glorious gilded altar, under three arched domes. Colorful streams of light bled down into the room from the stained glass angels above.

Saffron pacing back and forth like a rabid dog as she ranted at, well, no one.

I stood there, watching the aggravated woman vent.

Ah. Now I get it.

"What did I do? What have I done wrong? I tried so hard to be a good person. To be a good mother and wife. To provide for my family. To provide for the community. That is what you asked of me, wasn't it? What you ask of everyone?" She dropped to her knees, eyes upward at the altar, she pressed. "Did I fail you? Am I being punished? Please, please ... Why did you take them from me?"

I hung my head, quietly slipping into a pew. And waited. She needed to go through this. No one can make the trip to acceptance easier; it was a path she must walk alone.

More pews ran perpendicular to the main aisle. These had rows of seating above them, braced by grand, oblong arched pillars. Paintings lined the walls below. To give Saffron some privacy, I wandered quietly, viewing the pictures as if in a museum. It took me a moment to recognize the Stations of the Cross. Itemized glimpses into the final moments of Christ's life.

The first station: Jesus is sentenced to death and crucifixion. A robed man bound at the wrists, led by a Roman guard. The second: Jesus is given his cross. The man, wearing only a drape over his hips, carries his heavy wooden load, his face contorted just slightly by the burden ... Burden? My heart skipped a beat. I quickly moved to the next station. Jesus falls for the first time. A man on his knees, the cross an oppressive weight on his back. The falter!

The sentence, the burden, and the falter make three.

The fourth is where the next clue will be.

I dashed to the fourth station: Jesus meets his mother. I looked around the floor, the walls, I peeked behind the picture—no disk. Exasperated, I put my hands on my head. "You put it in a church? Will, do you have any idea how many Catholic churches there are in New Orleans?"

"Over twenty within a mile of your house." I spun to see Saffron, arms folded angrily. "What are you doing here?"

I glanced over my shoulder to make sure we were alone. "Asked the woman who's got people trying to kill her." I closed the gap between us. "You agreed not to leave the manor without telling me!"

"I'm a prisoner, then?" Her eyes were puffy and red. She wiped her nose with a tissue.

The sight cooled me. "Of course not, but one of us should be with you at all times." I took a moment to look around, letting both of us calm down. "It's a beautiful place."

"It's close to my restaurants so we worshipped here frequently."

"How'd you get here? Now, I mean."

"Street car."

I looked beyond her to the immaculate altar. "Did … you get any answers?"

Saffron sighed. "What do you think?"

"I refuse to believe you're being punished."

She licked her lips but had no response.

I put a hand on her elbow. "Come on. Let's go. That is, if you're finished—" A wind came up from behind me with a shimmer around it. Wildly, I looked around to see if there were other witnesses in the church at the same time I pushed Saffron behind me. A portal had formed.

I backed up, pushing her along as I inched toward the door.

"What the hell? That's one of those bubbles!"

I hushed her and glanced around for any kind of weapon. "Of course, it has to be in a church," I sighed.

Fully formed we waited, but nothing happened.

THUMP THUMP THUMP.

"Theodore!" I called, angrily. "Really? Right now? Do you know where we are?"

He stepped through. "Hiya, Winki. Wow," he looked around. "What are you doing here?" Another goblin stepped through behind him. Bigger, nearly twice in width, but all muscle. "This is my brother-in-law, Grunik." Grunik. Now that was a goblin name! "And that's Saffron Jolly, the cooking lady I told you about."

Saffron lost all patience. "That's it! There's no way any magician could have set up anything here in this church. What the hell is going on?" Her eyes raged at mine.

"Fine," I said, and I grand swept my arms. "Magic is real."

She rolled her eyes and folded her arms.

"Happy now?" I turned to Theodore. "Grunik, nice to meet you."

"Likewise," he growled.

"He's the vendor," Theodore said. Not exactly the best time to get this done, but … "He raises the best frogs we've ever eaten. They're fat, and juicy, and—"

I held up my hands. "Yeah, yeah. I got it."

"It's in the water, ya know," Grunik added. "Grow 'em right here in Louisiana. The bayous are perfect. Good mud." He spoke with a heavy Cajun accent.

"And what do you want for the frogs?" hoping to end this conversation before Saffron bolted or someone else walked in.

"Help."

I twisted my face in confusion.

"I need help to catch 'em."

"People?" Dang. I was hoping for emeralds. The harder the better. I really wanted to see what hoops Nathan would jump through to get this done.

"People are fine as long as I don't have to deal with 'em. Goblins and people have history." At the word *goblins* I brought my finger to my lips trying to hush him, thumbing at Saffron.

"You need some workers for gigging?" Saffron stepped beside me. "How many?"

"Not giggin'. Catchin'. Frogs need to be alive. Enough to catch three hundred of 'em. A couple of days, maybe a week, I'd reckon."

She looked at her watch. "Almost seven. I can have them at your place tomorrow night. Would that work?"

"They good with frogs?"

Saffron nodded. "I have a manager who handles staffing. Hires whatever and whoever we need. I have several ranches and farms supplying my restaurants, so he's used to dealing with different jobs. Catching frogs is a bit odd, but I'm sure he can make it happen. He'll find folks who can handle the frogs and treat your land with respect."

Grunik nodded. "That will work for me."

"Got an address?"

The big goblin reached into his pocket and pulled out—I kid you not—a business card. "Have them come here. Land's all mine up and down the coastline on the lake side. They can just start hunting and leave their catch in the bin by the road. They'll know which one."

"You got a deal."

The goblin spit in his hand, then extended it. Before I could argue, without hesitation, Saffron spits in hers and they shook.

Theodore waved his arm in a big circle, creating his exit. "I got a good feeling about this, Winki," he said. "In fact, I'm just gonna get started right away. I'll let you know anything as soon as I find out."

"Thank you, Theodore." I offered a fist bump. He took it.

As the goblins left Grunik said, "What was that? That fist thing you did?"

"It's called a fist bump; see I do this—," and they stepped through.

And disappeared.

I stood there for an awkward moment, wondering what I should say.

"I'm going to wash my hand," Saffron said as she brushed past me. "And don't insult me. *Magic is real,*" she huffed. "I'm not a juvenile."

I had no idea what she thought she just saw. But her willful blindness worked for me.

Once she cleaned up, we hustled back to Nathan and the scientists.

"Where is he?" I asked as I stuffed Saffron in the van.

Mr. Smith looked at Saffron, then me, seeking permission. "Um.

Minnesota."

I gave him a blank stare. According to Jeeves, there were five nexus points on this plane; Prague, Bangkok, Natal, a small island of Hawaii whose name I can't pronounce, and New Orleans. These areas emanated powers or energies that balance our plane, Midland. All of the houses in our plane were located in those cities. "Like the state?" Nothing of import should be there. Or so I thought.

"Hey, at least he's still in this plane."

Nathan, hearing our open conversation in front of the normal, rubbed his eyes with a heavy sigh, looking over his shoulder. He tried to change the subject. "Saffron, what the hell were you thinking, leaving the manor without telling anyone?"

"I've already talk to her," I defended.

"Got a phone?" Saffron asked me. "I can call my manager, Robbie." I stared blankly. "Catchin' frogs for the little green men?" I'd lost track of the earlier conversation already. So much for multitasking.

Nathan's eyebrows shot up, his hazel eyes piercing my own.

"Ah." I handed her my phone, trying to ignore my brother-in-law. "You don't have one of your own?"

"Used to. Too many sympathy calls … Hey, Robbie. Saffron Jolly, how ya doin'? Yeah. I know." She grimaced, slowly dropping the phone to her chest, and sadly shook her head. It seemed obvious that Robbie offered condolences, and Saffron was tired of hearing them. Finally, she raised the phone. "No, I'm here. Sorry, look, I got a job for you …"

I whispered to Mr. Smith. "Where in Minnesota?" He pointed to the small green blip on the screen. The three dimensional map view showed not only a building, but a location on a particular floor. The title on the monitor read Rochester, Minnesota.

"He's moving," Mr. Smith announced as the green blip made its way through the building. The signal vanished.

"Why did it stop blinking?"

"Either he's moving through another portal," Mr. Smith answered, "or he's dead."

I gave his arm a sharp smack. "Don't even joke about such things." I caught Nathan's "I told you so" look in the rear view. "I'd be worried if any of you went missing."

During the next ten seconds, which took an eternity, I tried to sort out my feelings. I felt responsible for Jack. It was only fair. I had, after all, screwed up his life. When I discovered what he was at the last tournament, I promised I'd never tell, only to out him to my staff within moments of returning home. I'm sure the vibrations Nathan had picked up were generated by my crazy amount of guilt.

The green blip reappeared. The displayed map zoomed up and out of Minnesota, down the country's center, back to Louisiana, into the New Orleans CBD. Back to the building he'd entered nearly an hour before.

In a few minutes the van door opened. Jack smiled smugly, hands in pockets, rocking back and forth on his heels. "Well. I've got news."

Chapter Twelve

SAFFRON PULLED TOGETHER a fabulous late-night dinner of honey baked ham, biscuits, collard greens, and baked beans. We'd forgotten how good a fresh-cooked meal tasted. Everyone ate with gusto, including Saffron.

After a heated debate while she cooked, I decided to include her in the following discussion. Surprisingly, Jack argued for her, since it was Saffron's life at risk. Of course, the presence of a normal would make some explanations and parts of the story impossible to tell. I promised I would handle those situations, and backed the need for Saffron to hear what's going on. So it was agreed.

Around the overly long dining room table, Jack told us his tale.

"Apparently, the Asclepium Order never fell. Decimated, they went into hiding. Only a few, a dozen or so, still survive. Their role, as they see it, is to monitor healers. They keep meticulous records: when healers are born, who they serve or what they do, and how and when they die. They even know," he cleared his throat, "whom healers assist at tournaments."

"Whoa," Nathan said. "That's huge. How do they know that?"

"I'm sorry," Saffron said, leaning forward. "I know I'm new, but what is a healer, exactly? Are we talking doctors?"

"Yes," I answered her. "A kind of doctor. But not a go-to-school-and-get-a-degree kind; these are special people born with an innate ability to know what's wrong with you and how to fix it." Saffron seemed satisfied so I urged Jack on. "How do they know who healers assist at tournaments? Isn't that very hush-hush?"

"Sadly, they didn't trust me enough to divulge their information. I confess, I do believe them."

"And why is that?" Mrs. Black asked, peering through her coke bottle lenses.

"They told me whom I'd assisted at tournament for my entire life."

"This is kinda good news," Nathan mused. "They know who served Will at his last tournament."

"Yes. They do. They agree he was framed and unjustly exe—" His eyes found Saffron. "Eliminated." Thankfully, she hadn't realized what had almost been said.

I gave Jack a "that was close" look. Best not to freely throw words around like *executed* in front of a normal.

"But before we can negotiate with them," Jack continued, "they have a serious problem. With Mrs. Jolly."

That got her attention. She looked up. "Why? Wh ... why me?" she stammered.

"According to the order, there was a prophecy," he started. "It warned of a normal—by that I mean someone outside our community—who, in the midst of their deepest anguish, creates a poison that destroys all healers. Until recently, they assumed the threat would be someone intentionally targeting healers, perhaps believing them to be the source of his anguish. But given Mrs. Jolly's situation, they are convinced that she is the one." He looked Saffron in the eye. "The despair of losing one's entire family is the deepest pain any person can possibly suffer."

"How ..." Saffron swallowed. "How do I convince them they're wrong? I mean, I'm not really cooking anything anymore, certainly not creating anything. And I don't want to hurt anyone. They had nothing to do with my husband's and kid's death, right?"

"True. In fact, given the prophecy, if they'd known in advance it was you, they would have done anything and everything in their power to protect your family."

"What if I talked to them? I could convince them—"

Jack raised his hand to stop her. "We're past that point. There is only one thing they want: an absolute assurance that you will never create anything again." He frowned. "Certainty that to them requires your death."

"Typical," Mrs. Black spat as her fork clattered onto her plate. "In order to save their own skins, they want to kill an innocent. Healers! Oughta be horse-whipped, the lot of 'em." She timidly looked at Jack. "Present company excluded, of course."

"Of course," Jack solemnly echoed.

We all sat there quietly, nervously avoiding the accused woman's eyes.

"Take me to them," Saffron whispered.

"What?" Nathan barked.

"Take me to them." She looked around at us. "Look, I have no problem with dying. And if my death saves people, then I'm more than happy to do it. I want to die. I want to be with my family."

I swallowed, not knowing exactly how to tip toe through these tulips. I looked up, hoping to find the right words. I found my husband. "Look at that portrait," I started. "Did I ever tell you who that is?"

"No."

"That's Will. That's my late husband." I decided to skip the part about that *really* being my husband ... "I sit here everyday, every meal, and sometimes just to think, all to stare at that wonderful man. He died November before last. He was murdered, taken before his time."

"I thought you said it was an accident."

"Nothing can be proven, but I know. *We,*" I gestured to the table, "know. So when I tell you I understand your grief, I really do. Death is a given, Saffron. Death is a certainty. And while the separation is excruciating, death will come to you. What's important, what's really, really important is what you do with this time."

"Apparently, I'm going to kill a whole bunch of people. Seems like an easy trade off."

"And what if it isn't? What if you're just seeing it as a loophole to get you where you want to go? Are you absolutely certain that's the answer? You'll only get this one chance."

She thought for a moment. "I don't want to create anything that kills innocent people."

"We'll make sure you don't. That is, if you let us."

Defeated, Saffron lowered her head.

I looked at Jack. "Do you have a recommendation on what to do next?"

Before Jack could answer, we all heard a tiny French voice, "*Ma chére … ma … chére!*"

"Hercule?" Everyone except Saffron looked around them to spy the little guy.

With grunts of effort he appeared on the table. "*Sucre … sucre!*"

"Whoa!" Saffron stood, knocking over her chair to get away from the bug.

Jeeves retrieved a saucer from the buffet. He splashed some water into it and added a cube from the sugar bowl. Hercule gasped and stumbled his way to it. We could hear him chewing the grainy substance.

I pursed my lips already seeking some explanation before I looked at Saffron and her wide-eyed stare. "Did … the roach talk to you?"

As my mind raced for rational words, Jack asked, "You heard him?" He looked at Nathan. "Is that possible? I just assumed only the talented could hear."

We both looked at Nathan for an explanation. He raised his hands. "Look, in the last couple of days I've learned that a mythical organization actually exists, that Mother Earth herself deems me irrelevant, and *her* thoughts," he thumbed Saffron, "have enough power to kill me. I'm so beyond understanding what's *possible*."

"We can hear him," Mr. Smith interjected. He pointed to his partner. "We're normals."

"Really?" Jack said. "I had no idea."

"Yeah, but only in the house. We get nuthin' outside," Mr. Smith said with his mouthful.

Saffron spoke up. "My ... my thoughts can kill you? And the cockroach talks?" Her eyes bounced between us all. They landed on me last. "It *is* real. Isn't it?"

I half-expected her to run screaming out the front door. It was, after all, exactly what I'd done when I realized magic was real.

"We call it talent," I said softly. "An ability out of the ordinary. One of Nathan's talents is the ability to——"

"Read minds? He can read minds?" I could see her panic swelling like a tsunami, even without his talent.

"He can hear what's being broadcast loudly," I put it. "And your grief registers at about eleven."

"That's what this is for," Nathan pulled the amulet from under his collared shirt. "It dampens everything around me." He twisted his face. "And I still hear you screaming. I know you are tired of sympathy because it's a constant reminder of what you've lost, but I am so, so sorry. You see, I *know* what kind of pain you're in."

"I didn't know anyone else was suffering." Saffron gave a wan smile. "I'm the one who's sorry."

"Okay, little chimpanzees around the table," Hercule announced. "I am back. Does anyone want to know what the little *cafard* discovered, hm? Why he flew and ran as fast as he could all the way home?"

I consoled him. "Of course, Hercule. What did you discover?"

"A dark truth. One that will bring even more grief to the woman you call Saffron Jolly." After a small dance to think, he turned to Saffron. "This will not help take your pain away. However, you need to know."

Nathan braced his palms against his temples. "Okay. I'm ready."

Hercule's antennae bounced to and fro. "Your brother, *mon ami*. He is the one ... who did this to you."

Saffron sat back in her chair as blood drained from her face. From shades of grim to confused, her eye narrowed. "Simon," Saffron stammered quietly, "wanted them dead?"

"No, no. He wanted only for you to suffer. But the devil your brother went to, the devil who assisted, she knew the prophecy, *oui?* You understand now?"

The word *she* rattled around in my brain. The *she* devil the brother went to ...

"But how?" Saffron shook her head in blatant disbelief. "How could he have killed them? They all died in separate accidents. Simon was nowhere near any of them."

"He didn't have to be," Mr. Smith said nonchalantly. "If he went to the darklings they use a ghoul as a kind of hit man. Ghouls can take over a person and make them do, well, anything. Like run their SUV off the road, or be the driver of a hit and run, or make people climb onto rooftops."

"Or drive into an oncoming semi-truck," Mrs. Black offered.

I should have heard her clearly, since she spoke of Will but ... "She? The *she* devil?" I whispered, fighting the hot white pinpoint of pain in my stomach.

"Uh, hold on," Nathan said. "I don't understand. You're saying someone knew about the prophesy and used Simon's desire to hurt his sister as an opportunity to, what, make it come true? Kill all the healers? Who in their right mind would do that? *Why* do that? You eliminate the healers, and the entire structure of the tournament falls apart. We all go back to ..." Nathan stopped cold, his breath labored. "By the damned Dark Lords."

"Who's the devil?" I asked, the pinpoint in my stomach growing to the size of a fist, burning my heart and lungs as well. I was barely aware of the whispers and mutterings of the others.

"War," Hercule said to Nathan, a little too gleefully. "We all go back to war. Mayhem, bloodshed, agony, despair ... *oh*, the resplendence of it all."

Mr. Smith nodded. "Dark Ages, two point oh."

"The end of this plane," Mrs. Black said. "The end of *all* planes."

The white fire shot up to my brain. I slammed my hands on the table, no longer willing to be ignored. I stood as I screamed, *"Who's the devil?"*

Everything went quiet. All eyes fell on me. I stood in a rage, panting like a rabid dog, looking at the bug on the tablecloth.

Hercule turned to me. Hesitating, he admitted, "Esmeralda, *bien sûr.*"

The name hung in the air like a guillotine blade, sharp, bright, terrifying. I saw her with my mind's eye, laughing at me, laughing at my tortured husband, laughing at the broken bodies of Saffron Jolly's family.

Red. My entire field of vision went red. I swept my arm over the table, throwing everything onto the floor. I remember screaming, but have no idea what I said.

My mind made a tactical list, all on its own. *Armor, hammer, halberd ... I just need a portal to the Radiant Plane ...*

Someone called my name. They grabbed my arm and spun me away from my goal.

Get off me! I've got a witch to kill!

They held me fast ... I threw my fist to free myself ...

Nathan fell back, holding his newly clocked jaw, tumbling down the stairs, saved by Jack from breaking his neck.

Once he stood on his own feet again, he looked up at me, holding his new bruise.

I saw his eyes. All their eyes. They all saw me punch him: Smith, Wesson, Mrs. Black, Jeeves, Jack, and Saffron. "Don't tell me I just sit by. Don't tell me I just take it! That *we* just take it."

Jack casually put his hands behind his back and walked up the steps to me. "Yes, ma'am. You do. They get to lie and cheat and kill. And we, ma'am. We take it."

I searched his blue-green eyes for something more, some explanation, some reason, some clarity. "Why?" I finally whimpered.

"Because we are a white house. We always play by the rules."

Saffron was the last person I saw before my vision blurred. "I'm sorry," I said to her. I turned and ran for my bedroom. And I cried. I cried for my husband and I cried for Saffron. I cried for her family I never knew. I cried from the rage I felt inside me, the intense anger that I'd been warned about. I cried because I wanted to embrace it. Dammit, I wanted to kill the red-haired witch.

I cried because it would be so easy, too easy, to do.

I took a deep, calming breath. Hatred is the path to the darkness, someone told me. They hurt you, you hate them, you do something rash, and ... you become them. How could I possibly win? Moreover, this wasn't just an individual choice, it wasn't just me I was choosing for. I was the champion of the house, and each of them within it were tied to it, to me.

If I damned my own pathetic life, *I damned them all.*

~ ~ * ~ ~

I stood at the top of the stairs, barefooted. I could hear them talking, Nathan and Jack. The long day bore down on me, my eyes heavy. But sleep would elude me until I said what I needed to say. Mustering my courage, I went down the steps and into the living room.

Nathan wore his glasses as he read some document. He rubbed his chin. I stopped before he saw me.

"I can heal that for you," Jack said, out of my view.

"I know. But it's not that bad," he mumbled without looking up.

As I entered the room, both men looked up. "Jack? May I please have a moment with Nathan?"

"Of course, ma'am. As a matter of fact, I will retire for the night. I will see you both in the morning."

Once alone with Nathan, I didn't know how to ... "How's Mrs. Jolly doing?" I asked. *Coward.*

Nathan glanced over his glasses, but quickly retreated. "Surprisingly well. Better than I would under the circumstance. Better than you did." He flipped a page. "But then again, she has you. You're good at coming up with plausible explanations."

"Nah. I think she's just desperate enough to let herself be distracted." An awkward silence filled the room. I took a breath for courage. "I want to apologize, Nathan, but words won't be enough." I waited until he looked at me, reluctantly. Just another quick glance. "Don't ever let me do that again."

"Blocking punches is a helluva lot easier when I see them coming," he said nodding towards his amulet.

"That's not what I'm talking about." I back peddled. "Well, yeah, that too. You know it's easy for me, easy to slip into rage. Easier than I want it to be." Nathan wouldn't look at me. "Don't let me walk that path, Nathan. Don't let me damn this house."

"Yeah. Like I could stop you. I couldn't stop Will, and you're a thousand times stronger." He kept his focus on the paper.

I hung my head. It wasn't true, thankfully. So far I had very little talent. I was a one-trick pony. "Is this what happened to Will? Is this what pushed him down the path? Did they push him—?"

"You already know the answer. You beat on a little kid enough he grows up to be an angry man." His heavy words came with no emotion, as if they were practiced.

"I want to know—"

"Stop," he held up his hand. Now his eyes bore into mine. I dropped my own. "You don't. It won't make a difference because he wasn't you. Everyone follows the path in different ways. Who knows how you'll ..." He gruffly set his glasses aside and poured himself a shot of bourbon, swallowing it with one gulp. "You don't listen. You never listen. I'm terrified of you, Mrs. Witherspoon. Absolutely terrified. You have no idea what you're capable of. You went to your first tournament a complete beginner and left rated in the *mid-thirties*. That's unheard of. That's like getting off the couch with the decision that you're going to compete in the Olympics just for fun, and winning a bronze medal. And that's with one talent, your first, which is—to those of us who have been raised in this community well know —your *weakest*. The easiest one to access. And what's your starting skill? To manipulate a fundamentally *un*manipulatable constant in the universe." His voice raised. "And your next trick is making matter move across time and space." He let that sink in, glaring at me. "Are you starting to see a pattern here? I ... I can't even fathom what's coming next!" He poured himself another drink.

I swallowed. *No one had ever told me this before.*

He waved his drink dramatically. "Do you know what my greatest talent is?" Under his scrutiny my mind went blank. "My *shield*. It's maybe the strongest one ever manifested. Bullets can't penetrate it. Will had a talent he called *spark*. He could throw small lightning bolts. Two formidable talents. Together we could defend the house with ease. But they're nothing compared to yours. With more to come!" His eyes twinkled in the dim light, his fatigue showing in the dark rings under his eyes. The black and blue bruise on his jaw looked angry, nicely matching his mood.

My mind whirled. *I* was no one. *I* was nothing. I was so new to all of this, how can he possibly be afraid of me? But I heard him this time. His frustration pulsed through the room like—A flash appeared outside, and to make the point, thunder rocked through the room.

"So, Mrs. Witherspoon," he said coldly, "don't look to me to be your guide or your conscience. I can't possibly be your anchor. Because when your tide rises, I'm going to drown, just like everyone else in this house." He threw his drink back and smacked his glass down. Leaving the room he turned, stepping backwards, "Hell, who knows? My soul was damned once before. I'm certain it will be easier to cleanse a second time round!" He left me alone while torrents of water poured down the windows.

And my cheeks.

Chapter Thirteen

I DIDN'T JOIN them for breakfast the next day. Nathan's words still rang loudly in my ears. I laid in bed, staring at the roach on the ceiling.

"You feel sorry for yourself?" Hercule said after hours of staring down at me.

"No."

"Good," he danced. "Nothing I hate more than sniveling primates."

With a sigh I rolled over, ignoring him. Someone knocked on the door. "Who is it?" I asked, half heartedly.

"It is I, madam." Jeeves. "I brought you breakfast."

"I'm not hungry."

"If I may be so bold, once you see it you will be. Mrs. Jolly prepared us something this morning. I am quite impressed."

That piqued my interest. Jeeves was hard to impress. I got up and draped myself in a thick, terry cloth robe. "Come in," I said, seating myself at my table.

Jeeves carried a silver platter with a silver dome. The strong scent of coffee filled the room. I sighed, contented. Once he removed the top the smells of bacon and pancakes joined the air. My stomach growled.

"That looks fantastic," I said. "Are those bananas?"

"Indeed, madam. Banana pancakes with peanut butter. Mrs. Jolly said she created them years ago after a visit to Graceland." He stood erect after he set the dome aside and pulled out a small pad. He waited, pen in hand. This meant Jeeves had news for me.

I took a sip of coffee as Hercule climbed onto the table top. Out of habit I scooped up some Steen's syrup and put it in my cup's saucer for him. The bug had a sweet tooth. Antennae. Whatever. "Please," I gestured, "what's up today?"

"Mr. Smith and Mr. Wesson have created something they call a *barrier booster*. They would like you to test it with them this morning."

"What's it do?" I said, mouth full of wonderful hotcakes with sweet peanut butter. Heavenly!

"They believe it will boost your conjuring ability; get you, as they put it, 'over the hump.'"

I smiled with my mouth full. I loved it when Jeeves used slang. Had to admit, with the tournament just four months out, I really wanted this talent in my back pocket. That is, if it was mine to have. "Fine. I'll meet with them around nine." I checked the clock on my mantle. It was already eight thirty. "Make that ten."

"Also," he said, "Mr. Marble wants to have a word with you this morning."

Just one? "Mr. Marble had plenty of words last night. I don't need to hear anymore today, thank you."

The butler put his hands behind his back. "You two had an argument?"

"Jeeves, I punched him in the face. No one in this house should be punching anyone else in the face." I took another bite. "We both need cooler heads before we talk." I changed the subject. "How is Mrs. Jolly this morning?" Judging by the food, I'd say awesome.

"I was rather surprised to find her still here, to be honest. She's taking this all quite well."

"I think she needed to be out of her own house. Lots of ghosts there. Lots of memories." I could relate.

"Hm," he mused. "Ghosts there, goblins here. I must warn you, however," he said, "normals shouldn't know too much about the community."

"Talented people want to kill her. Shouldn't she have some understanding of them? Or why?"

Jeeves had no answer. "One more thing, madam. I am to remind you that tonight is the dinner in the Citadel Plane." I grimaced. I'd completely forgotten. "I've been asked by Mrs. Black for a list of your party. She will put together their attire. Whom do you want to attend?"

I shrugged. "Who do you recommend?"

"*Whom*," he corrected and I rolled my eyes. "It is not my place to say."

"Do you want to go?"

"Not particularly, no, madam."

"Well, for the record, neither do I. Ask Nathan. He knows this stuff better than me. Whatever he says is fine."

"Madam," he sounded displeased, "you need to start making these decisions."

I rolled my eyes with an irritated sigh. "I'll talk to Nathan and get back to Mrs. Black before I see Smith and Wesson. How's that?"

"Satisfactory, madam."

My words had come out so fast I was surprised he understood them. "Glad it is for someone," I muttered.

I finished my breakfast, got presentable, and headed downstairs for round three with Mr. Marble. As I'd scored it, we were one and one; I'd got in a good punch, but he'd came back with a swift kick to my stomach. I hated being angry with him. I hated it even more that he was angry at me.

Nathan and Jack stepped over the threshold on their way out. "Nathan! Wait!" I called.

"Wait in the car, would ya?" he asked Jack, who gave me a "Good Morning" nod before he trotted down the porch steps. "Mrs. Witherspoon. Did you sleep well?"

His face had swelled significantly from the blow. The circles under his eyes looked darker and bluer than they did last night. "Nope. Yourself?" Didn't appear to me he did either.

"I've had better."

I licked my lips. "Dinner tonight at the Citadel. I assume we want to distract the Chancellor and his staff enough for Hercule and the spiders to snoop?" If I were in a better mood I would have pointed out what a great band name that would be: Hercule and the Spiders.

"That was the plan."

"Then what if Jack joined us? A healer being present might be a distraction."

With a thoughtful nod, Nathan said, "That ... would do it. I'll talk to Jack. He's going to hate that."

I gave a mockingly sinister smile. "I consider it a bonus." *Why shouldn't he join in the fun?*

"You *do* want him to like you, right?" He shook his head and turned to leave.

Okay, we got the chit chat out of the way. I followed him onto the large patio. "Nathan, would you just stop?"

He did without looking at me.

"You're right. I need to have my emotions in check all the time. There's much more at stake with my decisions than my own ... situation. I have more than my life to consider."

He didn't move for a long, painful moment. He set his satchel down, turned, and said, "No."

I hung my head, crestfallen. What more could I have said?

"*You're* right." He put kind hands on my shoulders. "You're still new and innocent and overwhelmed by everything around you. Your emotions stem from your untrained and uneducated reaction to all this. The rest of us have had trained for that all our lives. So it's up to us—this house, this staff, and mostly me—to guide you through it. To tell you when you're wrong. To keep you, and us, safe." He shrugged. "So, what if we throw some punches? We kick each other's ass almost every evening."

"Never when we're angry," I said, sternly. "And especially never when we're angry at each other. I'm sorry."

He gave a small nod. "Let's make that a rule, then. We can yell and scream and call each other names, but nothing physical. Not outside the ring."

"Agreed."

Nathan bounced on his toes. "And how about a second rule that says we have to work it out before either of us goes to sleep?" He gave a half-grin. "I tossed and turned all night long."

I blew some hair off my face. "I predict some long nights, but agreed."

With a kind hand he took the back of my head and leaned me into him so he could kiss my forehead. "Eight oh two this evening. Sharp. That's when we leave for the Citadel. Until then, have a good day, Mrs. Witherspoon."

"You too, Mr. Marble." I could tell by the light and airy steps he took that he, like I, felt infinitely better. "Nathan?" I stopped him. He looked up. "Can your shield really stop bullets?" Okay, it wasn't what I really want to ask but I did want to know.

"Yes."

"Then why didn't you use it last year? Why didn't you save yourself from me and Mama? You could have stopped ..." I swallowed. "You know. When I shot you."

I could see the wheels spin, looking around the vast front yard, as if the answer hid there. Seconds passed. "Everyone in this house, the people I loved and try to protect, everyone I would die a thousand times for … they all thought I'd betrayed them." He shrugged. "Frankly, I didn't want to live." He was off again.

"Nathan," I stopped him again.

"I need to get going, Winki," he said, looking back at me with a grin.

I swallowed, unsure I wanted to know. "Are you really afraid of me?" That was what I wanted to ask him.

"No." He took a moment to straighten his jacket. "I'm utterly *terrified* of you. That's the cold, hard truth. But," he waved his hand between us, "that's what makes this all the more exciting. That's also the cold, hard truth." He strolled around the corner. I heard him open the car door, turn over the engine, and the car crunch its way down the seashell driveway.

Even after they'd gone, I wondered if I could handle the cold, hard truth.

With Nathan and Jack off, I, as promised, told Mrs. Black that the three of us would be going to the Citadel tonight. Then, I diligently visited the laboratory of my two mad scientists in the basement. Yes, a basement. It contained, well, anything we needed whenever we needed it. Sometimes the lab, the workout ring, most of our weapons, or space for a decent obstacle course that I ran frequently while being shot at by my various opponents, like Nathan and my mad scientists.

Every time I amble down those stairs I recall that I'm going under water. *Below* sea level. I reflect that, since New Orleanians buried their dead above ground, that I, as part of the living, should also stay above ground. *Above* sea level. Needless to say, I often find myself distracted.

"Mrs. W," Mr. Smith announced as I entered the lab. "Right on time. Please, follow me."

"What devious and painful plan have you for me today?" I asked.

"Nothing painful. I don't think, anyway. All you have to do is sit in here." He'd led me to a small phone booth-like set up in the center of the laboratory. "It's a sound booth we modified," he explained. "All you need to do is sit in it and summon that knife." Just outside the box sat a stool, and on it sat a knife, the one I won during last year's tournament. Beautiful little thing, double edged, with a blade about five inches long. White pearled handle with silver inlay. "We're going to sit out here. You do the summoning when we ask, and we're going to modify some of the energy signatures around you."

"So," I stepped into the box, "this is gonna hurt." Modifying the energy around me sounded a lot like being electrocuted.

"Mmm," he hedged, "probably. Just don't dwell on that. Now, take a seat and let us know when you're ready."

I did, perching myself on the stool in the room. When I closed the door, my ears roared in silence. "I'm not wild about the room." They didn't respond.

Then Mr. Smith voice came through a little speaker. "Oh, push the button if you need to talk to us."

I spied said button, just next to the window. "I'm not wild about the room," I repeated.

"Your ears will get used to the quiet in a few moments. Now, if you're ready, focus on the knife."

The two men sat behind a table facing me, covered in computers, monitors, keyboards, and pads. Neither looked at me. Probably didn't matter.

I stared at the knife. The last time I summoned anything was also the first time. The item was a gun. I had never seen the thing before, but at the moment I wanted it. I wanted a gun, and one appeared. Knowing that, I held out my hand, wanting the knife. I filled my mind with need, desire. I filled my mind with intention and image. I tried to feel the knife in my hand; its weight, its handle, its cold handle. But nothing happened.

I pushed the button. "Nothing."

"Just a sec," Mr. Smith answered. He held the "talk" button as he discussed things with Mr. Wesson. "Right there," he pointed to a monitor. "Let's amp up that frequency ... and that one, too."

I felt a tingling sensation up my spine. I didn't impact me physically as much as emotionally. I suddenly felt cranky. I told them so.

"Cranky is good. Remember, just focus on the knife. We're ready when you are."

I closed my eyes and repeated the process. The knife, the weight, the touch, the cold ...

Something was in my hand. I opened my eyes wide. "Uh ... guys?"

Both men stood. Yes, there *was* a knife in my hand, just not the one I wanted. My knife still sat unmoved on the stool outside the booth. The one in my hand felt sticky, and the blade had residue on it of some kind. I recognized it as a butcher's knife; heavier than mine, longer than mine, completely shiny silver or stainless steel, unlike mine. Even the handle felt warm, like it had been used recently. Also, unlike mine.

"So ..." I stammered as I left the booth and presented the dirty object to them. "Success?"

"Where did you get that?" Mr. Smith asked me.

"How should I know! You two amped up something. I did what I always do."

Timidly, Mr. Smith came to see it up close. "May I?" he held out his hand. Mr. Wesson joined him as he took the knife, and handed me some hand sanitizer, which I immediately used.

Mr. Smith turned the knife in several directions. "Anyone recognize it?"

"We didn't recognize the gun I summoned either. Maybe I can only get things I don't know about, or haven't seen before?" *I summoned. Holy guacamole! I did it.*

"That makes no sense. There's got to be millions of knives in New Orleans alone. Why did you get this one?"

Someone came down the steps. Saffron Jolly followed Jeeves. He cleared his throat although they already held our attention. "Pardon me," Jeeves said. "But Mrs. Jolly has experienced something unusual. Go on, madam."

"Hey, I'm sorry to bother y'all," she said, "but the strangest thing just happened and *hey!* That's my knife! How did you guys get it?" She looked angered. "Is this some kind of magic trick y'all are working on?"

"What … um," Mr. Smith looked at the knife again. "What were you doing with it?"

"Getting dinner ready. Cutting up some pork chops. Why?"

To Wesson, he said, "Can you pull up the news from the day we came back from the tournament? Any missing guns?"

"You mean," I asked, flabbergasted, "we didn't check for missing guns when this happened the last time?" Saffron shifted her weight, nervously.

"Of course, we did," Mr. Smith said, looking over Mr. Wesson's shoulder. "But we're looking for something specific, now. We have some new information, thanks to Mrs. Jolly."

"Missing gun?" Saffron started, then held up her hands "Never mind. Can I have my knife back?"

"Just a sec," Mr. Smith told her. Saffron and I joined the view of the monitors as Mr. Wesson scrolled through headlines involving missing guns. "That one, check it," Mr. Smith pointed. A click later displayed the article that talked about a gun disappearing while in use. The man who fired the weapon got off on an attempted murder charge as the gun had never been found. "*In use,*" Mr. Smith said as he retrieved the stool from the sound room and set it next to the one that held up my prize weapon. "Can we borrow you for just a quick moment, Mrs. Jolly," Mr. Smith said as he looked around and found some fig-filled cookies that he and Mr. Wesson kept for snacks. "Do me a favor and cut these cookies when I tell you. Mrs. W? Back in the booth, please."

"You can't eat these after I've cut them," Saffron informed. "The meat on this blade was raw."

"We won't. We promise. You ready?" he asked me.

I pushed the button. "Yup." Again a tingling shot down my back, again I felt irritated. I sneered at them.

I saw Mr. Smith wave a hand, instructing Saffron to cut the cookies. Over the speaker he said, "Focus on *your* knife, Mrs. W. Just like the last time."

I closed my eyes. I *wanted* the knife. A moment later, Saffron's knife was in my hand.

Smith and Wesson jumped, like school girls, up and down with glee, high-fiving each other and giving pats on the back. Once Saffron saw her knife in the booth she jumped back a little with her eyes darting between her hand and mine.

Leaving the little room I gave her back the cutlery. "Can Saffron go back to work now?" I asked the celebrating men.

"Oh … yeah. We're done here. We understand it now."

Saffron smiled. "*That* is a really cool trick. How the hell did you get that out of my hand? No one touched me, I'm sure of it. No one came near me, even."

"Smoke and mirrors," I smiled with confidence. The geeks smiled, too, still bouncing with glee.

She scratched her head and shrugged. Pointing to the cookies she said, "Don't forget to throw those out, now." Jeeves escorted her out of the room.

Arms folded, I patiently waited for the ongoing celebration to end. Eventually, they would realize I was still there.

"It's simple, really," Mr. Smith finally said. "It isn't the weapon, per se. It's more that you want to use it. When you wanted to shoot someone, you got a gun that had already been fired. Don't you see? The weapon you summon needs to be already in use. The one nearest you is the one you'll get." He pointed back at the article. "The gun came from just three blocks away. You wanted a gun; at *that* time a gun was in use; *poof!* You gotta gun."

"That doesn't sound useful," I said. "If I can only summon someone's else's tools."

"Well, firstly, that's pretty damned useful," he assured me. "For example, let's say at tournament you can only bring in one weapon to the bout. But if you can disarm your opponent—"

"By summoning his weapon, now I have two and he has none." I beamed. "Okay. Way more useful."

"One more test," he said, "just to make sure. Back in the booth, please."

I did; closed the door, gave a nod, felt the tingle. Mr. Smith, using my knife, cut up the cookies. I summoned the knife. It came to me.

This time, the celebration was mine. I clapped my hands and jumped with joy. Hats off to the stars! *I was a conjurer.* Provided, of course, I was tucked in my little booth with some particular energy signature "amped up", but hey … we've worked with less.

With a well-defined starting point, Smith, Wesson, and I summoned a variety of things: weapons, pens, chairs, cookies. Each time they tweaked down the energy in the room, and the tingling got less and less, until I failed to conjure. Then we'd start over. I shifted my focus from the object I wanted to the tingling sensation I needed to feel, making me feel it myself. And after four grueling hours of work, I stood at the top of the staircase into the basement and summoned my knife. It still had to be in use—one of the lab monkeys were hacking away—but I could do it.

I could conjure items out of thin air.

Chapter Fourteen

BEFORE LEAVING THEM, I asked Smith and Wesson to keep my progress a secret. I really wanted to show off to everyone later, but right now I had things I wanted to do before our Citadel dinner.

I'd worked so long with the geeks I missed my lunch, and the pit-like sensation in my stomach stopped me cold at the top of the stairs. I wolfed down a late lunch—a muffuletta Mrs. Jolly had set aside for me—then dashed to the garage to fire up the Duck. I had a few hours to check a couple of churches for Will's disk before I getting ready for this evening's dinner.

I had a plan, a map of churches and cathedrals I wanted to check first, listed from those closest to the manor and then outward. From past experience, I knew there had to be some reason why Will selected the church. He wouldn't have put it in just any church for me to find, on that I felt confidant. As I rolled up to the first, I looked the edifice up and down, trying to recall a memory or a reason. Did someone we know work here? Was there some event we participated in? Nothing came to mind.

I entered, quiet as a church mouse, and slipped along the wall bearing the first stations of the cross. When I got to the fourth, I looked around. Nope, nothing, not even a reasonable hiding place.

Undaunted, I proceeded to the second church, which was much smaller and less ornate. While walking through, I couldn't recall any reason for being here, or why Will would have selected such a place. I made my way to the fourth station again, and again, left the building in disappointment. Really, Winki? Are you going to search every church in New Orleans? It was a Catholic community; there were thousands. I mounted the Duck and rested my head on folded hands across the handlebar. We weren't even married in a church.

My cell rang. "Yeah?" I answered the call.

"Winki? Nathan. Look, uh, I got some bad news. Last night Jack and I decided we'd question Simon again this morning. We were hoping we'd convince him to turn himself into Detective Duplantier, maybe put Saffron's angst at rest a bit. Uh, anyway, he's ... missing."

"Missing?" Great. And just before we need to leave. "How do you know?"

"Not at home, not at any of the restaurants. He was supposed to be at Plates this morning but never showed. Not answering his cell, either."

I recalled Hercule's story last night, about Simon making a deal with Esmeralda. I freaked out before I knew the details. "How did Hercule know about Esmeralda? Did Simon contact her?"

"Oh, yeah. I guess you left before that part. Hercule followed Simon to Ravenswood." Malador's manor. "Given Hercule plays on Team Winki, he's not able to go in without invitation, but through a window, he saw Malador's butler contact the Radiant Plane. You can see how he made the connection." I didn't bother asking how Hercule could tell it was a portal to the Radiant Plane; they all looked the same to me. Esmeralda's realm exists in the Radiant Plane, and she's Malador's sister.

"But he didn't see Simon leave, either through the front door or through the portal?" I asked.

"No. Because he came home."

"What do you think we should do?"

Nathan fell silent for a moment, thinking. "Normally, I'd say we go look for him, but we can't. We've got to make that departure time to the Citadel. I'll have Jack contact Detective Duplantier. We'll tell her Simon's missing and let her know where we found the micro chip you found in the desk. Who knows, maybe the NOPD will get lucky."

I licked my lips. "What do we tell Saffron?"

"We don't have anything to tell her right now. She's been through enough already. Her brother could be out walking around the Barataria for all we know."

I had to agree. After I hung up I headed back home, empty handed and heavy-hearted.

~ ~ * ~ ~

Nathan and Jack stood in the living room, waiting for me at the base of the staircase. They looked absolutely dashing in their black tuxes, with red bow ties, matching cummerbunds, and a splash of red on their jackets where a crimson kerchief peaked out of a breast pocket. The only difference between their garb was Jack's kidskin gloves.

"You two clean up nice," I said as I carefully made my way down the stairs. The caution was warranted as I rarely wear heels, which Mrs. Black had deemed necessary. I wore a blue dress, high collared, long sleeved, perfectly fitted through the waist and hips. A silver band of mesh snaked around my body, starting at my shoulder, winding around my bosom, my hip, and along one leg and down to the floor.

The men hadn't responded to my comment. I had expected wisecracks at my outlandish dress. Their silence stopped me. I realized they were gawking at my outfit.

I tilted my head to the side. "Oh, sure, it's stunning but completely impractical. What if I have to fight one of those bone wraith thingies? I can hardly walk in this, let alone run. Heck, I'm not sure I'll make the trek off the mountain without breaking my neck."

Jack regained his composure. "I think I can speak for both of us when I say your dress's impracticality was *not* what we were contemplating." He bowed. "You look exquisite, ma'am."

Jeeves added, "I will send you to their door, madam. No *trekking* will be needed."

"Jeeves? If you please," Nathan turned away abruptly to the man.

My butler's eyes turned bright green and he turned to face the living room and raised his arm in one grand sweep. The room started to shimmer as a portal began to form.

"*Whoa.*"

We turned to see Saffron peeking out from around the doorway. "How did you do that?"

The men looked nervous as their minds raced for explanation. I smiled. "A good magician never reveals his secrets. We'll be back soon," I told her once the portal finished forming. "But don't wait up."

With a small step, Nathan, Jack, and I left the Midland Plane and set foot in the Citadel Plane, about a hundred feet from the massive black wood doors into the Citadel itself. I'd know the place anywhere, the uniformly orange sky, the black soil and rocks and edifice, and one lone green tree, now dotted with delicate blossoms.

As we closed the distance between us and the five people standing by the Citadel's entrance, I wondered why we didn't do this all the time, rather than slog our way down the rocky hillside.

"Every house comes through the same portal location," Nathan explained to me quickly. "That way no two portals collide accidentally."

"Makes sense," I nodded. I looked at him. "You heard me?"

"Yeah. We're outside the walls. All our talents work here. They're only stifled in the Citadel."

"I know that. But aren't you wearing your amulet?"

He stopped short, and placed his hand over his chest, validating its existence. Nathan narrowed his eyes. "Huh."

"Greetings, House of Gateway." Before us stood the Chancellor himself, frail in stature, a little hunched, and bearing more wrinkles than Keith Richards. One eye was bright and clear, the other a milky white.

I watched as his eyes fell on Jack; they widened a bit in shock. He did a remarkable job of regaining his decorum. With a forced smile he gestured to the Mage Council who stood in a row, ready to greet us.

"Winki Witherspoon, Champion of New Orleans," the Chancellor started, "may I introduce you to the mages of the Citadel." Trembling as he walked, the slight Chancellor gestured to the first lady, a plump woman with short brown hair that paged around her face. She wore a black laced jacket over a bright green satin skirt that draped to the ground. "This is Lady Safina, Viscountess of Pisces, Champion of the Coral House in the Aqua Plane."

I'd been prepped by Mrs. Black ad nauseam about official introductions, something to do with a grand curtsy, but given my attire, and my propensity to mock authority, I ignored her recommendation and did what I always did; I put my hand over my heart and gave a deep and surrendering bow. The Viscountess responded with a heart warming smile and a giggle, and even offered her hand to me which I took. "Very nice to meet you at last," she said.

"Very nice to meet you as well, Lady Safina."

"This," the Chancellor shuffled us along, "is the Lady Jezebel, Queen Mother of Diamond Realm, Radiant Plane." Diamond Realm ... wait, great gravy, Queen Mother? Esmeralda's *mom?* I immediately saw the family resemblance, the pale skin and the fiery red hair, as I bowed. I hoped my boiling blood didn't show. Lady Jezebel gave a single nod back.

The Chancellor continued, leading us to an absolutely uninteresting man. I recalled when I first saw him that he looked like an insurance salesman. Balding head, featureless face except for the thick black glasses, average height and build. He wore a frumpish sable-colored suit with an equally lifeless tie. "This is Lord Edmund, Viscount of Mace Realm, Phantom Plane." *Phantom Plane?* I'd fought a number of liches from the Phantom Plane but had no idea that anything remotely "human" in appearance did, or even *could*, live there.

I bowed before him. He gave me a wink in return. Gotta admit, kinda creepy.

"And this," the Chancellor said, "is Lord Victrol, member of Harmony House of Nebulous City, Zephyr Plane." *Interesting … Member, not champion nor king nor viscount?* The lord looked like a character out of *Chitty Chitty Bang Bang*, the evil candy man that captured children for the Queen. Black brittle hair poked downward from under a black top hat. Predominant cheekbones almost perforated his skin, and his curved beak nose made him look like a hawk. Black tails fell a bit short in the sleeves, in an failed attempt to make him look bigger. His small and diminutive stature just sold his not-to-be-trusted demeanor. I bowed humbly before him. He bowed with a grand flourish, tossing his tails behind him.

Jeeves had taught me that the Counsel Mages were the best of their times, undefeated for years, even decades. They are asked at that point to either retire with *clean rights*, meaning no house or realm could ever attack you, or to serve on the counsel. Other than judging the tournaments, I had no idea what any of these people did. Or if they were *people* at all.

"Before we begin our meal," the Chancellor, "we've gathered out here so you can to test whether the Citadel Plane is safe for this year's competition. We certainly don't want you, or any of the patrons to feel ill at ease."

Nathan bowed. "Thank you for the invitation. We only want to ensure its safety and security before the next tournament."

"We discovered," Lord Edmund said to me, "that there was a significant amount of damage done to the Great Tree. We've taken great care in mending it, and we believe that has solved the inconsistencies you and your party noticed last year."

"We're not convinced the tree is the problem—" I started, when Nathan took me by the arm, a gentle reminder of my place here.

"Oh?" Lord Edmund said, stepping into my personal space. I didn't retreat despite the great desire to do so. "And you thought what, exactly?" He gave me a condescending glare, which made my hackles bristle. Suddenly, this seemingly innocent and harmless man looked like my worst enemy.

I kept my tone even and cool. "We believe there was an injustice done. That a healer was executed for a crime he didn't commit."

"Really? An interesting, even fantastical explanation considering you very well may have been the person who damaged the tree. We've attended to it and healed it, and now the plane is stable. How do you explain that?"

Lord Edmund had stepped even closer, puffing his chest, and using all of his alpha-male body language to intimidate me. I kept my eyes on his and stood a little taller myself. I was never one to kowtow to intimidation. I said, "A band-aid on a gaping wound will slow the bleeding but won't fix the problem."

His mouth twisted a bit as his common brown eyes stared into mine. To the Chancellor he said, "Perhaps the demonstration is in order?"

"I don't really think *this* is necessary," said Lady Safina, with a nervous laugh and a gesture behind me.

Her lack of confidence spoke volumes. I followed her hand. I'd been so fixated on Lord Edmund I didn't see, I didn't hear … Jack and Nathan knelt on the ground, held down by half a dozen bone wraiths. Cloudy black bands from the creatures bound their arms to their sides. One nebulous arm wrapped around Nathan's mouth. His eyes remained calm and trusting. Jack avoided my eyes by hanging his head.

Heatedly, I turned back to the Mages, expecting to see Lady Jezebel smile in glee, like her daughter would. To my surprise, she wore a frown of dismay, her arms folded. So did Lord Victrol, his eyes narrow and angered. Based on appearances, if asked which of the Mages were friend or foe, I would have given completely different answers.

"What is the meaning of this?" I growled. I could feel uncontrollable heat in my stomach.

"A simple test," the Chancellor waved his arm. The bright orange sky over the Citadel suddenly darkened. Bone wraiths, sentries of the Citadel, emerged from out of nowhere. Hundreds, possibly thousands, of them, swarmed in the sky, like angry bees seeking a new hive, yet eerily silent. They headed for us.

Not only did my fears of my completely impractical dress haunt me, but I had no weapon. And none were in use nearby to summon, as far as I could tell.

But that's what they wanted me to do, wasn't it? Was it really a test or just an attempt to entertain themselves, possibly eliminate the few persons who could truly damage their reputations, damage the fundamental core of the power they wielded, damage the honor of the tournaments?

"Go on," Lord Edmund smiled. "Slow them down. Use your talent. See for yourself the plane is fine."

"She could do that without—" Lady Safina started, but stopped when Lord Edmund shot her a heated glance.

Angered, I let the sky darken. I folded my arms and watched

them. As blackness shrouded us, I kept my eyes on Lord Edmund's. "No," I said softly.

"No?" he smirked. "Are you sure? They will die."

I took a cocksure step towards him letting my shoes touch his, ensuring he felt me in *his* personal space. "Let me tell you what's going to happen next. You and the Chancellor are going to call off the guard and we're all going to smile, shake hands, and call this a misunderstanding. Then we're all going to go inside and have the nice meal we were invited to."

"Look, *little girl*," he threatened, "you have no authority here to tell anyone what to do."

"No?" I smiled sweetly, "Perhaps you'd rather my party and I return home and contact all the other white houses with our story of how we were lured to the Citadel Plane months before the tournament only to be ambushed by the Council and their guards?" He looked like stone. "Or did you intend to kill us all? Thinking the Gateway Manor's presence in this year's tournament would not be missed?"

"Did we agree to so many?" Lord Victrol mused out loud as he looked upward to the darkened sky.

"You've lost, Edmund," Lady Jezebel piped with a broad smile on her face. "Free them, and call off the wraiths."

"You wanted the demonstration," Lord Edmund said to her.

"No. *You* wanted the demonstration. *I* already know what's wrong here."

"I thought just a dozen or so," Lord Victrol said to no one in particular.

Lady Jezebel turned to the Chancellor. "Chauncey," she seethed. "Stop this now before—"

One swooped down towards Jack. Out of the corner of my eye I saw him drop his shoulder, preparing for the attack while I kept my intense vision on Lord Edmund's eyes. I held up my hand, thinking

No! The wraith stopped mid-flight, hovering in place, it's bony razor sharp fingers just inches from Jack's throat.

Lord Edmund's eyes widened and he stepped back, craning his head toward the sky. The entire sky had frozen; the hundreds of bone wraith perfectly still, their smoky bodies hardened in foggy shapes, some bony protrusions visible beneath the billows of mist. I hid my own awe. I had no such strength. I stopped Mother Witherspoon in the crypt which I passed off since we were in a closed space. But … this? I stopped them. *All of them.* I had no such power. Whatever they'd done to "fix" the plane was drastically over done.

"Perhaps," the Chancellor said in tremolo as he limped his way to join me, "you are right, good Champion. This was just a misunderstanding. Our apologies."

Lord Edmund shoved his hands in his pant's pockets as he spun on his heels and blustered towards the Citadel, gruffly demanding the doors to be opened so he could storm inside without breaking stride.

With a wave of the Chancellor's hand the binding wraiths released Jack and Nathan. They didn't move. Nothing did.

I grabbed the one nearest Jack and pulled it away from my healer. That act popped it back into time. Without so much as a whisper it fled upwards, dodging its frozen kindred, and disappeared. I did the same for the creatures that held Nathan.

The two men lumbered back onto their feet. Nathan brushed off the dirt from his knees. "Well, now," he said in his annoying voice, "isn't that a fine turn of events? We come all this way and get treated like—"

I stopped him. "It's been covered." I leaned close to him and thought, "Let's just go inside and have a nice, long meal, like we planned."

He chewed his lip and gave a reluctant nod.

"Jack," I turned to him, "you okay?"

"I'm fine. Thank you for asking, ma'am."

"Lead on," I said to the Chancellor.

"Um, would you mind?" He gestured to the still frozen guards looming in the sky.

"No. I rather like them that way." Fact was, unless I touched them, I had no idea how to unfreeze them. Eventually, it would just wear off.

Ladies Safina and Jezebel exchanged coy glances with smiles as we all walked inside through the massive doors.

The nearly black interior was illuminated only by torch sconces that dotted along the stone walls. The Chancellor led us through the maze of hallways until we reached the grand dining hall. No one said much. Only the echoes of our footfalls reached our ears. After minutes we arrived.

When I last attended a meal here, the room was full of tables, one for each competing house. Now just one lonely and lost table sat in the expanse of the room, smack in the center of the five sided cavern.

I froze when I saw the large picture that hung on the wall. Every year it predominately showed last year grand winner. Malador's portrait. The smirk across his lips beckoned for a swift kick. Of course, that could have been just my bias.

"I hadn't realized," I said to Nathan quietly. "I never even asked."

"Who won the tournament last year? No, you didn't ask. And I never volunteered."

Little silver name plates directed who should sit where. My tag read, "Champion, Gateway Manor." The labels on either side of me read "Guest." We three were on one side of the long table and the two ladies sat across with Lord Victrol in between them. The Chancellor and Lord Edmund sat at the heads.

As we all settled, a mix of goblin and human waiters entered with toasty bread baskets and soup.

While the mages had been introduced to us—well, me—the Chancellor hadn't finished his introductions. "My apologies, mages. Not only are you in the presence of Winki Witherspoon, but this is her brother-in-law, Nathan Marble."

"Brother-in-law?" Lady Safina's eyebrows shot up. "As in Will's brother, Edward Witherspoon?"

How did the Chancellor know?

"Long story, that," Nathan smiled and cleared his throat. "Technically, no. Not only is my name changed but my talents as well. The White Lords cleansed me, creating a new man entirely."

"They *regifted* your energy," Lady Jezebel said. "How fascinating!" Sounded like she meant it, too. Something in her gaze at him made me think they'd known each other before. "You don't look like Edward. Well," she tilted her head, "maybe a little around the eyes. Yes, I think I see it now."

"I had some work done. I needed to hide myself. For Will's sake."

"And," the Chancellor broke in, "this other fellow is Mrs. Witherspoon's healer."

To that eyes raised all around. "You have your own healer?" Lord Victrol mused. "How very intriguing. Did you catch him?" He rubbed his hands over one another—yeah, I thought that was stereotypically creepy. "I've always wanted my own healer."

"No. He came to me, asking for protection."

"A healer? Came to you?" Lady Safina nearly drooled. "That's unheard of. They strive for anonymity."

I looked at Jack, but he didn't want to talk. "I'm afraid I foiled that for him. I recognized him at tournament last year. In his frustration, he decided that if *I* did, others might as well. So he asked to be in my employ. And protection." True, that was a very loose interpretation of the history, but good enough for dinner chat.

After the soup came salad, and after salad came appetizers, and after appetizers came the main course; a large meat pie. I didn't ask what kind, and they didn't volunteer. Maybe best, that.

Throughout dinner, topics remained uncontroversial, and conversation remained friendly. I tried to suss out the mages. By appearance, Lady Safina looked to be "good" (perky, happy, and fair of face), but after I saw her undress poor Jack with her eyes a number of times, I changed my opinion to "evil." Lady Jezebel, who I deemed as "evil," spoke about justice and happiness, with such conviction that I started to doubt my classification. She admitted to being Esmeralda's mother, so surely she, like her daughter, was dark and wicked. As far as I was concerned, Esmeralda was the poster child for wicked.

Meanwhile, it was clear that boring Lord Edmund had a deep, dark, and nefarious streak to him, while Lord Victrol, the sunken-eyed, beaked-nosed, straw-haired, black-tailed devil of a man seemed, well, mannerly. *Can't judge these books by their covers.*

I decided it was time to kick the beehive. The topic of the healer was why we were here. If I could shine light now on the poor man's unjust end right now, there'd be no need to proceed with "plan B," even though it was in full swing as we spoke.

I brought up the request to have Will's healer, the one who was mercilessly executed for a crime he didn't commit, vindicated. Lord Edmund emphatically disagreed.

"What is really the harm?" I asked. "Consider, for a moment, the consequences. If you are right, and it was the damage to the cherry tree that caused the plane's inconsistencies, then you've already fixed the issue, and no one's the wiser. But if I'm right, and you choose to ignore that possibility, then the plane itself could crumble. In just a matter of years, as I understand it, destroying centuries of peaceful bouts between the dark and light sides. While you may think that's improbable, even a remote possibility is worth some investigation, isn't it?"

"You're missing the point," Lord Edmund said as he noisily took a deep drink of wine. "Even if the healer was innocent, his death doesn't matter. That's not enough to destroy everything you see around you. Healers are nothing to the fabric of the plane. They are insignificant."

I sat upright. "And yet Lady Safina and Lord Victrol would love one of their own." I looked at each with a smile. "How can you say such a thing? They are *the healers*. Without them, there is no tournament." I looked for some kind of support from the other mages. "You honestly believe the tournaments would be better off without them?"

"Of course not, child," Lady Safina sung. "His point is that innocent or guilty, the death is without consequence. It is little more than killing a fly."

A fly? I glanced quickly at Jack, who did a damn fine job of tuning out the conversation around him. He ate methodically, stacking pieces of cut asparagus on his fork to make a perfect bite.

Nathan sat unusually quiet, letting me do all the talking. He gave a tiny shrug when I looked at him. I took that to mean I should run with my idea.

"While here, that man, whoever he was, was a healer. But he was a man the rest of the year. He had a life, a job, a family. That alone should matter." Nothing. No reaction. "I know I'm new here, but it seems to me, while healers may be lesser beings in the eyes of the talented community, they play a key role in the success of the tournament. Ensuring fairness to them seems obvious, if not critical, to me."

I sipped my own wine, watching the others.

Lord Edmund dropped his fork onto his plate with a clatter, wiping his hands. "If you feel that strongly about it, perhaps you'd like to make a wager?" The words hung in the air. Both Jack and Nathan froze, eyes on me and Edmund.

"A wager?"

"Yes. Put your conviction on the line."

"I'm listening." I put my fork down, certain that, in a moment, I would want to retch what I'd already eaten.

"Let's wager on this year's tournament. You win, and win cleanly, without the antics of last year, and I, *personally*, will look into the death of the healer."

Okay, there's the carrot. Now for the stick. "And if I don't win the tournament?"

"You give me an object of my choosing. A possession of yours. Something you care deeply about."

Nope. Didn't like that. "You'll have to be much more specific, dear Lord."

He nodded and casually said, "Very well. Your *healer*."

To that Jack lowered his hands. His eyes dropped toward his lap.

I laughed out loud, as if he'd told a joke. I knew he hadn't. I just wanted to call out his ludicrous idea. "Let me see if I understand you. You believe healers are about a valuable as flies, but you want me to give you mine?"

"No, I want you to wager yours. I think he's nothing, nor more valuable than a trinket, but clearly you think he's of some great value. I know that because you've hesitated. He means something to you."

"He is a person. I'd no more wager his life than that of my brother-in-law," I thumbed Nathan, "or my staff, or my friends. No. No deal. I don't believe people are bartering objects. Or objects at all."

"Says the woman who owns a man," he smirked.

I shook my head. "I don't—"

"Very well," he let out a dramatic sigh, then took a deep drink of wine. "What does that say about a champion, unwilling to put their beliefs on the line?"

"What does that say about the great mages, that they are willing to put the safety of the Citadel beneath their own glory?"

Lord Victrol cleared his throat. "Perhaps not all of us agree on that point, good lady," he croaked. "Just give us some proof, anything pointing to that poor man's innocence, and *I* will give you the healer's name."

"You have no authority," the Chancellor boomed.

"I do. I am a Council Mage, which entitles me access to all your documents, including that ledger of yours, dear Chancellor. I won't be stepping on toes if she can produce proof."

The only thing I had was Will's claim. Not exactly "proof."

"Take the deal." All of us turned to look at Jack.

"What?" I said, completely dumbfounded. "No way—"

"Take the deal. A healer for a healer. Unorthodox but fair to me."

The smile on Lord Edmund's face frightened me.

"Jack," I stammered, "we'll find another way—"

"Please," he stopped me. "Take the deal, ma'am."

"Jack," Nathan finally weighed in, "you want to trade a living, breathing being, *yourself*, for chrissake, for what … some *information*? That's crazy. There's no guarantee he'll hold up his end when he loses, but there's every reason to think he'll take his reward. Besides, as soon as we leave here, they'll arrange the games in such a way as to exploit Winki's weaknesses. You know the tournaments change every year. This will only give them a reason to take advantage of her."

The words quieted the table. I had to agree: Making the games exceptionally difficult for me to win seemed more than plausible. I'd say it was a certainty.

Lady Jezebel broke the silence. "We could tell you now what we have planned for the participants." She looked around at the other mages. "We agreed on it just today, did we not?"

The Chancellor shifted uneasily. Lord Edmund scowled but nodded.

She continued. "We wanted something unusual this year, something that the competitors would find challenging but have control over."

"The second phase," Lord Victrol said, "would be similar to last year. We'd hand out your fighting rosters that have your bouts assigned. But then …," he smiled and clapped his hands in glee. "My, I can't even wait!"

Lady Safina took over. "But in the third phase, challengers will get to pick their battles. Each competitor will get three choices. If selected, you must fight."

"So some competitors," Lord Victrol said, with a little too much glee, I might add, "will only fight three battles of their choosing while others may get selected a great deal."

"Like me," I whispered.

"Perhaps," Lord Edmund said. "Also, in order to eliminate the shenanigans of last year, no one can forfeit any fight. Whether selected by us or themselves, they must fight."

Last year, I threw a couple of fights to lower my rating so that when I battled Esmeralda and beat her—surprisingly satisfying—she lost greatly in her ratings. But once that was understood, my fellow fighters threw some of my battles, allowing me to regain lost ground. Touching, really.

Nathan shook his head. "As your lawyer," he said to me, "I'm telling you, no deal. We're talking Jack's life here."

Jack sat tall. "Look at the picture on the wall." Nathan and I turned to gaze at the great and mighty Malador. Last year's winner. I'd already beaten him when he attacked my house last year. I even beat him at the Jolly residence. But he bested me outside the Citadel when both our talents were weakened. I didn't see an obvious win, simple or easy. "Ma'am, please. Take. The. Deal."

I looked at Nathan, who looked at Lord Edmund. "I want it in writing, everything. Including the structure of the games this year," he said.

I watched the other mages, whose eyes were on Jack for some reason. Lord Edmund held his hand in the air and flicked his wrist. With a flash of light a piece of paper appeared in his fingers. *Ah, a conjurer.* He handed it across the table to Nathan and said, "I've added a gag order on the games description. You're not to share that with anyone."

With a gulp, Nathan pulled out his glasses and started to read. I took this time to implore Jack. "Listen to me, we can explore other ways to get this man's name."

"Ma'am," he nodded to the painting, "it's Malador."

"I know who it is. That's not the point. This is ... off. He's up to something."

"I agree."

I glanced at the smug mage. "Jack, this just isn't worth your life. We have *other ways.*" Hopefully, we were undergoing one at this moment, I tried to remind him. "Besides, this guy's from the Phantom Plane. What kind of existence could you possible have there? The air is toxic. You will be locked away in a box, a *real* cage."

"Then you'll have to prevent that from happening, won't you?"

"Nice touch," Nathan sneered to the Lord. He handed me the parchment. "It's straightforward. If you win, he pledges to name Will's healer, and will do so before the tournament next year. If you lose, he gets the body and soul of Jack Frost." He looked pensive. "Don't ask me how he knew Jack's name."

"He doesn't get to sit on the information for a whole year. No deal. You want Jack? I want the name before I leave these hallowed halls."

Lord Edmund and the Chancellor looked at each other. The Chancellor nodded. "Done," Lord Edmund said.

Using his own pen Nathan modified the agreement. He handed me the document. "If you agree, you must sign it ..." he hesitated.

"You must sign it in blood. *Jack's* blood. As your lawyer, I *strongly* discourage you from doing this."

Jack took a steak knife and sliced his palm. He cupped his hand, letting the blood pool. He moved his palm toward me. "I'm happy to be a catalyst for justice."

With another flick of the wrist Lord Edmund produced a plumed quill and handed it to me.

I looked up at the picture again. Such a pompous potato-head. I wanted to trust I could win the tournament. Yes, my talent was strong, and no one yet knows of my conjuring abilities, including the two men that flanked me. And Jack believed I could win. Confidently believed. I looked in his eyes, searching for any hesitation. I saw none.

I dipped the quill into Jack's blood and signed my name.

Winki Witherspoon.

Chapter Fifteen

WITHOUT JEEVES, ONE of the mages had to open a portal for us to return home. Standing outside the Citadel after such a cold dinner, needless to say, goodbyes were curt and brief. The Chancellor waved his arm in a broad sweep, constructing the bubble. We three stepped in and returned home.

The dark house surprised us all. Time in the Citadel Plane runs faster than here, so despite the hours we spent away, we should have only been gone five, maybe ten minutes tops. We all looked at the grandfather clock and the tale it told. It read four fifteen in the morning.

"How is that possible?" Jack asked as he daintily rapped on the clock's glass with his index finger.

"I'm not sure. Something's off. Is everyone okay?" he asked us.

I shrugged. I felt fine. "Why?"

The lights flicked on. "What the hell?"

The three of us jumped, startled by the voice of Saffron Jolly. She held a rolling pin threateningly in her hand, lowering it once she saw us. "Oh my god. It's you!"

My mouth gaped when I saw her. Her hair, which had bobbed about her face earlier today, hung just at her shoulders. Before I could express my shock, Jack beat me to it. "Have you changed your hair?"

Footsteps running down the stairs interrupted any answer. The rest of the staff, Jeeves, Mrs. Black, Smith and Wesson, all donned in robes or pajamas, came trundling down like a herd of irate buffalo. Mrs. Black ahead of the others, threw her arms around me as if I'd returned from the dead. "Oh, my dearie! I missed you!"

I held her back, "Oh … kay. Good to see you, too!"

Mr. Smith was handing Mr. Wesson some money. "Off by a day," he muttered. The comment perplexed me but I didn't get a chance to ask.

"Jack, Nathan," Jeeves exhaled. "We were so worried!"

"Why?" Nathan asked, eyes narrowed. "What's going on? Why is it so late? We were there for just a few hours."

Jeeves stood before Jack, putting his hands on his son's shoulders. "I'm so glad you're all right, my boy. It is wonderful to see you."

Embarrassed, Jack cleared his throat. "Father, what is going on?"

"You don't know?" Jeeves said.

"That's plenty clear," Saffron said.

Nathan thumbed the clock. "Is that the right time? Is it really past four in the morning?"

The robe-clad group exchanged glances, each searching the other for something to say. Mr. Smith stepped forward. "The clock is right."

"That's impossible," Nathan scoffed.

"That's not the impossible part," Mr. Smith said. "You've been gone for over four months."

Nathan, Jack, and I took stunned steps backwards.

"What?" Nathan gasped.

"In fact," Mr. Smith said, gesturing into the room, "we leave for tournament tomorrow! At this point we just assumed we'd meet you there."

We three turned, following his wave, to see the stack of items collected in the center of the room. Due to the darkness, we hadn't noticed it before. Assorted sleeping bags, tents, cookware, and boxes formed a heap. I remembered that from last year – we spent the last couple of weeks prior to departure preparing for the journey.

"We *hoped* we'd meet you there," Mrs. Black corrected. "Since no one contacted us on your whereabouts, we only assumed you were fine. But," she stammered, "we did fear the worst."

I spun to Nathan. "Did they do this on purpose?" I yelled. "Was this a sure way to win the wager?" My eyes briefly darted to Jack. "To screw me out of four months of training?"

"You mean you guys really didn't know?" Mr. Smith said. "Even the spiders had an inkling."

"No! Of course not!" I hollered back, not really angry with him, just angry with the deceit of the mages. I took a break, recovering. "I'm sorry, Mr. Smith. We were only there for dinner, nothing more."

Mr. Wesson scribbled on his pad with Mr. Smith watching over his shoulder. As he worked, Nathan answered my initial question. "I don't know how they could do this on purpose. A portal's a portal. Just a door. I don't know of anyone who has the power to point the door into a different time. A different place, a different plane, yes. But a different time? That's a new one on me."

"You'd have to admit," Jack said, "this works well for Lord Edmund. The timing couldn't have been more perfect."

"He could have made us miss the tournament altogether," I grumbled.

"We think there's something going on at the Citadel," Mr. Smith broke in. "Something wrong." He pointed to Mr. Wesson's data. "Like a chronometric fluctuation on their side." He turned to me, knowing I would need the explanation. "The Citadel Plane itself sits in its own plane, one that runs on its own time. Much faster than ours, of course, which is why the two-week-long tournament only takes four of our days. But if they've changed the fabric of the plane, that could cause time to run slower, thus causing the time shift."

"A perfectly-timed time shift," Jack scoffed.

"Yes," I said to Mr. Smith. "There is definitely something wrong with the Citadel Plane." I turned to Nathan. "I assure you, they're mucking with it."

"How do you know?" he said, undoing his bow tie.

"Firstly, you could hear me even when you wore your gonzo. Secondly, The *demonstration*, Nathan."

"You stopped the wraiths from attacking us."

"I froze them. *All* of them. I don't freeze things. I slow things down, and if I'm very put out I can slow down twenty, maybe thirty objects. But tonight? *I froze them all.* Hundreds. I don't have that kind of …" I cast a glance to Saffron, "strength."

Jack cocked his head to the side. "I fail to see your point, ma'am."

Nathan smiled, joining my train of thought. "Whatever they did is affecting our talents, boosting them. And, it's affecting the Citadel's time, too."

"And it wasn't just 'fix the tree.' They had to have worked some mojo to heighten the plane's energy *whatever*," waving my hand at Smith and Wesson, "which not only resulted in my talent being twisted, it screwed up the chrono …thingy."

"Chronometric fluctuations," Mr. Smith corrected.

"Yeah. That. The mages know something's wrong with the plane and used some magic patch to fix it."

"You mean," Jack said, "the demonstration wasn't really for our sake, but for theirs. So they could tweak the plane before the tournament."

"Good thing, too," Nathan shook his head. "Otherwise everyone who showed up for tournament would have returned home having ten years pass them by."

"So as it stands," I added, "*if* they fix it to run correctly and get it right, only we will know there's anything wrong. They still have plausible deniability." I shook my head. "I just don't get it. If simply acknowledging an unjust death fixes the plane, why not do it?"

Nathan explained. "I don't know much about the politics of the mages, but it would be my guess that some of them would want to do just that. But others ...," he gave Jack an apologetic look, "others would find that appalling, since it was a healer. Maybe all five have to agree on such things, and they don't. So, here we are."

Dissatisfied, my eyes roamed. They stopped on Saffron, who had her arms folded and wore a scowl on her face. "Saffron, I'm so sorry we were gone so long. I'm amazed you stayed ...How are you?"

She shot Jeeves a heated look. Jeeves cleared his throat. "Mrs. Jolly remained here ...with *prejudice*, I'm afraid."

"With ... prejudice?"

"I can't leave," she exploded. "This stupid house won't let me."

"I ... don't ... what?" I stammered.

"It is true, madam. Every time Mrs. Jolly tried to use a door—"

"Or window," Saffron interjected.

"Or a window," Jeeves acknowledged, "the manor would shut the opening, locking it. Anyone else could unlock it and move outside, but Mrs. Jolly was prevented."

"We kinda had to tell her ...um, everything," Mr. Smith said.

"Everything?" Nathan's eyebrows shot up.

"Hell," Mr. Smith laughed, "she figured out something was up when the doors shut on their own."

"Yeah," Saffron growled. "Watch this." She walked to the front door and as she approached we clearly heard a soft but audible click. Saffron grabbed the doorknob and pulled, pulled with all her might, her body leaning back for leverage and her bare feet firmly planted on the ground. She even put a foot on the door jamb.

The quiet Mr. Wesson trotted over to the door. Saffron stepped away, and the little man in bunny slippers grabbed the knob, and opened the door just as easy as pie. He seemed so proud of himself.

Door wide, he stepped away and gestured to Saffron to walk on through. Saffron took one step and *—wham!* The door shut emphatically on its own. They both raised their arms in a "Ta Da!" manner.

Nathan, Jack, and I all gulped at the little show. "So, uh," Nathan stammered, "when you say you had to tell her everything—"

"The poor woman was stuck here for four months," Mrs. Black defended. "Of course she was upset. So we did the best we could to make her feel at home. That included answering all of her questions. About the manor, about Will, about us, about the tournament, about Hercule, about you," she pointed to me.

"I dare say," Jeeves stopped him, "Mrs. Jolly knows more about us than you do, Mrs. Witherspoon. She is an astute student."

Great. Just when I felt like I wasn't the newbie anymore. "What about the spiders? Did they come back?" I asked.

While Nathan, Jack, and I had dinner with the mages, Hercule and a few spiders checked out the Chancellor's office, looking for possible locations for the healers' ledger. That's why we stayed as long as we did; we needed to give them time to get in, look around, and get out, while we had all the mages distracted. Otherwise, after the wraith "demonstration," I'd have punched Lord Edmund in the snoot and demanded to leave.

"They returned last month," Mrs. Black nodded. "Unharmed," she added.

"That's when we started theorizing about the Citadel Plane," Mr. Smith added. "We've been working on this for weeks, now."

Mrs. Black continued. "They found a number of—"

"What is everyone doing up at this ridiculous hour—oh. You're back," Hercule yawned as he crawled up the wall. "Is it not possible for you monkeys to keep it down? Some of us are trying to sleep."

I ignored the grumpy *cafard*. "You were saying, Mrs. Black?"

"They found a number of—"

"No, no," Hercule interrupted. "I will tell the story, since you already have me awake. We found three—not one, not two, but *three* —different safes in that room. *Absurde!* What does one person need with three different safes?"

"Well," Mr. Smith mused and counted on his fingers. "One for valuables, one for weapons, and one for documents."

"That was a question *rhetorical, monsieur!*" Hercule snapped. "I did not want an answer."

Smith and Wesson both gave me a shrug. The bug could be so contrary sometimes.

My head of security, the spider Annabelle, joined him, drifting into view from a gossamer strand. "We returned with some numbers that helped Mr. Smith and Mr. Wesson identify the safes. They are very old. They should be easy to get into, we think."

"Thank you," Nathan said. "But now we have no time to figure out how to break into them."

"Again, the timing seems particularly advantageous to the mages," Jack sighed.

As I took off my shoes, Mr. Smith said, "We're on it. We have a couple of ideas already packed and—"

That's the last thing I heard. As soon as my bare foot touched the floor every cell in my body exploded in energy. I felt myself falling, swimming, pushing through wave after wave of sights, sounds, and smells. I saw Detective Duplantier talking to Saffron, delivering the news that her brother Simon was nowhere to be found. I saw Smith and Wesson in their lab with a new amulet for Nathan, and it sat untouched, collecting dust for weeks. I saw Mrs. Black weeping, night after night, worried by our absence. I saw Jeeves walk by his son's bedroom door and place a caring hand upon it. I watched, after hundreds of attempts through doors and windows, Saffron slowly joined the household, becoming comfortable with a cockroach that argued in the kitchen. Every movement, every moment, every conversation, every coming and going, everything that passed during the last four months all slammed into my brain within seconds.

Clearly, the house had much to tell me.

But I couldn't handle it, the sheer volume of it all within the moments it took. Humans aren't supposed to be present, in all moments, throughout the many and varied rooms of the entire mansion.

I cried out as my brain's synapses struggled to keep up, to comprehend the enormity of the information. I was drowning. I was dying.

Mercifully, I passed out.

~ ~ * ~ ~

"Winki? Can you hear me?"

My eyes didn't want to open. I felt warm where I was. It felt cold where I was going.

"Ma'am? Take your time. There's no hurry."

Warm hands with long, thin fingers cupped my face. Jack. Someone moaned. That might have been me. I keenly felt each beat of my heart, aware that it shoved blood through the tiny vessels in my swollen brain, each pulse a miserable throb. My mind, meanwhile, sorted all of the new data, compartmentalizing what had been "downloaded" into it. One memory flashed across my field of vision, something different and out of place. I think it was Will, but I couldn't be sure. Ladened by effort, I let it get filed with the rest of it. As moments ticked by, as my heart beat slowed and steadied, the pain subsided, and ultimately vanished.

I opened my eyes just as Jack removed his hands from my cheeks. "What happened?" I mumbled.

"We don't know, ma'am. You passed out."

I sat up. I still wore my gown, one shoe adorned a foot. I nodded, recalling the memory. I winced. "The house got … gabby." I blinked a few times, letting my eyes truly focus back on the here and now. No matter where I turned my gaze, another concerned face met me. I held out my arms. "Help a girl up?"

Nathan and Jeeves obliged, each by an elbow. I stumbled, lacking grace wearing only one shoe.

"Are you okay?" Nathan asked.

I didn't know how to answer him. On the one hand I felt better now that the pain had gone away. It was a curious sensation to reflect on the months that passed with such clarity and such completeness. Kinda nifty, really. On the other hand, why? Nothing truly outstanding had happened. Usually, when my house shows me a memory or event, it's meaningful to the house, or the house believed it would be meaningful to me. The only thing of import I remembered involved an argument between the goblin, Theodore, and Jeeves. As I stood there, my one foot on the warm wooden floor, I received another wave, visions of people across several eras embracing, crying, and apologizing. The house's way of showing me its worry, its fear, and its apology.

"The house missed me," I answered. "I'm fine." I turned to Jeeves. "Theodore was here?"

He stiffened, casting a scolding glance to the house. "Yes, madam. He claims to have *intel*—his word, not mine—about Malador, but refused to share it with me."

I nodded, looking at the stacks of gear packed to go. Four months! That meant tomorrow was the first day of Summer. *Four frickin' months!* I could have used the time to go after Esmeralda, confront Malador about Simon Jolly, negotiate with the Asclepium Order, find Will's DVD, or just *train*, for mercy's sake. Now I would be going in completely cold. And a human being's freedom dangled in the balance. "I can't believe I missed Mardi Gras this year," I grumbled. "I feel snookered."

"And Jazz Fest," Mr. Smith added. "It was awesome."

Mr. Smith lacked the finer points of making someone feel better.

Well, not completely cold. No one knew, yet, no one other than Smith and Wesson. I had a new, strong talent. It would get me far. It might be enough.

"What happened, if we may ask, at your dinner?" Jeeves politely asked.

Nathan, Jack, and I exchanged glances. Nathan filled everyone in by recalling the night. As he spoke, we all drifted to the dining room and took seats. The retelling became heated once he got to the part about the wager.

Jeeves protested. "Nathan!" he yelled, "he's my son!"

"I know, I know! Jeeves, look——"

"How could you let that … *monster* disguised as a man make a contract for his life?"

What an intriguing description of Lord Edmund.

When the arguing reached a certain volume, I called from my seat, "Enough." No one heard me over their roars. "Hey! I said enough!" They heard me that time. A quiet settled in the room filled only by the dulcet ticking of the grandfather clock. "While I know all of you are upset and excited about the wager, believe me," I moved my gaze to each of them, "I will move soil and sea before anyone takes Jack from this house."

"But you'll have to win the tournament, madam," Jeeves pointed out.

"And we know," Mr. Smith said, "Lord Edmund isn't an honest man."

"And on top of all that," Nathan added, "the Citadel Plane's not stable. You can't count on anything being what it seems to be."

All eyes were on me. I looked at the man in the portrait. The subtle smile. The confident eyes.

Wait … the house showed me Will, I'm certain. I closed my eyes for a moment, recalling the memory. Will and Nathan, just a few years ago, and a discussion, no, an argument about ... of course! *I get to pick my competitors.*

"Winki?"

No. No, I *didn't* have to win the tournament. I just had to ...

"Exactly," I whispered.

"What to you mean, *exactly*?" Nathan asked.

"Mrs. Jolly? Would you please make a fresh pot of strong coffee? We have a long night ahead of us." I looked around the table at my staff, my friends, and my family. "None of you are going to believe this," I thought out loud, "but I have a *cunning* plan."

Chapter Sixteen

"WE STAND STRONG!"

The words echoed in my head as we made our way down the black, rocky, switch-back trail that wound off the hill, heading toward the grand edifice called the Citadel. Hard to get excited about it this time, I was just here yesterday.

Moments ago Nathan had given a rousing speech in the manor, meant to motivate and encourage, something he does well. After, my entourage and I stepped through the portal, leaving Mrs. Black and the spiders to defend the homestead.

Saffron Jolly, too, joined us. There was much debate on the topic. Frankly, the safest place for her to be was within the mansion's walls. But she had made an impassioned plea to, and I quote, "Get the hell out of this house." Moreover, given the Citadel's instability, we might not be back for years! And so she walked beside me.

Nathan, Jeeves, and I, wore enormous red crushed velvet robes, with ample sleeves and overly large cowl necklines pulled up over our heads as hoods; my familiar perched on my shoulder. My scientists wore their usual lab coats. Jack wore the customary brown cloak that identified him as a healer, despite an argument that I wanted him to wear red—apparently that would insult the other healers. Whatever. Saffron was the only one dressed normally. Since Saffron traveled as our cook, she could wear a robe too, but found garb way too cultish.

I had to agree.

Of the three in red robes, Nathan's stood out. A heavy and bulbous piece of jewelry adorned his attire, a gold necklace bedazzled with fleur-de-lis ornaments. It clear to all he was my orator; if you wanted an audience with me, you had to clear it with him.

"Where the hell are we?" Saffron nervously asked. The Citadel Plane has that effect. The sky was a bright and solid orange, in every direction, the source of light eerily unknown. It contrasted with the ground, stretching black in every direction. Only a few large, dead trees, whose gnarled and twisted branches reached out into the orange atmosphere varied the rocky landscape. The air around us shimmered as if the day was hot, but the temperature felt pleasant enough. Saffron reached out a hand, testing if heat caused the illusion. "Are we on another planet?" she finally asked.

"No. Another plane. I thought you were told all this." I then muttered, "Some best student."

"I guess I just didn't understand what 'another plane' meant. I half-thought we were going to Nebraska or something. They have plains, right?"

"Lady," Mr. Smith laughed. "We are *so* not in Nebraska."

"Looks like a hellscape to me." I had that reaction the first time I saw it, too.

As far as my eye could see, portals popped into view disgorging red-clad individuals starting their journey to the looming Citadel. Gathering at the entrance, the jumble somehow became five rows. We joined one.

Saffron scanned the black castle, shaking her head. "How does it stay standing?" It was a fair question. Many of the towers that poked out of the asymmetrical structure did so at odd and illogical angles, almost as if they defied gravity.

"Magic," Mr. Smith eagerly nodded, watching for Saffron's

reaction.

"Knock it off," I poked him. "What happened to the logic guys? You were on my case constantly about using the term *talent* and saying, 'it's just science.'" I tried to mock Mr. Smith's voice.

"Aw, we were just joking." he said. Mr. Wesson nodded heartily.

We slowly shuffled forward, as group after group got checked-in and entered the Citadel. It felt slower this year, more disorganized. I even overheard another party whispering something similar.

At the entry, a bone wraith, with shining purple eyes and the wispy black-smoke body, waved a desiccated hand over its little crystal ball. Saffron's own eyes nearly popped out of her head.

I took her arm encouragingly. "On my first trip here," I leaned to her, "Jeeves told me to convince myself it was all CGI stuff and elaborate costumes. I suggest you do the same."

She fell in step behind me. Close behind me.

Nathan took the lead when we were next, gave a deep bow, and said, "Gateway Manor, New Orleans, Midland Plane."

The wraith waved his bone hand over the ball, and after several slow moments finally gave a small nod. In a gravel voice it rasped, "Welcome, House of Gateway. Proceed to the Obsidian Tower."

I rolled my eyes. *We weren't so welcomed last night.* I wondered if this very being was among those I froze.

"Sir," Jeeves said to Nathan, "That seemed to take an inordinate amount of time."

"I agree," Hercule said. "Something is wrong."

Once through, Nathan led us through the familiar maze of dimly lit hallways. It started to come back to me, the location of my home-away-from-home. "We are always in the same suite?" I asked Jeeves.

"Yes, madam."

"Seems bad. How do we know Malador didn't put any eavesdropping tech in our suite before we showed up?" I refrained from using the term "bugs" on purpose, so as not to offend the one on my shoulder.

"No one is allowed into the Citadel before the tournament," he puffed.

"*We* were. Just yesterday," I pointed out, but let it go. I'd have Smith and Wesson check it out later, now that I've discovered a new level of paranoia.

Overhearing us, Nathan added, "That's one of the jobs of our host. Ensuring privacy."

At last we reached our tower. Without pausing, Nathan thrust open the massive wooden doors that led into the cavernous common area. A man robed in emerald green velvet beamed when he saw us. "Nathan! Winki! Wonderful to see you both! Welcome back." His eyes positively twinkled, and his rosy cheeks puffed just over his white beard.

"Jeff," Nathan said, arm extended for a hand shake, "so good to see you again." The two greeted each other warmly.

"Wow," Saffron whispered, "Looks like Old Saint Nick."

"As far as I know, he is," I laughed. "Sweet, too."

Jeff gave me a welcoming hug. "Champion Winki! Ah," Jeff said, once we parted, "I see you have your own healer this year. Good for you. More trustworthy, I think."

My healer asked me before we left not to introduce him to anyone. He wanted to remain as anonymous as possible, hiding behind the large hood that covered his face. I did, however, introduce Saffron. "My new chef," I said, "This is Jeffery, Master of the Obsidian House". They shook hands, heartily.

"Anything you need, dear lady, anything at all, you just let me know. Well," he said as he rubbed his hands together, "you know where to find your suite. Everything is ready for you. Number seven, at the top of the stairs."

Everyone left immediately, but I took Nathan by the sleeve and turned to Jeff. "Is everything all right? Checking in seemed to take much longer at the front."

"Oh, yes," he said grandly, then waved his fingers to bring us closer to him. He whispered, "There is some disorganization this year. No one had details, but the mages are very behind. Keep it to yourselves, though."

We nodded, thanked him, and headed for the sixteen flights of stairs.

"All interesting," Nathan said while plodding away. "That supports Smith and Wesson's theory, that our coming home so late was because the plane's been tampered with. I suppose you should feel better that they didn't take away four months on purpose."

"Hm."

Reaching our door we entered our ample, two-storied suite. Downstairs included the kitchen and dining area—determined by the large, hefty picnic table with matching benches—and a small living area, now full of our packed belongings. It also included a small cot, which my healer took immediately. The rest of the bedrooms were upstairs by way of a staircase that looked more like a twisted tree.

We all began unpacking cookware, setting up our makeshift kitchen. We had packed several outdoor portable stoves, all gas, since the Citadel lacks electricity. "How did this stuff beat us here?" Saffron asked.

I just shrugged. Didn't really care, so long as I didn't have to carry it. "Once we set foot in the plane," Nathan answered, "retrievers are sent for it. They're responsible for making sure it's safe."

"So, these retrievers are the Citadel's equivalent of the TSA?" I snarked.

"Basically."

Mr. Wesson yawned as he pulled out his pad. The two scientists had worked through the night and the morning preparing for the added responsibility I'd foisted on them last minute. Given there was no power at the Citadel, they scoured the city looking for batteries and power packs for the computers and laptops they brought.

Normally, by this time, their work was complete. Their job was to prepare me for anything and everything the mages could throw at the champions. Once done, they come to observe the occasional bout and make a friendly wager or two. They'd do only the former this year, with laser focus. I wanted them watching, calculating, and theorizing about one particular competitor. Only *one*.

The first phase of the games always started with a great and glamorous dinner. This year only four of us were attending; Nathan, Jeeves, Saffron, and myself. As soon as things were unpacked, we dressed for the gala. The men wore tuxedos. We women dressed in gowns. Mr. Smith, Mr. Wesson, and my healer had already begun their research. So engrossed by the time we left, I don't think they noticed when we shut the door.

Was I confident? Not hardly. I couldn't worry about the days to come, not yet. First, I had to make it to the dining hall without breaking my neck tripping over the flouncy, silver gown with my sparkling, silver high heels. My feet still hurt a bit from last night's footwear.

I huffed after stumbling the third time. Mr. Marble offered me his arm, which I took. Why did Mrs. Black always dress me like a high-fashioned doll?

Chapter Seventeen

SINCE WE DIDN'T finish the tournament last year we were punished with a lower rating. As you win bouts, your rating increases; the highest, as far as I know, is level fifty, indicating you're undefeated. I had achieved a level thirty-two (at least, that's what the last score board read before we abandoned). But it wasn't official. This year, I would start at a rank of seventeen.

Mr. Nathan Marble once told me, "It's not how you're ranked going into the tournament, only how you rank when you leave." None of it matter, not to me anyway. My low rank meant my early bouts would start pretty easy. That is, if this year's tournament's anything like last year's. If this year's tournament goes *as promised*.

Last year we were the defending house so we entered the dining room last, with all other participants already seated. This year we entered closer to the middle of the ceremonies. By the time we made the walk to address the mages, the venue was half full.

Protocol dictated we enter when called, simply bow to the mages, then take our seats.

I've never been one for protocol.

The grand door before us opened, and a voice boomed, "May I present Mrs. Witherspoon, Champion of Gateway Manor, New Orleans, Midland Plane." I led my party straight toward the center table, now on a riser to stand above the rest. I gave a broad smile and said with a burst of enthusiasm and a voice everyone could hear clearly, "Did y'all get a good night's rest? We're plum tuckered, ourselves. We barely had enough time to get changed!"

I didn't have to look to see the confused glances the seated parties gave each other. I could hear the rustle of seat shifting and the murmur of whispers. My eyes stared only at the Chancellor in front of me, my grin wide.

He cleared his throat and gave an irascible look. Nope. Not gonna rattle his chain.

I made a quick curtsy, then followed the maitre d'—a tentacled octopus-type creature in a tux, which just couldn't have been comfortable for the guy—to our table.

"Well done," Nathan whispered as we sat ourselves. Hercule, who rode upon my shoulder, chuckled in approval.

I watched our guide slither away back to the head table to receive the next champion. I was mesmerized by his movement. So was Saffron.

"Wh-wh-what was that?" Saffron stuttered, clutching the table.

"Exactly," I answered.

Jeeves patted the back of her hand. "Please, dear lady, don't dwell on what you don't understand."

I added, "Just think of this as an example of Mother Nature's great and varied imagination."

Surprisingly, that worked. Saffron Jolly sat back and watched in awe as announcement after announcement, man, beast, troll, goblin, lich, wraith, elemental, and whatever else entered the room. Champions all.

"How does this work again?" she asked.

"The tournament is made of five stages," I explained in a hushed voice, so as not to interfere with the ongoing announcements. "This is the first stage, a grand dinner. From here on in it's all about kicking butt. The second stage battles determine our rank, effectively how strong we are. The third stage determines our standings with each other, like a final sorting. The fourth stage is the elimination round, kind of like the NBA's Sweet Sixteen. The fifth and final stage is the big battle between the best of the light and dark houses." Or so I'd been told. I had yet to see it.

I paid closer attention this year to the champion introductions. After Mrs. Black's and Jeeves's teachings I was more curious about the other houses in my own plane. Those from the Czech Republic, Brazil, Thailand, and Hawaii. I didn't know any of them, which was a shame, I thought. I should at least be acquainted with them. Come to think of it, after last year's tournament, I never spoke to Colonel Mustard or his anyone from Magnolia House, and they lived right in New Orleans. After this was over, I aimed to change that.

The second to last announcement introduced the creature I affectionately call Archy. "May I present the Arch Lich, Champion of Eidolon Castle, Cardamom Realm, Phantom Plane."

"I love cardamom," Saffron said.

"I know, sounds delightful, doesn't it?"

Nathan sighed while rolling his eyes. He leaned close to me. "Are you sure about this?"

By now we'd seen a number of liches take their tables. Lobster-like in appearance, these creatures seem more to scurry than walk on six legs. Most have a single large claw, a smaller hand-type appendage, stand roughly two feet taller than me, and are golden or brown in color.

But Archy was ... more. Black, three or more feet taller than the rest. Broader all the way around, too. He sported two giant, sharp claws. I swallowed when I saw them. They'd severed my head from my body in a bout last year. "Our plan sounded so good last night," I said to Nathan.

We all watched as Archy, amidst hisses and boos from the other patrons, shuffled his way to his table. He sat alone.

"Why are they booing?" Saffron asked.

I let Nathan explain, my throat oddly sore all of a sudden. "Every year, he shows up and completes all of the bouts asked. He beats everyone. Every year, rather than stay for the final battles, he ups and leaves. No explanation. Everyone hates that."

"Why? If he beat them, he'd be the winner, but since he's leaving, they get to win. Why dislike that?" Before Nathan could answer her eyes went wide. She looked at me. "Wait, *that's* the guy?"

I took a deep breath, forcing air past my aching neck. "That's the guy." Nathan gave my back a comforting and encouraging rub.

Presented last because he won last year's tournament, Malador was announced. As he marched his way to the mages, Saffron's eyes lit up. "I remember him. He was the one who came to my house." She turned to me. "He wanted me to go with him."

I didn't respond. Having her here was a risk, admittedly. If Malador still wanted Saffron that would add a layer of complexity, not to mention a burden of security, to protect her. On the plus side, within the walls of the Citadel, his talents, like mine and everyone else's here, were bounded. They were only at our disposal within the arenas. Lacking his incubus sway he remained should-be-illegal gorgeous.

"His portrait hangs on the wall," Jeeves pointed out to Mrs. Jolly. "Didn't you notice it, madam?"

"No," she looked at it now. "I was too busy looking at all the people and creature at the tables."

Malador bowed grandly to the mages, dramatically brushing back his black cape as he did so.

"Bring on the food," I said, barely hiding my disgust for the man.

The Chancellor addressed the room in a booming voice. "Greetings one and all to the opening ceremonies of this year's tournament. Before we begin I'd like you all to raise a glass and join me in a toast." The room rustled as all the attendees stood and raised glasses into the air. "To a fair and noble tournament. May fortune favor you all, and your houses prevail in peace."

"In peace," everyone echoed. We drank and the banquet began. The first wave of food came out, the droves of waiters carrying bell shaped, jewel encrusted, cloches over their heads, streaming to each of the tables. Our first course was a hearty barley soup. Next to us sat a table of goblins. Their first course—which I knew from experience was the same as every other course they would receive this evening was frogs. Just like last year, one of them slipped away, leaping for freedom toward our table.

"Ah," I said, as some clammy creature rummaged near my feet, "this is some kind of tactic."

Undaunted, Saffron picked up the little leaper and handed it to a green goblin, who profusely apologized for any inconvenience. I opened my mouth to warn her to look away, but it was too late. The goblin ate the amphibian in front of her.

"Oh!" she cried out, covering her face.

Jeeves shooed the goblin away. Disgruntled, he asked Nathan. "Must this happen every year, sir? Is there nothing we can do? Request a new location? File a complaint?"

Mr. Marble smirked. "Yeah, I'm sure Chauncey would make that a priority."

After the main course of steak and potatoes, which was what we had, everyone milled about and mingled. I asked Nathan to join me and excused us from the table. I left the bug chomping on a piece of bread.

As we walked around, he again offered his arm to improve my stability. I thanked him. "Any one in particular you want to visit?" he asked.

"Colonel Mustard," I said. "He came to our table last year. It occurred to me that I haven't seen him since the last tournament."

"We're the Gateway House," he said casually as we strolled.

"That makes us no one's ally."

"I don't understand."

He licked his lips. "As a rule, it's best to keep what you are and who you are to yourself. For example, I haven't told you what all my talents are. Nor has Jeeves, nor has Mrs. Black. In fact, I've prevented myself from using them, unless it's a critical situation, so you don't know."

That hurt my feelings a little. We sparred almost every night. Had I offended him somehow? I frowned. "Why?"

I could see it pained him to talk about it. "It's, well, a reflex of sorts. A safety mechanism. The more you know about a person the more likely you can use that to your advantage. Especially if you change sides."

"Wait," I stopped and looked him in the eye. "You're afraid I'll become evil?"

"I didn't say that. We just never know what the future holds." I opened my mouth to protest but he cut me off. "I've already been through this with Will. We grew up together. We knew everything about each other. If we had walked separate paths, we would have torn the house apart. That experience was enough, however, to know that keeping your cards close to your chest is in everyone's best interest." I dropped my head, hurt by his words. Nathan put his hands on my shoulders. "You asked why the Colonel never visits. That's why. Keeping his distance keeps him safe. Again," he lifted my head to look at him with a gentle touch beneath my chin, "I learned this from experience."

I searched his glassy eyes and recalled what little I knew of my late husband's past. "Will did something terrible to his family," I whispered.

Nathan let a few beats pass so my words could make their sharp and damaging point. He softly said, "All is forgiven between us. But it will never be forgotten."

I nodded, but no longer able to look him in the eye, my vision wandered about the room. They found Archy, alone at his table. Liches don't use chairs. With his giant claws he tore some meat off the bones of whatever he'd been served. Despite how awkward the claws looked, he moved with speed and grace.

"Having second thoughts?" Nathan asked, after he followed my gaze.

"Does he always come alone?"

"I don't ever remember him bringing an entourage."

"Mrs. Witherspoon, I greet you in peace."

I turned to face the deep, luxuriously southern voice. It belonged to the Colonel himself. Colonel Mustard stood tall and proud, dressed in a seersucker suit and a cane, which I knew he didn't need. As the name would suggest, his thick hair was blond with a few gray streaks. Meanwhile, his thick mustache was opposite, gray with a few blond streaks. He looked the picture of a proper Southern gentleman.

I put my hand on my heart and bowed to him. "In peace."

"How lovely it is to see you again, madam."

"And you, Colonel." I extended my gloved hand, which he took. He bent and brushed his mustache against the back of my hand. "We were just on our way to see you at your …" My eyes flew wide. Next to him stood a ghost. I inhaled in surprise.

"Ah," the Colonel said, "I see you've noticed my new valet and orator. Not to worry, madam. You're not hallucinating." His voice soothed, so slow and deliberate. "TJ, may the gods rest his loving soul, had a twin brother. This man is Thomas. Thomas, may I introduce you to Mrs. Winki Witherspoon, the champion of Gateway Manor."

The handsome black man next to him smiled with beautiful, pearly whites. He gave a deliberate nod. "It's an honor to meet you."

"And you," I said. He and Nathan introduced each other and

shook hands. "You gave me a fright. You are the spitting image of your brother." TJ, or Tony Jones, died last year. He protected me in a late night gun fight at Audubon Park. As a consequence of helping me, he was murdered. As the memory came back, I fought to raise the corners of my mouth. "TJ saved my life," I said. "I can never repay that."

"He was a good man," Thomas said.

Then it hit me. "Thomas … Tom Jones?"

With a shrug he said, "It's not unusual." He winked.

I laughed. Everyone here used a pseudonym as far as I could tell. Except me.

The Chancellor clinked his glass. "If I may have your attention, please," the frail man bellowed, "the time has come to cover this year's rules."

The moment of truth, I thought. Part of me hoped they didn't hold up their end of the bargain and changed the rules. That would put an end to this stupid contract, and we'd have a real out for Jack.

We bade farewell to our neighbors and made our way back to our table.

"Firstly," the Chancellor started, "proxies will be allowed this year, for the qualifying phases. The fourth stage and final battles, however, will be fought one on one."

A few people applauded this news. It made no difference to me. A proxy was an individual who suffered for you, as I understood it. They took the pain of your beating while you fought. That sounded like a benefit, especially if you lacked a good healer, however, if your proxy was weaker than you, you could lose the fight faster. I was pretty strong, given the training I had from Smith and Wesson, Nathan, and Annabelle. There was no one in my party that could last longer than me. Well, maybe Nathan. My eyes fell on him. I raised an eyebrow.

"Don't even think about it," he feigned insult.

"As a result," the Chancellor continued, "competitors of the second stage will need expiration to win."

"Expiration?" Saffron asked.

"Death," I said coldly.

"You *kill* each other?" she exclaimed.

"It's not as bad as it sounds," I quipped. I reflected back at last year's battles, my eyes upward. "I take it back. It's awful."

The Chancellor added, "This year we've decided to take a different approach to eliminations in stage three. Rather than assign your competitors for you, we're allowing each competitor to pick their opponents. Each of you will choose three competitors." There it was. Just as they promised. "Some of you, as you will be selected more often, will fight quite a bit, while others perhaps not at all."

I sat back, unsure if I was happy about their honesty or not.

"Your scores will be monitored accordingly. The top sixty-four champions will go onto the final battles. Winners of the fourth stage will be determined by the last man standing. Orators, please give your selections to your chamber host by end of day, tomorrow."

The murmur throughout the room made me think no one was happy about the arrangement.

"Lastly, there is a limit of two weapons and two talents for each stage this year. I suggest you choose wisely." Everyone chuckled. "If there are any questions, orators are encouraged to ask when they pick up their champion's assignments. Now." He picked up a scroll from his table, unrolled it, and began to read. "House of Ravenswood, please come forward."

This was really happening. I glanced at Archy again. And sighed.

I didn't trust Lord Edmund or the mages, even if they'd kept their word so far. We needed to discover the healer's name for ourselves. So, while I spent my time fighting the biggest and baddest competitor, distracting the elders with my efforts, my *spies* could rifle through the Chancellor's safes and find the name of the executed healer.

My plan hinged around fighting one, and only one, champion, ideally beating him. Ideally because that would give the mages pause on taking any kind of retribution on me or my house. Important, given we were doing some breaking and entering.

But it wasn't the sexy demon who swaggered up to receive his own assignment. Only one creature came year after year for nearly a century, kicking everyone's keister. Only one stood utterly and completely undefeated.

All I needed to do was beat the Arch Lich.

~ ~ * ~ ~

"In the name of the Father, the Son, and the Holy Spirit. Amen."

I looked around, startled by the words. I stood, one among a crowd of people, just in front of a hard, wooden pew. I'd never attended a mass, but I'd been here before. St Patrick's Cathedral, Saffron's church downtown.

"You may be seated."

I looked up at the priest standing in front of us. There he was, dressed in a black robe, fitted through the chest and abdomen, which widened in a pleated skirt below the waist. His collar was white. His eyes were blue.

Will.

I'd been looking forward to going to sleep tonight. Will told me last year that we could see each other but only one night a year, the shortest night. The Summer Solstice. I don't know if these visits were just dreams, or some magic-reality glitch, but it had felt real last year. It certainly felt real now.

The room rustled as everyone took their seats. I remained standing.

"What are you doing?" I called to him.

The offended room turned towards me.

"I'm conducting a mass. What do you think I'm doing?"

"Will, you're not even Catholic." I scooted out of my row to the aisle and walked to my late husband.

He spread his arms in gesture. "*This* is called a clue."

"Yeah, way ahead of you. I know you left the DVD in a church," I said as I walked up the steps to stand in front of him. "I need to know *which* church." I swept my hand over the now empty pews behind me. "I know it's not this one."

"See?" he smiled. My heart skipped a beat. *Will I ever get over loving this man?* "You're my clever girl." He took my hand, curled my fingers over his, and kissed them.

I miss you.

He gestured behind me. "Take a seat." As we did, he said, "I won't solve your riddle for you, but ask me anything else. You look troubled, Winks."

Where do I start? "I blew it, Will. You told me the death at the Citadel was important and I dropped the ball." I swallowed. "I keep giving Jack reasons to hate me."

"Is that important to you? That Jack doesn't hate you?"

"I don't like anyone hating me."

He scoffed. "You're in the wrong line of work."

"Let's review: I didn't choose this. Any of this."

He patted my leg. "Winks, it was a joke." Nothing funny about it, I thought. "I get that you and he are in a bad situation. Both of you are trying to make the best of it. If you worry about his feelings, you're going to make bad decisions. For him. For yourself. You're just letting yourself get distracted. That is, unless …"

"Unless what?"

"Unless there's a reason he's so important to you."

"What do you mean?" I asked, confused.

"Winki, its okay to fall in love with someone—"

I didn't let him finish. "I'm not in love with Jack. I'm not in love with anyone."

"I'm not … I didn't … Look, all I'm saying is that it's okay if you are."

"Will—" I argued.

"Sooner or later, Winki, if it's Jack or whoever, you're going to fall for someone. That's okay. Great, actually. I want you to be happy. I want you to find someone to share your life with."

I want to share my life with you, what's left of it. I want you back.

"Can't happen, Winki. We had our time together. Maybe this," he gestured between us, "these annual meetings are a bad idea. Maybe seeing me won't let you heal and move on."

My gut wrenched a bit. *No. I need this.* "I'm healing just fine," I defended. "I don't want to move on." He frowned. "Will, my life with you felt like a bolt of lightning."

"Terrifying and dangerous?" he asked with a crooked smile, one a little larger than in the portrait.

"More like a long shot. What are the odds I would have such happiness? What are the odds of it happening again? Lightning never strikes twice. I don't even want to try."

He stroked my face gently. "Today. You don't want to try *today*. Just keep an open mind. And heart." He shifted a bit. "What else is bugging you?"

"I made a deal."

"I know. Next time, by the way, if Nathan says don't sign the contract, take it from me. Don't sign the contract."

"Not useful now."

"I like your thinking, though. Beat the Lich. Could work. Won't be easy."

"Did you ever get close?"

"Hell, no."

That depressed me. Will reigned over the tournament for eight years. "Has anyone?"

He took a deep inhale. "Two come to mind who managed to last a bit longer, without getting killed right away. Both had the same strategy. Since Archy, as you call him, has a rather quick technique, some thought if they could avoid him they'd wear him out. One was a goblin whose name I don't recall, the other, King Hector. Didn't work, though. Archy just stood there, waiting for the opportunity to cut off their heads."

I winced. "Yeah. That happened to me last year."

"Happens to everyone. Every year. Head. Or an appendage so you bleed out." He cleared his throat. "If you're going to exhaust him you've got to make him move. Remember, he's completely resistant to any magic of any kind, so don't even try. Just don't. You'll only give him time to act, and he's damned fast. I think the only thing to do is fight him. Really and truly fight him. Take your weapons and leave everything else outside the ring. That includes pride and ego."

"I have no pride. Nor ego."

He raised an eyebrow.

"Not much ego."

"What I mean is, don't worry about what everyone else will think or talk about. If you challenge this guy multiple times, that's going to attract a lot of attention. Let it."

Kind of the plan.

"I'm curious," he tilted his head. "What made you think of it?"

"Beating Archy? Well, you."

He raised his eyebrows.

"I saw a vision of you and Nathan arguing about him. And that just got me thinking—"

"You have visions?"

"Yes. Well, no. I mean, the house shows me stuff."

He smiled. "Really? Winki, that's fantastic. The manor and I were close, but it never volunteered information. I always had to ask. I'm thrilled you two are getting along."

That was cool to hear, and I beamed. "Hey, if this was a dream then you'd know all this. Is this really real?"

Something flashed out of the corner of my eye. We both turned toward the altar, which now glowed hot, consumed in flames.

"Huh," Will said casually. We stood, my mouth agape. He pointed to the fire. "I need to go take care of this."

And I woke up.

Chapter Eighteen

AROUND THE MORNING breakfast table, Nathan listed my competitors for the next five days.

"Even though these are going to be relatively easy fights, especially at first," Nathan said to me, "you have to win them."

"Yeah, yeah," I said, devouring my pancakes. "Trust me, I'm doing nothing to forfeit this stupid contract." With a finger I scraped up some maple syrup and smeared it on the table in front of Hercule.

"*Merci!*"

"That's not what I meant," he said.

Mr. Smith, briefly breaking from wolfing down his plate of pancakes, chimed in. "Since you're planning on challenging the Arch Lich, you want your own rating to be as high as possible going into stage three. That will increase both your life points, making you harder to kill, and increases your ability to resist his talents." As he spoke, the silent Mr. Wesson stole part of Mr. Smith's breakfast for himself. He raised a finger to his lips when he noticed me notice.

"The larger those numbers are," Nathan said, "the better your chances of beating him. Or just staying in the ring."

"Or prolonging your suffering before he cuts your head off," Hercule added.

Mr. Smith scratched his head, looking at his empty plate. "Can I have some more?" he asked Mrs. Jolly. "I'm real hungry for some reason."

Jeeves asked, "Have you had any luck determining how Mrs. Witherspoon will succeed with the Arch Lich?"

As Saffron heaped more 'cakes on his plate, Mr. Smith said, "Um, not yet. We're running a program right now that analyzes the anatomy of liches and similar crustaceans. It looks for any weaknesses and calculates the probability for success attacking those areas. Should be done in a day or two."

"I usually split their heads, right between the eyes." All of us looked at Saffron, who voiced the wisdom. "But I put them in a freezer for a couple of hours first so they don't, you know, move around."

Jeeves cleared his throat. "Mr. Smith, Mr. Wesson, and I will attend all of his bouts during this stage. I hope we can determine some strategy for you to use, madam." He looked at the chef. "Since we lack a sufficiently large freezer."

"Mmmmm," my *cafard* familiar said as he licked his maple-syrupped antennae. "I, too, will do a bit of the … what is the term, *mon ami*, 'recon?' We will find a way to succeed!"

Hercule's role, his sole purpose for the rest of the tournament, was to post himself in the Chancellor's office and find the ledger. We'd decided before we left we would never speak of what he was up to, just in case we're ever overheard by eavesdroppers. "I want you to take extra care, Hercule."

"Bah!" he snipped. "I've done this type of snooping decades before you were born, *ma chére*. The Great Hercule knows how not to be seen."

"What I meant was," I said, offering a palm for him to climb onto, "that I'd hate for anything to happen to you."

"Ah. Well. In that case," he stood up onto his hind legs and, like a proper gentleman, gave a little bow. "*Merci, beaucoup.*" I set him down, and he dashed off the table saying, "Hercule knows all the little corners and cracks to hide, no? For he is a cockroach, and that is what we do. Keeping our ugly selves hidden from the view of the insipid monkeys who somehow have managed to rule the world ..."

Nathan pushed his empty plate away. "Time to get going, Mrs. Witherspoon." I rose, bidding everyone a good day while I went off to get my head banged in.

We walked side by side, my silent healer just a step behind us. I wore my baby blues, clad in leather from head to toe. My hammer dangled off my right hip, a small knife tucked in the belt on my left. "There's something you need to know," I told Nathan.

"Oh?"

"I, um ..." I had told neither Nathan nor Jack that I, indeed, had a new talent. As we entered the arena for my first battle, I was about to say the words, "I have a new talent," when Mr. Marble beat me to it.

"I see you have a new talent."

Above the arena boards inform the opponents and viewers of important information about the combatants. Sure enough, mine read:

Winki Witherspoon, House of Gateway
Level: 17
Life Points: 184
Talents: Time Guardian, Conjurer
Weapons: Knife, Hammer

I pointed to the board. "But ... How ...?"

Nathan scratched his head. "I'm not sure. Maybe one of them has a talent, similar to mine, but more powerful. A super *thought catcher*?" He continued as we entered the five sided, roped arena, just like the one we had at home. "That would explain how they knew Jack's name."

"The Chancellor knew his name. He checks these guys in every year."

"True, but he's not supposed to share that with anyone, including other mages. That information is for the Chancellor only." He looked at the board again. "I got to say, Mrs. Witherspoon, I'm a little hurt you didn't tell me."

"What? That I can conjure? I only learned it, what, yesterday? Then there was the dinner here, then the bet, then losing four months, then ... whatever. Between the whirlwind of hoopla we've had to deal with these past two days, it didn't seem a priority. Besides," I said as I watched my competitor, a troll named Nubbick, enter the ring, "that's protocol, right? We keep such things to ourselves."

He dropped his gaze and gave a sad nod. "*Touché.*"

I wondered if I looked as hurt at the dinner as he looked now. "It's not that powerful," I offered as an explanation. "It's limited."

He nodded at the troll. "Show me." He and my healer walked off.

I had the honor of fighting a couple of trolls just last Halloween, but the sight of them still felt daunting. He stood about the height of a man yet was two to three times as beefy. His skin was gray and thick, like you'd expect on a hippopotamus or elephant, and was hard to pierce. He had no hair on his head. A telltale characteristic of a troll were two tusk-like teeth that protruded so much that he couldn't keep his lips over them. Unlike a wolf or a snake, the ivories came from his lower jaw. Quite a creature.

We took our places at opposite sides of the ring. He sported a broadsword in one hand, halberd in the other.

Hm. Halberd.

An ethereal voice said, "Begin."

Nubbick let out a raucous war cry as he spun the halberd over his head. He came rushing at me. I could hear the blade cutting the air as it swung towards me.

I didn't slow time down. I didn't have to. After the months of sparring with Nathan I could easily duck and spin out of the blade's path. I concentrated on that feeling we practiced days ago, that annoying buzz in my spine, and I imagined the halberd in my own hands, the feel of the wood, the weight of the weapon. I fluidly moved, continuing in a circle, swinging the now present weapon in my palms.

Nubbick found his blade tucked between his ribs. He looked up, jaw dropped, eyes wide. Almost comically, he fell backwards.

"Winner," said the voice. "House of Gateway."

I stood in the ring, watching as Nubbick's healer did what healers do, joined by Nathan and Jack.

"Nothing wrong with that talent," Nathan said, patting me on the back. "That seemed to work very well. I'm proud of you."

"The item has to be in use. That's the catch."

Nubbick stood up, a bit shaky. I approached him, held my hand over my heart, and gave him a bow. I'm not wild about the killing we do here, even if it's temporary, even if it's just for show. It feels wrong to take a life, and I want my fellow champions to know that.

The huge, gray man walked up to me and offered his fist. I bumped it with an understanding grin. He lumbered off.

"Well," Nathan rubbed his hands together. "You got some time to burn. Let's go see something, shall we?"

We went to the arena in the room next door where Malador fought a wraith. Tricky creatures, those. They look like the bone versions we dealt with last night: cloud-like form, black with bright purple dots for eyes. But lacking, of course, bones. Having fought a cloud recently in the cemetery, I shuddered at the memory. If you cut through them, they just reform. This one seemed to be giving Malador a bit of a time.

We took seats in the bleachers, which were mostly empty.

Everyone fighting their own battles kept viewership to a minimum. When Malador walked around the arena, he saw me in the stands. He smiled and winked, and tossed his long, black curls from his shoulder.

My heart skipped a beat. *Damn, I hate this guy.*

A ball of fire formed in his hand. With a casual flick his wrist he sent it hurling toward the wraith. It, however, didn't see that—it got distracted by Malador's flirting and turned to see me, only to burst into flames. Poor thing.

"Winner. House of Ravenswood."

Malador strolled ringside and leaned on the ropes. "Thank you, my love. Your timing was impeccable." He blew a kiss.

I'll play. "How is it you won the tournament last year when you can't beat a lowly wraith without my help?"

"I have other tricks. You just made it convenient." He slipped through the ropes and approached. "I'm so glad you stopped by. I have something I wish to discuss with you."

As he approached me, my healer quickly stood up, placing himself between Malador and me.

"Call off your guard dog. I come in peace."

I put a hand on Jack's shoulder. "It's okay." He took a step back. Jack and Nathan closely flanked my sides. "I know I'm *so* going to regret asking, but what do you want?"

"Oh, you know what I want, my bride-to-be. The joining of our houses … our bodies—"

Nathan put a hand on him, pushing him back. "Never gonna happen."

"But that's not what I wish to talk about at the moment," he said, brushing Nathan's hand away. He looked into my eyes. "I know you brought the girl. You know I want the girl." I gulped. "And I know your healer's fate is on the line with these games." *How …? Good news travels fast.* "You know as well as I do, ultimately you'll have to beat me to win the tournament." Malador stepped a little closer and spoke in a quiet, sultry voice. "A final battle I can throw, and would, *just for you.*" I searched his eyes. "You keep your healer, win some wager you have with Edmund, and, as an added bonus, you get your first tournament win under your belt. All I get is the girl. Almost seems unfair, really, what I'd do for you."

"Back off," Nathan said, pushing him again, attempting to widen the gap that managed to get smaller.

I consoled my Orator. "That's okay. Malador, firstly, *she* is a woman." The champion rolled his eyes. "And, secondly, I've learned my history since the last tournament, and I know that your sister is more likely to win the games this year. Seems you two like to trade off." I'd been told when Will fought the final battle year after year, his opponent alternated perfectly between Malador and Esmeralda. "And thirdly, why? She's a normal. A fabulous cook, true, but a normal. Why does she interest you?"

"Ah," he smiled—again my heart skipped a beat, even though he stood outside the ring where his allure was greatly diminished—and said, "I'm so glad that dull household of yours has finally found the time to teach you anything. Regarding sister-of-mine, she isn't interested in winning this year." He turned his attention to Nathan, staring him dead in the eye.

In the few beats of silence, Nathan moved away from the dashing villain, just slightly. The blood drained from Nathan's face, turning him gray. He swallowed as the two men stared at each other.

"Sister has bigger fish to fry," Malador smirked. Nathan's jaw clenched.

My eyes darted between the two men. *Now* what the devil was I missing? What did Esmeralda have to do with anything?

A smarmy, sinister grin spread over Malador's face, one that forced me to fight my own emotions to keep from trembling. I'd never truly felt afraid of this man. Until that moment.

When Malador turned back to me, I saw Nathan deflate, just slightly, out of the corner of my eye. "As for the girl, she interests me. That's all you need to know."

"Before I hand the *woman* over," I clarified, "I need to know why. I'm not about to give you someone to torture for eons."

"Very well. I wish to have her prepare me something unique. Something ... *special*." He gave a small shrug, keeping his perfect smile.

"Like a barley soup? An alligator stew? Or ..." I snapped my fingers. "Oo. How about a poison that kills all healers?"

For a brief moment rage flashed across his face. He recovered quickly, bringing back his cheshire grin. That gorgeous and dangerous smile.

"I see you have learned a thing or two. Delightful. My offer stands as such: I throw the fight, you win your wager, and I get the girl. And trust me," He leaned in close, his lips to my ear. "I know the difference between a *woman*," his breath tingled my neck, "and a girl." He stood back, bow deeply, rolling his hand from his forehead, and hastened off.

Once out of earshot I turned to Nathan. "Okay. Spill."

Transformed back to his lawyer self, Nathan laughed it off. "It's nothing." He left the room, his red cloak billowing behind him.

Jack came to stand at my side, the two of us watching the door close behind him. "Any guesses?" I asked.

In typical healer fashion, quiet and brooding, he offered a single shake of his head.

As if I didn't have enough to worry about already, keeping Saffron safe, keeping Jack in my house, and now this.

I had to keep Esmeralda from Nathan.

Chapter Nineteen

THE REST OF my day was uneventful. Thankfully.

I wanted to press Nathan about what transpired between him and Malador, but he managed to avoid me, only appearing when I needed my Orator at the start of bouts. I thought about talking to Hercule, who would surely know something, but he would only return when he had any information about Will's healer. That left Jeeves, but I knew from experience he was not a good source of information; discretion being the better part of a butler's valor. For the moment, I had to accept myself being left in the dark. Pretty much my state of being since joining Gateway Manor.

Equally uneventful were the second and third days. I easily managed to get my seventeen rating up to twenty-nine. I felt stronger in the ring, a curious sensation. Even my armor gained strength and resistance. During one battle, I missed blocking a swinging axe, which hit me full on the back. The blow knocked me to the floor, but the blade didn't pierce my suit. As of yet, I had yet to receive a cut.

That made it a boring tournament for my healer.

On the morning of the fourth day, Nathan, Jeeves, my healer, and I had gathered in the lobby, seated around the heatless hearth in the center of the room. The Chancellor, with his creepy milky eye, and his lap dog Lord Edmund visited to tell us "the good news."

"It isn't fair," explained the Chancellor, "that you continue to fight those ranked so much lower than yourself."

"Sounds like you guys shouldn't have ranked me so low to begin with," I retorted.

"Winki," my Orator scolded me. "My apologizes, Chancellor. We're happy to accept a new schedule."

They handed Nathan a scroll and left. He unrolled it and frowned.

He handed it to Jeeves, whispering, "Last bout today."

Jeeves looked it over. "Only fitting, I suppose." He sighed and gave me an apologetic look. "You will be fighting Esmeralda."

Of course I would be. I closely watched Nathan's expression, searching for clues for whatever might be going on. He revealed nothing.

"We're off," Mr. Smith announced as he and Mr. Wesson came down the stairs to join us in the comfortable lobby of our tower. They each clutched a laptop computer. "Archy's first battle starts in a few—"

A small noise stopped him. We all turned to see an envelope had been pushed under the lobby door from the hallway. Mr. Wesson retrieved it. He held it up for all to see the word clearly written across the face.

Winky.

"Hm," I said when he handed it to me. "Someone doesn't know how to spell my name." I opened it and jumped to the bottom before reading it. "It's from Theodore." My goblin bud. It read:

Winky-

I heard this morning you were to battle my new employer today, so I wanted to

```
warn you. Do not recognize me when you
see me. I will avoid you also.
I've followed leads that have lead me to
Esmeralda. I'm "working" for her now.
She has Simon, brother of Saffron Jolly.
He isn't being well treated.
Ez and Mal are planning something, but
they haven't shared details with any of
us. I will try to keep you informed.

Please be careful today. She has
something up her sleeve, I can tell.
-Theodore
```

"What's it say?" Nathan inquired.

I tucked in inside my jacket. "He knows where Simon is."

"Where?" he asked. Even Jack perked up, sitting more erect. He looked at the staircase ensuring that Saffron remained upstairs in our suite, cleaning up after breakfast.

I whispered. "With Esmeralda."

"Not Malador? Wait, *here?*" Nathan pointed to the floor.

"He didn't say." I didn't think so, but it was a fair question. "Why would she bring him to the tournament?"

"I can say with confidence, madam," Jeeves added, "none of us ever understands why she does anything."

"He only says Simon's been mistreated," I added.

Nathan shook his head. "Dammit," said under his breath.

"You two need to go," I said to Smith and Wesson, who'd stayed to listen. They both nodded and left. I focused on Mr. Marble. "Nathan, what do I need to know about you and Esmeralda?"

"Nothing." He stood. "We need to leave, ourselves."

"Nathan." I looked him hard in the eye. "I'm going to fight her this afternoon. What's going on? Last thing I, no *we*, need to have is to be blindsided because you failed to give me all the facts."

"Mrs. Witherspoon, there is nothing you need to know in order to defeat her today."

When Mom doesn't give you the answer you want you go ask Dad. I spun to Jeeves, butler scruples be damned. "What happened between Esmeralda and Nathan that I need to know about? There's something going on."

Nathan's eyes stared hard at Jeeves, but he gave no physical signal, no shaking of the head, no mouthing of words, no waving of hands. Just a hard glare.

Jeeves stiffened, straightened his butler vest, and calmly replied. "I can honestly tell you, madam, that nothing has transpired between Mr. Nathan Marble and Esmeralda."

The words felt cherry picked. *Ah.* "I don't suppose if I rephrased the question about *Edward Witherspoon*, you'd give me a different answer?"

"Madam, I'd prefer it if—"

I held up my hand to stop him. "Never mind." I had enough for now. I looked at Nathan, whose eyes were closed. He exhaled. I knew relief when I saw it. "Jack, let's go." Before I entered the hallway I turned to the room. "I'm so sick and tired of being left in the dark!"

~ ~ * ~ ~

Nathan caught up as I stormed with long strides to my first game of the day. Without a word, he jogged ahead. That was the Orator's job. The torch-lit halls buzzed with activity, small parades of threes milling in every direction as Orators led their Champions and Healers to their next destination.

As usual we arrived early. We stood outside the ring, avoiding eye contact, saying nothing. Neither Nathan nor I wanted to go into the ring. Once there his *thought catching* talent would become active. I didn't want him reading my anger and frustration any more than he wanted to.

Other folks came in, taking seats in the stands. My bouts always seemed to attract a crowd, more so than what I'd noticed for other champions.

Nathan caved. "Look, Winki, I swear to you, this isn't anything you need to worry about. It has nothing to do with you." He did a double take, his eyes bulged, looking at something behind us.

Something big.

Something looming.

I knew who it was, having noticed him moments before Nathan did. I slowly looked over my shoulder, then jumped, feigning fright. "Archy!"

He brutally brushed Nathan aside with a swipe of his giant claw so he could stand in front of me. "You have challenged me."

I'd never heard him talk before. I longed for that lack of knowledge. His deep voice grated, having a tactile quality, like nails on a chalkboard, with such intensity my teeth buzzed. Sort of like listening to the combined voices of James Earl Jones and a Dalek. I couldn't keep my skin from crawling at the noise. Jumpin' Jimmy Legs, if he had that affect on me simply by talking, what chance did I have fighting the guy?

I forced—literally, through my grinding teeth—a smile. "Long time, no see!"

"You have challenged me."

I couldn't resist the involuntary twist that developed in my neck. "Yeah, about that—"

He pointed a claw at my chest. "No tricks. No magic. Play the game."

"G-g-game?" I stammered, fighting for control over my tongue and teeth. My face scrunched, puckered as if I just ate a lemon.

"Play the game." As he lumbered off, his rigid lobster tail swept my feet out from under me. My healer caught me by the arm before I hit the floor.

Jack helped me stand up and put his hands on my face. I took a few calming breaths and felt the warm, wonderful peace of his touch. My concentration returned.

"You managed to piss him off," Nathan said, eyes on the door after Archy left.

I gave Jack an "I'm fine" gesture. "Never mind his thick exoskeleton and razor sharp claws, Nathan, how do I keep him from talking to me."

"I never heard him speak before." He opened his jaw as he rubbed just below his earlobe, as if trying to pop his drums. "That's a toughie."

My opponent entered. I was grateful for the distraction, feeling my chances of success wavering. A fire elemental. According to the board his name was "Fire." So much for creativity.

Never fought one of these before. He looked like a man constantly burning, orange and red flames lapping his entire body. My instinct was to dowse him with a bucket of water.

"Suggestions?" I asked Nathan as we entered the ring.

"Keep your distance and make it quick. He often uses a hug as a way of winning, so don't get close."

"So he has substance? He's not just flame?"

"He has some substance some of the time. Be careful."

I learned from last year that the higher your opponent's rank, the more likely they could resist my talents, or develop resistance as we fought. As a result, I don't often open with moves like slowing time. I engage first, testing their fighting skills against my own.

My weapons for this bout were my knife and halberd. The hammer is my strongest but required me to get up close and personal, and that, I reckoned, would give the Heat Miser opportunity to inflict damage.

Hey, at least Jack might get something to do.

As soon as the bout started I realized I was in trouble. Fire launched his body at me. I managed to dive out of the way, but ... The guy wasn't just on fire, he was fire. Getting within ten feet of the guy made my eyes water and my skin all but blister. His pungent sulphuric scent assaulted my nose, making breathing a chore.

I kept my distance as best as I could. All he needed to do was advance, and I was on the retreat. My leathers overheated, making it hard to concentrate on anything other than leaving the ring and take an ice bath.

He lunged over and over, and I jumped, ran, ducked—anything just to keep my distance. I would took a swipe or two with my halberd, only to watch him duck, dodge himself as my blade passed through his body without effect. How the hell was I going to beat this guy?

I could no longer resist the urge to use my talent. As he lunged for me again I held my hand up and thought, "Stop!" He didn't, but he slowed. That gave me enough time to simply catch my breath, which I desperately needed. Hands on my knees I hunched over, panting, while I watched Fire out of the corner of my eye.

"How do you fight fire?" I gasped to myself. I knew it would be just moments before the spell wore off and I'd be on the run again. I kept a watch on Fire as he slowly drew closer.

My talent worked. Which meant I could use my summoning talent on him, too. Not that I could use it—

With fire.

The craziest thought entered my head. Could it be that easy? I summon items but could I actually summon fire, his fire. Perhaps, if I took it quickly enough I could extinguish him. Suffocate him, sort of.

I liked the idea but it had a problem. When I summon an item, I get the item. I certainly didn't want to get near the guy let alone possess his flame myself. It made no sense to turn this into a race for death, him dying from lack of fire, and me from setting myself alight.

Maybe I was thinking about my talent all wrong. Maybe this wasn't so much about acquiring things, but moving them. I'd just only focused on moving things to me. What if I tried to move things, well, away?

I looked into the bleachers that surrounded the ring. There. There was an open space, where no one sat.

Fire regained his composure. He laughed at me, making another dash, arms wide.

Getting that annoyed feeling was trivial. I stood upright, and concentrated on the heat. And the bleachers. Both my hands pointed at those targets, Fire the Elemental and where I wanted his fire to end up. See them, Winki. See them on fire!

My suit blistered. Even my hair started to singe. I felt searing arms wrap around me. I wanted to run, to scream! But I kept my eyes on the bleachers, wanting them to burn ... willing them to burn.

They smoldered first. Then ... flames.

Those nearest the small inferno gasped and leapt to safety. The benches exploded from the heat, the flames leaping high and hot and spread quickly.

Within a beat, the source of the fire became apparent. The moving swirl of flame that left Fire's figure looked like a narrow tornado that vertically spun out of the ring. Those beneath it cleared out as well, eyes wide and mouths dropped.

My own pain subsided as Fire let go of me. His body contorted under the intense suction. He tried to flee, but his feet couldn't gain traction; he looked like he ran in a wind tunnel, striding quickly but making painfully slow progress against the current. Desperately, he gripped the ropes and cried out as the last of it left him, his body bending backwards from the strain.

A husk of a man stood there, charred and frail and unmoving, hands wrapped around the ropes, head bent severely back, mouth open wide toward the ceiling. I cautiously approached the ghostly remains. Fire, no longer on fire, was gone, and a perfect statue of ash remained.

I blew on it. It disintegrated into a pile on the floor.

The room cheered so loudly that I almost couldn't hear the words, "Winner. House of Gateway."

The pile re-ignited, and Fire stood before me. Instinctively, I took a step back, but now he gave off no heat. Only the vision of fire. I raised my hand, attempting to feel any warmth, but none existed. I put my hand on my heart and bowed to him. He gave a subtle nod, then, with a small puff, simply vanished, as if he never existed.

I limped my way to my healer, who already jogged toward me. Jack made his way over my body, tenderly touching my burns, delicately handling each wound in such a way as to reduce what pain I felt. He healed everything, including my armor. I watched the process, fascinated.

I caught Nathan watching us. Watching Jack. His face bore a look I couldn't identify, hurt perhaps? Anger? He kept his distance, waiting for us to finish. He'd expressed concern over Jack just days ago. Could he honestly think Jack was doing anything other than healing me?

Once my healer completed his task, Nathan approached.

"You lied to me," Nathan said.

"How so?" Was this about Jack?

"You said your conjuring talent was limited. But that?" He pointed to the still smoldering section of bleachers, "That was incredible. I fail to see any limitation."

I gave a wan smile. "I'm thankful it actually worked."

He gestured out of the ring. "Shall we?"

Esmeralda. Next on my list.

"Let's go," I told the men as we left the arena.

Chapter Twenty

THE PACKED ROOM hummed with anticipation. I stood in the center of the arena waiting for the arrival of Esmeralda and her entourage, spinning slowly in a circle to see the audience. "Don't these people have their own battles?" I asked Nathan.

"Apparently not."

Even my own entourage attended. In the front row sat Smith, Wesson, Jeeves, and Saffron.

I leaned on the ropes and addressed the geeks first. "Don't you two have somewhere else to be?"

"Archy doesn't have a bout for another hour yet," Mr. Smith answered. "And we don't get to watch you in action often. Wesson wanted to come." Mr. Wesson smiled with a "thumbs up."

I rolled my eyes. I looked Jeeves, nodding at Saffron. "Are you sure she should be here? These aren't happy events, typically."

Saffron answered. "I got bored sitting in that room by myself all day. I wanted to see what you do."

Jeeves added, "Did you want me to chain her to the stove, madam?"

Before I could retort—and I had a good one—the door slammed open. Every head turned.

Her Orator, face hidden behind his ample red robe, raised his arm grandly. "All hail, Queen Esmeralda, Ruler of Diamond Realm, in the Fourth Plane of Fire!"

I gave Nathan a swat with the back of my hand. "Why don't you do that for me?"

He gave a sigh before slipping through the ropes to take a seat next to Jeeves. My healer sidled close. "Are you all right, ma'am?" he whispered. They were the first words he'd spoken since we arrived here days ago.

"I'm fine for now. Stay frosty."

He bowed and exited the arena as the grand lady entered it. "The Queen" strutted around the five-sided ring, arms wide, letting everyone have an unfettered view. A bit over the top, if you ask me. Meanwhile, her entourage paraded past the stands, while dragging some poor guy...

"Simon?"

I turned at hearing Saffron's voice. My group stood to see.

"Oh, god! Simon?"

Led by a noose around his neck—by Theodore, of all things—the poor brother shuffled behind Esmeralda's group. His hair tousled, longer than I remembered, his once well-groomed beard now thick and unkempt. His hands were bound behind him.

Saffron leapt from her seat, only to be held back by Jeeves and Nathan. My stomach roiled.

"Please," Jeeves implored her, "let us take care of this."

"What's to take care of?" she cried back, struggling against them. "I want to see him! Simon!" she jumped up and down, waving.

Simon glanced frightened eyes over his shoulder. Once he saw his sister, he dejectedly hung his head.

C'mon. Let's do this dance and get this over with.

Esmeralda finished strutting and took the center of the ring. "As is my right," she bellowed upward, to the ethereal voice we only ever hear, "I choose a proxy."

Are you kidding me?!

"Name your proxy," said the voice.

"Him." She pointed to Simon.

"What's that mean?" Saffron asked, hysterical. Her emotions justified by the uproar in the audience. "What's a proxy?"

Esmeralda didn't shy from pain, this I knew from past experience, so choosing a proxy, someone to suffer and die in her stead, well, I should have seen that coming. Not only would it torture Simon, it would torture me, too.

"Really, Ez," I said chided, "can't it be just us girls?"

"Proxy accepted," said the voice.

Crap. I could just throw this, and not hurt him.

I swallowed. Lord Edmund made it clear that throwing any bout would cause him to win Jack. I looked at my healer. I looked at Simon. Lastly I looked at Nathan, who wrestled with our struggling chef.

He said just three words. "Make it quick."

Simon was led to a space reserved just outside the ring. His hands were freed and his noose removed. He turned around in an attempt to flee when a round structure blinked into place around him, like a man-sized bell jar. It shimmered with energy, however, instead of glass. His hands searched the tube shape, trying to find a door. Almost mime-like. Some of Esmeralda's goblins laughed at him.

Saffron screamed, "*Noooo!,*" all the while fighting Nathan and Jeeves, who desperately tried to calm her. At one point Nathan wrapped his arms around her waist as her feet and arms reached out for her imprisoned brother.

"Begin."

We stared at each other as we paced a circle. She lifted an eyebrow. "I see no special shield this time."

"Nope. Just me."

Within a blink she came at me, her fingernails raised. She swiped at me, but I rolled out of the way, whacking her in the back with my hammer as I passed.

I heard a grunt, but not from her. Simon slammed into the invisible shield of his confines.

Saffron held her hands to her face, eyes big and tearful.

This was truly gonna suck.

Something cut the back of my leg, sending me to the mat. Dammit! I got so distracted by Saffron and her brother I took my eyes off Esmeralda.

That's a big ten-four—this was truly gonna suck.

Get yourself together, Winks. You can beat this whack-job.

Before I regained my feet, she came at me again, fast and furious. I dodged her as my hammer made perfect impact with her knee.

Simon screamed as he collapsed to the floor. He held his leg, grimacing. He barely had enough room to sit in the space.

"Stop! Stop this!" Saffron screamed, her body shaking, her face red, and her eyes brimming. Not that I noticed her. I tried to keep my eyes on the red-haired witch.

"Time out!" Esmeralda called.

"Time out granted," said the voice.

She approached me, which raised my hackles. "Pity, isn't it, how that poor man has to suffer."

"So release him. Let's do this, just you and me. I'm game." I knew it was futile to ask.

She took a deep breath, as if thinking about it. "Perhaps we can come to an accord." I really didn't like the direction this headed. "I tell you what. How about a trade?"

"A ... trade?" My mind raced for answers, hoping to see the trap she set. *What the Hades was she doing?*

"Yes. I'll release Simon, for your cook's sake, but you give me someone else to serve in his stead."

"Someone else ...?" I closed my eyes. I knew who she'd name before I even heard the words. I swallowed, my gaze landing on the poor man.

"Nathan," she said.

Nathan and I stared at each other. Even though he was out of earshot, he knew, he *knew*, what the conversation was about.

"Only fair, I should think," she luridly said. "Simon isn't part of our world. He shouldn't have to suffer in it."

"Why him?" I asked. "Why Nathan?"

I quickly regretted that.

She softly answered, "I love to hear him scream."

My body shuddered.

Nathan watched her, unwittingly releasing Saffron, who ran to the bell jar weeping and collapsed in front of her brother. She put her hands on the shimmering surface that separated them.

Meanwhile, Nathan and The Queen remained locked in a heated stare. He purposefully avoided looking at me. He gave no hint, nor help in the decision. He let me know it was all mine.

The memory of him in our own ring flashed through my mind. My halberd in his side, my guilt, his suffering. In the safety of our own home, with only us as witnesses. But this? This would be for the masses, for entertainment. Despite the crowd of creatures, the room was deathly quiet. All eyes on me. I could scarcely breath the thick air.

Forgive me. "Nathan." He looked at me. I nodded to the bell jar.

He nodded back and handed his robe to Jeeves as he kicked off his shoes. Head high, he walked to the prison, rolling up the sleeves of his collared shirt. With a soft pop bell jar disappeared. Simon slumped to the floor into his sister's arms, moaning as he cradled his knee.

I didn't have to tell Jack what to do. He was on his way, followed by his father.

I exchanged my hammer for the halberd. It took a few seconds for Jack to heal the man. Jeeves and Saffron helped Simon to their seats as Nathan took his place.

"Healer, stay with Nathan. Get ready."

The bell jar reformed around Nathan.

I heard Archy's voice in my head, "Play the game."

I understood it then. No tricks, no talent, just battle. "Let's get this over with," I hissed.

She smirked.

"Begin," said the voice.

My rage took over, and I attacked, no longer wanting to wait. I raised my halberd, spinning it in my hands, and swept down at her.

She moved as I expected, dodging the blow. To my horror, she was precise. Esmeralda avoided the kill but managed, intentionally to let herself be gashed. I split her arm open. I thought I had; as the weapon passed through her skin it closed immediately.

Nathan tried hard not to cry out as he held his own wound. Blood oozed between his fingers.

Again, I attacked, and again she moved, precisely placing herself in danger but not death. I forced myself to shut out the scream from the slash across my brother-in-law's abdomen.

I grunted with frustration. I raised a desperate hand, trying to slow her down so I could finish her. It didn't work. Attack after attack, blow after blow, even when I knew how she'd move, how she'd duck, how she'd avoid me, I only could damage.

I panted with exertion, standing with my weapon. Esmeralda just stood there, smiling. She didn't move, didn't advance. She never attacked at all. She didn't want to win the fight. She only wanted Nathan to suffer.

For some reason I looked up at the boards. Her life points, *Nathan's* life, were falling, steadily. If I did nothing now he'd be dead in a minute, maybe two. I could just wait it out. Deprive her of more satisfaction.

I turned my attention to Nathan. Crimson ichor smeared the bell jar. He rested on bloodied hands. His body heaved as he gulped for air, every pained exhale audible to the room. Jack, too, knelt next to Nathan with his hands pressed on the energy, showing concern and solidarity. Every passing second felt like an eternity. I couldn't let him suffer more than he had to.

She joined me. "I told you he had a wonderful scream. Luscious, isn't it?" Her words dripped like honey. She genuinely loved watching him languish.

"No," I said. I spun quickly and smacked my knife into her heart.

Esmeralda staggered back, blinking at the hilt in her chest. I assumed the blade of it was in Nathan, really.

"I learned that trick from your brother," I growled.

"Winner. House of Gateway." The room erupted in cheers and applause.

Once Nathan slumped lifeless to the floor, my healer went into action. I clutched the ropes watching him work. A crowd gathered around the two of them, blocking my clear view. I saw Nathan's knee move, a hand twitch.

She was leaving the arena when I caught up to her. "Why? Why him?" I grabbed her by the arm. "Why was this important?"

Her Orator took great offense at my action, unsheathing a sword from his side.

She stopped him, and pointed to Simon, still seated with Saffron. "Go. Collect our dog," she told him.

I heard Saffron's raised voice. Out of the corner of my eye I saw her fighting off the Orator, trying to keep her reclaimed brother.

Esmeralda turned to me. "He means something to you?" With her long and elegant arm extended pointed at Nathan who was being helped to his feet.

"He's my husband's brother. Of course he means something to me."

She gave me a wicked smile, one that rivaled Malador's.

Inwardly, I cringed. "He means something to me, too."

I braced myself.

"He's my fiancé."

I didn't see her leave. I don't know how long I stood there, trying to remember how to breathe, gripping the ropes with my fists. My mind reeled, trying frantically to find some logic, some argument to explain how this was not my fault.

Nathan was not her fiancé. That I knew. But *Edward?* Could it be? It was he that had the poor judgment to follow Will into the darkness; maybe he entangled himself in her web as well. I couldn't fault him for that, though I tried. The fact was, until last year, until Nathan declared that he was Will's brother, everyone thought Edward was dead.

Everyone thought Nathan was just a lawyer.

But now? Now everyone knew.

And that *was* my fault.

Chapter Twenty-One

UNDERSTANDABLY, SAFFRON COULDN'T cook that evening. She locked herself in her room and sobbed. How could we explain that there was nothing we could do? We were not in a position to rescue her brother, not here. Not now. Esmeralda brought him here, he'd have to leave with her. Stupid tournament rules.

Jeff, aka Santa, said he'd watch over her while the rest of us went to dinner in the Grand Dining Hall. It was always open, like a constant Vegas-style all-you-can-eat buffet. I'd never been since we always had our own cook.

I didn't feel like eating. Apparently, neither did Nathan.

The two of us sat quietly as the rest of the group fended for food, joining in the thrums and murmurs and laughter around us. Our heads bent forward. Nathan strummed the tabletop with his fingers.

I wanted to apologize. I mean, how do you say "I'm sorry" to someone you just sliced? To death? In front of a crowd?

Clearing my throat I said, "Nathan, I—"

He raised his hand. "Don't."

I licked my lips. "We agreed we'd talk when we're angry with each other."

"I'm not angry," he droned. He strummed some more, thumping. "I just can't talk about it."

I sat quietly for several moments, but that's not in my nature. "I knew I cost Jack everything when I outed him. All this time I'd felt guilty about what that meant to him."

"Winki," he growled, rubbing his face.

"But I didn't consider you. I mean, I knew I cost you everything too, that you separated yourself from your family, that you wouldn't see them again—"

"Please …"

"—but I never thought about the rest of it. I never thought "

He abruptly stood, slamming his hand on the table. "*Dammit, Winki!*" he screamed.

The room fell heavy and silent.

"You *don't* listen! You *never* listen!"

He charged off, leaving me the glue for all the faces in the room. Not that I could see any of them through my blurred vision.

I swallowed the sore lump in my throat, set my elbows on the table, and buried my face in my hands. Slowly, the conversation picked up around me.

Judging by the gentle clatter of a plastic tray placed on the table, someone sat next to me. "Madam? May I bring you something to eat?"

"No. I'm great, Jeeves."

The others followed closely behind, everyone taking seats.

Much like me, Mr. Smith dosen't like silence, which was curious since his best friend and partner never says a word. He broke the quiet. "We found a weakness."

To Archy, I assumed. "Finally."

"Took a while. Mostly because we didn't like the answer we got, so we kept re-running the problem, narrowing parameters, constricting the algorithm—"

"Just get to the point," I stopped him.

He looked at Wesson, who shrugged. "Right between the eyes. Just like the chef suggested."

Mr. Wesson put his pad on the table and brought up a drawing of the Arch Lich. My eyebrows shot up at the quality of the image, like looking at a blueprint of the giant lobster, complete with dimensions and descriptions. He pointed to the place, just above his eyes.

"That's the softest part of his shell. And conveniently where his brain is located. So, just one good shove—*ugh!*" He demonstrated for affect. "Your small knife should do the trick."

I could see why they were unhappy with the answer. *I* was unhappy with the answer. "Should I just ask nicely for him to stand still while I get close enough with my little knife to lodge it into his head?"

"Sure. Give it a try."

My humor was often lost on him.

~ ~ * ~ ~

Nathan sat alone in the lobby with a book on his cross-legged lap when we returned from dinner. We made our way to the stairs, me trying to get to my own room as quickly and quietly as possible.

"Winki," he said softly. "A moment?"

Drat. Everyone said good night as they passed, spiraling themselves up the narrow twist of staircase. On numb legs, I took a seat in the middle of the sofa opposite him, my palms perfectly placed on my thighs and my eyes on the floor.

He closed his book and set it aside. "I'm sorry. I didn't mean to snap at you."

I raised my hands. "Not necessary." *Can I go now?*

"I mean, I *did* mean to, but it was wrong to. I mean, the relationship between an Orator and his champion ..."

"Nathan. It's okay. It's not your fault."

"No. My lack of control is my fault."

That stupid painful lump was back. "Got a lozenge?"

He tilted his head to the side and gave a small smile. Nathan moved seats, joining me on my sofa. "Come here," he said, and he embraced me.

That act of tenderness did me in. I nestled my face into his shoulder as tears escaped my closed, wet eyes. My brother-in-law hushed me as he gently rubbed my back, consoling me.

"I'm sorry," I sniffed.

"You've done nothing wrong."

"I screwed up your life."

"*I* screwed up my life," he said softly.

"You used to be happy. " I pushed him away. "I ruined everything. You had a wife, and kids, and a dog. *I saw the pictures!*"

"Come here," he said, pulling me seated next to him, so my head rested on his shoulder. "Come here and just listen."

I didn't fight. Didn't want to. I took a sobering, deep breath.

"I made my family disappear with a single phone call. I was able to do that because I set it up years in advance. I knew, I've always known, that at any given moment, I'd have to make them disappear. If I were found out, they'd become my greatest weakness. I had to get them away from this crazy life of ours to keep them safe. To keep me from being vulnerable. That was not your fault. It was my fault. I insisted on having a family, knowing the tremendous risks. That's all on me, not you."

"Will had a family," I pointed out.

"It's different when you're the champion. But, more importantly, he didn't. He had you. He had a wife, but no family. I suspect even he couldn't bring himself to endanger his own kids. So, he didn't have any." He kissed the top of my head. After a moment he said, "I do miss that dog, though."

I gave a small laugh as I wiped my eyes and sat back up. I leaned my head against the sofa, finally finding the courage to look at him again.

His gaze wandered, looking at some distant point. Seconds of uncomfortable silence filled my ears. These are the moments I would normally feel the need to speak, but I bit my tongue. And waited.

"I was young," he started, speaking so softly I could barely hear. "I was so young and so stupid and so very easily impressed. Looking back, I'm not sure how much of my infatuation for her was my own. When she touched me ..." He rubbed the bridge of his nose, eyes clenched, fighting his own headache. "This is why I'm so adamant you stay away from Malador. She can do to men what he can do to women, okay? She can make you feel so ..." he swallowed. "So damn good. You'll *do* anything, *say* anything," his eyes narrowed, *"suffer* anything, just to feel ..." he let out a shaky exhale, "so damned good." He looked at me. "I screwed up my life. I did it without any help from you."

I laid my fingers on his face, he put his over mine. He gave me a forgiving smile and an encouraging squeeze.

"What will you do now?" I asked.

"Well," he shifted, "there's only two things I can do. Either I go to the Dark Lords and ask to break the engagement, or ..." He swallowed. "Or, I marry her."

"So, option A, then."

He stopped, his mouth twisted a bit. "I don't like the idea of dealing with them. Typically they want something in return. Something horrible. Like feeding them," he said, recalling Will's deal. "Maybe I should have Smith and Wesson make me a mirror of my own," he nervously chuckled.

As with most humor I could feel the hint of truth to the jest. "What can I do?" I asked. "How can I help?"

"Thank you for asking. But first things first, Mrs. Witherspoon. Let's end this tournament, end this matter with Jack, end the matter with Saffron and Simon. If we're still alive after that, we'll talk.

Deal?" He held out his hand.

I shook it.

Bring it on.

Chapter Twenty-Two

TODAY, IT REALLY started. Today was the first day of stage three.

Today I faced Archy in our first battle.

Much to my surprise, no one wanted to challenge me. I felt a bit disappointed, really. I at least expected Malador to challenge me. I dreaded that Esmeralda would, making me trade someone else in lieu of torturing Simon.

Speaking of brother Simon, what a problem! While Ez and I fought, Saffron and Simon had talked at length about how they each came to the tournament. He broke down, confessing to her that all of this was his fault; that in a drunken, weak moment of stupid sibling rivalry after her latest recognition (some award from the Food Network, of all things), he had bitched to some guy occupying the bar stool next to him about how *she* had everything and wouldn't give *him* a dime. I'm guessing said stool's occupant was Malador. Jawing turned to camaraderie, camaraderie to dealing, and the deal took on a life of its own. He'd give anything—his life, his blood, his freedom —if he could just take it all back.

Saffron was, in my opinion, a frickin' saint. She forgave him. Right there, on the spot. Simon took her family, her husband and kids … and she forgave him.

I'd have sent him back into the bell jar.

But as she told us the tale she wept, explaining, "He's the only family I have now."

I saw her point.

All this happened over breakfast this morning. Now, Nathan, my healer, and I stood in the arena waiting for the arrival. *His* arrival. I shook my hands out, loosening them for my first bout with Archy.

"Between the eyes?" Nathan asked.

"Just above. Not that it matters, really. I'm just going to figure out how I can get that close to him this time."

"Smith and Wesson had no suggestions on that front?"

"On the contrary. They were very useful. They recommended avoiding the claws." I chuckled a bit as I shook my head, "Was this a fool's errand? Am I out of my mind here?"

"You've been unchallenged. That means no one wants to fight you, which means they don't think they'll beat you. You should take that as a compliment."

"That's all well and good if I had stayed the course and just attended the tournament like everyone else here. Do you think I can beat him? I want an honest answer."

He inhaled deeply. "Honestly, yes. The only issue is time. The question is, can you do it in these three bouts? But there is no doubt in my mind that if anyone can do it, it's you."

The doors flew open with a cacophonous boom. We spun, startled, to face him. The big, black lobster raced into the room, shrieking as he moved. His cry felt as grating and piercing as his speaking voice. Everyone covered their ears, trying to prevent their ear drums from bursting. He came at us. He never slowed. He ran straight at Jack, Nathan, and me. Idiot men that they were, they jumped in front of me. I had no idea what they were thinking. With a broad sweep, Archy flung them both high up into the air and out of the ring. And still he approached, a black lobster tornado.

I raised my halberd and angrily screamed, "Hey! Spanky!"

He stopped, almost pausing mid-stride, as if I froze him. I didn't.

He glared at me, only inches away.

I pointed upward. "We wait for the little lady to talk before we start!"

As if on cue, the ethereal voice said, "Begin."

What?

I ran in the opposite direction, trying to get just a little bit of distance on him. I'm used to the protocol, addressing your opponents, a moment to assess them, but this start, this explosion of lobster mayhem, rattled me.

And I never recovered.

Before you could say, "I need a healer," Archy had his claws around my waist and snapped my body in *half*.

"Winner. Realm of …"

I never heard the rest.

~ ~ * ~ ~

I fought to stay in the black numbness, struggled to return to that peaceful, inky dark, the leaden cessation that was death. It felt nice there; warm, and pain free …

With that thought, that realization, a flood of complete and excruciating agony coursed throughout my body. I drew in a deep breath, which I quickly regretted. I screamed.

"Winki! Please stop!"

The memory came next. The Arch Lich. Cut in half …

"That's it. Stay calm."

Why does this hurt so much? I tried to look around, but my eyes couldn't focus, couldn't get passed the pain. *Make it stop! Make it go away!*

"I am. I'm trying. I needed you awake, forgive me."

Jack.

The agony subsided just enough for me to experience the

penetrating chill that enveloped my core. At first I trembled, then quaked, then nearly convulsed in the frigid sensation. My teeth chattered with so much force, I nearly bit my tongue.

"You lost a lot of blood. Just breathe. It will pass soon."

"Why?" I asked. I don't think the words really came out. I heard something more like a mumble.

Jack hushed me, soothingly. "It will pass soon."

Not soon enough. I distracted myself from the cold and pain by focusing my vision. I moaned as my eyes adjusted to the constant orange illumination. In my room, in the tower.

Usually, I wake up on the mat of the ring. *Why am I here?*

Usually, I'm healed in seconds, maybe minutes. *Why is this taking so long?*

"This was worse," Jack whispered. "Much worse."

Last year I got my head cut off by Archy. How could this be much worse than that?

"Lots of muscle," Jack whispered, "internal organs, bone, blood, nerves … so much damage." He whimpered.

I felt that. A sting, sharp and bright, on my right side.

My eyes, dimly able to focus, found my healer. At my side. His eyes were closed, but tears flowed down his cheeks. His chest heaved as he took large, deliberate lungs full of air. Blood covered his chest, stomach, and arms. He wore no robe.

"It was in the way," he spat.

He could hear my thoughts? Only when connected could he …

I looked down. His hands disappeared, lost in my abdomen. We cried out together as some shot of nerve, hot and fiery, came back to life. Now, we both breathed, panting in unison.

I covered my eyes with an arm, my bent elbow hiding my face. He was healing me, and I was torturing him. He felt what I felt. He had to suffer the wound for me to get better.

"Better," he whispered. "That's much better."

Yes. I felt something warm deep in my stomach. Much better. I exhaled, sweet relief.

He retrieved his hands, dripping with my blood, as he took a few, collected breaths. Once he gathered a bit of composure he reinserted his hands.

On, it continued. Jack would "repair" something, lots of pain, or cold, or intensity, he'd take a small break, then repeat. The process went on for what seemed like hours. Both of us, gasping, moaning, breathing.

Connected.

Finally, after he assessed me for a third time, ensuring all the blood vessel and organs worked, he set out on my skin, sealing it all together.

When Jack finished he collapsed forward, his head on the blanket next to my hip. I didn't feel healed. I felt weak. And guilty. I stroked his head, his short blond hair tacky with the sweat of his toil.

"No!" he snapped upright, pushing my hand away. "Don't … touch me …" Like a newborn foal he stumbled across the room, catching the window ledge to steady himself. I watched him breathe. Slow, long, deep inhales. Slow, long, deep exhales. Rhythmic. Mesmerizing. Peaceful. Moment by moment he gained strength. He stood a little taller. Straighter. Eventually, he no longer needed to brace himself.

I, on the other hand, felt terrible. Weak. Tired. "What's wrong with me?" I asked.

With my basin—we have no running water at the tournament—Jack washed away my blood from his body, arms, and face. He donned his robe. "Nothing," he finally said, softly. He pulled the spacious cowl over his head to hide his face, returning to the unknown, unnamed "healer." "Nothing now, anyway. But the process took time, which meant you lost a tremendous amount of blood." He knocked on my bedroom door, alerting those on the other side. "You need a good night's rest. By this time tomorrow you'll be one hundred percent."

The door opened. Nathan, dressed in his Orator robe, poked his head in. He looked me up and down. To Jack, he asked, "You all right?"

"I admit, that was quite a challenge."

My Orator looked at me. "How 'bout you?"

I came up onto my elbows. "I could use some water."

Nathan looked at Jack, concerned. Jack nodded. "That's a good sign. She can eat something small, something plain, right now. She can have more in a couple of hours, if she feels like it."

As he passed Nathan to head out, Nathan stopped him. "Jack?" The brown robed man faced him. "I will *never* doubt you again. Thank you."

The healer gave a small bow and left the room. I overheard someone down stairs say, "Some crackers or bread, and some water."

Nathan sat on my bedside. "How are you … I mean, really?"

I flopped back onto my pillow. "I keep forgetting that he has to go through everything I'm going through."

He looked over his shoulder, into the hallway, presumably to watch Jack descend the small, winding staircase. "The Chancellor volunteered two additional healers to help you out, but Jack wouldn't …" He smiled at me. "That was a tremendous act on his part. In fact, I didn't think it was possible for just one man to heal so much … I was worried."

"Jack's good."

"Amazing, is more the word. If you want to thank him," he leaned forward a bit, *"don't let Archy do that again."*

Simple words, I thought.

Jeeves brought in a tray. I could smell the toast as soon as he entered the room. I hoisted myself up to sitting and Nathan propped up my pillow for my back to lean against.

"I'm so very glad to see you awake, madam," Jeeves said.

"Thank you. And thanks for the food."

"My pleasure." He bowed and left.

"So, uh," Nathan said as I munched, "you should be proud of yourself."

I nearly choked on my food. "Proud? The bout lasted, what, ten seconds?"

"Seven. But you're focusing on the wrong thing."

I shrugged. Not sure what more there was to focus on.

"Do you remember what happened?"

With a swallow I said, "He came at me like a mad hatter—"

"Stop. Before that."

I recalled the events. Archy burst open the doors and came at me. "I'm sticking to my mad hatter metaphor."

He rolled his eyes. "When did the bout start? When did he come at you?"

"Right away. He attacked before we started."

"We call that *cheating*, Winki. He came at you before he had cause, before he had permission. He came at you, he assaulted your Orator and healer,"—oh, yeah, they were tossed out of the ring —"and all before either of you were given the 'begin.'"

"Okay," I nodded. "So?"

He gave me a big, broad, happy smile. "Winki. He *cheated*." He let the words sink in. "The Arch Lich. The big, undefeated Champion, the meanest, most formidable opponent ever to darken these dreadful halls, *cheated*."

Still not following.

"Why?" he pressed. "He's never had to cheat before. He shows up, he kicks butt, he leaves. So why?"

I furrowed by brow, following Nathan's bread crumbs. "He had to?"

Nathan clapped his hands once, startling me. "Yes! He thinks it's possible. He thinks you can actually beat him. So he rattled your chain. He broke protocol, and came at you to put you off guard."

I wanted to share in his enthusiasm, but it was hard to feel good about what happened when I lay in a bed, my injuries taxing my healer, and still woozy with the loss of blood. "It worked," I muttered. "I still lost. I never even got close to him." I didn't get a single swing in, let alone determine how I'd get close enough to kill him.

With folded arms, he leaned against the window casing, looking out over the expanse of nothing that stretched as far as the eye could see. "I wanted you to be surprised at your next bout. I wanted you to see it on the board. The Chancellor told me, and only me. I haven't shared the news with anyone else."

"What?" I couldn't tell if this was good or bad news.

"You're a level forty-seven."

Mid-swallow when I heard this the toast suddenly stuck in my esophagus. I spasmed, coughing wildly. I gulped some water, and cleared my throat. "What?"

"They take everything into account. And not just the battles you've won. But your opponents. How they treat you, for example. You're unchallenged. No one put you on their list of opponents, which spoke volumes to the mages. Now this. Even they noticed Archy's behavior. That, too, spoke volumes. Add to that your two talents—"

"Which everyone seems to be able to resist," I blurted.

He ignored me, "—makes you the second highest ranked champion in the Citadel."

Archy was a level fifty. The highest possible rank.

"Even Will, who reigned supreme winner for eight years, never ranked higher than forty-two."

I heard the words, but as I lay in my little bed mending from being severed into two Winki pieces, I couldn't share in the joy. It meant nothing. How could I be so strong and yet so weak?

Nathan turned to leave. Before he opened my bedroom door, he said, "As your Orator, your brother-in-law, and your friend, I could *not* be prouder."

The door gently clicked behind him.

But I didn't do anything!

Chapter Twenty-Three

SINCE I STOOD unchallenged, I had the rest of that day and all the next to recover. I needed the time. With every passing hour, my strength returned. True to my healer's words, I felt fine the next day.

My next bout with Archy was scheduled for the Great Arena. I'd never been there and never saw it before. We left last year before the final battle. The one Malador won.

Unlike the smaller arenas, surrounded by a few bleachers for viewers, this arena was dwarfed by its surroundings, just a tiny dot of a stage in an grand amphitheater.

"The final battle is fought here," Nathan explained. "The seating is ample since everyone else is done fighting and typically wants to watch the last round."

"So, why are *we* here?" I asked, spinning slowly to look at the room, which was nearly half full by now. This wasn't the final battle. Hopefully.

"I'd guess popularity. The two highest ranked beings in the Citadel are going to fight." He chuckled. "Come to think of it, I can't remember when that's ever happened, since Archy never stick around for the final battle."

"Great," I muttered. As moments ticked by, as more and more attendees filled the stands, I felt manipulated. How did I get ranked so high? I didn't feel different. Sure, I felt stronger once I stepped into the ring, but my skills were the same, right? And while I appreciated the attendees's eagerness to see me ripped in half, we're still in stage three. Most of them should have their own battles.

"The mages rescheduled them," Nathan said.

I tilted my head. "We need to talk about mental boundaries."

"Sorry."

"What was I ranked before my slaughter with Archy?"

"Thirty-eight. Why do you ask?"

"That's a huge jump, isn't it? Thirty-eight to forty-seven? In just one bout? That I was annihilated in?"

I could see Nathan agreed, but he didn't admit it.

I just couldn't shake this feeling that I was being set up. But I couldn't see how it was to anyone's advantage.

Firstly, there was Lord Edmund, a mage. He and the other mages determined the rankings of all the champions. Assuming he wanted to win the wager—and who wouldn't want their own healer, especially one who single-handedly can put two halves of a being back together—a lower rank for me would ensure his victory, right? Perhaps the other mages didn't want to see him win the bet?

Secondly, there was Archy. My ranking was a direct consequence of his behavior. He'd won every battle he ever fought for the last, what, century? By rushing at me, by attacking before the fight began, he boosted my rank. So, why'd he do it? What did he gain by having a tougher opponent?

And why here? Why am I standing in—?

"Okay, stop," Nathan moaned. "You're giving me a headache."

Speaking of the devil, in he … crept. Slow and controlled this time. He stepped over the ropes as if they weren't there.

Before he got too close, I inserted the earplugs given to me by Smith and Wesson. Nothing fancy. Just those foam ones. It was the best they could do on such short notice. No one had any idea Archy's voice would be so debilitating.

"Good luck," Nathan patted my back as he and Jack slipped out of the ring.

I faced the lobster. He faced me.

"Begin."

I took a wide-legged stance, my halberd in my hand, its head lowered. If he rushed me now, I'd poke him in the eye. At least, I kept telling myself that.

He didn't move. Fine. I'll play.

I adjusted my weapon, holding it like a spear. I threw it at him, aiming for the soft spot in his head. I knew it wouldn't work. I just wanted to make him move.

He did. With a claw he swiped the air, knocking the item out of the ring. With that motion I dashed towards him. He swiped at me with the other claw, open to grab me. I jumped out of its way, into his face.

He backed up, and I reached out to grab … anything. I found something. I felt a pop in my hands, before stumbling to the floor.

Like everyone else in the auditorium, I held my ears, trying to protect them for the blood-curdling wail that filled the room.

Archy shrieked. Trying to collect myself through the head-splitting pain, I dropped something that, apparently, was in my hand. An antennae.

Liches feature six spiky protuberances upon their heads. Archy now had five.

While he screamed, my body seized. The earplugs helped with the sound somewhat, yet the painful vibration coursed through my skull. Every muscle in me clenched to the noise, his cry so abrasive, his volume so bone chilling. If he came at me now, I'd be done for. *I couldn't move.*

He didn't, though. He seemed to collect himself, which gave me a moment to get back on my feet. *Why on earth not?* My knees wobbled. My teeth ached. I was a sitting duck, for Hades sake.

Archy paced the ring, goading. He charged with claws snapping, each loud click a testament to his strength. I softened my vision, keeping my eyes on the destination, the floor in front of me. One claw neared—I ducked. The other swiped—I jumped, and I dove under his belly. I swiped my knife upward, hoping to cut his underside.

I left a scratch that looked like I keyed a car.

Agony gripped my foot. I flailed, grabbing at anything as he pulled me out from under him. He held me in the air, dangling upside down in front of him. By my ankle.

Which he severed.

My turn to scream now. I crawled on hands and one foot away from him, leaving a bloody trail. He came at me. I could hear his pointy feet ticking on the mat as he drew closer. I turned around, my knife poised.

I thrusted as the same time he did, me with my knife and Archy with a sword-like leg. My arms wasn't as long as his leg. I stood no chance.

He stepped on me. Threw me. His leg punched down with ease, like a hot knife through butter.

"Winner. Realm of Cardamom."

With a grimace, I laid my head on the floor. *Forty-seven, huh?*

I didn't notice Jack kneel down beside me. But I was fully aware when he stuck his fingers into my stomach. *Didn't we just do this?*

I turned away in an attempt not to watch. Archy slowly turned, head hung, to leave the arena.

"Hey," I called to him. A mistake. A rip of electricity shot from head to toe. I heard Jack grunt.

It got Archy's attention. The massive crustacean turned to face me, and patiently waited while Jack sealed me up.

I sat upright while my healer moved onto my foot. I had tons of questions. "Why did you rush me?" "Why didn't you kill me when you used your voice?" "Why do you show up year after year and never claim the prize?" But I decided he'd never answer any of those.

I reached out, grabbing the antennae that lay near me. "You forgot this." I tossed it to him. He caught it, put it back in place, and healed *all on his own.*

Archy turned and left.

∼ ∼ ⚭ ⚭ ⚭

Another day to recover. I pushed my peas around my plate, lost in my thoughts and unaware of the chatter around me. He could heal. All on his own. That explained why he didn't bring a healer, or request one from the Citadel. He could do that whenever he wanted, including during a battle.

Any injury I gained had to wait until the end.

What chance did I possibly have?

"Did you hear me, *ma chére?*"

"Hercule!" I sat upright, happy to see him. Yes. That's right. Happy to see a cockroach.

"I see you wallow in your failures, hm?"

"Something like that," I confessed. It dawned on me. "Please tell me you didn't fail."

"Perish the thought! The Great Hercule never fails!"

I beamed. Finally, some good news.

"What now?" Nathan asked.

"Mr. Smith, Mr. Wesson? Get ready for Phase Two. Hercule, please go with them."

"Also, I have brought with me some interesting news, *mes amis,*" the bug said. "All is not happy in the Citadel."

"We knew that," Mr. Smith said. "That's why you … you know," he waved his hand.

"No, no. But I mean something more." Hercule sat up in front of me. "I overheard the Chancellor and Lord Edmund. They argued, with much heat. Apparently, the lost four months was, in fact, an error. The wraiths and mages have been scrambling to be ready for the games. The Chancellor said it was a minor miracle they pulled it off. That was why checking-in was so slow this year, *comprenez vous?*"

Admittedly, I felt a little better. I looked at my healer. "At least the time loss wasn't an attempt to cheat."

Though I couldn't see his face, I'd bet he rolled his eyes.

"Thank you again, Hercule. Now, off with you three."

No one talked of details, no one asked specifics. We couldn't be sure of what privacy we genuinely had in the Citadel. I didn't need to know what Hercule found out, I didn't need to hear the name.

But if all hell broke loose, everyone else would.

~ ~ * ~ ~

Back in the big ring for the third bout we waited. "Three's a charm," Nathan told me. I think for the third time.

The auditorium brimmed with hushed murmurs, as if waiting for the curtain to rise. I suppose they were. I, on the other hand, waited for the guillotine to fall.

My eyebrows lifted as I noticed Lord Edmund enter the auditorium. He made a beeline to the arena, all the while un-excitedly clapping his hands. "Well done, Mrs. Witherspoon! Well done."

Nathan and I exchanged glances.

"I've come be to congratulate you on your brilliant strategy. Well played. It's almost a certainty you'll win the tournament now."

So ... why did I have a sneaking suspicion things were about to go very badly very quickly?

"I admit, the idea of challenging the undefeated one to boost your ranking was truly magnificent. Once he abandons, and we all know he will, it will be you everyone has to beat."

"Um, that was the plan."

"All you have to do is finish the games. Isn't it?"

I nodded, and gulped, at the same time.

He took a seat, interlaced his fingers, placing the tips of his indexes on his lips. He gave me a wink. Every inch of my skin crawled.

What was I missing? I had that sinking feeling I'd forgotten something important, something critical.

I looked at Nathan. He, too, watched Lord Edmund. In a hushed voice he said, "We are about to get blind-sided." He trotted to another side of the ring. "Jeeves?" The butler stood. "Do me a favor? Go back to the suite. Make sure everything is okay?"

"As you wish, sir." I watched him leave, an effort that reminded me of salmon swimming upstream as he struggled against the tide of spectators coming in.

Nathan turned to me. "You know, I long for the good old days of the tournament. We'd come, we'd fight, we'd leave. The last three years have been like playing a game of chess with half the pieces behind a curtain. I just can't see what's going on."

"I can't even play chess," I sighed.

The room fell quiet. Archy had entered the venue and climbed into the arena.

Nathan took my elbow. "I'm going to go back to the suite, too. I gotta bad feeling ... You good here?" He looked at my healer and me.

We nodded.

"Break a leg," Nathan said as he left, trotting up the bleachers and out the door.

I should be so lucky.

With a smile I looked at the black, giant lobster. "Archy!" I bowed.

He growled.

Jack put a warm hand on my shoulder, gave a confidence-building squeeze, and exited by slipping through the ropes. I twisted my woefully inadequate earplugs into place, and readied my knife and hammer. Oldies but goodies.

"Begin."

I took a settling inhale, and as I exhaled, I heard Nathan's voice in my head. *"I want you to watch where my feet are. I want you to know what step I'm going to take next."* I softened my vision, focusing on nothing in particular. And yet I saw everything. I saw Archy sway his massive claws, I saw all six of his legs, adjusting, shifting ... they charged.

Ducking one claw, I leaped over the other, spun and smacked Archy across the face. With a somersault, I scurried out of his reach and readied myself again.

The room erupted in applause as Archy moved sideways, all the while keeping his fierce claws facing me.

I repeated my new mantra in my head: *Soft eyes. Soft eyes. Soft eyes.*

Archy swayed, his massive body fluidly moving left and right. He was trying to hypnotize me. Had I been watching him, I'm confident it would have worked. But I watched, well, nothing. I noticed when he charged.

I evaded him again. I spun three-sixty and used that momentum to swing my hammer. I connected with something solid but yielding.

I broke one of his legs. His shrieking crippled me. It crippled everyone in the auditorium, but only I was at his mercy. I couldn't look up. I couldn't stand up. Hell, I couldn't move. I felt his voice like a giant knife piercing my skull. I clutched my head and dropped to my knees.

Surely, this time, he'd finish me.

I waited for the explosion of gore; a claw around my waist, or a leg through my torso. But it never came.

Once he stopped screeching I quickly stood, scrambling a safe distance from him.

Why didn't he kill me? Why didn't he take advantage of my helplessness?

Why was everything about fighting this guy so blasted confusing?

As I watched, I noticed the broken leg moving. *Healing.*

I had a small window of advantage. I took it.

Dashing around him, I moved toward his injured side. Archy responded slower than usual. He reached out with a claw, I bashed it out of my way, spun and jumped, and used the bad leg as a step. With my entire body I reached up, stabbing at the lobster with my knife, trying to hit "the mark."

He ducked, spun, and the centrifugal force flung me into the ropes. Before I could find my feet, his tail swatted me, sending me sailing out of the ring.

Kind hands and bodies caught me, as if I landed in a mosh pit. I rode a wave of hands, tentacles, and talons back into the ring.

Not that I really wanted to go there.

My time out was enough for Archy to fully recover. I lost my advantage.

We circled each other again, like distant dancing partners.

Archy attacked me several times, and each time I barely avoided getting killed. To my chagrin, I never had an opportunity to reach the height of his head, let alone stab him in the soft spot. We must have sparred for nearly an hour, and as Will suggested, I kept him moving, kept him working. But he showed no signs of slowing, no signs of fatigue.

Unlike me.

After an hour of blocking, jumping, spinning and running, my lungs ached for air and sweat stung my eyes. I had avoided injury, but gained nothing. I really missed those four months of training time. *Curse you, Lord Edmund.*

The lobster advanced. I dodged, spun, struck at his leg with my hammer, but missed, hitting his exoskeleton hard. It felt like I'd hit a block of cement. The result made my skull rattle.

I dropped the hammer and stumbled back, stunned.

A claw closed around my throat.

Oh, no ... not again ...

With ease he lifted me off the ground. My feet flailed as I kicked, trying madly to connect with something. Anything!

He drew me in to him, face to face. I wrapped my hands around the claw, pulling up to lessen the strain on my throat. Why didn't he just do it? *C'mon, already, just snap the neck and be done with it!*

"You," he said, his voice causing me to convulse. "You just might work."

"W-w-work?" I gasped. Not easy talking with a claw around your neck.

Airborne. I flew fast and hard. I noticed the crowd below me, the myriad of attendees, their faces upturned as they watched me soar through the air.

Into blackness.

Chapter Twenty-Four

Jack and I sat in the empty auditorium, our backs against the wall, our knees drawn up under our chins. Sulking.

We hadn't moved from the spot where he healed me, my neck broken from the impact of hitting the wall. The healing took just a few minutes. When he'd finished, people were still leaving the room. I sat up, he joined me, and there we sat. Did I mention sulking?

"I'm sorry," he whispered, being the first to break the silence.

"What for?" I asked. "None of this is your fault."

"I encouraged you to sign the contract. That put an added and unnecessary burden upon you."

I patted his robe-draped knee. "It's not your fault we lost four months, Jack. As it is, I'm in a good position to win this thing. I've beaten two of the elementals now, Air and Fire, both of which are among the toughest competitors. And my rank is crazy high, thanks to Archy. It didn't go the way we hoped, but I'm feeling confident." A lie, but I passed it off with a sound voice.

He pulled his hood back. I tried to hide my shock at the maneuver; Jack was a stickler for rules, and exposing one's face as a healer was a big no-no.

He said, "I want you to know how deeply I appreciate your efforts, ma'am." I looked into his blue-green eyes. "No one has given so much of themselves for me before."

I wanted to quip, to make light of the situation. But he rarely opened up to me. "You're welcome."

The door flew open, and Jack quickly covered himself.

A man in a blue suit said, "There you are!"

It took me a moment to recognize him. He traveled with a competitor who also resided in our tower.

"You need to go to your rooms, quickly. Something's happened!"

Cripes! I forgot Jeeves and Nathan left the game early.

We followed the informant and trotted down the torch-lit hallways until we reached our tower.

A rock developed in the pit of my stomach as I laid eyes on the small crowd milling about outside our tower's door. I excused myself repeatedly as Jack and I wiggled our way into the lobby.

Which was trashed; furniture broken, walls holed (consider, for a moment, that these were stone), debris strewn everywhere. Several people, Jeeves included, knelt around someone sprawled on the floor. We quickened our step as we approached the butler, who looked up at us.

"Thank goodness you're here, Jack," he said to the healer. "Please. He needs help."

Dorm master Jeff reclined, unmoving on the floor. A gash across his normally jolly cheek oozed red fluid. Not blood … exactly.

"Yes," I told Jack, unsure if he needed my permission. "Heal him." I asked Jeeves, "What happened?"

"Griffins, madam." *Griffins?* "Several of them burst in and attacked everything and everyone. I realized it was a distraction when two started upstairs to our suite. I followed, but we couldn't stop them before … I'm afraid to say, madam, but they took Mrs. Jolly."

I sucked in my breath. "Took her? Where?"

"I regret that I don't know. Just outside our window was a waiting portal. They flew into it, but without my talent, I have no idea where it lead."

Before I could turn to check on the rest of my group, in they walked. The grand Chancellor and best bud, Lord Edmund. "What is going on here?" the Chancellor looked around, eyes wide. If he was acting, he would have gotten an Oscar. I believe this took him by surprise. His sidekick, on the other hand, didn't strike me as surprised so much as angered, like this wasn't part of the plan.

Jeff stirred, moaning as he recovered. I resumed my dash upstairs.

Our room, too, had sustained damage. The large table lay on its side, pots and pans littered the floor, even the staircase banister was broken.

"Winki!" Mr. Smith called from somewhere. I moved towards his voice, spying his arm waving over some debris. He and Mr. Wesson knelt over the body of …

"Nathan!" I screamed out the door, "Jack! Jack!"

I put a hand on his face. His skin felt cool and looked ashen in color. Sweat beaded on his forehead.

"He's not dead. He was bit," Mr. Smith said quickly. "One of the griffins bit him." He pointed to Nathan's arm and the tidy triangle of red dots exposed under his torn robe. "They're crazy poisonous."

Jack reached us, taking just two long running strides to kneel next to his partner. He looked at the bite and placed his fingers over it. A moment passed, then another. Nothing happened.

He sat back. "I can't heal him, ma'am, I'm sorry."

"What do you mean, you can't heal him?"

"Poisons are tricky. But griffin poison … is impossible. It's more like a curse than a poison. I'm so sorry."

"He won't die, right? I mean, there must be something—"

I stopped when I saw him enter the room. Prowled, really. Lord Edmund, eyes on Nathan, crept towards him, like a cat towards an unsuspecting mouse.

Hands in his pockets, he stood tall, looking down on Nathan and me. He clucked, insincerely. "What a tragedy. I give him two, maybe three days before he dies."

I couldn't shake the feeling he knew about the attack before it happened.

"No one's dying, pal," Mr. Smith said. "There are several cures," he said, reading over Mr. Wesson's hand as it scribbled on his computer pad. "For one, we could destroy the griffin that did it; that would break the bond. Or ... or ... that's it?" Mr. Wesson solemnly nodded.

I needed to get to the Radiant Plane, and now. "Jeeves, make me a portal—"

"Interesting," Lord Edmund said. I froze, sickened by the tone. "If you leave now you abandon the tournament. That means ..." His eyes wandered to Jack. "Well, I think we all know what that means."

Molten lava coursed through my stomach. "You can't hold me to that contract when—"

"But if you stay, and fight, and finish, well, your Orator will perish." The bastard smiled.

I clenched my fists. *Yes, this definitely went according to his plan.*

Lord Edmund stood in my personal space. "I'm not a heartless being, Mrs. Witherspoon, so I'll agree to modify our arrangement. Let's put all the chips on your next battle, how's that? You lose, I get your healer. You win, you get the name you wanted, and you'll still have time to save your Orator." My mind raced, trying to find the loop hole. Dammit, I really needed a lawyer right now. "Agreed?" He offered me his hand.

I looked at Jack, then Jeeves, then Smith and Wesson, then the placid face of the man on the floor. I couldn't pick any one person to sacrifice; not Jack, nor Nathan, nor Saffron. If there was a chance I could save them all, how could I not try? Besides, I consoled myself, I was highly ranked now. One battle, not the whole tournament, so victory should be mine. Right?

I hope I don't regret this. "Agreed." We shook. I already regretted touching his clammy hand.

"By hell's night!"

I looked up at the Chancellor, who raced into the room. "What's happened here?" he exasperated as he looked around.

I thrusted my chin at Lord Edmund. "Ask your friend."

The Chancellor scowled. "Edmund? Do you know anything about this?"

Before he could answer, Jeeves offered, "Griffins, Chancellor. I'd guess about five of them. Two of them came up here and attacked Nathan …" His eyes widened when he saw our Orator on the floor. He regained his composure and continued, "Nathan and our cook, Mrs. Jolly. They took her," he pointed out the window, "through there to a waiting portal." Jeeves looked at me. "Madam, when I left to go downstairs he was fine. I don't understand."

"Griffin bit him," Mr. Smith growled.

"Where was the portal going?" the Chancellor asked.

"I don't know, sir," said Jeeves.

Lord Edmund smiled, coldly calm. "Griffins come from the Radiant Plane. Perhaps we should speak to those competitors?"

"Indeed." To me the Chancellor said, "We can move Nathan to my office. He'll be safer——"

"He'll stay here," I fumed. "The damage is already done."

"As you wish. I'll gather the names of Radiant competitors and send out the wraith to ask questions. If I find out who's done this, Mrs. Witherspoon, you will be the next to know." He took a step away, looking down at Nathan. "I'm so very sorry." He tisked. "And we came with such good news."

"What news, sir?" Jeeves asked.

"We've had a special request." He gestured at Lord Edmund. "Under normal circumstance we'd be inclined to ignore it, but this stage of the tournament has proven rather, how shall I say, *thrilling.*"

I gathered by his tone that I, for one, would not be thrilled.

"If you recall, we had asked the competitors to give us their three choices for battle early in the second stage. But we received one recently. By a competitor who, prior to now, had not given any names."

"Let me guess," I said. "They chose me." I cast a quick glance at Lord Edmund. He knew. He knew before he offered me a new deal. He knew *exactly* who my next battle would be against. *Winki, you're an idiot.*

"They did!" the Chancellor nodded. "And we wanted to know if you'd be willing to appease them. There will be no penalty on your part for declining, I assure you. The choice is all yours."

Not now, it wasn't. "Can I ask who challenged me?" Esmeralda? Malador? Someone trying to "make their bones?"

He and Lord Edmund exchanged looks. "Why, the Arch Lich, of course!"

"Archy?" I repeated.

"Who's ... Archy?" the confused Chancellor asked Lord Edmund.

"The Arch Lich," the Lord condescended. "That's her pet name for him."

"Ah. Yes. Archy, then."

If only my eyes could kill. I stared at Lord Edmund. "When?"

"Well," the Chancellor stammered, "given this is the last day of the third stage, and we do like to keep to a schedule—"

"Tonight," Lord Edmund burst. "After dinner." He gave a sinister smile, one only I could see.

My eyes darted across the faces of my staff. All of them looked at me. All of them had heard the deal I just made. All of them knew what was at risk.

That bastard Edmund, he *knew* my next bout would be with the Arch Lich, the one competitor I can't beat. Hadn't beat.

Slow down, Winki. The deal was on the *next* bout. Just because this came up didn't mean I had to accept it. The Chancellor made this *my* call. I could decline to fight the lobster and wait for the next bout, which surely would be easier.

However, that might not be soon enough. I might not fight in the next couple of days, once we start stage four. In fact, I'd wager Lord Edmund would somehow manipulate my schedule to ensure exactly that. Nathan didn't have days. Saffron might not, either.

No. I had to get out of this tournament now.

"But under the circumstance," the Chancellor said, "this might not be the right time. I suppose—"

"Yes," I said flatly. "I accept."

"Um ... Very well. I'll make the arrangements." The Chancellor turned to leave but hesitated, and bowed before me. "I'm so very sorry for all this, good Champion. I will get to the bottom of it, I promise you. Edmund? Are you coming?"

Lord Edmund nodded to me. "I'll see you in a few hours, good lady." He bowed, "And gentlemen."

Once I felt confident they were out of earshot I spoke to Smith and Wesson. "Please tell me everything is in order?" My eyes were fixed to my unmoving brother-in-law.

"Yes, ma'am," Mr. Smith whispered, still watching the door the Chancellor and Edmund left through. "Just the push of a button."

"Good," I exhaled a heated breath. "Bring everything that's important with you to the next fight. Win or lose, all of us—we're getting out of here."

Chapter Twenty-Five

I DIDN'T KNOW if the roomful of people knew what had happened to our house, that griffins attacked and took one of our own. I didn't care. I just wanted to end this, right here, right now.

My entourage occupied the front row. Jack and Jeeves sat on either side of Nathan, propped in a chair. He looked like he'd just nodded off, except for his waxen skin. Hercule took a position on Nathan's shoulder. Next to them sat Mr. Smith and Mr. Wesson, with several backpacks and bags scattered at their feet. We had brought only what we could carry, what we cared about most.

I leaned on the ropes in front of them. "Just to be clear. As soon as the outcome is announced—"

"Yeah, yeah," Mr. Smith said. "We got it. We got it fifty times ago."

Nathan looked peaceful. "Is he suffering?" I asked them.

"No, madam," Jeeves answered. "Those who've been aroused from the Griffin Slumber only recall sleeping."

A cold comfort, I supposed. I kept myself from looking into the crowd. Everyone was here this time. I didn't want to see Malador or Esmeralda or give anyone an opportunity to rattle or distract me. I was doing a fine job of that myself.

My hands quaked. I couldn't feel my feet. It felt so wrong to be in the ring waiting by myself, as if abandoned. Jack had offered to stand with me, but I wanted him to be near Nathan. Just in case.

Applause erupted from the crowd as Archy climbed over the ropes. Finally. But that wasn't who received the applause, I realized. From the other side of the ring, the great Chancellor entered as well.

I heard Archy sigh, expressing the same frustration I experienced. *Delays.* "I'm with you, brother," I huffed.

"Greetings, one and all! It is my pleasure and honor to share this unique opportunity with you, a grand battle between good and evil, between the Midland and Phantom Planes ..." and on and on.

I lolled my head back and said to Archy, "Just kill me now, please."

"Hm," he growled somewhat jovially. "Patience."

After what seemed like hours the Chancellor finally said, " ... Mrs. Winki Witherspoon, and the Ruler Of Cardamom Realm, the Arch Lich!"

I envisioned it one last time as the frail Chancellor shuffled himself off the floor. Each move, each stroke, each step ... I rehearsed it over and over in my mind. Will was wrong. Archy couldn't be exhausted. I had to do it quickly. My one shot. If it failed, I would be completely open and exposed and ...

I was about to disappoint everyone here, because it would only be seconds before, either way, the bout was ended. A lot of hype for something so quick.

But I at least, for the first time in days, knew what to try. *My one shot.*

Finally, he left. Finally, we two stood alone in the ring. I didn't bother to put in my earplugs this time, for all the use they'd had been.

"Begin."

I advanced, which immediately took Archy by surprise. He backed away, his immense claws wide and waiting. One swiped, I ducked rolling towards him, the other swiped, I leapt up, and grabbed some plating on his chest, raising my legs just out of the way. He shook, trying to dislodge me, and I used that momentum to swing, flipping my body up and onto his neck. I straddled him as he bucked and spun, much like riding a mechanical bull. He raised a claw to reach me. With my left hand, armed with my hammer, I blocked the blow, and my other—*and with every fiber of my being*—I thrust my dagger between his eyes.

My own head nearly burst from the agonizing shriek, the long and guttural, deafening cry that shook my core, shook the floor, shook the walls and chairs and bodies of everyone and everything in the room.

I don't know how I got to the mat, cowering there, holding my head to keep it from splitting into a million pieces. That didn't help the electric rattling of my bones. *Damn, that lobster's voice!*

It abruptly ended. Everyone watched as the hulking, black crustacean, like a felled tree, toppled to the floor.

"Winner. House of Gateway."

The room exploded in noise again, but this time from people and creatures applauding, cheering, waving their arms, and jumping up and down with such enthusiasm as to shake the room.

I paid it all no mind. I rushed to the ropes and hollered to my entourage, "Move! Move! Move!" as I thrust a thumb toward the ring.

Jack shifted Nathan over his shoulder into a fireman's carry as they all clamored over the ropes and into the ring.

"Jeeves," I ordered. "Now."

Once in the ring where his talent was active, Jeeves swept his arm wide and summoned a portal, our way back home.

Lord Edmund and the Chancellor climbed into the ring. "And where are you going, Mrs. Witherspoon?" Lord Edmund asked.

"Home. Kidnapped cook, griffin's poison, work to do."

Jack started towards the portal.

"Halt!" Lord Edmund called to him. "If you're leaving you owe me a healer."

"Um," I pointed to the black lobster, who occupied over half the ring reclined, "maybe you weren't paying attention, but I won that bet. As a matter of fact, you owe me a name." I waved my fingers in a "give it to me" manner.

"As a matter of fact," he said, stepping closer, "the healer is mine." I lowered my eyebrows. "We never modified the contract."

"We shook on it."

"Hand shakes mean nothing in the Citadel."

I folded my arms. *Meathead.* Sadly, I wasn't at all surprised. And I didn't have time to argue. So, I spoke loudly and clearly. "You're not going to honor the death of an innocent man, nor the unbinding of the fabric of the Citadel, nor a deal we secured with a handshake? None of those things mean anything to you?"

That got everyone's attention. The entire room, still full of attendees, stopped to hear the conversation. Some of them began concerned whispering.

"Mrs. Witherspoon, we told you," the Chancellor added. "There's nothing wrong with the Citadel."

Lord Edmund never responded. He didn't have to, I knew his answer.

I pointed at Jack and nodded to the windy sphere. "Go," I commanded, and he disappeared through the portal, Nathan over his shoulder.

I addressed the Lord. "Let me make myself clear, Edmund. As long as I am alive, the healer is mine. I never expected you to be honest, but I did think, as a mage, you'd be fair. A handshake may mean nothing to the Citadel, but since you offered it, it should mean something to you. To reneg now, since you clearly lost, is called *cheating*." I shrugged. "But, then again, I cheated, too." Eyes on the Lord, I pointed to the lab coat. "Mr. Smith?"

My geek raised his hand, which held a small remote with only one red button. He pressed it. As the noise started, he and Mr. Wesson stepped through.

Will's voice came through loud and clear. *"Listen to me. It wasn't the healer. They killed him on my behalf, before I had my faculties back to defend him. I'm asking you, please. Don't let that poor man, Reggie Walters, go unspoken for. Clear his name. Make sure they know. They killed an innocent man in the Citadel."* Pause. *"Listen to me. It wasn't the healer. They killed him on my behalf..."*

Over and over my husband's voice repeated with the name dubbed in.

The Chancellor and Lord Edmund looked at each other, eyes wide. "How did she—?"

"I don't know!"

"Turn that off!"

I gave a small bow as I backed myself toward the portal and my butler, who "held the door open" for me. Together, we stepped through.

Chapter Twenty-Six

ONCE HOME, JACK and I threw some water on our faces. Jack changed into more appropriate garb for our hot destination. I still wore my baby blues, still stained with Archy's black ichor. I confess, I looked like the lich bringer-of-doom, which suited my mood—instead of wallowing in worry for Nathan and Saffron, anger seemed a preferable option.

Only thirty minutes later, we took our first steps into the Radiant Plane. Once the portal popped out of existence, I took in my surroundings.

I'd learned from Jeeves and Mrs. Black that the five dominant planes were variants of our own plane, other versions of our own planet. The Radiant Plane was what our world would look like if it were stuck in the dark ages with no industrial revolution, and the sun were a good deal closer.

We set foot in a little town that reminded me of a Clint Eastwood spaghetti western. We stood on a narrow dirt road. Brick and adobe buildings lined the street, gapped with missing windows and doors, some in ruins, becoming one with the dusty ground. Wooden walkways had eroded into holes, splinters, and timber shards.

Thanks to my leathers I felt little of the relentless sun on my skin. The stifling heat scorched the air, burning my nose, the back of my throat, right into my lungs. A sickly, bright red glow illuminated everything. A not-at-all-refreshing breeze whipped a fine layer of dust upon us, tossing dried thistle across our path.

I knew exactly where I was. Every nexus point was the same on every plane, so the five hot spots of my world (New Orleans, Natal, Prague, Bangkok, and that small, unpronounceable island in Hawaii) aligned with the same five hot spots here. I didn't need to read the half-fallen sign to know I was in New Orleans.

Which was a good thing, since the sign read *Bucktown*.

"New Orleans is a swamp," I remarked as we walked over the sandy landscape.

We watched another tumble weed blow by. "Apparently not here," Jack surmised.

I was glad Jack changed. He wore a long-sleeved white linen shirt and matching white linen pants, made to completely cover his body yet remain cool. I had gave him the outfit for Christmas last year, since healers need to be clad as much as possible—another silly healer rule—and New Orleans' summers were both sticky and stifling. He had never worn it until now. It had an SPF rating of 45, otherwise Jack's usually pale skin would become painfully red in moments. Even so, we needed to get out of the blistering sun and heat as quickly as possible.

I'd asked Jeeves to drop us at Esmeralda's front door, but he couldn't. He explained that she, too, had a doorman who would alert her, and we'd be instantly captured. Or worse, killed. Thus, the hike.

Jack and I faced our direction of travel. "Ravenswood should be over there," I remarked.

"Diamond Realm, ma'am."

"Whatever. Evil … This-a-way."

As we passed the last building in Bucktown, I noticed the cross atop what was left of its steeple. My head filled with memories.

My vision of Will as the altar burst into flames … hearing my own voice say to Jeeves, "The Radiant Plane is known for its mastery over fire" … "The Radiant plane is the fourth plane" …

The fourth is where your next clue will be.

"Ma'am? Are you all right?"

I pointed to the church. "Here. It has to be here."

Dashing into the lopsided and wholly unsafe building, Jack followed, close on my heels. As my healer, he wouldn't let me out of arm's reach. Especially after the graveyard incident.

Gingerly, I made my way over the partially fallen stone walls. The wooden roof had long since caved in, half of it clinging to the high walls by sheer force of will. I managed to get a fair bit into the building, all the while looking for what I thought might be Will's choice for the perfect hiding place.

Jack forged ahead, shuffling his way to the back. He peered under a portion of fallen roof. "Ma'am? I may have found something."

I joined him, leaning over to see what lay under the dusty slats. He hoisted them higher, kicking up a plume of dust, revealing a delicate and ornate silver tabernacle.

"Can you lift a little higher? Please, be careful." None of this looked solid, nor safe.

He managed, barely allowing me to reach the tiny little door of the metal box. It clicked open.

A DVD.

With a smile, I waved it in front of him.

Jack slowly lowered his load. As he scratched his head, he said, "I must confess, I'm still quite befuddled by the riddle. But congratulations, ma'am."

"*The sentence, the burden, and the falter make three,*" I explained. "Those are the first three stations of the cross. He was telling me I'd find it in a church. The last line told me which church. The church I'd find on the fourth plane." I tucked my prize under my leather jacket and led the way back out … when … I sneezed.

"Bless you, ma'am."

"Yes. Bless you."

We froze. We turned.

Malador.

Unlike I'd ever seen him before. His eyes glowed hot red. His arm shot forward, unleashing a gush of fire flowing as if from a massive hose, perfectly tubular and deadly precise. Jack and I hit the floor, barely escaping the rush of heat that scorched our backs.

Gathering my wits, I waved my hand and slowed him down. We collected our feet beneath us, getting out from under the molten-looking stream of fire, and ran as fast as we could over the broken boards and slats. Jack's foot broke through the brittle timber, effectively tripping and trapping him. Using my hammer as a lever I jammed it into the wood, attempting to free his leg.

The daylight around us dimmed, which offered some relief from the wicked sunlight, but felt unnatural. We both looked up.

Griffins. Hundreds of them.

The griffins neared us, shrieking. Their leathery wings *whomp*ed with every beat. They circled so chaoticly I wondered how they kept from knocking each other out of the sky. Closer and closer they hovered, spiraling to the earth, filling our ears and blackening the sky.

Two swooped down on us like leathery lightning, with ear-piercing cries and sharp talons exposed. I swished my hand, both to defend myself as well as slow them in mid-flight. Jack twisted and pulled, freeing his ankle. We ran from the structure, trying to get out from under the angry birds. More swooped down, and again, with a wave of my hand, they paused, swaying in mid-air.

They didn't look quite as I expected them to. Each had a massive cat-like body, enormous leathery wings, and a serrated beak of a nose. But they had no fur. Just skin, and lots of it; ample quantities of thick and coriaceous hide that wrinkled over massive muscle, like the skin of an elephant or rhinoceros. Perhaps the creatures were expected to grow more and fill it out.

"Stay behind me," I called to Jack.

My talent, while powerful, has a limited range. Any griffin outside its radius stayed quite nimble. If I missed by a fraction, an unaffected birds would quickly halved the gap.

But I had a handy hammer. I would slow 'em with one hand, whack 'em with another. Swish and strike, twist and turn, swish again. I found a rhythm in it. Eyes alert, movement fluid ... I could do it all day long. I mean, *I* could ...

"Ma'am! Ma'aaaaam!"

From over my shoulder I saw Jack in the talons of two griffins. With just a few beats of their immense wings, they swept Jack into the claret colored sky. *No!* That moment of distraction was just enough for something to whack me from behind, sending me to the dusty and broken floor below. I jumped to my feet, readying myself to fight the griffin that buffeted me with its wing. But none came. All the creatures backed off, either hovering just out of my reach or retreating to the broken walls around me.

I looked to the sky. Jack and the two griffins who captured him were just a spec in the distance. My mind filled with horrible thoughts. *What if they bit him? What if they ate him? What if they simply let go?* A heat of rage and guilt pulled the corners of my mouth painfully low. *Stupid girl.* I could have noted the DVD's home and come back for it when I'd done what I *actually* came here to do. But no, I had to get it now.

Malador clapped his hands and laughed. "*Pft.* This from the mighty Winki Witherspoon, the woman who beat the Arch Lich?"

I kept my eyes toward the noxious rouge sky, purposely avoiding his gaze. I seethed, "Bring him back."

"How terribly disappointing," he added, ignoring my demand.

"If you want to do a round with me, I'm happy to oblige, Malador," I said. I could really stand to take this guilt out on someone about now. I pointed to the ever-shrinking speck. "You bring him back."

"Oh, I think not. Sister-of-mine is waiting. Besides. He's fine. He'll reach his destination unharmed. Once there, however …" He gave a fiendish smile. "Best to hurry."

I wanted to do just that. I decided, however, not to show my worry, which would be acknowledged as a weakness, so I busied myself by dusting off my clothes. Moreover, I wanted to stall looking at him. I knew the effect his gaze would have. "Where are they taking him?" I finally looked up. "You hurt him, so help me, I'll kill you."

"Well, good news for me, then, as I have absolutely no intentions of harming that man in any way." He pouted as he made a small X across his chest. "Cross my heart."

I glared at him. Damn that gorgeous face … How was it possible to want to kill and kiss a man at the same time? I glanced again in Jack's direction. He was no longer in view. I hung my head, ashamed of my failure.

"Come now, my love. It's not all bad. They're taking him to the castle, and as it happens, I'm on my way there, now." He offered an elbow. "Care to join me?"

"Castle, yes, You, no."

"I promise, no harm will come to you."

I shot him a hot look. "You just shot fire at me."

"I missed on purpose. Please. Give me some credit."

I showed no signs of accepting his offer.

"Winki … may I call you Winki?"

"No."

"Winki, how many times do I have to tell you? I don't want you dead. I want you by my side. I want your house and my house to align, more so now that you've proven yourself to be the strongest among us. Together we could rule, not just our world, but all the planes uncontested. No one would rise against the great Queen

Winki, and her dashing, roguish King. That would be me, by the way."

I bit my lip, fighting the warm vibration that flooded my body. *Those soft locks of hair, those chocolate pools of eyes, that perfect chiseled jaw ...*

I turned my gaze, before I did something I regretted.

"Take my arm and come with me. No tricks, I swear."

"I've made way too many deals with you darkling devils already this week."

He winced, "Yes, that bit with Lord Edmund." He let out an audible shudder. "Even sis and I keep our distance from him when we can." He made a grand sweep with his arm, forming a portal. Malador offered his elbow again. "Take my arm. Come with me. Or ..." He nodded in a direction. I spied the line of griffins that perched along the wall like blackbirds on a telephone line. "Or travel there in the same manner as your healer."

I weighed my options.

"I am better company, I assure you."

Malador or the griffins. Hard call. While the griffins kept me out of his reach, they could bite me, or dump me in a pit somewhere. Then I'd be of no use to Saffron or Nathan. Or Jack.

Or go with Malador.

True, he only needed to touch me to "turn" me, which he made clear was his intention. But both of us were clad from from head to toe in our leathers. We'd have to be cheek to cheek to touch, and given he was a good bit taller, well, surely, I could see that coming, right?

I considered the windy orb. While I didn't like the idea of taking his arm, it was a little bit of insurance. The other side could be the bottom of some ocean. Going arm in arm ensured that, whatever might lie on the other side, we'd face it together. Moreover, since he had opened the portal, it would close once he stepped through, leaving me in the heat and dust and a mile from the castle.

So. Together.

With my right hand on my hammer, I threaded my left though his arm.

Side by side we stepped through.

Chapter Twenty-Seven

WHEN THE PORTAL behind us disappeared, we stood before gilded gates hinged on stone walls. An enormous symbol I didn't recognize adorned them, nearly blocking the view beyond. But I could make out a stretch of long and winding road, made from paving stones, leading to a crystal edifice.

The castle, I had to admit, was impressive. It positively twinkled in the dazzling, red sunlight, probably an optical illusion from the heat shimmers. Though I stood a fair distance away, it loomed tall and proud, with five spires, each a different height, and each capped with a shiny, green cones. Such an odd contrast, this elegant and opulent structure, with the surrounding desolation, decay, and disaster.

"Whoa," I couldn't help but utter.

"You're impressed?" Malador asked. "Don't be."

"It's a crystal castle, for cripes sake. I mean, I love my house, but it's a house."

"It's an illusion," he sighed. "Trust me. The place is brick and mud, just like all the other structures on this forsaken plane."

Distracted by the glistening building, I missed the tiny and unassuming house squatting next to the gates. It blended into the wall so well that, until Malador spoke to the man inside it, I didn't know it was there.

"Gatesman, sister-of-mine is expecting me," Malador said with an air of snobbery.

Sitting just inside the open door stood a guard, clad in leathers. Well, *half* a guard. The other half lacked skin and any muscle, just bloody bone with bits of draping meat, as if his flesh had been torn from his body. Yesterday.

I turned away, trying to hide my disgust. I'm sure, however, I grunted my revulsion.

The gates grandly swung inward, groaning a bit as they moved. I focused on them and the task at hand, trying to remove the image of that poor man from my mind.

Malador noticed my reaction. As we crossed beyond the castle walls, he explained, "The people here have learned never to cross my sister. *That,*" he thumbed behind us, "is an example of what happens to you."

I didn't respond out of fear that I would retch, right there in front of him.

"She doesn't kill you, nor your family. She makes you live in misery. Effective. Not my style, but effective."

I changed the subject. "I'm curious, since you live on different planes. Are you and Esmeralda really brother and sister?"

"Half. Same father, different mothers."

"So your mom isn't a mage, I take it."

"No. And *thank you* for bringing up a such a sore subject."

He squeezed my arm a little too tightly. Not my intention to irritate him, but it felt rather good knowing I'd found a button. Didn't feel so good on my arm.

With a deep, cleansing breath he expounded. "I'm a bastard. Both figuratively and literally. In fact, the family wanted to forget I even existed."

He fell silent for a few steps, which made me look at him. A mistake. My heart raced, my skin heated. "You're not close to them, then," I said, mostly for my sake, keeping my mind busy with idle conversation to help calm my stupid hormones.

"Much to their dismay, I am powerful. Very powerful. That makes me hard to ignore."

I shook my head, and changed the subject. "Why are you here, Malador?"

"You're here, aren't you? Once you left the tournament I had no reason to stay. So, I came here."

"You followed me?" I asked.

"You flatter yourself, my love. True, your movements intrigue me, but I came here to collect what is mine."

Saffron? "You weren't a part of the raid on our suite, then?"

"No. Again, not my style."

"I remember," I nodded. "Your's is the attack-when-your-prey's-outside-the-Citadel style."

"Guilty as charged," he nodded grandly.

I recalled the incident when Hercule and I had left the safety of the Citadel at last year's tournament to search for the first DVD. We'd waited until everyone had gone to sleep. Apparently, not everyone had. "Who told you," I asked him, not really expecting an answer, "that I left the Citadel? That night, I mean. Not now."

"Your cook, of course."

Of course.

"She was all too keen to keep me in the loop." He sounded rather pleased.

I stopped, dead in my tracks. "Wait, Esmeralda is here, too, right now. She left the tournament as well?"

"Yes."

"How long? How long had she been here?" I started to worry. I knew each plane has a different pace of time, but it never occurred to me that, despite my thinking it's been only a few hours, Saffron may have been here for *years*.

"Several weeks now." I winced. He smiled. *Weeks!* "I have it on good authority the cook is fine. I'm here to claim her. And might I say, again dear lady, you really need to hire competent staff. You should know all this."

I rolled my eyes. "Why do you want the girl so badly? Why does your sister?"

"*Woman,* I've been taught," he said, smugly. "There's this prophecy—"

"Yes, I've heard all about the stupid poison that kills the healers. What I want to know is why? Why do you want to destroy healers?"

"My dear lady! I don't."

I gave him a quizzical look.

"I want the *ability* to destroy the healers."

That didn't change my look.

"It's the same reason mankind developed the atom bomb, my love. They didn't really want to end their enemies. They just wanted everyone to know they could."

"Power," I thought out loud.

"Power." He licked his lovely lips. "Sway. An undeniable bargaining chip. That's very much my style."

"And Esmeralda?"

"Oh most definitely, she wants to destroy the healers. She wants the chaos that comes from eliminating the Citadel. I've argued at length with her that she doesn't need to hasten the events that are already unfolding, but she's hell bent on—"

"Wait," I stopped him. "You knew?"

He rolled his eyes. "Of course. As well as you do, its fabric is crumbling. Wasn't that the point of your little *tell all* in the auditorium?"

Um, yes. It was.

He continued. "Not that I had to be told. I've known since our little fight outside the Citadel walls last year. I had you. I *touched* you.

You should be mine. And yet." He continued walking, pulling me along in his elbow grip. "The only reason my touch didn't have its usual lasting effect is because the matrix of the place is tearing. Weakening."

"So, the mages know," I said.

"They'd have to be idiots not to. They live there. For what it's worth, I think you are correct. I think an innocent was destroyed there, not the bit about the tree. That didn't help things, mind you, but it wasn't the cause."

I wanted to ask more but our progress had brought us to a set of enormous glass doors, the official entry to the castle. They appeared to be thick, like glass block, with streaks of red and orange and gold glitter. As we walked up to them, they opened inward without any command. We never slowed or broke stride.

Along the path to the castle, Malador and I had walked alone. Once through the entry, however, rows of knights, metal armor from head to toe, stood erect and still along the path we traveled. They did not look at us. Heads high, shoulders square, and spears at the ready. The first guard looked human, at least I thought so, but past them stood rows of un-humans, a mix of goblins and trolls, wearing red leather pants and matching vests adorned with a round griffin emblem. They held an assortment of weapons, from swords to maces to halberds.

So effectively intimidating were the royal guards that I didn't get a good look at the room we traversed. Probably the point. They were a reminder that I would be hard pressed to escape without a fight. *Whose plan was this, anyway?*

I focused on the man beside me. "I got to admit, I'm impressed," I said. "You haven't tried to touch me on this walk." I gripped my hammer tighter, fully understanding that I'd just invited an unwelcome move.

"You're not ready yet."

"Uh … Excuse me?"

"You're not ready. Not at the moment. But you will be. Soon. I've put things in motion, and when you are ready, my love, you will come to me. You will beg me to kiss you, to turn you," he gripped harder, "to take you."

"You clearly have me confused with someone else," I scoffed, attempting to hide my concern.

"A wise man once told me that if you stand still long enough, everything will come to you. I've learned to be a patient man. Mark these words." He looked at me. He had the faintest hint of that smile, the one he gave to Nathan, the one that made me recoil ever so slightly away from him. "You will beg me."

I forced myself to look ahead. A row of guards lead to a closed wooden door. *Put things in motion?* His absolute confidence rattled me. I swallowed my apprehension, feeling, yet again, I was in over my head.

Two guards opened the way, letting us into …

I couldn't help but gape in awe. Before us spanned a cavernous space lighted by whimsical stained glass windows seeping color between exposed mahogany beams. Decorative banners in deep azure and gold hung from each beam, identical in shape and size. A court of people stood along the red carpet dressed in the latest fashion circa 1623. The women wore gaudy gowns in a rainbow of colors, bedazzled with brilliant jewels. The men wore equally colorful tunics, cloaks, trousers, leggings, and shoes with big buckles. All of them watched as we strolled up to the Queen herself, seated on an opulent golden throne, laced in filigree and glistening rubies. Everything precise, pristine, and perfect. Disney couldn't have created a better court. Except for the people part—here it was goblins, trolls, and deformed humans.

Trumpets blared from somewhere. The Queen stood as we approached.

Malador released my arm, took a step forward, and bowed deeply in front of her.

"Brother-of-mine, I see you come bearing gifts." She looked me up and down, heaving a burdened sigh. "I am disappointed. This isn't the one I wanted."

"My apologies, dear sister-of-mine." Malador uttered the words while inspecting his fingernails, as if he just had a manicure. Not sure what he saw through the gloves he wore.

"Where is Edward?" she demanded.

I shot my arm up into the air and did my best Horshack impression. "Oo oo oo! Madame Queen Lady?" That got a disapproving murmur from the court, and a hot glare from the Queen. "Nathan's not here because he's in a coma." She raised an eyebrow. "One of your griffin-thingys bit him."

Someone snickered. She shot a bitter glance in their direction. "Is this true?" she hollered, facing upward. I followed her gaze to spy the rows of griffins clinging to the rails of the gallery. They shuffled about, insecurely. "You were told not to bite anyone!"

A scuffle of griffins, pushing and shoving, resulted in a singled lion-bird-lizard thing struggling to fly to the ground near me. One of its wings bent a bit, giving it an asymmetric and pained appearance. My imagination filled in the blanks; I envisioned Nathan doing some damage to the creature, and it retaliated with a chomp.

"Did you bite Edward Witherspoon?" the Queen growled.

It cowered meekly, kneeling in apology and pitifully flapped his broken wing. Despite the fact it poisoned Nathan, the thing got my sympathy.

It received none from her. Her hand flew out, a jettison of flame enveloping the griffin. It roiled, shrieking in agony for several heart-breaking, gut-wrenching moments, then dropped, unmoving and smoldering.

I began to appreciate Jack's position on vegetarianism as wafts of cooked griffin filled my nose.

Focus on the positive, Winki. If I understood things correctly, Nathan would wake from his poison slumber with the death of the creature. Yes, *I* wanted the thing dead. But why did she?

The Queen stalked over the smoking remnants. "I have great plans for Edward, my pet. Glorious plans. And I have none for you. Take it away!"

A couple of leather tunicked trolls carried the still-smoldering griffin from the room.

The green-eyed, flame-haired Queen turned her attention to me. She did look remarkably like her mother. "Well. I do have a surprise for you."

Being somewhat familiar with "surprises," like unexpected parties and friends that just drop by, I suspected this was none of these, and I wasn't going to like it.

"I'm having a special dinner tonight, one your very own healer will be the center of."

Yep. I didn't like it. "You realize you just dangled a preposition."

"You realize, of course, you are going to be punished for your insolence."

I gripped my hammer tighter as she approached. She blinked, and I mean a "I Dream Of Genie" kind of blink; big and deliberate. When she moved within range, I threw my arm up to slow her down …

Wait … It didn't move. Nothing moved. I commanded my body and *nothing moved.* I used my mind, and thought, "Now! Now! Now" but nothing happened. I couldn't slow her down. Until this blasted moment, I didn't realize I needed to move to manipulate time.

In front of me, Esmeralda slowly, with the thinnest of grins on her face, removed her glove. Finger by finger, tugging, exposing …

My heart raced. My muscles filled with adrenaline and still they refused to move. *C'mon, Winki, you're stronger than this! Move!*

"Poor child," she sickeningly sang, "bound in place. This was how I subdued your dear husband."

With fast and deep breaths I watched as she moved her hand about, as if admiring her razor sharp fingernails. "Bind is such a small talent. But can be very powerful if you have no resistance to it."

I cursed my stupidity. *Way to walk into a trap, Mrs. Witherspoon.*

"Do not fret, though. I have no motivation to turn you, unlike my brother. I rather enjoy good enemies. But —" She grabbed my face with her bare hand. *I am so screwed.* "But I want to give you a small taste of what your husband suffered at my hands for days. What his brother is about to suffer. For *eons*." The silky sound of her voice poured into my ears, and filled my stone-like body with a potent mix of terror and rage.

For one clear moment we looked each other in the eyes. I read in her gaze, her absolute, complete, and repulsive malevolence. Her eyes showed nothing but the diabolical.

Every molecule in my body exploded at exactly the same moment. From my littlest toe to the top of my head, from my internal organs to the expanse of my skin, every little gray cell in my brain, every tendon, every ligament, every muscle, every bone, *everything*. Nothing was spared the sharp, bright, stab of high frequency vibration, as if every cell had a dentist drilling into it. I couldn't move. I couldn't scream. I could only feel the pain, its completeness, its flawless and exhaustive sensation. My blood pressure soared, my pulse galloped, my over-burdened lungs wheezed. *Stop! Stop! Please! I'll do anything!*

My eyes couldn't move. They fixed on hers. Her gleeful, joyous, happy eyes.

My overtaxed body couldn't keep up with its own demands. My vision turned to stars, my body quaked, my muscles seized from lack of oxygen and blood. And still the torture continued, undaunted, unfaltering, unrelenting …

I understood the complete horror of it, what Will went through at his last tournament. The pain was perfect. She could keep me in that space, that knife edge between consciousness and madness, for as long as she wanted. As long as it entertained her.

And there was nothing I could do.

Chapter Twenty-Eight

SHE HELD MY face. I had the strength to move now, despite the darkness I found myself in. I pushed it away, but she held fast and hard.

I heard my name, muddled in the distance. A familiar voice …

"*Get away from me,*" I raged, and I fought the grip. I kicked. I screamed. *I hate you!*

"Ma'am! Please, it's me. *It's Jack.*"

The words echoed in my head, bouncing around my sore brain, as I continued to struggle. But I weakened, so damned fast. I had no strength. It had all been ripped from me.

Arms secured themselves around me. "It's me, ma'am. It's all right now."

Jack. *Wait … I know that name, that voice.* "Jack?"

"Yes, ma'am. I'm here. You're safe now."

I surrendered, largely out of exhaustion. I waited for the trickery, but none came. Just arms around me, a tender but secure hold. A snug and safe embrace.

Waves of relief and self-pity crushed me. I sobbed. I lost all control and sobbed. "I would have done anything …" I wept.

"I know. I would have, too."

Even my grief succumbed to my complete lack of energy. Within moments I didn't have a cry left in me. I felt like a soggy, dirty rag:

limp, useless, and tossed aside.

I finally heard his words. "What do you mean, you would have too?" With effort I pushed myself away to face him. "She touched you?"

Jack hesitated to answer as he reached for my face. I stopped him, holding him by his forearms, noticing the dirt and tears of his linen shirt. "Yes," he whispered. "She bound me, and tortured me, too."

Unlike me, that meant Jack woke up alone. I hung my head, shame flushing my face, wrenching my gut, squeezing my heart. I failed him. I failed myself. I failed *everyone*.

He reached for me, but I pushed him away. *I don't want to be healed. I don't deserve it.*

Persistently, he reached again. In honesty, I lacked the strength to avoid him. His warm hand touched my face, his palm against my cheek. I felt a flush of heat, warm and caring. If love itself could manifest physically it would feel just like Jack's gentle touch. He pulled me into him. I collapsed, defeated.

We sat on the dirt floor, his back against a stone wall, cradling me in his arms. I didn't know how long we remained that way. I didn't care. I hadn't been consoled with such tenderness since, well, since Will. It didn't feel like a betrayal now. It felt like a necessity. To hear another heart beat. To feel the simple movement of breath. I needed to be held by another caring human being.

Through the warmth of his touch I regained my strength. I pushed myself up a bit.

Filth and dirt and darkness surrounded us. A single torch fastened to a wall lit the room. Our cell, it turned out. With the exception of a small barred window and a thick wooden door, nothing but stone surrounded us.

"Let me finish healing you," he said, sensing my will to leave his side. "I just need a moment." He pressed his hand on my neck.

Abashed, I cursed myself. *What kind of champion are you? Stupid girl.* I ran off to rescue Nathan and Saffron, and did what, exactly? We were jailed. We were trapped. *We're dead.*

"We're not dead yet."

I wanted to laugh since he'd said it with perfect Monty Python inflection. I didn't have the strength.

My connection to him saved me the effort of speaking. I thought, "I'm sorry. I'm so sorry."

"This is not your fault."

"It's completely my fault." Images filled my head; Nathan, pale and lifeless on the floor, Jack whisked into the sky by griffins, Saffron being tortured by Esmeralda, just as we were. "Some champion I turned out to be."

"We don't know about Saffron, ma'am. The Queen needs her to be alive and useful to make the poison. Besides, you've only been at this for two years. Cut yourself some slack," he whispered. With a sigh he added, "I don't think anyone could have been prepared for this."

"What do you mean?"

"As I've been sitting here, I've gone through these events in my head. The poisoning of griffins. The appearance of Malador. The bind of Esmeralda. I've concluded hardly anyone knows how to handle true battles anymore. Think about it. Since the inception of the Citadel, over a thousand years ago, good and evil have camped themselves solely in their houses. They don't really plot or plan or war anymore. They only fight yearly in the restricted space of the arena with restricted rules and restricted weapons."

I understood his argument but not his point.

"Consider my father, for example. He's served Gateway since, well, before Nathan and Will were born. He served other houses prior to that. Do you honestly believe that he'd let you and me come here alone if he thought that it was absolutely futile? Of course not.

Wouldn't he have told us we needed a gonzo, or talisman, or medallion to prevent her bind talents? He just didn't know, ma'am."

"Really?" I asked, tilting my head. "How can that be? I'm not blaming him, mind you, but he had to know she could *bind*. As you've pointed out, he's seen her in many battles over the decades. She had to have used it."

"She probably did," he said. "So what? You had *bind* this year, remember?"

"I did?"

"Yes. After your second bout with the Arch Lich."

"I need to pay attention to those information boards," I muttered.

"*We* knew it was a talent you were awarded, and only available in the Citadel. Using a talent during the tournament does not mean you actually have that talent. It's my belief that was done intentionally. So one knows what talents any of the competitors genuinely have. We don't track what skills competitors use."

"Sounds like we need to."

He shook his head. "It shouldn't be necessary. That was the point of the Citadel. Fights, domination, wars … all of it was to be replaced by the tournament. We all could just live our lives the rest of the time."

Before I could consider this, he quickly dropped his hand and hastened to put his gloves back on. Then I heard it, too. Noise outside the door.

"Look. We don't want any trouble," called a voice.

We stood. I squared myself to face the visitors as the door opened, rolling my head to loosen my neck. I felt infinitely better and ready for a fight.

A goblin and two big hulking trolls entered the cell, blocking the exit. They all wore matching red leather vests and pants with griffin crests on them, the uniforms of the guards. I blinked in surprise. The goblin was Theodore. He didn't look particularly friendly. I wondered how much loyalty three hundred frogs really got me.

Theodore moved in front of the two gray goons and spoke. "The Queen sent us to bring you to her party. We're just trying to do our jobs. We don't want any trouble." He opened his vest just slightly to display, tucked through a loop in his breaches ... *my hammer.*

I barely hid my glee.

"Pink boy," he addressed Jack. "Step away from her."

I gave Jack a reassuring nod, and he separated himself from me.

"Turn and face the walls. Both of you. Hands behind your back."

We did as instructed.

The trolls stood nearby as Theodore, dangling some hefty handcuffs, came toward me. I heard the clank of metal but felt the heft of my hammer being placed in my hands. My hands were not bound, but I played along.

He spun me, my hands behind my back, so the trolls could see the "chained" prisoner. He cuffed Jack, unfortunately, in earnest.

"You," Theodore said to one of the trolls. "Take the pink one to the kitchen. You," he said to the other, "take her and come with me."

With a massive gray hand on his shoulder, Jack was led out of the cell. His troll led him to the left.

I gave Theodore a quick glance. He shook me off. I was being told to wait. I frowned as Jack disappeared from view.

"Lead the way," Theodore called to my guard, who replied with a grunt. We turned right.

After a series of turns, we made our way through a long, empty tunnel-like hallway, walking single file. Theodore prompted, "Winki, now!"

I tapped the troll in front of me with one hand, and when he turned to look, I swung a right hook with my hammer. The ground shook when the massive being hit the floor.

"What about Jack?" I turned to my rescuer.

He looked left and right, then waved me out of the hall and into a darkened doorway, out of view. In a hushed tone he answered. "Jack's gonna be fine in the kitchen, trust me. That's where Saffron Jolly is. Here's what you need to know."

I knelt down to get in better hearing range as Theodore brought me up to speed. The Queen had been using Saffron's brother, Simon, as leverage to get her to make the healer-genocide poison. While they'd only been here a few weeks, "Well," Theodore winced, "you know how persuasive the Queen can be."

"Saffron did it?"

"Apparently so. That's what the celebration is for. It's the unveiling of the poison. The Queen's calling it 'the Age of Anarchy.'" Theodore mimicked her voice, sounding a little like Julia Child. "She intends on using it at the party in a grand demonstration. On *your* healer."

"You just sent him—!"

He held up his hands. "At the party, Winki. He'll be fine until then." He leaned back a little, nervously scanned our location and ensuring our solitude. "Look. Your best chance of getting you and your healer out of here is at the party. I've already arranged for a distraction—"

I could see by the look in his eyes he meant just the two of us. "No."

"No?" he asked, blinking.

"I can't leave Saffron and Simon here. I have to get them home."

He rolled his eyes. "Live to fight another day!"

I hadn't finished my point. "And I have to stop this … Age of Anarchy. I can't let Esmeralda have that kind of power. I have to find the poison and maybe destroy it."

"You won't have a chance. Right now the captives are under tight lock-down until the party, then they're going to be seated with the Queen—"

A black, gloved hand reached around the corner of our hiding place, clasping over his mouth. I jumped to standing. As the little green man struggled, I readied my hammer, left hand raised, ready to slow down and pummel his assailant. He slowly appeared, sauntering around the corner, keeping his grip on the goblin. Tall, dark, and evil. Sadly, amazingly handsome.

"Clearly," Malador said, "you two don't understand the concept of how to remain hidden. It largely involves being quiet."

Ignoring him, I tensed, hammer raised. My mind raced trying to think of how to get out of here without him running to his sister. And her thousands of guards. *Blast all, we'll never get out now.*

"I'm not going to harm you. Or your friend. As I promised," he looked down at Theodore, whom he continued to clutch.

I stood still as stone, ready to lay the whammy on him.

"By the dark night," he spat, rolling his eyes, "I was on my way down to the dungeons to rescue you! Why else would I be in this dreary place?"

Nope. Not moving.

"Woman, right now we are allies, you and I. I don't want my sister to have that potion any more than you do."

"*You* want it," I accused.

"We can argue about what to do with it later. Right now we need to get it out of her hands. Then, side by side, we can leave, just like we arrived."

"I need to rescue Jack, Saffron, and Simon, too."

He opened his mouth to say something, thought better of it, tried again, stopped again. He looked down at his goblin hostage. "This was where I walked in, wasn't it?"

"Uh-huh," Theodore nodded under his glove.

"Fine," he huffed, releasing the goblin. Theodore rushed to stand beside me. Malador put his fists on his narrow hips. "Have you ever heard the adage, 'Live to fight another day?'"

"That's what I tried to tell her!" Theodore said, exasperated.

"If you don't want to help me," I spat, "I'll do this alone." I started to storm off in the direction I saw them take Jack when Malador stepped in my way.

"How? Let's assume, great warrior that you are, you can fend off the over five thousand guards—"

"Eight thousand," Theodore corrected him.

"The eight thousand guards she has in this castle. Her powers are without limit here, unlike what you've had to deal with in the tournament. She doesn't have to be in the ring to bind you. All she has to do is see you. *Miles away.*" He took a slow step nearer. "You can't do it alone, Winki. Let me help you." Another step. I felt flushed with fever. "Then, after we've escaped this damned plane we can ... hash out who will get what." He licked his perfect lips. "Maybe over a quiet dinner?" Another step. My heart pounded. "Some wine?" And another. Beautiful chocolate eyes ... "Candlelight —"

"Hey," Theodore pressed in between us. "You got a plan, dark man? Because where I'm from, we got a saying: you don't start organizing your victory celebrations until the ogre's dead."

I exhaled my relief. I hated how easy it was to get lost in his tantalizing incubus charm. "Yeah. You got a plan?"

"Yes. I do," he smiled. From under his jacket he retrieved, and dangled, a golden necklace, with a round medallion bobble on the end — some kind of gonzo. "But you're not going to like it."

Theodore recognized the amulet at once. "Isn't that the Tempest Veil?" he asked astonished at its presence. "Did the Queen let you borrow it?"

"It is. And no. I stole it."

"Tempest," I squinted, as if painfully pulling out a memory from Jeeves's teachings, which I was. "Isn't the Tempest House in the

Zephyr Plane?"

"Ah! Very good. And do you know what this little trinket does?" He waved it in front of me.

"Invisibility!" Theodore blurted out, like an enthusiastic student.

We both shot Theodore a glance.

"Yes," Malador said. "And no. You see, in the Zephyr Plane it works precisely as you'd expect, which is to say the wearer stays invisible the entire time they're wearing it. But you may have noticed we're not in the Zephyr Plane. *Here* the effects are limited."

"How limited?" I asked.

"They will only work for a short time. An hour at most."

I took the item from his hand. "That's all I need—"

My little body guard grabbed if from me. "No no no. Tell her the rest!" He wagged and angry finger at the gorgeous man.

"The rest?" I raised an eyebrow.

Malador shrugged. "It's ... poisonous here. It will only work an hour because after that you'll be dead," he said frankly. "But once removed, however, all better. There are no lasting effects. Provided we work quickly, you should be fine." There was the frightening smile again. "Let's talk about this *conjuring* talent you have, my love."

Malador was right. I didn't like it.

Chapter Twenty-Nine

MALADOR LED ME as a prisoner of the Queen through a maze of hallways with a goblin escort. Submissively, I kept my eyes on the ground in front of me, my white hair falling forward, covering my watching eyes. Malador nodded, and Theodore bowed, at every guard we passed along the way.

This was Theodore's idea. Said he saw it in a movie once. If I could have, I would have mewled like Chewbacca.

We arrived at a wooden door with two sentries. Their eyes widened at the sight of Malador. However, as he moved to enter, they blocked his way.

"Stand aside, you fools," Malador commanded. "Sister-of-mine has another prisoner for the scullery." He shoved me forward to make his point.

With an exchange of nervous looks one answered, "We beg forgiveness, Prince Malador, but we were told that no one—"

"Look. You and I both know she changes her mind fifty times every minute. Step aside."

"I ... um ... we ..."

Malador leaned closer to the man and ominously whispered, "We can both take a walk to see *The Queen* where you can explain why you denied *her brother* access to the kitchen."

The guard gulped. He moved aside. So did his partner.

I couldn't help filling my nose with the brume of cooking meat and savory spices, the scent nothing short of amazing. The room, however, was as dark and dreary as our cell had been, and proved Malador right—the entire building was just brick and timber. A wood-burning stove spanned one side of the room, and along the other arched an enormous hearth, housing a blazing fire. A cauldron dangled in its center. The ceiling timbers held stacks of dried herbs, suspended upside down in bunches. I couldn't tell how deep the room ran since it was filled with shelving, brimming with pots, pans, lids, utensils, books, jars, and whatnot. Three tiny round windows high on the wall allowed some fresh air to come into the room, but given their height offered no view.

In the center, at a large wooden picnic table, sat Jack. Opposite him, with his back towards us, sat Simon. Saffron stood by the stove, stirring a cast iron skillet.

Jack moved to stand when we came in. A guard's hand pressed him roughly back into his seat. My healer reacted with a frown, I think. Hard to tell—he often wore a gloomy scowl. He continued eating his piping soup.

Guards stood by each of the prisoners. Recognizing Malador, they stood even taller.

"Don't let it boil too long," came a voice from behind the shelving. I couldn't see the face. But I didn't have to. I recognized the voice. Soft, deep, with a sultry island accent.

She stepped out from behind the bookcase. Our eyes met, hers bulging, as if surprised. They weren't, that's just how they always looked.

Mrs. White.

A flash of rage coursed through me as the memory possessed me: holding the gun, pointing at Nathan, the terrified look in his eyes, hands raised and begging for his life. I could still feel the resistance of the trigger. *I came so close to pulling it.* Then realizing the truth, the betrayal … it all had unraveled from that point, that sharp point in time, when Nathan admitted his relationship to Will, and Jack became my … my …

"Well, child," she smiled at me, pearly whites exposed. "Isn't this a pleasant surprise? It is good to see you again."

She sounded so smug, so cocky. Her smile so fake, her lilting voice gloating that she'd beaten me.

The heat of my stomach spread quickly throughout my limbs. My jaw and fist and stomach ached from clenching. *This woman, she did it, she set me up, she betrayed the house … she killed my husband!* I stamped my foot so hard on the floor, releasing my hatred, my anger, that the items on the shelves rattled.

Everyone froze.

Not slowed, but *froze*.

In the distance, I heard the rumble of thunder as the room darkened from gathering clouds outside the small windows.

I didn't dwell on the outcome, just took advantage of it. I touched Jack first, releasing him. He looked around, slowly standing. "Ma'am?" he asked, gingerly.

I pointed to the man across from him. Simon's sported a black eye, swollen shut, and a long scar that ran the length of his head, crusting his cheek in red. One arm, supported by the table, looked abnormally twisted and swollen. "Heal him," I said.

Jack touched the man, and shook his head. "I can't seem to—"

Before he finished I touched Simon, snapping him into time. Another rumble of thunder happened at that very moment. Outside the room I heard shouting guards run past the closed door. Only the people in the kitchen froze, apparently.

Jack placed his hands on Simon, who looked around wide-eyed. "What the …?" He turned to his frozen sister. That's when I noticed the chains. A shackle clung around one of her feet, affectively chaining her to the stovetop.

"Where's the key?" I asked him as I inspected it.

"Uh … that guy!" Simon pointed to the guard that had been behind Jack.

Before checking his pocket, I liberated my hammer, which I'd hidden beneath my jacket. Thunder roared close as I filled myself with anger before I unleashed my weapon into the troll's snoot.

He snapped into time just as his body hit the wall, generating a troll-shaped cloud. I rifled through his pockets and retrieved a set of keys.

Once he healed Simon, Jack joined me at Saffron, and diligently inspecting her condition as I unshackled her. When I touched her, she gasped in surprise. "What the …?"

"Saffy!" Simon rushed to her, embracing as if they hadn't seen each other in years.

"Please, Mrs. Jolly," Jack said, "let me take a look at you."

With a satisfying click, the metal cuff released and fell away. "I'm fine," she said to Jack. "Now, I'm fine …"

"Saffron," I asked, "where's the potion?"

As she and Simon broke their embrace, I got a good look at her. Saffron looked as she had when I first saw her. Eyes red and sunken, patchy complexion, dirty hair, sallow skin, but much thinner, almost frail. "They took it. The guards came and … I … I have no idea where it is now," she stammered. To Jack, she said, crying, "I'm sorry. I'm … so sorry!"

Crap! I had to find that stupid potion.

I touched Theodore. He whistled in appreciation at those still frozen around him. "That is such a cool talent!"

"I need you to make a portal to Gateway Manor. Take Saffron, Simon, and Jack home."

Theodore nodded and immediately waved his hand, jumping high to make it, larger than himself. As the air started to swirl into formation, Jack protested. "Ma'am, I have to stay with you. I have the chip—"

More thunder. More guards ran nearby, sounding panicked.

"Jack, get home and heal them both! I want everyone out of here now. Theodore can take me home."

"But—"

The portal loomed, ready to go. I pointed at it with each word, "Jack. Go. Now."

He frowned in earnest as he gestured to Saffron and Simon to enter the sphere. Saffron cast me one last glance. "I'm so sorry," she said, stepping out of the Radiant Plane arm in arm with her brother.

Out of the blue, Jack gruffly grabbed Theodore and shoved the goblin through the portal. The sphere immediately shrunk behind him, closing with a soft pop.

"Dammit, Jack!"

"Ma'am, protest to your heart's content and punish me at a later time, but I'm staying here with you. Their cuts and bruises can wait for my administrations. Any injury suffered by you, however, cannot."

I folded my arms, wanting to argue, but knowing full well there was nothing I could do now. I cast the unmoving Malador a glance. He could make portals. I could have him make one to send Jack home … but knowing Malador, he'd want something in return. Like me. The threat of his setting things in motion made me gulp. As I stared at the handsome prince, I realized I'd have to break his spell in any case. Only he would have an idea of where the poison could be.

Thankfully, touching didn't require any skin to skin contact to break the freeze. I whomped him in the shoulder to get him into my time.

"Ow!" he said, rubbing his shoulder, although I didn't hit him hard … or as hard as I wanted.

His head jerked upwards, reacting to the rumble outside. His eyes snapped to the windows. He backed towards the door, mouth agape, as if he'd never heard thunder in his life. He lived in New Orleans, for pity's sake. We sometimes get days of storms.

"What is wrong with you?"

"Nothing," he recovered, looking a bit sheepish. He looked around at the frozen guards and Mrs. White. "I see you've rescued the brother and sister."

"Yes. But the poison isn't here. Ideas?"

When he didn't answer right away, I felt frustrated. I just wanted out of this damned plane! Another crack of thunder pealed followed by the hush of rain.

His neck craned to the ceiling as Jack and I exchanged befuddled glances. "You don't understand," Malador said, as if that explained his reaction. "It never rains here."

"First time for everything, darkling." I snapped my fingers with the words. "Poison. Where?"

"Sister-of-mine must have it, since I doubt she'd entrust it to anyone else. Follow me. That pendant may come in handy yet."

As we headed out the door, I looked back at Mama White, the betrayer. For a moment I was back in Will's hospital room; nurses scrambling, orders called, someone hollered, *"Clear!"* I could strike her down right now.

I heard Nathan's voice in my head, as he looked at me with his black eye. "When your tide rises, I'm going to drown."

C'mon, Winki. Leave her here. She's not worth it.

With a cleansing breath, and not another thought, I turned and followed the incubus.

Chapter Thirty

MALADOR LED JACK and me up a series of staircases that wrapped a five-sided tower. Without rest, we climbed as fast as Malador could go. Up a long flight, slight turn to the right, and up again.

Initially we crossed long landings, where panicked people ran like headless chickens. We no longer needed the ruse of my being a captive. All the guards and castle employees ran around so terrified that, short of blindly running into us, they never noticed us.

All the while, Malador grumbled. "How is it you don't know?" he spat over his shoulder. "I've told you before, woman, you need to fire your staff. There are certain fundamentals everyone needs to know, and the persistent, constant, eternal lack of rain on the Radiant Plane is one of them!"

Too bad Jack couldn't just catch my thoughts. I'd ask for ideas on how to get Malador to shut up, since racing up the stairs didn't hamper the stream of complaints.

The storm sounded like it was dying down. I hadn't heard any thunder since we left the kitchen, only the steady thrum of rain. Tiny rivulets spilled their way down the very steps we chugged up. Clearly, no one ever thought of waterproofing the place.

Finally—and my legs couldn't express their gratitude enough—we reached a dead end at a lone door. Across from it a window, more of an opening, really, gave us a view of the gray sky beyond. Our attention was drawn to the closed room, and the ranting from within. Esmeralda. Using language that would make a longshoreman blush, she, too, fretted over the rain.

"Are you ready?" Malador asked me. He wasn't even panting.

As I took some deep breaths to help my quads, I pulled out the amulet and nodded. "Put it on, and follow me in. And you," he said to Jack, "get ready. Once the gonzo comes off, she'll need some healing."

I hesitated a moment upon hearing that. Not sure what disturbed me more; that wearing the gonzo would make me sick enough to need a healer, or that Malador expressed what seemed like genuine concern for me.

I took a deep breath and donned the necklace.

Immediately my stomach convulsed. A thick wave of nausea squeezed my insides.

"Ma'am?" Jack asked. But he didn't look at me. Not directly, anyway.

It worked! He couldn't see me. I raised my hand in front of my face. I couldn't see me either.

I groaned as another wave clutched my internal organs.

"You said an hour?" I sputtered. "I don't think I can wear this thing longer than a couple of minutes."

"Then we'd better hurry," Malador said. "Follow me. And stay quiet, my dear. Otherwise, all is lost." He grabbed Jack by the neck, opened the door, and brusquely shoved my healer into the room.

Jack, taken by surprised, was unable to collect his feet down the small stairs, and sprawled without grace on the floor before the Queen. Malador walked in, and I slipped in behind him.

Her opulent bedroom was larger than the average shotgun home in New Orleans. It was five sided, like the rings we fight in, but sunken by three steps. That made the space look like an arena, and the steps could be seats for viewers. Colorful and elegant swaths draped a myriad of directions, covering all of the walls. Dressers, vanities, settees, and the like dotted the space. In the center splayed a large five-sided poster bed. The sheets and pillows looked unmade and dirty with patches of ocher and red stains. I winced at the site of blood. Long chains with manacles ran from each post, and several nearby small tables supported items you'd more likely find in an operating room. Some of the tools, too, were stained. I shuddered at the sight. Could have been from the amulet, though.

"Where is she?" Esmeralda screamed at her brother as he danced down the stairs. "Where's that little harlot of yours?"

"She's not mine," he defended. "Not yet."

"She's doing this, Mal. She's making the rain!" Her wide eyes were filled with hate.

"Impossible," he said. "No one's that powerful."

"Explain it then!" In her fury, she attacked one of the innocent vanities, throwing it and its contents to the floor. Shards of mirror and bits of colorful bottles slid in every direction.

Jack found his legs and, upon seeing the bed and its enhancements, backed away from it. He suddenly stiffened, his arms and legs binding together.

"You!" Esmeralda sneered, approaching the poor healer. "You will pay for all this!" She placed a hand on his face. He flinched just slightly, unable to react, unable to move.

Leave him alone. I raised my hand to freeze her when another wave of nausea hit me, hard. It was all I could do to keep my feet. Whether the amulet or the sickness stifled me, I had no talent. I wondered what else Malador had failed to inform me.

I had to find the poison and fast. I *had* to take this thing off me.

I tiptoed around the room as quickly as I could without making noise, keeping an eye on the floor now littered with bottles of perfume, jewelry, mirror shards, and cosmetics. I didn't want to kick anything. Or slip.

I heard Jack whimper. I clenched my jaw, trying to ignore it. *Ignore him, just get it done.* But I knew what he was feeling, what he was going through. That complete, perfect, penetrating pain of a million needles … my anger flared.

A new crack of thunder rocked the outside.

"Ez, this won't help anything," Malador implored. "How much more can the castle stand of this?" He put his hand on her shoulder. "Please. We need to get out of here."

She bore her teeth at my healer, as if straining. He responded with a guttural noise as his eyes rolled up into his head.

Jack collapsed to the floor.

She didn't just kill him, right?

Heated, I raised my invisible hand, but only the thunder and the nausea responded. A tide gripped my throat. I wavered in step, and crushed a piece of broken mirror.

"Sh," she snapped her head in my direction as the thunder rolled into silence.

"Let's go," Malador prodded. "It was just—"

"No. Be quiet. She's here, somewhere." Esmeralda looked in my direction.

Bloody hell.

"I know you're here, Witherspoon!" she called into the room. "You'd never leave your precious healer in my care, would you?" My gut tightened. I nearly lost my stomach. Thunder cracked outside. "I offer you a deal. A trade, if you will. You stop this wretched storm you're creating and I won't kill your healer." With those words, she produced from the folds of her skirt a petite vial, an ampoule made of purple glass and slightly translucent. The liquid within glowed a bright green. It sloshed thickly in the container, leaving residue on the ampoule's sides.

Of course she had it. Winki, you're an idiot.

No reason to remain hidden now. I had a fighting chance of

using my powers without the stupid necklace, not to mention ending this miserable sensation.

"Show yourself, Witherspoon."

I reached around my neck for the chain. I couldn't find it. My fingers could feel my shoulders, my neck, but the jewelry just wasn't there. *Dammit, what the hell is going on?*

The delicate cork on the vial yielded to her thumb with a small pop. "I'll give you to the count of five," Esmeralda growled, "then I pour this down his repulsive throat."

My hands flailed around my neck, desperate to feel metal, links, chain ... anything! But nothing was there. I lost my balance when the next revolting wave tore at my insides, and I staggered noisily toward a bed post. *I had to get this stupid thing off me!*

"One." *Come on, Winki. Get it together.*

"Two." *You're losing. Again. To this stupid, sadistic, witch of a woman!* I hoisted myself to full standing, letting the bed post support me. With effort I managed to get one leg in front of me ... my throat and stomach cramped hard ... I clawed at my neck and shoulders.

"Three." She knelt beside the unconscious man and opened his mouth with her fingers. I wanted to move, but my stomach ... the world was spinning ... *Get this thing off me!*

"Four." She brought the vial to his lips. *Please don't hurt him ...*

"Five." *No!* I stamped my foot. A bolt of lightning slammed through the room, tearing through the stone block ceiling. I instinctively ducked. So did Malador and Esmeralda. Blinded by the bolt I couldn't see, the taste of ozone coated my tongue, I covered my ears, trying to protect them from the blast of noise, and my body cowered in an attempt to hide from the massive blocks that, like the pouring rain, hammered down upon us. It lasted for minutes, or so it seemed, a never ending stream of water, mud, and rubble.

When the chaos settled, rain pelted down on me. I timidly raised my head toward the gray sky that replaced the ceiling. Rain started to pool in the sunken room. Within seconds, an inch already gathered.

Another wave of nausea cut through me. I emptied my stomach, clutching my abdomen. The relentless pummel dripped down my back and pasted my hair to my soaked face. I trembled, gasping gulps of air to recover.

Pushing my pain aside, I focused on what was left of the room. Jack still lay unmoving on the floor, gobs of mud covered half of him. Out from a nearby mound of rocks and debris peeked an unmoving hand. Where Esmeralda had just been. In her clutch still loomed the bottle, inches from Jack's mouth. The poison poised above his lips. If Esmeralda came to, or even stirred, she'd kill him.

On hands and knees I crawled toward him, splashing through the rising pools, hoarsely calling him name.

Something hard pressed down on the small of my back. I collapsed under the pressure, my belly flat on the floor. I strained to raise my head out of the water to allow myself to breathe. Beneath the pressure, I flailed like a helpless turtle. With a moan I craned my neck upward to see what held me there.

Malador smiled down on me. "In the water, my love, I clearly see you."

"Let … me … go …" I wanted to say more but my stomach churned again. I uttered a cry.

With gentle clucks, he shook his head. "The amulet has ill affects, doesn't it? Although I have to say, I thought you'd be able to handle it better than this. Well, live and learn."

"I can't …" I gasped through the pangs, " …take it off …"

"Of course not!" he laughed. He removed his foot from my back and, on one knee, knelt in front of me, inadvertently splashing water in my face. "Did I forget that part?" he said, overly thoughtful, with a finger on his lips. "So sorry, dearest. You see, the person who places the amulet, either on themselves or another, cannot be the one who removes it. Only someone else can." He looked upwards. "Odd rule.

Probably why I forgot to mention it."

I felt a stab of pain, heightened by my own stupidity. *If I get out of this I will kill this man.*

Tugging at each finger, he removed his glove. Boy, the bad guys just love that move. "Now, my beloved, I'd be more than happy to free you of this burden. But you know what I want."

He tucked the glove in his belt and extended his hand. It looked helpful. It looked like salvation.

I tore my eyes from him to look at Jack, still motionless. The poison loomed near his lips, and the water rising around his face. *Move your feet, you fool!*

"I want to hear you say it," he cooed. "You want me to touch you. You want me to turn you. I want to hear the words." He leaned closed to me and whispered, "I want to hear. You. *Beg.*"

I looked up at the open, gray sky above his head, the rain dripping through his beautiful ringlets. Those chocolate eyes. Those perfect lips. Chiseled jaw ...

My breath was labored. By the illness or him, I didn't know. What struck me was, despite the miserable burning in my stomach and esophagus, I so wanted this man. *Surrender, Winki. Give yourself to him ... you can still save Jack.*

"I ..." I stammered, trying to speak through the agony. *Just do it, Winki.* "Please ..."

I moved my hand to near him, dragging it through the water. I felt something move, something I accidentally pushed. A long shard of mirror. My hand shook with effort as I quickly grabbed the fragment. I clutched it tightly.

I slashed with everything I could muster.

Malador fell backwards with a splash, stunned. His face started to ooze crimson along the perfect slice across his cheek and nose. Rain instantly smeared it along his jawline. He wiped the blood from his face and inspected his palm. Red eyes fiercely glowered at me.

"How ... *dare* you," he roared as he grabbed a sword from his side. I had nothing left. As the nausea clutched me again, I tried to back away, tried to move—

Something hot and wet startled me as it slapped across my cheeks and throat. Shocked, I scrambled back, eyes gawking at the large blade that stuck out of the darkling's chest. Malador slumped sideways and collapsed into the rising waters, exposing a figure behind him.

I recognized her bulging eyes, her dark skin, her warm smile ...

"Mama?" My voice cracked, my body shaking uncontrollably. I wiped my face and my hand came away, visible from blood. Malador's blood. My body convulsed again.

"Come here, child. Let me get this off you." She reached out, patting my head as she tried to find my neck. "I would have thought you had more sense than to listen to that pompous *couillon*. Ah!" I felt her fingers grab onto the chain and—*sweet relief!*

I filled my lungs with glorious, sweet air. The clench of my stomach disappeared instantly.

On hands and knees, I wallowed my way through water and mud towards Jack and snatched the potion from Esmeralda's limp fingers.

"What are you doing, child?" Mama asked as she stood, her soaked shirt plastered to her legs. "Oh, I see. But there was no need. It was not real."

I lifted Jack's head onto my lap and out of the rising water. "What do you mean?" I asked.

"It does not work. I made sure of that. That's why I'm here. That's why Nathan sent me here. " She tilted her head. "Didn't he tell you?"

I'd forgotten how comforting her Jamaican accent sounded. She frequently used "d"s in place of "th"s, so *this* was *dis*, and *that* was *dat*. But at the sound of *Natahn's* name, I tensed. This woman had fooled me more than once already in my lifetime.

"Aren't you tired of blaming him for everything?" I muttered.

I heard a very distant, almost soothing, rumble of thunder, just above the hush of constant rain.

"The wicked Queen was right about one thing," she pointed upwards. "*This* is you."

"Ridiculous." I turned my attention back to Jack and shook him gently. "Jack? Can you hear me?"

"You must listen, child. You must calm yourself before you destroy this castle. With us inside it." She held out her hand to catch some rain.

Jack moaned as he grimaced, tossing his head. Water splashed around him as he moved. I think the wetness helped. His eyes roamed the room, trying to focus. The first thing they landed on was Esmeralda's hovering hand. Eyes wide with panic, he scooted himself away, off my lap. "Bloody witch!" he seethed.

"It's okay, Jack. We're good. You're good."

Once comfortably clear of her, he tried to take in his surroundings; the rain from above and the lack of ceiling. "What's happening?" He saw the blood covering my chin and neck. "Are you bleeding? Are you hurt?"

"Not mine." I helped him to stand. The water came up midway to our calves. The stupid arena design of the room was turning it into a pool. "Time to leave."

Mama continued her accusations. "This is you, Winki. You must clear you head. You must—"

I ignored her and asked Jack. "Are you all right?"

"I will be," he said. "What is going on here?" He jutted his chin at Mrs. White. "Where'd she come from?"

"Your mistress is killing us all," Mama stated enthusiastically. "She's making the rain. This world cannot absorb the water. The castle will fall if it don't stop."

She had a point. The remnants of walls that remained after the ceiling fell began to slump and erode. "Jack, where's the portal? Jeeves said he'd know. How is this supposed to work?"

Jeeves and the geeks had instructions that when we needed a portal to return home, they'd make one. My butler confidently said he could sense our desire to come home from this plane, and since Jack was still "lo-jacked" from the chip Smith and Wesson injected last week, we could be located. Well, here we were. Ready to go. Anytime now …

"I don't understand," Jack said. "It should have been here by now." He looked at me gravely. "Something's wrong."

I spun to the Jamaican traitor. "What have you done?" I accused.

Admittedly, the woman just saved my life. But that in no way made up for the world of anguish she had caused me and my house. Her own nefarious plans might depend upon my survival. Moreover, she was the only unanticipated element in our plan. It didn't seem outlandish to suspect her of interfering.

"Not a thing," she objected. "If the butler said it would be here, it would be here."

A guttural rumble, not thunder, vibrated the floor and water below us. One of the five standing walls, the only wall with an exit, melted away, slurrying into heaps of smothering ooze. Once it vanished, the water, now above our knees in depth, found an exit. In a massive tidal surge, the pool turned into a torrent, racing to the gaping exposure, taking some nearby furniture with it. It happened so quickly, none of us were prepared for the surge. Our feet slipped out from under us. We were immersed in the massive tide, tumbling with the angry flow that took us to the breach. I waved my hand, trying to freeze the water. But no dice. I was in it, touching it. Frantically, we clawed, fighting our way to the other side of the room, which finally got easier as the gush ebbed and the water drained away.

I pressed my hand to the block wall nearest us. It yielded to my touch, like a sponge. Soaked.

Unfortunately, that wasn't our biggest problem. The missing wall —while giving us an absolutely stunning view of the wet world outside—unveiled the great height below us. No more door, no more stairs. We were stuck in the very tall, very wet tower. If another wall gave way, we'd fall to our deaths, buried alive in the mudslide far below.

The rain continued to pelt us. I futilely wiped my face, trying to see any options out of here. "Jack?"

"I ... don't know what to do." In all that we had been through, I'd never seen real panic on his face. Until now.

"Can you make a portal?" I asked Mama.

"No," she said, "I do not possess the talent." She moved closer and held out her hand. "But you do."

"I wish!" Desperately, as a matter of fact.

"You do. I swear you do."

More wall washed away, and the floor nearest the expanse started to crumble. A vanity and settee fell from view. The poster bed tilted over open space. More and more floor chunks fell away, the chasm growing closer. Large boulders dropped with heavy thuds, further covering the Queen and Malador.

"Hold my hand," Mama said softly. "And take his. Remove your gloves!" she commanded him.

Was this some kind of trick?

Jack failed to believe so. Without hesitation, he removed his gloves and took my hand and hers. My eyes wandered about the decaying room. We had just seconds left. I hesitated to take Mama's extended palm.

Jack jerked with his hand. "Try it, ma'am. We'll die here if you don't. We have no choice."

No pressure. With prejudice I took her hand. "What do I do?"

"Think about the person you long to see the most."

"What does that mean?"

"That's how the talent works. Focus on the one you love. See them clearly in your mind. The talent will take you to them."

I thought of Will. I filled my head with the image of his portrait. I even said his name out loud.

"No, child. They have to be real. Tangible."

The rain and wind whipped through the room. A boulder thudded, just feet from Jack, taking a chunk of floor away as it continued downward. He jumped closer to us.

"Concentrate, child!" Mama scolded.

I longed to see the house. I longed to see my friends. My new family. But the thumping of my heart and the droplets dripping down my face kept distracting me.

Then I saw him clearly in my mind. Many images flashed through my memories; swirling his bourbon in his glass before shooting it down his throat, pushing his reading glasses on top of his head, spinning his halberd while taunting me in the ring, angrily slapping the table top as he yelled at me at the tournament, lying there pale and unmoving, poisoned by the griffin …

"Nathan," I whispered.

From behind closed eyes, I saw a brilliant flash of white and yellow, simultaneously hearing a thunder clap as my feet washed out from under me … as my stomach rushed up to meet my ears … as Mama and Jack cried out.

And we fell …

Chapter Thirty-One

I'D FORGOTTEN HOW to breathe. The impact felt so hard, *I'd forgotten how to breathe*.

"Winki? Winki!"

I recognized the carpet below me as I struggled to hands and knees. Suddenly, my body recalled the simple act, and I filled my wanting lungs. My nose took in a thousand scents—wood and polish and mildew and mold. I knew immediately. *Home! Ay, Caramba!* We'd landed in the living room of my beloved home.

Mama, Jack, and I lay sprawled on the floor, dripping wet and covered in thick mud.

"Hey!" I smiled as I sat on my heels, ready to congratulate myself on our achievement, however it happened. I recognized the small crowd of people nearby. Nathan, Jeeves, Mr. Smith, Mr. Wesson, and Mrs. Black all sat in dining room chairs placed in a row. But ... they were bound with rope that wrapped around their torsos way more times than necessary. And they weren't alone. Also bound, to my shock and awe, was our *good* neighbor, Colonel Mustard and his valet, Tom Jones. Mr. Jones and Nathan wore their leather armor. The Colonel sported an elaborate military outfit, also made of leather. Out of the corner of my eye I noticed the black ceiling, but I didn't call attention to it.

"Hey?" I stammered, scanning the room.

Nearby, standing with hands raised, were Saffron, Simon, and Theodore.

Lastly, I noticed the brown-robed individuals, fifteen or so of them. I couldn't see any of their faces. The coffee-colored drapes they wore were tied closed with common rope around the waist. *Healers?*

I let out a deep and audible exhale of frustration. I just escaped the icy grip of Esmeralda, the lustful grip of Malador, and being buried alive on the Radiant Plane only to come back to a home invasion. My stomach churned.

"Hey!" I uttered, angered, "what the—?"

A distant rumble of thunder filled the room.

"Winki," Nathan stopped me. "Did you get it?" It. Get *it?* I couldn't take my eyes from his face. Above one of his eye's oozed a thick, bloody cut. "The poison?" He pressed.

Oh. I'd almost forgotten. From my pocket I produced the purple vial and shook it slightly, it's glowing contents thickly covering the bottle's interior.

Nathan twisted to look up at the cloaked person nearest him. "There, you see?" he said pleasantly, "I told you she'd get it."

I didn't see any weapons, but I had to assume, given the situation, the household surrendered for some reason. My house was strong. I felt another wave of rage fill me. Again thunder clamored, closer this time.

"You brought the storm with you?" Mama muttered as she struggled erect.

"I don't believe this," Jack said to the terrorists once he recognized them. He stood up off the floor. "You invaded my home?"

"This is not your home," the one over Nathan said. "*We* are your home. *This* is your prison."

"Brother Bartholomew, please keep your tongue," one of the

cloaked men said.

Healers! I must have said that out loud.

"Quite right, good lady," Colonel Mustard puffed. "Allow me to introduce you to the Asclepium Order. I only just today was informed of their existence."

"What are you wearing?" I asked, looking at his military outfit.

"My armor, of course. We were on our way to join you on the Radiant Plane when these hooligans barged in."

"Why have you come?" Jack asked the brothers. "I told you I'd bring the poison to you."

"We waited for months. We didn't hear from you. We assumed your master made you change your mind."

"We had months stolen from us," I defended. "Untie them all now."

No one moved.

"Seriously?" Jack scoffed. "This is how you chose to handle the situation? To barge into this house and take hostages? To cause them pain and injury?" He pointed at Nathan. Jack shook his head in irritation, waiting for one of them to answer. The healers looked at one another.

"This woman," Jack nodded at me, "went to great lengths to find and release the name of the healer, one of you. *One of us.* To redeem him. To clear his name from that of the stained traitor."

"She did that to save the Citadel Plane," one of them retorted.

"No," Jack hollered. "She did it because it was the right thing to do."

Jack's eyes looked truly crestfallen. I think he had wanted to believe the healers were better than the rest of us, that they'd never resort to violence to solve a problem. Yet, here they were. Invading our house.

The lack of any justification *irritated* me. For Minerva's sake, I was exhausted. When was the last time I slept, truly slept? Or ate, for that matter? But, no, I came home to this … this sickening display of brutality, by an organization I believed to be noble and caring.

"Do any of you know what kind of day I'm having?" I asked. "I mean, I return from the Radiant Plane where I was tortured by the Queen, imprisoned, escaped, rescued these two," I waved my hand at Saffron and Simon, "found the poison, only to be tricked by Malador into wearing the Tempest Veil, which nearly destroyed me, then I came this close," I parted my thumb and finger just a small distance, "to getting *buried alive* in the mud that was once Esmeralda's castle. Not to mention that, when my day started what seems like years ago now, I was on yet another plane and fought the Arch Lich, not once, but *twice*. That, as it turned out, was the easiest part of my damned day!" By the end, I was screaming, finding my own rage. Thunder rumbled loudly, a constant backdrop to my diatribe. "Now, I'm home and I find my own staff and allies and guests tied up and held captive to a bunch of raggedy, out-dated, out-classed, robe-clad, two-bit healers." I held up my hand. "I'm not saying you guys don't have any reason to be royally pissed off, but you have absolutely no reason to barge into *my* home and make an enemy out of *this* house. Or me."

I hadn't come to grips with the complete chaos my life had become until I replayed the last day. Suddenly, my exhaustion piled on me like a mud castle melting in the rain. I put a hand over my eyes to hide my fatigue, pushing away the tears of weariness and distress.

Everyone in the house exchanged glances. The robed men looked at one in particular, the leader I guessed. Still no one moved. *I mean, what was it gonna take!*

My exhaustion gave way to anger, which quickly gave way to rage.

"Let them go now or I'll destroy this house and everyone it in!"

I snapped my arm straight up into the air and the sky responded with a profound flash and deafening of thunder.

Whoa.

I swallowed, trembling with rage.

The leader bowed. "Well?" he asked his followers. "Do as the master of the house orders. Don't tarry now, boys. Brother Charles, Brother David, please heal any who need it."

Brother Able, Bartholomew, Charles, Daniel ... yes, I saw the pattern.

As the ropes fell away from the captives I turned to Jack and whispered. "Please, tend them. And watch the healers."

"Yes, ma'am."

I wiped my eyes again, trying to stay ahead of the building torrent of tears. My knees felt weak. *I'm so damned tired.*

"Well played, madam," said the head monk as he approached me. "Winki Witherspoon, I presume?" He held out a gloved hand.

I folded my arms, refusing his gesture. "I am Winki. And you are?"

He lowered his hand. "I am Brother Able, patriarch of the Order. We did not come here to hurt you or any in your house."

I sighed. "I confess, at the moment," I eyed my staff, "I don't believe you." As the steady rain fell against the panes of the large window seat, I jutted my chin to Nathan receiving Jack's ministrations. "How did he get the cut on his eye?"

"*I* confess," the brother said looking over his own group that clustered together, distanced from my staff, "we were a bit over zealous in our attempts to convince your house. My sincere apologies," he bowed again, "but it was our intention to heal any who needed it before we left. I assure you."

"Why are you here?" I said without emotion.

"For the poison ... and the girl."

Why does everyone insist on calling her a girl? "You can have what I brought back but I don't think it is the poison." I gestured to Mama, who'd never moved once she stood up. "She claims she assisted Mrs. Jolly in its making and sabotaged it."

"This is truth," Mama whispered.

I handed him the vial. "But whatever it is, it's yours."

"I ... thank you. But we cannot leave without the chef."

"Get used to the disappointment," I said flatly.

"Madam, please understand our position—"

I raised my hand. "I said no."

"If she can destroy an entire populace of "

"*I said no!*"

Lightning cracked, blinding everyone. An oak tree just outside the bay window exploded, sending a small rain of bark and bits to the ground. I didn't move. Everyone else jumped and shuffled away from me, including Brother Able.

"Winki."

I jerked toward the voice that called me. Nathan reacted by raising his hands in the air, as if I were going to shoot him again. "Winki, try to calm yourself," he said softly, matching the slow steps he took toward me. His eye had been healed, and now both of them looked at me wide open. Afraid.

"They're not taking her!"

"Okay, okay. You're right, you are, you are—"

I recognized the squawky Boston accent of his talent, the voice of reason. "Don't use that tone of voice with me!" I shouted, pointing at him.

He clenched his eyes and cowered, certain I would strike him where he stood. His hands, still in the air, trembled.

"They're not taking her," I snipped. "And don't you dare try to convince me otherwise."

He gulped and licked his lips. "Okay. I just want you to—"

"What? Calm down?" *Yes. I'm losing it.* "They're going to kill her."

Again lightning blinded the household, and the subsequent clatter shook the walls and windows. A mirror shook loose from the wall and crashed to the floor.

I thought he'd retreat, but Nathan stood his ground. In fact, he stood taller. His wide eyes narrowed. His face turned red, bursting with fury. "*Then knock it off!*"

Nathan's rage completely shocked me. I took a small step back.

"You get a grip *right now*, Mrs. Witherspoon," He took defiant steps toward me. "Take a breath. Take a nap, for god sake's, but get your *damn act together.*"

I swallowed, embarrassed. My ears felt hot and flushed. I struggled to find my voice. All eyes in the room were on us. On me. "Nathan, I just—" I really hated it when he was mad at me. I dropped my gaze. Thunder grumbled distantly.

"No," he growled, "in fact, I insist. You've done your part. You did what you set out to do. But threatening to kill everyone in this house, Mrs. Witherspoon? That crossed a line. So," he said sternly, "get out, before you make that a reality."

His eyes bore into me. I shifted my feet, like a punished child.

He was right. I had crossed the line. In my head, I heard his words, "When your tide rises, I'm going to drown, just like everyone else." Killing was the A-number one way of becoming a darkling, and I just let everyone in the room know I was about to take the first step, and drag the house along. Nathan was doing exactly what I had asked him to do; stop me from making that move; keep me in line. Even at the risk of his own life.

Probably harder than me protecting my stupid ego.

"Sorry," I managed to squeeze out. I swallowed the large lump in my throat. I shuffled my leadened feet and made my way up the staircase.

Chapter Thirty-Two

THE SOFT AND soothing sound of distant thunder roused me from my sleep. Everything splashed around me. I jumped, sure I was still in Esmeralda's castle, sure I was drowning. I flailed, splashing water everywhere—

"My lady. My lady! You're fine."

I gripped the sides of the bathtub, filled with cold and filthy water. I panted and shivered. It all came back. I had peeled off my clothes and drawn a hot bath, wanting to soak off my rage and worry. Apparently, my exhaustion overwhelmed me, and I had fallen asleep in the tub.

I spied the spider dangling just above me. "Annabelle?"

"I watched over you. I wanted to make certain you didn't accidentally drown."

On its own, the tub started to drain and the spout ran with steaming water. My house. I put a hand on the wall. "Thank you." I looked at Annabelle. "Thank you, too."

"Do not be so quick to thank me," she said, swinging her way to the tile on the wall. "I ... I've come to apologize."

As the water warmed, I reapplied soap. I hadn't actually cleaned myself, having fallen asleep so quickly. "Apologize?" I asked, lathering my hair.

"Yes, my lady. The house security is my priority. Mine alone.

Those men should never have been able to get in the door, let alone hold our people hostage."

"Annabelle, it's not your fault." I stopped her. "I saw the spiders on the ceiling." I had noticed the black of a million bodies, the spiders waiting for my call to attack, but I hadn't look at them. I hadn't wanted to give them away to the intruders. "You were ready."

"It should never have gotten that far. Once Mrs. Black and Nathan got hurt, I should have ... we should have ..."

"Hey," I tried to console. I'd have given her a hug if I could.

The spider continued. "I always know my enemy. But I didn't know them. I don't know healers. Would our venom kill them? Would they infect us? Would they be immune and kill us all? Those doubts made me ... hesitate. Then it was too late."

"I understand, I really do. You don't need my forgiveness because you did nothing wrong. Waiting was prudent." I watched as swirls of blood and mud made rivulets between my feet and down the drain. What a mess. "If anyone's to blame, it's me. We met with the healers, yet we had no idea they'd attack our house. If I'd had any inkling, I would have warned you." I sighed, thinking about their action. "I think that was very out of character for them." The spider remained squatted, still looking upset. "But now we know."

Fully cleansed, I stood and wrapped a fluffy robe around me. As I toweled my hair, I asked her to fill me in. "How did it happen, anyway? I mean, Nathan is formidable on his own. How did the healers manage to subdue them all?"

She spoke, making her way around the walls as we went into my bedroom. "It started once Nathan woke up," she said. "We were all so relieved."

I sat on my bed where I could press my hand against the wall ...

In a blink, the house took me into the past. I stood in the foyer as Nathan rushed down the stairs, already dressed in his black and red armor. He looked at the grandfather clock. "Where are they?" he called behind him. "What's taking so long?"

Nathan called Colonel Mustard, Annabelle explained, sounding like a voice over in a dream. *They were going to meet you in the Radiant Plane. Nathan didn't want you to be there alone. He'd dealt with the Queen before.*

"They said they'd be over as soon as they could, sir," Jeeves answered, trying to keep up with Nathan without killing himself on the staircase. "They are arriving now," he affirmed.

A portal formed in the living room. Out from the windy ball stepped Colonel Mustard and his valet, Tom Jones. Mr. Jones' leathers looked like a coffee-colored version of the outfit Nathan wore, the color perfectly matching his own skin tone. The Colonel, on the other hand, looked like a leather version of a civil war re-enactor; high collar, blazing gold buttons, oversized gauntlets, and epaulets on each shoulder. His leather pants pouched over his thighs, tucking into his leather riding boots. Even a thin sword dangled from his hip.

The Colonel and Nathan shook hands. "Thank you for coming," Nathan said.

"My pleasure, dear boy. Shall we be off?"

Nathan turned to Jeeves. "If you would be so kind?"

The butler changed his appearance and waved his hand in the air. Nothing happened. "I don't understand," Jeeves said, tilting his head. "There's too much … I think someone's coming."

The house bell rung.

Impatiently, Nathan said, "What's the hold up? Winki and Jack are alone. Open a portal, first." He turned to the maid who watched from the massive door jam. "Please, Mrs. Black, answer the front door."

She gave a small curtsy and turned away.

Meanwhile, his dazzling green eyes twinkled as Jeeves waved his arm in a grand circle. Again nothing happened.

Nathan shifted in frustration.

"I don't understand, sir. Unless ..."

"Unless?" The lawyer waved a hand in a hurry-up movement.

"Unless someone is trying to open a portal here—"

What's going on? I asked the spider.

Annabelle said, *In reflection, I believe Jeeves got confused by several things happening at once; the healers at the front door, people returning from the Radiant Plane at the same time he tried to open a portal the other direction.*

Mrs. Black cried out as she was shoved into the room. Before the frail woman hit the floor, Nathan managed to catch her. He didn't look up fast enough to see the brown-robed men pushing her into the room, one holding something pointy under his robe, thrusting it forward like a gun. The healer closed the gap quickly and landed a swift punch to Nathan's face sending him and Mrs. Black sprawling. Thus, the gash over his eye.

Reacting to the assault, I took my hand from the wall, interrupting the vision. That's why the Order was able to take the house. Its defenders were distracted, trying to get to me. Trying to help me.

"It looks like it wasn't your fault at all," I whispered to her. "Looks like it was mine."

"How so?"

If they weren't worried about me, if they'd had the utmost faith that I *was* their champion, that I *could* rescue Saffron and Simon *all on my own*, the monks wouldn't have gotten past the front door. But I couldn't speak the words. I had no reason to blame them, really. Just more bruised ego to go with the side of guilt. "Never mind," I cleared my throat. "After I left ... how's Saffron? Did the monks take her?"

"They did not," she said, accentuating each word. I placed my palm back on the wall.

Back in the living room I gasped at the vision ... of me. Covered in black lich ichor, dark mud, red Malador-blood. I stood there looking like death, slightly warmed over. My white hair was hidden by the goo and spatter. Blue crescents spread below my red eyes. Red and hateful. *By the stars, was that me?*

Nathan approached, "Okay, okay. You're right, you are, you are ——"

"Don't use that tone of voice with me!" she, I mean, I snapped.

Nathan cringed. Jeez, *I* cringed. Did I really look that angry? Almost inhuman?

I watched his face morph from fear to worry to anger. He yelled at the muck-covered woman, and she deflated like a popped balloon. Her shoulders slumped, her head hung, her spirit crushed. Within a heartbeat, she went from bringer-of-all-doom to scolded-child.

All eyes watched her slink her way up the stairs. I forced myself not to watch. I took in the room.

Jack moved from person to person, checking their well being. He spoke to Saffron and Simon while Theodore chatted with Tom Jones.

Nathan licked his lips with worry as his eyes watched her, me, ascend the stairs. His jaw clenched, his Adam's apple bobbed, and his brow hung low. Once I climbed out of view he collected himself. With a deep breath he turned to face the robed men, and—like a lawyer—his demeanor changed.

"Well, gentlemen," with a chipper smile, "let's wrap this up quickly."

Everyone in the room stopped milling about and watched.

Brother Able said, "Please, understand. We need the girl."

"Woman," Nathan corrected. *Yay!* "Not gonna happen."

"But—"

"Not gonna happen," he said louder. He turned his face upward as he pointed to Saffron. "Keep her here!"

The outside shutters slammed across the bay window and locked. Everyone jumped as all the shutters, all over the house, did the same.

"Stop!" Saffron said, running to stand between Nathan and

Brother Able. She held her hand up, as if trying to break up a brawl. "Both of you, stop. It's all right," she said, her eyes brimming. "I'll go with them."

"Saff!" Simon called.

"No, Simon. It's okay. I'll ..." She turned to the healer. "I don't want to hurt you. Any of you. After all I've lost, after all I've seen over the last, I don't know, six months? I don't want to cause more pain. I'm happy to go with you."

I frowned, standing there, unseen.

"Wait," Jack interrupted, joining the emotional fray of the room. "Can't we just talk about this?" He took Saffron by the shoulders, only to shyly dropped his grip. "You've done nothing wrong. Don't be quick to accept a death sentence for a crime you haven't committed."

"I appreciate what you're trying to do, but—"

"If you're so willing to give up your life then ...," He looked at Nathan, and Brother Able. "Stay here. Stay in this house. We still need a cook."

"I'm home now, healer," Mama argued. "The cooking is what I do."

Over my dead body.

Brother Able stepped forward. "You want her to accept the same terms as yourself. To be a slave in this house?"

"Not a slave, a paid servant. Just like the others. With a certain agreement in her contract that states she needs to stay here at all times, under our watch, care, and supervision."

"She's not a pawn," Simon spat, giving Jack a small shove away from his sister. "She's a human being. She has free will."

"I agree, but it would only be until we could find another solution. Maybe," Jack implored, "things will change, as they often do. At least she'd have her life." To Saffron he said, "At least it would give you a chance to be, well, somewhat normal again."

"I hardly think keeping her here will be protection enough for our kind," Brother Able pressed. "Our lives are already tightly restricted with rules and limitations. We cannot walk outside without being fully clothed, we cannot touch another human being or an animal for that matter, we cannot simply choose whether or not to participate in the tournaments. We hide our faces so we aren't discovered, lest we experience the same fate as you," he said to Jack. "Our lives are not our own already, but we do live. Yet, to add to our torment, here is this woman who has the means to wipe us out." He let a beat pass, ready for any argument. None came. I think that softened him a little, knowing he'd won some empathy, if nothing else. "I do not *wish* to harm the chef. We only wish to be safe. What assurances do we have she won't create another potion?" Brother Able asked.

"What assurances do *we* have that you won't come barging in here and attack the house?" Nathan answered.

"It is clear," the monk huffed, "you have the advantage. We understand that entering your home again would only result in our injury or death."

"So?" the green man retorted. I'd almost forgotten Theodore was there. "What does that mean to any of you? You're healers. You have nothing to risk."

"Please," Nathan held up his hand to the goblin. "Point taken, but let them continue."

"We can, and do, die, green one," Brother Able said. "Healing can be done only with our Mother's consent. Only under extreme circumstances do we even ask." He addressed Nathan. "You are safe from us. However, we cannot simply let her live freely. If she doesn't make the poison herself, she can tell others how. How can you guarantee she will not?"

"Perhaps I can be of service," the Colonel joined the group, Tom Jones at his side. In his basso Southern voice, he said, "Sir, I can give you my promise that any misbehavior on Mrs. Jolly's part will be met with a swift and just retaliation by the Magnolia House. We are allies with Gateway Manor to be sure. However, while I have no great love for healers—pardon any offense, sir—"

"None taken," Brother Able nodded.

"—I do appreciate the role they play in the peace between those of us who worship the light and those of us who linger in the dark. I vow my house to protect the honor and safety of the Asclepium Order."

Brother Able looked at his group of men. He regarded the vial in his hand.

"I'll have a contract made," Nathan offered, "outlining the terms of our agreement?"

Brother Able gave a slow, single shake of his head. "Contracts mean little to us." He folded his arms, hidden in ample sleeves. "Your word will do." Some of his tribe muttered. He raised a hand to quell them. "We have lost, brothers. We lowered ourselves to their level, acted as they would, and lost." He turned to Mrs. Black. "You can dismiss your ... um ..." he waived a finger at the ceiling, "we are leaving."

The ceiling was black, packed with our spider warriors and, while my house members knew they were there, it appeared no one else did. The other monks, the Colonel, and Mr. Jones all inhaled in awe. The ceiling shuddered in waves as the millions of spiders retreated.

Nathan cleared his throat. "Let me be clear. I regret that you're leaving here with the belief that you've lost. We have no conflict with you. We are on the same side. I have no ill will toward healers or the Order, and I have no intention of letting Mrs. Jolly, or anyone, harm any of you. Her being here, under our protection, is for your benefit as well as ours. On that you have my word," Nathan said. To the ceiling he called, "We're good. Everyone is free to leave."

The noise of shutters opening everywhere echoed through the

halls.

The cloaked man stood a little taller and gave a good-natured bow with his hand on his heart. "I will hold you to that. Come, brothers! Time for us to be on our way."

The brotherhood and Nathan walked to the front door, shadow-me tagged behind. The rain outside had slowed to a sprinkle, and the clouds started to separate, forming puffy windows for patches of starry night sky.

Nathan bade farewell to the Order, who walked down the driveway and onto the street, out of sight.

Colonel Mustard and Tom Jones followed.

"I apologize for putting you in an awkward situation, Colonel," Nathan said. "Thank you. For everything."

They shook hands vigorously. "I don't regret my participation, Mr. Marble. But you should know, Magnolia House just swore to protect the Asclepium Order. I take such allegiances very seriously." He leaned forward so only Nathan—and myself—could hear. "Do not put me in the middle."

"Understood," Nathan whispered. He took a deep breath as the two men made their way down the white driveway.

The goblin guest came next.

"You sure know how to show a guy a good time!" Theodore said.

"Thank you, for all your help."

"Call if you need me." He offered a fist, and Nathan bumped it. Theodore summoned a goblin-sized portal, bowed grandly, and disappeared.

Last out came Simon, with Saffron and Jack to see him off.

"I'm sorry," Simon said, probably for the millionth time. "God, I'm so sorry, Saff."

"Um," Nathan said, "Simon, the police are looking for you. Jack and I may have told them we thought you had something to do with the deaths of Saffron's family."

"They won't be able to prove anything, though," Jack added.

"I'll go to them now," he said and shrugged. "Not sure what I'll say."

Saffron spoke. "I'd go with you if I could. Send that detective to me if she wants to talk. I won't press any charges. Tell them it was just a miserable mistake. It was all just … a horrible coincidence."

"He's been missing for months," Nathan said the her. He shook Simon's hand. "They're gonna want to know where you've been."

"I'll figure something out," the brother gave a wan smile.

"I do have one question, though," Jack asked. "We found a micro memory card in your house, Mrs. Jolly. It had two recordings from your husband."

"Harry?" her eyes widened.

"One was a recording of him and Simon, arguing, and the other was a voice mail message he made for you, or so it appeared."

"I'll give you the card," Nathan added. "And you can listen for yourself."

"My question is, why?" Jack asked. "Why did he keep these recordings? The card was so well hidden even the police didn't find it."

"In the desk," she said to no one. "Harry …" she swallowed, and tried again. "Harry had memory problems. They started after his last concussion. One of many, I'm afraid. We kept it a secret from everyone, and he promised me that, after the next season, he was quitting the game. Anyway, he made recordings of things as a way to remember them. He hid them in all sorts of places, often forgetting where." She tilted her head with a small smile. "He thought I didn't know, but I did."

Simon put a hand on her shoulder. "I had no idea, sis."

"That's the way he wanted it."

He looked at Nathan. "Can I visit Saff? Can I bring my wife and kids? I know they'd love to see her."

"Sure," Nathan nodded. "I'm looking forward to meeting them."

As Simon crunched his way down the driveway, shouting from within the house made Nathan and Jack—and shadow-me—rush back to the living room. Mrs. Black pointed a gnarled finger at Mrs. White, yelling accusations. "You lied to us. You lied to me!"

"I did no such thing!"

"Hey!" Nathan called, raising his hands, "Everyone, calm down." He rubbed his neck. "Not now, okay? Let's do this in the morning. It's been a hell of a day." The women huffed at each other. "Please? For me?"

Mrs. Black hung her head, defeated. As she passed Nathan, she rose to tippy-toes and kissed him on the cheek. "Good night, my boy."

The last thing I witnessed was Nathan oozing up the stairs before I took my hand from the wall.

"Sorry," I whispered to Annabelle, "I got lost in the house's memory."

"I understand," she said, making her way up her thread. "You should retire in earnest, as should I. See you tomorrow."

Chapter Thirty-Three

I DON'T KNOW how long I would have slept if it hadn't been for the knock on the door. Incapable of forming anything like language I groaned.

"Madam? I have brought you breakfast."

I groaned again. My stomach, however, roared.

"May I come in?"

"Please."

Jeeves lofted into the room, setting my cloche-covered breakfast in place. With a grand *viola* move, he removed the cover, exposing hot oatmeal and brown sugar. *And coffee.*

My feet moved on their own, guided by my stomach. I sat and dug right in. I swear, nothing had ever tasted so good.

Jeeves remained poised.

"What?" I asked, shoveling heaping spoonfuls into my mouth.

"Mr. Marble has asked that you join him after you've eaten, madam."

I let out an audible moan. After being scolded by him in front of the household—not that I didn't deserve it, mind you—seeing him first thing wasn't top of my list. "Do I have to?" I whined.

"He's holding a house meeting." *Oh, good. All of them will be there.* "Your attendance is required, I regret to say."

I sighed. "Whatever. I'll be down in a few."

He bowed, and quietly left.

With each bite my appetite wavered. Eating when I'm sad never appealed to me. I only got through half of the bowl when I pushed it away, and set my head on the table.

Look on the bright side, I told myself. *You went to the Radiant Plane, you got the poison, you rescued Saffron and Simon … and Jack. Don't forget defeating the Arch Lich. So you threatened to strike everyone down in a blaze of lightning. Ha. Like you really could. It was an idle threat.*

Right?

Right.

Making my way downstairs with a cup of coffee in my hand, a whole new reason for worry dawned on me. *Mama White.* Making the turn into the grand living room, I saw her sitting on a single dining room chair in the middle of the room, when most everyone else sat on the regular sofas and chairs.

Nathan stood, dressed in a nice suit and tie, hands in his pockets, by the entry way. "Glad you could join us, Mrs. Witherspoon."

I really hated when he called me that. "What's going on?"

"We're about to discuss the re-employment of Mrs. White."

The plump woman looked at me, her face serious. I instantly flew into the memory; pointing that gun at Nathan, enraged by his betrayal, actually the illusion of betrayal *she* created. She had wanted to turn me evil. She came *so* damned close.

"Y'all have fun with that," I turned away.

"Winki, you need to listen to this." He gestured into the room. "Please."

"Why is this so important to you?"

"Please," he softly said.

As I looked around for my own place to sit, Jack stood and offered his chair. I thanked him and took it. "Go on," I said, Jon Stewart-style.

"I've asked you all to gather to discuss bringing Mama White back into our fold." A few grumbled or huffed. "Just to get an idea of what everyone's thinking, let's put it to a quick vote. All in favor of her coming home, raise your hand." Only Nathan held his hand up. "Opposed?" Everyone else. Everyone except Saffron and me. She had no reason to vote either way. I felt my position was clear. My hands remained tightly wrapped around my mug.

"You didn't vote, Mrs. Witherspoon," he said, having noticed.

"True. I didn't."

"And why's that?"

I looked at the faces in the room. Jeeves, Mrs. Black, Mr. Smith, Mr. Wesson, Jack, and Saffron. *Because this is ludicrous.*

Nathan sighed. "Please, say it out loud."

"Because this is ludicrous."

He nodded, and addressed the group. "Then I stand before you as Mama's advocate." He leisurely paced. "And I will ask each of you to tell us what your issues are, but I'm going to ask to go first."

"Of course you are," Mrs. Black grumbled. "So you can use that voice of yours to sway us." She pointed a thin and accusative finger.

"She's got a point," Mr. Smith said. His partner nodded in agreement.

Nathan took out a piece of paper from his briefcase, already opened and perched on a nearby coffee table. He raised it in front of them. "This is my opening argument on the matter." He handed it to me. "I'd like you to read it."

"Why me? She's the only impartial one here," I pointed to Saffron. "Have her read it."

"Please."

I started to.

"Out loud," he corrected. "To them."

I grunted in disapproval as I stood, setting my coffee aside.

I took a deep breath. "No one in this room has more cause to dislike, or hate, Mrs. White than me." I pointed at Nathan, making clear the "me" in question. "After, it was me she ultimately betrayed. It was me she undermined in the eyes of our new Champion, Winki Witherspoon. It was me she fingered as the traitor. It was me she wanted killed." I licked my lips, fighting the memory. "But more poignantly, and something none of you could have known, it wasn't me, Nathan Marble, she wanted to destroy. Not the lawyer, not Will's friend, not the executor of the house. It was me, Edward Witherspoon ..." I looked up at him. His arms were folded, his head cast downward. He rocked back and forth on his feet. I cleared my throat. "Edward Witherspoon, son of Charlotte, brother of Will, and the man she raised from a baby. That is who she wanted to kill. She recognized me within months of my showing up as Will's lawyer. She'd removed a wart I had as a favor, one Edward also had. Once she suspected my true identity, my gonzo's glamour no longer fooled her. Though she never said it, Mama has known, all this time, that I was Edward."

The staff cast glances at each other. I swallowed and continued. "In her journal, she expressed hatred for my cowardice, for hiding behind a new face and name. That she could have lived with. Until she realized that Will, too, knew who I was, and that we'd put together the will and testament leaving everything to his bride, and not me. That's when she acted, eliminating Will from our lives, certain I would come forward and reclaim the house. My failure to step up and reveal myself after Will's death spurred her to blame me for everything. In her eyes, I was weak, tarnished. The house should have remained in the Witherspoon bloodline, not just the Witherspoon name."

"That is not true!" the black woman protested as she stood. "I did not have Will *eliminated*." She waggled her head, at the word. "The Dark Lords were only supposed to test him, nothing more. I didn't think they'd take him, I swear to that."

The room burst with accusations and heated words. Nathan

whistled and hollered to gain control of the crowd.

"Go on," he said to me once all had settled. "Continue."

"I can't read anymore," I frowned, "I don't want to."

"Please," Nathan said, "it's important, Winki. Continue."

I did, begrudgingly. "So why am I standing here before you now, defending this woman? Because ..." Having read ahead, I took a deep inhale. "Because, that's what we do." I took a deep breath while watching the staffers. All eyes were on the floor, not me.

"We all witnessed the change in Will," I continued, "when he returned from his conversion, how happy and light and wonderful he'd become. And we welcomed the new master back into his home. While I understand Will didn't hurt us directly, I'd like to point out that we, those of us tied to the house, were forced into the dark when he crossed that line. Our hearts hardened, our thoughts blackened, and we all did things that remain unspoken. He hurt us. Yet once he converted, we continued to love him.

"I'm asking the same for Mrs. White, the most talented cook in New Orleans, a dizzying power with potions, and more importantly, our friend. Her conversion complete, she returns to us no less cleansed, cleared, and enlightened than was true for Will."

Tiny muscles painfully tugged the corners of my mouth downward. "I would defend any of you in a similar situation, because I believe first and foremost in redemption. I believe in second chances. I believe in the conversion. And I believe we are a white house, with clean consciences, with large hearts, and a propensity for compassion. I believe I am, in fact, the very man she raised and taught and loved." I sniffed. "And I wouldn't be standing before you now if it weren't for her. I want her to come home." Thank the stars that was the end of it, since my blurred vision stopped me from reading further.

I stood, thrusting the paper into Nathan's stomach, and left. I don't know if he even took it or if it fell to the floor. I didn't care. I walked across the entry and into the large dining room, still set up with silver sterno-warmed servers. After pouring myself another coffee, I sat at the table, facing the portrait.

That perfect face. Those perfect blue eyes. That small smile.

Taken from me by …

I'd almost killed Nathan because of her. I'd outed Jack because of her. I'd exposed Nathan because of her. *You're dead because of her. I just want to see you*

I'd forgotten all about it! I hadn't even noticed it when I pealed off the filthy clothing. I left the DVD in the inside pocket.

I ran up the stairs, two at a time, and removed the leather jacket from the hamper. Pulling the jewel cased disk from its safe harbor, I smiled, thankful. Yes. I'd found it. I'd kept it. After all I'd been through, I hadn't lost it.

Nathan waited at the bottom of the stairs, hands in his pockets. "Got a minute?"

Casting a glance at the DVD I shrugged. No. "Sure."

He broadly waved his arm, gesturing me back into the dining room. Mama was seated there, on the far end of the long table. Nathan took his favorite chair and nodded for me to do the same. With a frown, I complied.

"We took a second vote," he started. "They agreed she could stay."

"Was it unanimous?"

He frowned a bit. "No. It doesn't matter, though, because we all know it's your house. Your rules. So, your say."

Without looking at the woman I shook my head. "I say no."

"Winki—"

"Nathan, she killed Will."

Mama move to protest again.

Nathan stopped her. "Technically, that's not true. She just—"

"She killed Will. Your brother, my husband, *she*," I pointed without gracing her with my eyes, "killed him."

"Please, just listen—"

"Moreover, I don't believe her."

He cocked his head.

"That she's cleansed. She's already killed someone."

His eyes widened. "Who?"

Mama folded her arms. "I have not killed anyone."

"Malador," I answered. "She ran a sword through him." I nodded. "Not that I'm all that broke up about it. I kinda wanted to do it myself—" I noticed she sat back, with a soft smile on her face. "What?"

Nathan answered. "In the Radiant Plane? No, Winki. Evil can't die there. Didn't Jeeves cover this with you? Evil can be only destroyed in Aqua or Zephyr Planes." He gave a deep exhale. "Hell, we can only imprison it in portraits here. But evil can't be destroyed in either the Radiant or Phantom Planes."

That sounded familiar ... something about a "fundamental balance" that I passed off as "more stupid rules."

"Esmeralda had part of her castle fall on her head," I exclaimed.

"That will slow her down," he chuckled. "I only wish it could be that easy. Would have solved my problem." The two of them, each at the table's ends, stared at each other.

Oh, yeah. And that's another thing. "By the way, you clearly have had contact with her without my knowledge. She said you sent her to go work for the Queen and sabotage the poison."

He gulped. With a raised hand he stammered, "Not exactly—"

"Then how, exactly?" I scowled.

"I didn't send her there because of the poison. I sent her there because of the Jolly case—" He stopped himself with a huff, and pushed back from the table. As he poured himself a cup of coffee, he said, "Let me start from when Mama disappeared."

He brought the pot over, filled my cup, and took a seat. "I got word just days after she disappeared that she went to the Light Lords and threw herself on their mercy. She asked, begged really, to be converted. That's a rare thing, for someone to want to change. Not even Will wanted it." He muttered. "Will just wasn't given a choice." He sat forward, clasping his hands on the table. "I asked to be kept in the loop."

"But didn't bother to keep me in the loop with you."

"At that time, I didn't see any point. If the conversion didn't work, if she was tricking anyone, if she didn't want to come home, or couldn't, then I'd have worried you for no reason."

I folded my arms, slinking in my chair. "I should have been told."

"You might be right. Anyway, the conversion went well, or so I was informed. So, I ... visited—"

"You visited her?" I seethed.

"Yes. You kept hounding me to find us a new cook and what did I tell you? I was working on it."

My mouth dropped, dumbfounded. "For a lawyer, your attention to detail is pitiful. Or, we have very different definitions for the word '*new*.'"

He ignored me. "Then the Saffron Jolly case came our way, and when you told me Malador came to Saffron's house I knew, I mean I suspected, Esmeralda was probably pulling the strings. It felt like her. Taking that poor woman's family, that's right up her alley."

"Since you didn't see fit to tell me, I assume you let Jack know about this suspicion? You know, your partner?"

After several uncomfortably quiet seconds, he shook his head. "I hoped I was wrong. No. I thought I'd wait before sending everyone in a panic. The timing of it, I thought, was perfect. Mama was released, and so I asked her to watch Esmeralda, prove me right or wrong. I didn't know," he open-handedly waved at Mama, "she would get employed—"

"I didn't hear from you for months, Nathan. What was I

supposed to do? Ask to borrow a cup of sugar?"

He sighed, bobbing his head. "Then we got four months taken from us, and here we are."

"What else aren't you telling me? Because it sounds like I'm being kept in the dark constantly."

"I'm sorry, Winki. Please know, I don't make decisions to keep you in the dark or to undermine you or hurt you. Or Jack. Or anyone. I want you to trust me and trust that I'll do what's best for you and the house."

I didn't care about any of it. I thought loudly, "No." I knew the *thought catcher* would read that.

"Mama says she saved you. Is that true?"

I sat quiet, my eyes unfocused.

"She also says made sure the poison wouldn't work."

"I don't know about the poison. I'm assuming that's true. Otherwise I'm sure we'd have heard from the Order by now. She *did* take Malador's stupid necklace off me—"

"Why are you touching anything that man hands you?" he abruptly yelled, causing me to jerk with surprise. He dropped his head to collect himself and let out a heavy sigh as he massaged his forehead. "I'm sorry. Winki, I know you think he's a chuckle-head, but he's *extremely* dangerous."

"I know," I whispered.

"He's gunning for you. I worry about that more than Esmeralda gunning for me, or Lord Edmund gunning for Jack."

"I understand," I whispered, emphatically.

He, too, must have thought he'd made his point, or maybe just wanted to bring us back to the problem at hand. The one seated at the end of the table. "I think she's changed. I know from experience that those who've been converted are honest-to-goodness devotees. Moreover, Winki, this house will be stronger with her in it than without."

I looked up at the blond man forever stuck above the fireplace. His small smile beaming back at me.

"I'm glad you trust her, Nathan, but I don't." I stood to leave. "No. Send her on her way." I turned to leave.

"Winki, wait! Mama, would you please wait for me here? I'll be back in a few minutes."

Eyes lowered, Mama gave him a nod.

"You're heading to the media room I take it," he said. "I'll walk with you."

I didn't wait. I headed out.

With a trot, Nathan caught up to me. We traversed the house in silence, walking through several rooms to get to the media room. That was just how some of these old homes were arranged, so air could circulate within all the house once the windows were open.

I fiddled with the DVD in my hand. I really want to be alone. I knew he heard me. He was just ignoring me.

"I heard you made another deal with Lord Edmund," Nathan said.

Better than being berated again. "He offered to change the terms based on my final battle with the Arch Lich."

"You got that in writing, yes?"

I recalled our stupid handshake, seeing the event in my head.

He grimaced. "Winki. Handshakes mean almost nothing here in the Midland Plane, for chrisake. They certainly mean nothing anywhere else."

"They mean everything to goblins," I defended, "and it seems contracts mean nothing to the Order. Besides, I had witnesses." The whole thing pissed me off, so I changed the subject. "Since we're not going to talk about Mama, let's talk about the Colonel."

Nathan gave me a puzzled look.

"He came last night to help me. I thought they don't usually get involved with us. You know, keep to themselves, and all?"

"Everything's changed, Mrs. Witherspoon."

I hung my head. I really hated when he called me that. "What do you mean?" I huffed.

"Now, the Colonel is all too happy to supply help when we need it." I narrowed my eyes. "Because he knows what I know."

"Which is?"

We'd reached the media room. Nathan slid the pocket doors shut behind him, enclosing the chamber. "You beat the Arch Lich," he said sternly.

Yeah. I was there, so?

"Like me, the Colonel wants to make sure you stay on this side of the community fence. That's why he helped. He has a vested interest in you staying on Team Good."

"I don't understand."

"Because. He could never defeat you on Team Bad. We could never win. Evil would be infinitely powerful, and the world, every plane, would be shredded to pieces. Do you understand now?"

"Dramatic much?" I tossed my hair. "You seem to think I'm bucking to switch sides? Why do you think the worst of me?"

A sadness washed over his face. "Damn, where do I start? How 'bout this: You threatened to kill everyone in the room last night to get your way."

I scoffed. "That was a bluff—"

"The hell it was!" His face reddened.

I took a step back.

"You can't throw death around like it's the flu."

"It was a bluff—"

"It wasn't," he yelled and pointed to his head. "I hear you!"

I gulped.

"Just like I heard you when you pointed that gun at me. Killing is real. Killing will get you an all-expense-paid ticket to the dark world. Dammit, Winki! You think death isn't permanent? Go talk to your husband."

That was unfair. I stormed off to the other side of the room, arms folded to protect myself.

He didn't back down. "You can freeze time. You can conjure items out of the air—"

"It doesn't work that way—"

"—and you can control the frickin' weather."

"I cannot!"

"Yes," he calmed a bit. "Yes, you can. I noticed it last year when you possessed Jack. Whenever you're sad or angry, there's a storm outside."

I wanted to argue, but that did seem to be true. "We live in New Orleans," I offered in explanation. "Storms aren't unusual."

"It's you. I agree, control is a loose term, which is what nearly got me killed last night—"

"I wouldn't—"

"—but you're going to learn, and that's a promise. But first, you have to accept that your emotions affect the weather. Get them in check."

Those words and his tone of voice raised my hackles. Distant thunder grumbled. Nathan rolled his eyes.

"Okay," I nodded. I whispered, "Maybe it's me."

He shoved his hands into his pockets. "As amazing as that is, your fourth talent is quite unheard of."

I furrowed my brow, tilting my head.

"You can, with a blink of your eye and without the use of a portal, cross between planes of reality."

"That wasn't me."

"Both Mama and Jack both swear you made it happen."

"Talk to Mama about it, then. It was her idea to try. Maybe she did it."

He ignored me. "I mean, no one can do that. We don't have a

name for that talent because no one's been that powerful before. What the hell can possibly happen next?" He clenched his jaw, catching his breath. "You've got one more damned talent coming."

"Which apparently is to piss you off," I mumbled.

He hit the wall with the side of his fist. "Dammit, Winki. This isn't a joke!"

We both stood there for several seconds, letting the voices settle. I couldn't tell what hurt me more, his anger or his obvious fear of me. I saw it in his eyes last night. I saw it now.

He spoke in a low and serious tone. "This house won't save you, Mrs. Witherspoon. It will go as you go. That's its curse. It will protect you, and it will heal you, but it won't guide you." From the wet bar hidden within a large globe, he freed a bottle of bourbon and poured himself two-fingers. In one movement, he slammed the drink down his throat and with a hard smack, set the empty glass down.

"Nathan," I looked at the clock, "it's nine in the morning."

He glanced at his watch. "Good point," he muttered, and poured himself a second drink, which he swallowed with equal gusto. He clenched his eyes as the alcohol burned his belly.

I palmed my face.

He continued, whispering, "I can't save you either. I don't have the power. I don't have any leverage." He faced me, his eyes glistening. "Yes, I was scared last night. I confess. Not for myself. In fact, right now," he forced a laugh, "the best position I might be in is if you kill me." He darkened, pointing. "And that would be the end of you. God, that might be the end of the world."

With a flop, he sat on a leather sofa and kicked a foot over a knee. He avoided looking at me, keeping his eyes on the large flat panel on the wall.

I sat opposite him, slinking into the seat, as quietly as I could.

"I'm sorry," he said so softly I almost missed it. "When I'm scared, sometimes my voice kicks in out of desperation. I didn't mean to offend you last night."

I licked my lips. Apology accepted.

He took a deep, shaky breath. "The bottom line is only you can save you, but only if you recognize what's really at risk, here. Where the lines are, and when you're getting dangerously close to crossing them."

Arms folded, my eyes focused on the floor. Well, sort of ... stupid tears. "I don't want to be evil," I said.

"No one does. We just want to stop hurting. You were hurt and livid when you pointed the gun at me last year. You were hurt and exhausted when you threatened everyone last night. That's always the prod, the lure to take measures into our hands, the desire to quickly eliminate the problem, and that opens the door. "

Like revenge.

He continued. "You asked why having Mama come back was important to me. It isn't. But it's critical for you. You need to forgive her; forgive her for misleading you, for blaming me, for killing Will. The real reason she's here, Winki, is so I know you can forgive. Forgiveness is a key and fundamental code of conduct for the white warriors. If you can't forgive her—"

I winced, grimaced really. "She killed him ..."

He leaned forward and spoke softly. "If you can't forgive her, Winki ..." He licked his lips. "I need you to do this. I need to know you can do this. You need to know you can do this. Love and forgiveness are a part of you, and they're bigger than hate and anger. You need to know that you are as warm and kind and caring as I believe you are. As Will believed you to be." He bit his bottom lip, his eyes boring into my very soul. "For our sakes, Winki. I need you to do this. For the people you love. For me."

"That's why she's here?" I whispered.

"Please. Let her stay."

I looked at the DVD. Will's DVD. I waved it in the air. "My

husband's on this disc. This is how he communicates with me. Because he can't talk to me. He can't walk in those doors and talk to me." He hung his head, knowing he lost. "And she's the reason for that. Maybe, someday, she can come back. But not now."

He stood slowly and opened the pocket door. He started to close them, but stopped. "I want you to know I'm very happy you're back, safe and sound."

Folding my arms I said, "And not evil."

He frowned. "That's not what I meant."

Only once the doors closed did the little *cafard* make an appearance, crawling his way up the sofa and into view. "Where have you been?" I angrily asked.

"Seeing, *ma chére*. I see all."

"Seeing? There's been nothing but chaos here. 'Seeing' isn't really useful."

"Depends. You clearly do not see what I see. Besides, what would you have me do, hm? I have no venom like the spiders to protect this house. I can carry no weapon, like a wasp's stinger. While I like to think my words can hurt, they do little to harm. In short, I am useless except to do the hiding. And the seeing."

I hadn't thought about it before. "I'm sorry. I'm a little on edge."

"Bah!" he said, dancing back and forth. "I am the one who is sorry. I should have gone with you to the fire plane. I knew about the Tempest Veil. I knew it would make you sick, and someone else needed to put it on you so you could take it off." He sat still, and shook his little head. "*Je suis désolé, mon petit.*"

"Next time I will bring you. I promise." With a gentle finger I stroked his hard back. My eyes wandered to the door Nathan used to leave. "He's really mad this time."

"What was your first clue?"

I ignored the insult. "Is he right?"

"I have known Nathan for a good many years, both as Nathan

and Edward. I can tell you one thing with absolute certainty. Nathan is never wrong."

"Must be a real burden for him," I frowned. "Then you think I'll turn, you know, evil?"

"I honestly don't care, much like the house."

"Why not? You're supposed to be my guide."

"*Oui*, your guide. Not your conscience. No, no. I will tell you what options avail themselves, but I do not judge. I am rather looking forward to being dark again. It would be an interesting change, *n'est-ce pas?*" He let out a small ominous laugh.

I rolled my eyes and let my lips flap with a grand exhale. "Sometimes I really hate this place."

"I suspect it is sentiments such as that to which Nathan fully objects." When his little joke failed to lift my spirits he said, "Nathan has one flaw, I confess. He cares too much. About the house. About the staff." He paused as he danced. "About you."

"I know."

"I do not think you do." He sat up, and crossed his lower legs over each other and folded the other two pair. "You see, Nathan will do anything in his power to protect the ones he loves. If he had an inkling that you would walk the dark path, I predict he'd go to the Dark Lords and offer his soul over yours. I see the sadness in his eyes when you lose your temper. He knows he is to be damned."

What a horrible thing for the roach to say! "Hercule, what on earth would make you think that?"

"Because, ma chére," he sighed, collecting himself and crawling out of view, "he has done it before."

Chapter Thirty-Four

ONCE THE BUGS were dismissed and I was alone, I put the disk in the player, sat back, and hit *play*. Will's image filled the screen. *Man, how I miss those eyes and that smile.*

"Hey, Winks."

"Will," I mustered.

"So, I see you've been to the Radiant Plane."

Still reeling from my talk with Nathan, I wiped my eyes. "You have no idea what I went through to get it."

"You have no idea what I went through to put it there."

His smile warmed my heart. I smiled back.

"Some time has passed by now. What, are we nearly two years in?"

"You'll have been gone two years this November."

"That's good. Right on track, then. By now you've had a number of trials, some setbacks, some victories. More victories than setbacks, I'll wager."

"I guess," I shrugged.

"Hey. You need to acknowledge what you've done here. You started at zero. You had no idea that any of this existed, how any of this stuff works, or who any of these people were. You've created a circle of people who love you. I know you love them back. I know that because I know you, Winki. You have more compassion in your little toe than most people do in their entire bodies."

Scary he's saying this now. "I don't think I do, Will. I'm so angry sometimes."

"I know," he said, nodding slowly. "And I wish I could be there for you. But my time has come and gone. It's the nature of the beast, you know? We're born, we live, and we die."

"You died too soon."

"I had longer than some. And I don't regret a single day since I met you. I had a happy life, Winki. I want you to have a happy life, too. Just 'cause my heart stopped beating doesn't mean yours should. And it doesn't matter why it stopped, either. You're here. You're alive. It's time to move on."

I twisted my mouth. "Easier said than done," I whispered.

"What's wrong?"

"They want to bring Mama back, and I don't want her here. Just when I thought I could keep it in the past, it's all rushing back."

He gave a frown. "I'll be honest with you. The more time that passes, the more variables cloud the outcome of things, so I really don't know specifics about what's going on right now. But I suspect it's about my death, only because I know your death would have kept me angry for years, too. I can tell you with absolute confidence, I'd rather be in my shoes than yours."

I smiled, albeit dishonestly. "Lucky me."

"You've got two tournaments behind you now. How did they go?"

"I didn't finish either of them."

"You're blazing a new trail, one that's going to change everything. Right now it's all about gaining experience, taking lumps, and making your mark. Which I'm sure you're doing." He shifted a bit. "Look, I wanted to say ... wow, it's harder than I thought it would be."

"What is?"

"Let me get back to the point before, about you being angry. I don't want my death to cause you prolonged pain, Winki. You're still young and beautiful and you have so much to give someone."

"Wait. What?"

"Sooner or later, Winki, he's going to come into your life."

"Who?"

"Doesn't matter 'who.' That is up to you. Just know he's coming, and he'll make you happy."

"Will, I'm not going to fall in love again. Ever."

"See, that just makes me sad," he sat back. "I would never forgive myself if my death makes you afraid to give your heart to someone new."

"It's not your death," I corrected. "It was your life. I could never find anyone like you."

"I should hope not," he chuckled. "I don't want to be replaced, trust me. But I do want you to fall in love again. I want you to smile and laugh and love. Maybe not tomorrow, or the next day, but, well, keep your heart open. That's when you'll truly heal. You'll find that happiness again."

I wiped my face, and changed the topic. "Tell me about your conversion."

"Wow. That was weird. Why do you ask?"

"Is it real? I mean, can I trust someone who's been converted?"

Will looked off camera for several moments, reliving his own experience. "Yeah. It's real. If someone has come to you converted, you'll never meet anyone happier. Or more honest." He shook his head. "But if they were converted that means something terrible happened. Maybe that's why you're angry. I'm sorry, Winki. It can be a very confusing world. I can only say again, please, don't walk down the dark path. Not for anyone. It's not worth it, I swear to you."

"Things are getting scary here, Will." I wanted to talk about Lord Edmund and Esmeralda, but …

"Things are getting scary everywhere. That's why I made these DVDs. To keep you running between the lines. Don't swerve, and don't look back. You're doing great. I'm sure you're doing Nathan proud."

I scoffed. "I don't know. He's mad at me a lot."

"Ha," he laughed. "You don't know the half of it. That man would yell at me constantly. Damned if he wasn't always right. You gotta trust him. You have to put all of your faith into his basket, each and every time. *Nathan is always right.* If he says 'jump,' you jump. If he says 'zig,' you zig. If he says the answer is 'A,' and you know, you *know* with every fiber of your being that it's 'B', what are you going to do?"

I rolled my eyes. "Have a real big fight."

"And afterward?"

I surrendered. "Do 'A.'"

"Yes, you will. Nathan will see every angle, every time. He's a *thought catcher.* He hears everyone, he knows everything. Get it?"

"But he wants to bring—"

"Get it?"

I paused the recording. "Yeah," I whispered, pinching the bridge of my nose. "I get it." *Nathan is always right.* I shut off the TV.

I just didn't want to "get it." I mean …

Maybe Nathan was right about Mama; maybe I'd be a better person if I accepted her, and ultimately forgave her. But …

I couldn't shake the house's memory of how the healers got in. My staff got distracted. *Nathan* got distracted. He was so busy trying to get to the Radiant Plane, so sure I couldn't handle myself there, that everyone dropped their guard. What kind of champion did he really think I was? He said I was dark formidable, but didn't actually trust me to do anything. Which Nathan was right?

The Nathan who knew you needed to be saved. Stupid girl! You got caught. You got tortured. Hell, you got Jack tortured. Twice. I hung my head in my hands.

From nowhere, strong hands helped me to stand, and safe arms wrap themselves around me. Nathan held me tightly, his cheek in my hair. He said nothing. As my self doubt flooded my eyes, he stood strong. He didn't hush. He didn't console. He simply stood there, for me to lean on.

We stood like that, him supporting me, while my breathing slowed, my tears dried, and my quaking knees found strength to stand on their own.

I pushed myself away from him so I could wipe my eyes. He beat me to it, cupping my cheeks in warm hands, and his thumbs brushed the wetness aside.

"Never think that," he softly said. "Never think I don't believe in you. Never think that *I* think you're weak or incapable. I don't. You are the single most amazing person I have ever met." The kind words failed to console me. "I know what Esmeralda's touch feels like. I've experienced it myself. That's the reason I was in such a hurry to get to you. That's the reason I let myself get distracted. To warn you. To tell you. To help you succeed, not succeed for you. And, look!" He raised his arms wide. "You didn't need me. You did it all by yourself."

Not really, I thought to myself as I brushed some of the wet from his dampened lapel. If Mama hadn't helped … She stopped Malador, and she stopped the poison. I winced.

Nathan is always right.

"She can stay," I mumbled.

His eyes narrowed. "Are you sure?"

"Please, don't make me say it again."

He nodded. "I'll let everyone know." Quietly, he slid the door closed.

Taking a calming breath, I turned the screen back on and hit *play*. "I get it." I said as I hugged myself. All the aggravation and frustration welled up in me. "I want to talk to you. I mean, really talk."

Will smiled. "Well, keep in mind that, for years, I couldn't talk to you, either. I couldn't come home and brag how I won my sixth, or seventh, or eighth tournament. Or tell you how I worked so hard to keep the world a safe place for us. For you.

"Tell you what I did do, though. I'd touch the house, share my thoughts. I'd share my happiness and pain with it. It's big. It can handle anything. That's what you should do, too. Share your life with it. Even your sadness. It will make you feel better. It can show you such amazing things, probably already has. Seeing the world through its eyes always made me … warmer. And bigger."

"I'll do that. I promise."

"That's my girl. Now. Onto the next riddle."

"Already?"

"Yes. Pay attention. It's a toughie."

"Yeah. Because the riddles have been so easy so far."

"Ready?"

No. "Ready."

"*After the dust has settled, in the valley you've thrice walked through.*
Find the treasure, the one unnamed; That is who holds the clue."

"Uh," I moaned. "I don't think I like that one. Sounds like a lot of hiking. How about another?"

"You'll be fine."

"Easy for you to say."

He lifted the remote. "See you in a few minutes."

"For you, maybe." I swallowed.

"Goodbye, Winki."

"Goodbye, Will."

The screen went black.

** End Book Two **

ABOUT THE AUTHOR

Jax Daniels graduated from the University of California, Berkeley with a degree in Applied Mathematics. Thankfully, no one holds that against her. She was first published in 2014 with *The Dead Man's Deal*, book one in the entertaining series *The Witherspoon Mansion Mysteries*. She and her husband live in a New Orleans townhouse they call "The Tower" with their grumpy pug, Savannah.

Thankfully, no one holds that against her, either.

Tweet me: @JaxDNola
Like me: facebook.com/JaxDNola
Read me: www.winkiwitherspoon.com
Find me: www.jaxdaniels.com
… bug me: www.bugsmind.com

www.ingramcontent.com/pod-product-compliance
Lightning Source LLC
Chambersburg PA
CBHW071045250626
47159CB00002B/365

9 781946 236005